THE LITTLE BAKERY ON ROSEMARY LANE

Ellen Berry is an author and magazine journalist. Originally from rural West Yorkshire, she has three teenage children and lives with her husband and their daughter in Glasgow.

When she's not writing, she loves to cook and browse her vast collection of cookbooks, which is how the idea for this story came about. However, she remains the world's worst baker but tends to blame her failures on 'the oven'.

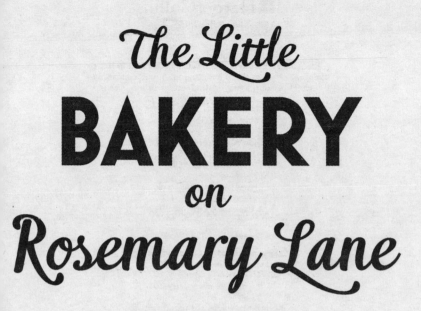

The Little
BAKERY
on
Rosemary Lane

Ellen Berry

avon.

AVON

A division of HarperCollins*Publishers*
1 London Bridge Street,
London SE1 9GF

www.harpercollins.co.uk

A Paperback Original 2017

1

First published in Great Britain by
HarperCollins*Publishers* 2017

Copyright © Ellen Berry 2017

Ellen Berry asserts the moral right to
be identified as the author of this work

A catalogue record for this book is
available from the British Library

ISBN-13: 978-0-00-815714-2

Typeset in Sabon LT Std by Palimpsest Book Production Ltd,
Falkirk, Stirlingshire

Printed and bound by CPI Group (UK) Ltd, Croydon CR0 4YY

MIX
Paper from
responsible sources
FSC™ C007454

Acknowledgements

Huge thanks to Chris and Sue at Atkinson Pryce Books, the wonderful independent bookshop in Biggar, Lanarkshire, where I've spent many a happy hour browsing and escaping from life. Incidentally, this bookshop 'magically' doubled in size! Thanks also to my ever-brilliant agent Caroline Sheldon, and to Rachel Faulkner-Willcocks, Helen Huthwaite, Sabah Khan, Helena Sheffield and all of the fantastic team at Avon towers. Many 'mwahs' to the ever-stylish Dame Wendy Rigg, who inspired me so much with her love of 'clobber' (and somewhat shakier relationship with kale). Big thanks to Tania Cheston for huge help in reading, checking and suggesting, and to Jen, Kath, Cathy, Michelle, Marie and Susan for being such brilliant friends since we all met in magazine offices way back in ye olden days. Finally, thanks to my lovely family – Jimmy, Sam, Dexter and Erin – and to Sheila, Ruby, Elaine and all the staff at McClymont House, who look after Mum with such thoughtfulness and care.

For Tania with love, hugs and sufficient fuss xxx

Prologue

Something peculiar had happened to Marsha Kennedy.

She had found herself editor of Britain's most popular fashion magazine. While she had already edited several publications, they had been in the diet and fitness markets, promising taut bodies and rapidly shed pounds; she knew virtually nothing about fashion and had even less interest in it.

'Don't you worry about that,' Rufus had said when he had first suggested she step into the role. 'In fact, view it as a positive. You're commercial, Marsh – you know how to sell copies and that's what this lot need. A kick up the backside, a wake-up call. They've had it too good for far too long, floating about and creating their . . . *pretty pictures.*'

As publisher at Walker Media Inc., Rufus was in charge of a whole raft of magazines, and as he said the words 'pretty pictures', his nostrils seemed to flare in distaste. Unconcerned by the creative aspects, his job was to ensure that his magazines raked in maximum profits. He was

1

also Marsha's married boss with whom she was having a somewhat frenetic affair.

'We need to be radical if the magazine's going to survive,' he'd added, twitching as Marsha traced a finger through the reddish, sweat-dampened hair on his slightly paunchy stomach.

They had been lying on plastic sun beds on the rectangle of Astroturf that covered her south-facing roof terrace in Dalston in East London. It was an uncharacteristically hot April day, and the pair had spent most of it massaging sunscreen into each other. Rufus had muttered that he would have to shower it off so as not to return home to his wife smelling of sickly shea butter. (His rather sunburnt hue would be a trickier matter, he realised, glancing down in alarm at his chest. He was supposed to be visiting his mother at her care home in Stroud, so how would he explain why his chest was the colour of bacon?)

'I want to put you in there,' he'd said, 'like a heat-seeking missile. If anyone can sort things out it's you, Marsh, sweetheart.'

'You really think so?' She'd twisted her shoulder-length chestnut hair into what she hoped was a cute little braid.

'Yes, why not?'

'Because it's not my market, darling.'

'Oh, come on. I know what you're like. You can do anything when you put your mind to it.' He winked, and she laughed. 'And believe me,' he'd added, pulling her close to his clammy chest, 'I'll make it worth your while.'

He had, too – financially as well as in other, more immediate ways. Marsha had now been installed at the helm of Britain's best-loved fashion magazine for two weeks. Although sales had dipped over the past couple of years, she was confident that this would soon be rectified.

Rufus had been right: *of course* she was capable of running a glossy fashion magazine. She just needed to scare everyone senseless. And, so far, this was working a treat.

First up, she had established a new start time of 9 a.m., instead of the more relaxed ten o'clock kick off. She had also introduced daily yoga classes, which were to be held on the office's scratchy grey carpet. 'It's optional, of course,' she had explained, baring her eerily white teeth at everyone, 'but I think you'll all benefit and I'll be *very* disappointed if you don't at least give it a chance.' Jacqui, the PA Marsha had insisted on bringing with her, had ordered in mats and bolsters for everyone, and booked two teachers to take classes on alternate days. To Marsha, who could conduct an important phone call while assuming a full headstand, there was something intensely amusing about watching the facial contortions of the less supple members of the team.

People like Roxanne Cartwright, the fashion director and longest-serving staff member, who had just this morning hurtled in, slurping coffee from her takeaway cup. Typical, Marsha thought. Everyone else was ready to start the session with their legs neatly crossed and eyes closed.

'Sorry I'm late,' Roxanne blustered, placing her coffee on the edge of Zoe the beauty director's desk, where it sat for a moment, half-resting on an eyeshadow compact before tipping over. 'Oh God!' Roxanne gasped, running to the kitchen and returning with a wad of paper towels. 'So sorry, Zoe,' she added.

'Rox, it's fine,' Zoe murmured from her mat on the floor. 'Calm down, darling . . .'

However, it *wasn't* fine, as far as Marsha was concerned. She sighed irritably as, with the coffee lake now blotted, Roxanne rushed off to change in the loos into her yoga gear. Apparently, she couldn't bring herself to travel to work in it as everyone else did. Finally ready for class and back in the main office, Roxanne assumed the required seated position on a mat next to Marsha. Funnily enough, that space was always the last one taken.

Whilst pretending to sit completely zen, Marsha snuck a glance at Roxanne, who was still panting a little. Marsha had already spent an awful lot of time observing her over the past fortnight. She was always running, Marsha had noted – off to appointments and shoots, cheeks flushed, hair askew, phone clasped to her ear. And she was in some state this morning. Her cheeks were bright red and her casual topknot was tumbling loose, with strands of fair wavy hair flapping in her face. However, although it pained Marsha to admit it, Roxanne was still striking for her age (when you were a mere thirty-three, 'late forties' sounded geriatric), her natural beauty quite captivating. Her light blue eyes were stunning and she was blessed with the kind of delicate bone structure that gave a person an air of elegance and dignity.

On top of this, Roxanne had a casual, bohemian way of dressing that Marsha could only hope to emulate – just how did one throw a perfect outfit together, seemingly without effort? Whenever Marsha tried to do that, the 'quirky' accessory – even something as innocuous as an Indian scarf – had the appearance of being flung at her by a passer-by as a cruel joke. As a result, Marsha tended to stick to the safe territory of fitted shirt in cream or white, plus black trousers; a uniform, really, which eliminated the hassle of thinking about what to wear every morning. Rufus had assured her that the editor of a fashion magazine was there to drive sales, not appear as if she had just stepped off the catwalk.

4

There was something else about Roxanne that Marsha had noticed, apart from the natural beauty and effortless style, damn her; she had a childlike enthusiasm that drew people to her and commanded fierce loyalty. Marsha had already had informal chats with Zoe and the other department heads, all of whom had been pleasingly compliant about the direction the magazine should take. Where Roxanne was concerned, she suspected things might not be quite so simple. Marsha's intention was to put a stop to the stunning fashion photography for which the magazine was known, and instead feature hundreds of cheap-as-chips outfits, promising figure-shaping miracles. Miracle knickers, bum-slimming trousers, boob-hoisting bras: *that* was what Marsha wanted to see. Of course, Roxanne would hate that. It hardly fitted in with her romantic aesthetic of achingly beautiful girls on horseback, swathed in chiffon – but who cared? Marsha's job was to sell more copies, reversing the circulation decline, and maximise profitability. This would secure her not only a whopping bonus but may also be the trigger for Rufus to leave that dreadful wife of his, and be truly hers. She loved the man deeply, and her favourite pastime was picturing the two of them – London's media power couple – scooping every accolade going at all the industry awards.

Whilst holding a perfect downward dog pose, Marsha glanced around at her team. All were obligingly trying their best, although she caught the odd anxious glance at the wall clock. Poor Tristan, the art director, was trembling visibly, a vein protruding from his neck. She caught a whiff of cigarettes from Grace, the beauty assistant, and Kate, the fashion assistant, let out a groan.

Meanwhile Marsha held the pose firm – muscles taut,

wobble-free bottom hoisted high in the air – as she glanced at her potentially troublesome fashion director. She would have to be tough with Roxanne, but Marsha wasn't fazed by that. In all areas of life – such as achieving a tightly honed body and stratospheric career success – she had a clear end goal in sight, and she wasn't about to let Roxanne Cartwright stand in her way.

Chapter One

Gently melt the butter, sugar and golden syrup in a small saucepan . . .

That sounded simple enough. This was a children's cookbook – a gift from her older sister Della, and intended as a joke. Roxanne was no cook. She couldn't see the point of baking anything you could quite easily buy from a shop. However, if a seven-year-old could manage it then surely, at forty-seven years of age, Roxanne could follow a simple step-by-step recipe without setting her kitchen on fire. Couldn't she?

Roxanne had chosen to make brandy snaps, her attention caught by the photograph in the book. As fashion director of *YourStyle*, she liked things to look pretty, and what could be more eye-pleasing than lace-textured biscuity curls? She opened her fridge, averting her gaze from the clear plastic sack of kale, which she had bought with the intention of throwing it into smoothies – to boost her energy and make her 'glow from within' – and which was now slowly decaying whilst awaiting a decision to be made regarding its destiny. Throw it away, like last time, and endure the wave of disquiet that was bound to follow? (*'I can't even get it together to use up my kale!'*) Or just leave it sitting there, quietly rotting? Deciding to pretend it wasn't there, she grabbed the butter, checked the use-by date on the packet and shut the fridge door. It was still edible – just. As Roxanne lived alone, a single packet could last her for weeks.

Not being in possession of kitchen scales, Roxanne estimated quantities, all the while picturing Sean's look of surprise and delight when he came over later and saw what she'd made for him. An edible love offering for his fiftieth birthday! How sweet was that? In the nine months they had been together, she had never made anything more complicated for him than toast, a coffee or a gin and tonic. 'My undomesticated goddess,' he called her, fondly, often teasing her about the kale supply: 'Why not just stop buying the wretched stuff?' Well, that would have been far too logical, and would have highlighted that she had given up on self-improvement. It would be like accepting she would never again fit into those size eight jeans stuffed in her bottom drawer and donating them to charity.

You kept them, just in case. Surely any woman understood that?

Anyway, never mind that right now. With all that syrup and fat, brandy snaps hardly counted as 'clean food', but on a positive note, an unusually delicious and heady aroma was filling her small, cramped kitchen.

While Roxanne might not exactly be glowing from within – a spate of late nights with Sean had dulled her light blue eyes and fair skin – she still experienced a flurry of anticipation for the evening ahead. Pushing back her long, honey-coloured hair, she smiled at the unlikeliness

8

of the situation: *Roxanne Cartwright, actually baking!* She owned just one saucepan, one frying pan and a single wooden spoon with a crack in it. As children, her big sister Della had been the one to potter away contentedly with their mother in the kitchen; she now owned a quaint little shop back in their childhood Yorkshire village of Burley Bridge, which sold nothing *but* cookbooks. Initially stocked with their mother's collection after she'd died, the shop was now thriving, a real hub of the close-knit community up there. Yet to Roxanne, that kitchen back in Rosemary Cottage had never felt welcoming. If she'd tried to help, she had botched things up and been snapped at by her mother: *For God's sake, Roxanne, how hard is it to chop a few onions? Oh, just give me that knife. Might as well do it myself!* At the sound of a bicycle approaching along the gravelled path, Kitty's expression would brighten. *Ah, that sounds like Della. Thank goodness someone around here is capable of helping. Off you go, Roxanne. You're just getting under my feet . . .*

'Getting under my feet.' How those words had stung. *I won't, then,* Roxanne had vowed. *I'll get well out of your way – as soon as I possibly can.* She had dreamed of escape and adventure; of stepping onto a London-bound train and never looking back. Her mother smacking her bare arm with a fish slice – 'Go on, scarper, can't you see I'm busy?' – had been the final straw.

Right here, in North London, was where Roxanne had landed at eighteen years old, having talked her way into the lowly position of fashion junior on a women's magazine. From her Saturday job in the newsagent's back home, she had saved up enough for an overnight coach fare to Victoria station and so was able to attend the interview without having to ask for money. Kitty had taken a dim view of the capital and all that she imagined went on there; 'That London,' was how she always referred to it. The intimidatingly chic magazine editor could hardly believe a fresh-faced teenager from a sleepy West Yorkshire village could be so keen to learn, so passionate about photography and fashion. She had gazed in wonder as this eager girl had spread all her sketches and scrapbooks over the desk. The fish slice incident had propelled Roxanne into action, and thankfully the editor offered her the job there and then. And here she still was, on a different magazine and fashion director now, with almost three decades of hard-earned experience to her name. Not that she was entertaining any fashion-related thoughts right now. She hadn't even considered what to wear tonight for dinner with Sean. Right now, she was focusing hard on the job in hand:

Allow to cool slightly, then sieve in the ground ginger and flour. Stir in the lemon juice. Line a baking tray with a sheet of parchment and drop on teaspoons of mixture . . .

Parchment? What was this, Ancient Egyptian times? Of course, they probably meant greaseproof paper or some-thing along those lines. She remembered that much from her mother's kitchen. As she didn't have such a thing – and Sean was due in less than an hour – she made do by liber-ally buttering her sole baking tray, then blobbed the mixture onto it and slid it into the oven. The used cooking utensils were dumped in the sink, and a tea towel draped over them for concealment purposes. *That* hadn't been too difficult, she reflected with a smile. Really, it had just been a matter of mixing a few ingredients together. Why did people talk about baking as if it were some mysterious art?

In her windowless bathroom, with the fan whirring noisily, Roxanne pulled off the indigo shift dress with pretty crocheted Peter Pan collar which she had worn to work, followed by her plain black underwear. She stepped under her rather feeble shower, sluiced herself down, then wrapped herself in a scratchy towel before making her way to her bedroom, where she flipped through the rail in her enormous antique French wardrobe.

A common assumption was that a woman in her position would live in a truly beautiful home, as photo-shoot-worthy as the models who trooped into her office on castings for shoots. Yet, perhaps because Roxanne lived and breathed her job, her domestic surroundings had always held little interest for her. Much of her furniture was, frankly, pretty scabby, having been hauled from flat to flat and more befitting her younger years as an impoverished fashion junior. In lieu of a proper bedside table, she still had a crate.

In fact, this wardrobe was the only item in her home which she truly cared about. With four doors and swathes of lavish carving, it was adorned with rococo swirls and carved angels picked out in gold. It was outrageous, really – an overblown folly crammed into the bijou top flat of a three-storey Victorian conversion in Islington. It was more befitting a French country home, somewhere with powder-blue shutters and gardens filled with lavender. It had been the flat's previous owner's, and once Roxanne had set eyes on it, she hadn't been able to focus on anything else. How could she possibly formulate sensible questions about boilers and council tax banding when she had fallen headlong in love with a piece of furniture? 'They did mention that they're quite happy to sell it,' explained the estate agent, catching Roxanne fondling it lovingly. 'It was a nightmare to get in – had to be hoisted through the window by a crane, apparently. You'll see a small chunk out of the left side. That's where it smacked against the

11

window frame.' Poor injured thing; she couldn't bear the thought of it being hoisted back out again, and possibly ending up being dumped. She had to have it.

With her wet hair bundled into a towel now, Roxanne pulled on her prettiest lingerie – scalloped indigo lace – followed by a simple bias-cut dress in charcoal linen. She blow-dried her hair upside down for maximum fullness, although, in reality, fullness was proving a little trickier to achieve than it used to. Where was all the volume going to? Perhaps it was time to consider subtle extensions? Her hairdresser, Rico, had already suggested she try some, in a way that had made it sound like a fun thing to do, rather than an emergency measure to compensate for middle-aged thinning. 'No woman has the thickness of hair in her forties that she had in her twenties,' he remarked cheerfully.

Now for make-up, with underplayed, natural eyes and strong red lips being her default look in a hurry. Forty-seven wasn't *that* old, she reassured herself. It was just that the glossy world she inhabited revered youth and made her feel quite ancient sometimes; she suspected that in fashion years, she was something like 167. However, she still scrubbed up okay as long as the light was right, and the restaurant she had chosen was *enhancingly* dim. Just last week, she and Isabelle, her seventy-five-year-old neighbour from the ground-floor flat, had had lunch at the local Italian Roxanne had booked for tonight, and barely been able to read the menu – which was a good thing, she decided, even if they had had to ask the waitress to read out the tiny print.

As she blotted her lips on a tissue, the intercom buzzer sounded. Was that Sean already? Roxanne frowned and checked her phone. Time had run away with her; it was

8.26 p.m. and their table was booked for 8.30. She scampered through to her hallway to buzz him in. She had seen him two days ago but still, her spirits rose like champagne bubbles as she heard the front door close behind him two floors down. No one else had ever had that effect on her. All the terrible boyfriends, the compulsive liars, drunks and narcissists (impressively, some of Roxanne's lovers had combined all three qualities): how joyful to be free of all that.

Once, her sister Della had joked that she had a talent for choosing men whose job titles required quotation marks: 'DJ', 'record producer', 'design consultant' – and, at one particularly unhappy point, 'socialite', which just meant he went out every night and could often be seen with cocaine-speckled nostrils, draped over models. Still, Roxanne had reassured herself: at least these men made life interesting – and what was so great about feeling safe and cared for and loved? Who really wanted a man who would cook for you and cuddle you when you were feeling down? Who'd show up when he'd promised to and didn't sleep with anyone else? What was so great about *that?*

Roxanne's own father, William, had plodded along, finally leaving her mother years after it had come to light that she'd had an affair with an artist from Mallorca. In fact, just a couple of years ago it had transpired that this artist, a man named Rafael, was Della's real father. Although shocking, the revelation had explained the perpetual tensions between their mother and William at Rosemary Cottage when the three Cartwright children were young, and the simple fact that Della, with her dramatic dark colouring, looked strikingly different to the fair-skinned and blue-eyed Roxanne and their brother Jeff.

For Roxanne, the most baffling aspect had been the

fact that William had known about Della's parentage all along – and chosen to bury his head in the sand. Roxanne *never* wanted a man like that. She was attracted to fiery, irresponsible types; like Ned Tallow – a 'party organiser' – who had once 'lost' a ready meal in his oven, having flung it in with such force, it had tipped over and gummed itself to the back. She had always found it almost impossible to resist the charms of the glamorous, the unhinged and frequently out of it – men whom she had supposed epitomised thrilling London life, in contrast to the rather safe and reliable Yorkshire lads she had known back home in Burley Bridge.

However, with Sean she had finally discovered how wonderful it was to be with a properly grown-up man who thrilled her yet still cared. He was cool, sorted and hugely successful as a freelance fashion photographer (in other words, he had a *proper* profession that needed no quotation marks). Clever, funny and charming, he looked as good in bespoke suits as he did in old, faded jeans, and the only Coke he acquainted himself with came out of a red can.

Sean's smiling, handsome face appeared as he hurried up the last flight of stairs towards her. It was his fiftieth birthday today, and Roxanne was determined it would be one he would never forget.

Chapter Two

'Hey, sweetheart. Sorry I'm a bit late . . .'

'That's okay. Happy birthday, darling.' Her lips landed on his, and his arms slid around her waist as he pulled her in tight. Sean O'Carroll's kisses felt so good. She stood back and smiled, still a little dizzy from the feel of his mouth on hers.

'Thanks, Rox. You look gorgeous. That's a very cute dress . . .' He glanced down. 'But aren't you forgetting something?'

'Oh yes.' She looked down at her bare feet and laughed, wondering if the attractiveness of his soft Dublin accent would ever wear off for her. His cropped dark hair was speckled silvery at the sides, and his wide, unguarded smile seemed to brighten the gloomy landing. He was wearing smart jeans, a pristine white T-shirt and a dark grey jacket.

Leaving him loitering in her living room, she hurried to her bedroom, deciding that her planned footwear – preppy lace-ups – looked too dumpy for the simple elegance of the dress. Dropping to her knees, Roxanne began to burrow amongst the muddle of shoes stashed in the bottom of her wardrobe, excavating deeper and deeper until a vintage suede sandal revealed itself like a prized fossil. She burrowed further amongst ballet flats, ankle boots, knee-high boots, loafers, stilettos, slingbacks, pumps, kitten heels, espadrilles, clogs – yes, actual wooden *clogs*; she had worn them just once and they had nearly hospitalised her – and every conceivable style of mule until the other suede sandal was found. Roxanne was not one of those highly organised women who stored her shoes in their original boxes with a photograph of them stuck to the lid.

'Aren't we going to be late?' Sean called out.

'No,' she lied, flicking through the tangle of shoulder bags which hung from the foot of her bed, and locating the correct one – a beauty in soft caramel leather – before pulling on her black jacket and smiling apologetically as they stepped out of her flat.

'So, where are we going?' he asked as they made their way downstairs.

'I told you, it's a surprise.'

'Oh, c'mon, honey. Are we getting a cab?'

She smirked. 'Don't need to.'

Sean shot her a quizzical look. In fact, there were so many restaurants within walking distance of her flat, they often spent half the evening debating where to go. 'Is it that Lebanese place?' he asked.

'No . . .'

'Manny's? Nonna's? Lol's Kitchen?'

She shook her head.

'Not that burger place?'

By this, he meant the crazily popular new restaurant at Angel tube station, where you couldn't book, and therefore had to stand outside for roughly fifty minutes and then, to add insult to injury, when you were finally allowed in, you couldn't sit down either; you had to munch your dripping beef pattie whilst standing at the bar. Roxanne felt far too old to stand anywhere. 'Just wait,' she teased him.

'Or that Nordic place where everything comes on a slab of rock?' His clear green eyes glinted with amusement.

'Nope, we won't be repeating that . . .'

'And not even your own, personal rock,' he went on, enjoying himself now, 'but a sharing one. Basically a communal paving slab for everyone to eat off. I blame Jamie Oliver.'

She laughed as his warm hand curled around hers. 'You can't blame Jamie Oliver for everything.'

'Yes, I can. Last book of his I bought, everything was presented on planks. He's single-handedly destroyed the crockery industry. Been in the china section of John Lewis lately?' She shook her head. It was not a department she frequented. 'It's like the *Marie Celeste*,' he added with a smile.

'Surely that trend must be coming to an end?' she suggested. 'Slate, wood—'

'I should hope so, but then, what's next? Bricks? Roof tiles?'

Roxanne chuckled. 'You needn't worry about that because we're going to an old-fashioned place where they wouldn't dream of serving your dinner on anything but a proper plate.'

'Oh, whereabouts?' His trace of cynicism evaporated immediately. Despite his high standing in the fashion world, Sean had no time for poncery where food was concerned. It was one of the countless things Roxanne loved about him.

17

'It's an Italian,' she explained as, still holding hands, they darted across the main road. 'You don't know it – neither did I. It's tucked down a little lane by the canal, just along here . . .' They turned off the main street towards the towpath.

'Really? I thought you knew everywhere around here.'

'I thought so too, but Isabelle came across it on one of her walks . . .'

'Isabelle?' He groaned. 'Christ, Rox, so she's managing our nights out now . . .' Roxanne smiled, well aware of how Sean viewed her elderly neighbour.

'No – listen. She finds places. That's what she does, she goes on these rambling explorations . . .'

'When she's not topping the bill at Ronnie's Scott's,' he cut in with a smirk.

'She's never claimed to have sung at Ronnie's Scott's.'

'Well, other jazz clubs, then. Any that'll have her . . .'

Roxanne smiled as he squeezed her hand. The late May evening was bathed in golden sunshine, and jovial groups had already congregated outside the well-kept Islington pubs, where hanging baskets were ablaze with freesias and petunias. Relaxed and companionable, just tipping into summer: this was the London she loved, and there was no one she would rather enjoy it with but Sean.

Roxanne had found him immediately attractive and charming when he had shown up in London five years ago after a lengthy stint of working in New York. She had booked him for a relatively low-budget shoot, and the elegant shots he produced had sparked the beginning of a fruitful working relationship. It had tipped from professional and friendly to much more when, after several margaritas, they had kissed like teenagers in the velvet-lined booth of a Hoxton bar and he had asked her back

18

to his flat. While there were no signs just yet of the relationship progressing beyond what it was now – he clearly valued his space, and they only saw each other around three nights a week – Roxanne had managed to convince herself that she should just enjoy things the way they were. They *were* having fun, and his busy diary was simply testament to his popularity; everyone loved him, from the interns in her office to the elderly fashion PRs who had been around since the 70s and were personal friends of Vivienne Westwood. Sometimes, she couldn't quite believe they were together.

'Don't tell me she's joining us,' he teased.

'Of course not,' Roxanne laughed. 'It's just us, sweetheart.'

'Well, that's a relief . . .' In fact, he was right to regard Isabelle as a whacky eccentric. A Londoner born and bred, she was suspiciously hazy about the venues she claimed to have performed at – and still sang at now, occasionally, or so she said – and a Google search of Isabelle Hudson had thrown up nothing of note. But who cared if she had fabricated an illustrious career as North London's very own Nina Simone? Squirrelling out delightful, tucked-away little restaurants and pubs – that was something she did for real, and from time to time Isabelle would invite Roxanne to try out one of her latest finds. She was just lonely, Roxanne had decided, when she had first moved into her top-floor flat twelve years ago, and got to know the curious single lady who lived alone on the ground floor. Apparently the great love of Isabelle's life had died before Roxanne had moved in, and although there was a son, there had been no visits that she was aware of. To say that mother and son weren't close seemed to be an understatement, as far as Roxanne could make out. In

19

fact, Isabelle barely mentioned him and gave the distinct impression that she wasn't happy to discuss him at all. It seemed to echo Roxanne's own, rather fractured family, and to her seemed terribly sad.

Sean's arm wrapped around Roxanne's slender shoulders as they made their way down the steps to the towpath. A few turns later, and there it was: the small, slightly shabby Italian, its hand-painted sign crying out for a freshen up, but still welcoming with the glow of orangey lamps inside.

'This is it?' Sean asked with a note of surprise.

'Yes, we were here for lunch on Sunday . . .'

'"We"?' he teased her. 'So you and Isabelle are a *we* now?'

'Oh, stop it,' she chuckled as they stepped into the hubbub, where they were immediately greeted by a cheery young woman, her sleek dark hair secured in a neat chignon.

'Hi, d'you have a reservation?'

'Yes, Roxanne Cartwright . . .' Roxanne glanced around the room. Its dark wood-panelled walls were hung with oil paintings of Italian coastal scenes, and shelves bore numerous, rather dusty-looking bottles of wine and leafy pot plants, which may or may not have been artificial. Apart from one vacant table right at the back, the place was full. 'Sorry we're late,' she added.

'Oh, don't worry about that – let me take your jackets . . .' As they were shown to their table, Roxanne glanced at Sean.

'Hey, this looks great,' he enthused as they took their seats.

'I knew you'd love it,' she said as they were handed unadorned hand-written menus. Sean smiled with approval as he registered the simple Italian dishes: not remotely trendy, and certainly nothing served on a plank. After the waitress had taken their orders, Sean clasped Roxanne's hand across the table and beamed at her.

'Maybe Isabelle does know a thing or two after all,' he conceded.

'Well, I hope it's special enough for your fiftieth.'

'I don't need special – you know that . . .'

'And you are having a *ridiculously* extravagant party tomorrow night,' she teased him.

'Yeah, but only because Britt forced me to. You know what she's like, taking charge of my life, saying she knows what's good for me . . .'

Roxanne nodded. Britt was Sean's formidable agent, and had poo-pooed his initial suggestion of a small gathering in the pub.

'I'm not planning to keep you out too late tonight,' he added. 'Remember you have that meeting first thing . . .'

'Yes, I know.' She grimaced. Sean was aware that her former editor, Cathy, had been shunted off without warning to be replaced by Marsha, who had come from the terribly depressing diet magazine that was published by the same company.

'I can't understand why she got the job, Rox,' he added. 'It seems nuts to me, and what about poor Cathy?'

Roxanne sighed. 'She's okay, apparently. She knew changes were afoot and she was given a huge pay-off. It *is* awful, but what can we do? All management keep saying is that we need to sell more copies if we're going to survive . . .' She tailed off, keen to change the subject. After a pretty dismal couple of weeks, during which the office had hummed with speculation about whose job might be in jeopardy, Roxanne just wanted to forget about work for one evening.

21

'I take it that optional morning yoga's still happening?' Sean asked with a smirk.

'Yes – you mean optional as in, it's the law?'

He nodded, amusement glinting in his eyes. 'I'd say that contravenes acceptable working conditions. It's blatant cruelty to fashion journalists . . .'

She chuckled and turned to thank the waitress as she poured their wine. 'But let's not talk about all that stuff tonight,' she added.

'Okay,' Sean conceded. 'But you do know everything's going to be okay, don't you?'

She didn't know, and, frankly, she *was* worried – but nothing would be gained from dwelling upon it now. 'Yes, of course I do,' she replied.

Their talk turned to fashion-industry gossip, and by the time their plates were set down, the crisp white wine – and simply being with the man she loved – had helped to convince Roxanne that, somehow, everything would work out fine. While Sean tucked into a retro chicken parmigiana, she had chosen a comforting spaghetti carbonara with lashings of cream. Hell, why not? Her many years of unrelenting dieting were behind her now. At her age, when she could no longer drop a few pounds by existing on black coffee and cereal for a couple of days, it was simply too misery-making to be perpetually ravenous. While she still tried to be 'good' – witness the purchase of kale – she now refused to deny herself the occasional bowlful of silken pasta or steamy, salty chips.

'That was amazing,' Sean enthused when they had finally finished. Roxanne smiled and studied his face. He was ageless, really, in the way that men blessed with striking bone structure often were; his hair showed no sign of thinning, and his green eyes had lost none of their sparkle.

She had seen photos of him from when he was much younger and, if anything, he was even better-looking now. How she longed for more time together, rather than just their nights dotted throughout the week. She had an urge to go away with him – to escape from their hectic London lives, just for a week or two, and be able to focus fully on each other. So far, they had yet to manage a holiday or even a weekend away together. Whenever she had mooted the possibility, Sean had proved impossible to pin down regarding possible destinations and dates. Of course, she understood why. He was incredibly in demand, and travelled constantly for work; even Britt complained that she had to beg him to take the odd break occasionally. However, Roxanne was finding it harder to ignore the persistent voice in her head which reminded her that going away on romantic little trips was something 'normal' couples did. Surely he could make the time for a night or two away with her, for goodness' sake?

'You don't fancy a weekend up at my sister's, do you?' she ventured as they were handed dessert menus.

'Uh, what for?' he asked.

'Remember I mentioned it? She's having a party at her bookshop . . .'

'Oh, yeah – what's that all about again?'

'Remember I told you she'd spent her share of her inheritance from Mum on buying the dilapidated shop next door, so she can expand her empire?' She beamed at him hopefully.

'Er, yeah,' Sean said vaguely, clearly not remembering at all. To him, Yorkshire was just part of that mysterious territory called 'The North' – supposedly cold and un-inviting, inhospitable to human life. Many of her colleagues were of the same opinion. Roxanne found it amusing and quite baffling, this fear of venturing further than a couple of hours' drive up the M1.

'Well, she's had the two places knocked into one,' she continued, 'and she's having a party to celebrate the opening of the new, double-sized bookshop.' She paused. She had mentioned this too – several times. 'So, d'you fancy coming up with me?'

He frowned. 'What, to your sister's? C'mon, Rox – you don't need me there.'

Frustration bubbled inside her now, but she tried to keep her tone light. It was his birthday, after all, and the last thing she wanted was a tetchy exchange. 'I don't need you there, but I'd *like* you to be. Why is that so weird to you?'

'Oh, baby, it's not weird.' He touched her hand across the table.

She forced a smile, trying to ignore the slight prickling sensation behind her eyes. 'So, why are you so reluctant to come to Yorkshire with me?'

'Because there's nothing there?' His crooked grin indicated that he was teasing.

'How can you say that?'

'Honey, I'm *joking* . . .'

'Don't you want to see where I grew up?' She paused to sip her wine. 'Aren't you *curious*?'

'Rox, darling.' He squeezed her hand tightly. 'You told me you couldn't wait to get away – that once you'd been offered your first London job you made a little chart to stick on the inside of your wardrobe, where you'd cross off the days . . .'

'Okay,' she conceded, 'but it still has charm – it's beautiful, actually – and I'd love you to meet Della and see her shop. She's put her heart and soul into it . . .'

24

'I know, it sounds amazing . . .'

'Shall we go, then?'

'Uh, sure, babe. We can go *sometime*. Just leave it with me, okay?'

But it's my sister's party! she wanted to add, trying to shrug off her irritation. None of her previous boyfriends had deigned to meet her family, even though she had tried to lure them north – so why was she feeling miffed that Sean was clearly un-thrilled at the prospect of a party in a cookbook shop? The only trouble with seeing a lovely, properly grown-up man, she realised, was that you started to hope for more commitment, whereas, with your Ned Tallows, you expected nothing.

She finished her wine as Sean studied the menu. 'Mmmm,' he murmured approvingly. 'Haven't seen these kind of desserts for years. D'you reckon they come on a trolley? Tiramisu, trifle, brandy snaps with whipped cream . . .'

Roxanne let her own menu drop. 'Brandy snaps?'

'What's wrong?' He frowned at her.

'Oh my God, Sean. I'm *so* sorry . . .' She scrambled up from her seat and glanced around in panic for the waitress. 'I was making some for your birthday. Oh hell, I can't believe what I've done!'

'You were making brandy snaps, for me?' He couldn't have looked more astounded if she'd announced she had bought him a camel. 'You mean you've actually been . . . *baking*?'

'Yes,' she barked, loudly enough for the couple at the next table to spin around, alarmed, 'and they're still in the oven. I'm sorry, darling, but we have to leave right now.'

Chapter Three

'Excuse me?' Roxanne waved to attract the waitress's attention. 'Can I have our bill please? We're in a terrible hurry . . .'

The woman nodded, signalling that she'd be over in a minute. She was carrying two cream-laden desserts and chatting jovially as she placed them on the customers' table.

Tension seemed to clamp itself around Roxanne's ribcage. Sean was murmuring something – telling her not to panic – but she wasn't really listening. The restaurant, which until a few moments ago had seemed so charming and intimate, now appeared to be criminally understaffed. For goodness' sake, the place was packed – surely they could employ some more people? And why was the sole waitress now chatting away about the couple's recent holiday ('If you loved Corsica, trust me, you'll adore Sardinia!') when the confectionery currently smouldering in Roxanne's oven could quite feasibly burst into flames?

'Rox, just sit down,' Sean hissed, trying to grab at her wrist. She shook him off.

'Please,' she called out, her voice rising in panic, 'I really do need our bill right now . . .' Despite having risen to lofty heights in the fashion world, Roxanne *hated* to cause a fuss. In a world where kindness wasn't always apparent, she was renowned for being a delight to work with, no matter how difficult or spoilt a model happened to be. On a shoot, she was virtually unflappable, even if the make-up artist fell out with the hairdresser, or a hovering seagull happened to do its business on a £1000 chiffon gown. However right now, she felt her blood pressure soaring. 'Excuse me!' she shrieked.

All heads swivelled towards her. The waitress widened her eyes.

'Sorry, but we really have to go,' Roxanne implored, conscious of Sean gawping at her.

'We can still have dessert,' he insisted.

'We can't. I'm sorry.'

'Rox, they'll just be a bit burnt. Nothing terrible's going to happen . . .'

'You don't know that!'

'Well, I don't want to seem rude,' he said, sighing, 'but I probably know ovens better than you do. How many times have you used yours?'

The waitress reappeared with their bill, and Roxanne snatched her purse from her bag. 'That was the first time,' she muttered.

'You'd never turned on your oven before?' Sean exclaimed.

'I've never needed to,' she mumbled, deciding not to add that she had in fact *used* it – continuously – as a storage facility for the vintage china tea sets she had taken from Rosemary Cottage when her mother died.

She handed the waitress her credit card and stabbed

her pin number into the little machine. 'Thank you,' the woman said primly. 'I hope you enjoyed—'

'It was lovely, thanks,' Roxanne cut in quickly.

'Sorry you're having to dash . . .' But Roxanne didn't hear any more as, rude though it was, she had blundered out into the humid London night without properly saying goodbye.

She wasn't a natural runner. Just as she had failed to fully engage with the new mandatory workplace yoga, so Roxanne had managed to get by for almost half a century without ever having participated in aerobic exercise apart from the occasional dash through the rain into a heated shop. However, she was running now, in a rather ungainly style, sandals clattering on the pavement.

'This is mad,' Sean exclaimed at her side. 'We don't have to run; it's not going to make any difference . . .'

'It might. What if the place is on fire?'

'Don't be crazy! It's just a few biscuits . . .'

Just a few biscuits! She must remember not to bother baking anything for him ever again.

'You'll break your neck in those,' he added, meaning her beautiful suede sandals which she had spotted in the window of a vintage shop, a size too small as it happened, but heck, she had managed to cram her feet into them and they'd eventually stretched enough so as not to be completely agonising.

She stopped abruptly and tugged them off. Damn Sean and his practical trainers.

'You're not going to run home barefoot?' he gasped.

'It's *fine* . . .'

'It's not fine. You'll cut your feet or stand in something disgusting. Come on, darling, put your sandals back on and let's just walk . . .' She glared at him, then realised

28

he was probably right and slipped them back on. Sean took her hand as they fell into a brisk walking pace. 'I still can't believe you were baking something for me,' he added, throwing her a fond glance.

'Hmm. Well, I probably won't again.'

'No, it's really sweet of you. But it's not very . . . *you*, is it?'

'Obviously not,' she muttered.

'I mean, it seems more like something your sister would do. Didn't she send you that tin of edible tree decorations at Christmas?'

'Yes. I didn't have the heart to tell her I hadn't got it together to buy a tree . . .' In fact, Roxanne had taken the delicious snowflake-shaped butter cookies into the office, and everyone had swooped upon them over drinks one afternoon. This was when Cathy was still editor and it was possible to have fun at work, in the days when there were frequent gales of laughter and the sound of a cork being popped.

'I'd never have thought of you as a baker,' he added.

'Yes, *okay*, Scan . . .'

'It's quite sexy actually,' he added, grinning now.

Despite the turn of events, she couldn't help smiling. 'I knew it. You actually want a wifey type in an apron, don't you? *That's* what you've been holding out for . . .'

'God, yes,' he teased. 'Floury hands and lipstick on, waiting for your man to come home . . .' He fell silent as they turned the corner into Roxanne's tree-lined street.

'Sean, look!' They both stared. A fire engine was parked outside her block.

'It'll be okay,' he said quickly, taking hold of her arm. 'It might not be your place. It could be another flat . . .' But this time, she shook him off and broke into an actual sprint. Despite her unsuitable footwear, she clattered towards the vehicle. She quickly spotted Isabelle, who was looking her usual elegant self – chic silver bob, simple navy blue dress – and hovering at the main door.

'It was Henry who called them, love,' she announced. 'I told him it'd be nothing – that you're always burning toast. A waste of resources, I said! I phoned your mobile a couple of times but it just rang—'

'Sorry, Isabelle, I didn't realise . . .' Roxanne hurried past her and charged upstairs. She always put her phone on silent when she was out on a date with Sean.

'I said you once burnt your fringe off the gas ring,' Isabelle called after her, 'when you were lighting a cigarette . . .' The elderly woman's voice faded, to be replaced by strident male tones on Roxanne's landing on the top floor: '*Sounds like someone's coming now – finally. Christ, what a bloody waste of time . . .*'

Sean had lagged behind. Roxanne could hear him being accosted by Henry, the boorish thirty-something solicitor who must have sprung out of his flat on the first floor, one short flight of stairs below hers. 'Sorry if I called them over nothing but the smell's awful. Emma's worried that her clients will complain. I mean, it's hardly *conducive* . . .' Never mind Emma, Henry's wife, and her psychotherapy clients. What about Roxanne's irreplaceable French wardrobe? She reached the top floor to find two firemen emerging from her flat.

'How bad is it?' she gasped.

The younger man frowned. 'This is your place?'

'Yes, it is . . .' Sean appeared at her side, catching his breath as she took in the damage. Her door was splintered, having been smashed open, and an acrid stench hung in the air.

30

'You're very lucky,' the fireman remarked as his companion made his way back downstairs. 'Your neighbour smelt smoke but there hasn't actually been a fire.'

'Oh, that's wonderful.' Roxanne felt like hugging him.

'But there *could* have been.'

'Yes, I know . . .' Impatient now, she peered behind him into her flat but this young man – this boy, who looked barely old enough to have any sort of paid job – was blocking her way.

'You need to understand that it's very dangerous to go out and leave something in the oven.'

She rearranged her expression so as to look suitably chastised. 'I do realise that, and I'm very sorry for taking up your time.'

He squinted at her, seemingly not done with lecturing her yet. 'You won't believe how many fires I've seen that have started this way. It's the fat, you see. Grease spits over the edge of the tray and then ignites . . .' He frowned. 'What were you making anyway?'

'Brandy snaps,' she replied, at which he looked baffled; well, of course he did, they belonged to a bygone era. This child before her had probably cooked nothing more taxing than a microwaveable pouch of Uncle Ben's rice – but then, neither had she.

He stepped aside to let Roxanne and Sean pass. 'Well, just make sure, any time you're baking in future . . .'

'Don't worry,' she said quickly, 'there won't be any baking in future, I can promise you that.'

She and Sean stood for a moment as the fireman clumped downstairs to join his colleagues.

'Okay up there, Roxanne? Need any help?' Isabelle called up from the hallway.

'We're fine here, thanks,' she shouted back brightly.

31

Sean shook his head and frowned. 'Bit of an over-reaction from Henry, wasn't it, calling the fire brigade? Look at the damage to your door . . .'

'Oh, it can be fixed. It's not the end of the world.' In fact, she surmised as they strode through to her kitchen, perhaps she had got off lightly. Apart from a terrible stench and the urgent need for a joiner, there was really nothing to worry about. The oven was open; the blackened tray of brandy snap mixture having being dumped in the sink and water poured onto it. The kitchen window had been opened, and a cool breeze was wafting in. She met Sean's gaze. 'I'm so sorry, sweetheart. This isn't quite how I imagined your fiftieth would turn out.'

'Hey, darling, it's okay.' He kissed her forehead softly, then wound his arms around her waist and held her close to his chest. 'I'm just relieved your place didn't burn down.'

She nodded and stepped away. 'I'd better see if I can find a joiner . . .'

'Yes, of course . . .' However, before she could even do a Google search, Sean had said, 'Hey, I'll do it,' and taken her phone from her, and was jabbing at it – because, of course, he was a man and this involved a tradesman with tools. *Blokes' stuff,* Roxanne thought wryly as Sean made the call on her behalf, as if she were incapable of communicating that her front door was broken. At least he was being helpful, she decided. What use would any of her other boyfriends have been, in a situation like this? They'd have laughed and called her an idiot, then raided her fridge for beer while *she* sorted everything out.

'Yeah,' Sean chortled into her phone, having lapsed into conversing-with-tradesman mode. 'Girlfriend left something in the oven, fire brigade called . . . yeah, you could say that, hur-hur-hur . . .'

She jammed her back teeth together. *You know what women are like,* was the unspoken theme.

Sean finished the call and beamed at her. 'Well, that was a bit of luck. He's local: says he'll be here within the hour.'

'Great.' Roxanne mustered a wide smile. 'Oh – let me get you your present.'

'Darling, I'm sorry.' He frowned in mock regret. 'I really think they're too burnt to eat.'

'That was just a little treat—'

'Come here. I want *this* kind of treat . . .' He grabbed her playfully and went in for a kiss, but she spun away.

'Hang on a minute . . .' She rushed off to her second bedroom – a box room really, that served as overspill storage for clothes and accessories – to retrieve the gift she had wrapped so beautifully in matt duck-egg blue paper with a perfect silver bow.

Sean was lounging on the sofa in her living room when she handed it to him.

'Here you go. Happy fiftieth, darling.' As she curled up beside him, she experienced a rush of pleasure at having tracked down a wonderful gift for a man who really did have everything.

'Thanks, sweetheart.' He peeled away the wrapping paper with care. 'Oh, wow! This is amazing, Rox. You know I love his work . . .' He gazed at the hefty coffee-table book of photographs by Laurence Grier, one of his photographic heroes.

She snuggled close as he turned the pages reverentially. Grier, who had been active since the 50s, specialised in black-and-white photographs of achingly beautiful women in rather shabby surroundings. They always looked as if they had been caught off guard, applying lipstick in a dingy cafe, or drawing a picture with a finger on the steamed-up window of a bus.

'Glad you like it,' she said with a smile.

'Of course I do. You're so thoughtful. I love you, babe.' He kissed her gently on the lips.

'I love you too, darling,' she murmured, beaming with pleasure. 'Look, there's something else too.' She leaned over and turned to the book's inside front cover, on which the photographer himself had written: *Happy 50th birthday Sean, with all good wishes, Laurence Grier.*

Sean stared at the inscription. 'It's signed! Is this for me?'

'Well, yes,' she said, laughing, 'unless it's a remarkable coincidence.'

His eyes widened. 'How on earth did you get this?'

'I bribed him with enormous amounts of money,' she said with a grin.

He closed the book and placed it on top of a muddle of magazines and newspaper supplements on her coffee table. 'Seriously? You actually met him?'

She nodded. 'Yes – when I was in Paris for the shows.'

'Really? Wow. *You* planned ahead . . .'

'It was just luck really,' she said quickly, a little embarrassed now: Paris fashion week was back in October. Did it seem overly keen to have planned Sean's birthday present seven months ago – and only two months after they'd started seeing each other? 'He was staying at my hotel,' she added.

Sean kissed her again. 'You're *amazing*, Rox. Gorgeous, sexy and amazing . . .'

She smiled and pushed back her tangled hair. 'And I noticed that he liked to sit with a gin and tonic in the hotel bar every evening, so I went out and bought a copy

34

and hoped he'd be there, just one more time . . .' She omitted to mention that it taken visits to four different bookshops before she had managed to track down a copy, and even then, it had a torn cover so they had to order another for her to pick up the next day.

The intercom buzzer sounded. Sean leapt up to answer it. 'That'll be Tommy!' he exclaimed.

She stared before scrambling up after him. For a moment, it seemed as if the excitement over the joiner's arrival had surpassed that of the photography book.

Sean hared towards the front door ahead of her in order to greet him. 'Hi, mate, that was quick . . .'

'Only three streets away,' Tommy replied with a grin. He had cropped ginger hair, a soft Liverpool accent and scratched at his stubbly chin as he examined the door. 'Whoa, that's some mess you've got here.'

'Yep, think the whole door needs replacing?'

'Yeah, for sure – but I can do a temporary patch-up right now, make it secure . . .'

'. . . And fit a new door at some point?' Sean enquired, as if this was *his* flat, and he was in charge here.

'Uh-huh, I can get you some prices . . .'

'That would be great,' Roxanne said firmly, forcing the man to register her presence. 'A temporary patch-up, I mean. It's actually my flat.'

'Oh, is it? Right . . .' Tommy darted a quick look at Sean as if to say, *Is that okay with you, her expressing an opinion?* before starting to unpack his tools. Roxanne gave them a cursory glance, then strolled away to get on with the business of chipping the brandy snap mixture off the tray, to the soundtrack of the two men bonding.

'*My* missus once left the iron on,' Tommy was saying. 'On our way to the airport, we were, in a taxi. "Christ,

35

Tommy," she screams, "I think the iron's still on!" So we had to turn around, get the driver to take us all the way back . . .'

'God, yeah,' Sean sympathised. 'I know that feeling . . .'

What feeling? Roxanne wondered, using a bendy kitchen knife to hack at the charred confectionery. She didn't recall that she had ever subjected Sean to an iron-left-on incident – although she supposed after tonight's episode she could hardly occupy the moral high ground.

'. . . And d'you know what happened?' Tommy crowed. 'We get all the way home and the iron's stone-cold . . .'

'It was off all the time? You're kidding me!'

'Nah, isn't that typical?'

'Did you miss your flight?'

Tommy snorted. ''Course we did! Cost us over three hundred quid for new tickets.'

Their laughter rumbled through Roxanne's flat as the two men revelled in that hoary old topic: the idiocy of womankind. Oh, what *fun* they were having. Roxanne understood what was going on here, as shards of black stuff pinged off the tray, occasionally hitting her cheek and landing in her hair. Sean spent most of his life in the company of rarefied fashion types. Most of his conversations were about whether the model's hair should be up or down, or if a necklace was required to finish the look. His professional life was all about capturing beauty, which was fine; there were far worse ways to make a living than photographing the world's most breathtaking women wearing exquisite clothes. Yet, despite Sean's creative talents, he was a pretty down-to-earth bloke, who had grown up with a ferocious single mother in an area of Dublin he always described as 'lively'. Opportunities to flex some masculine muscle were few and far between.

'So, what's your line of business?' Tommy was asking now.

'I'm a photographer,' Sean explained.

'Oh, right. Weddings, portraits, that kind of thing?'

'Well, I'm more kind of—'

'Would you do one of our Jessica? She's a right little character – just turned eighteen months. Me and my girlfriend, we'd love a proper picture of her to have framed for the living room.'

'Er, that's not quite my—'

'You know – looking cute, sitting on one of those sheepskin rugs?'

Roxanne chuckled to herself as she sensed Sean struggling to remain on his new best mate's good side. 'Uh, yeah, I know the kind of pictures you mean, but I'm actually more of a—'

'She's just *adorable*,' Tommy added fondly. 'D'you have a card or anything, so I can contact you?'

'Uh, not on me, no . . .'

'Aw. Well, I've got your number.'

'I called you on my girlfriend's phone,' Sean said quickly.

'Right. So, will you text me yours, so we can arrange to do the pictures?'

'Yeah, 'course I will . . .'

No, of course he won't, Roxanne mused as she sanded off the last of the burnt crust with a Brillo pad. *He happens to be a top fashion photographer whose latest campaign for a high-street chain is currently gracing enormous billboards all over Britain. Sean O'Carroll does not photograph babies on fluffy rugs.*

Drilling and hammering curtailed their conversation, and once Roxanne had finished cleaning the tray, she found Sean lurking in her living room. 'Why are you hiding in here?' she teased him.

'I'm not *hiding*,' he murmured defensively. 'I'm just letting him get on with the job.'

'Right. It's just that, a few moments ago, it sounded as if you were about to arrange a holiday together.'

Sean's eyebrows shot up. 'Don't be ridiculous!'

She laughed, just as Tommy called out to say he'd finished.

'So that's it secure,' he remarked as she inspected his work. Sean had failed to reappear from the living room.

'Brilliant, thanks so much – and, yes, I'd like to go ahead with the replacement door, please. Could you send me an estimate?'

'Yeah, no problem.' He seemed disappointed at having to deal with her now.

'Shall I pay you for this now, or will you invoice?'

'Now would be great, if you don't mind . . .'

'Sure, no problem.' She fetched her purse from her bedroom and doled out a bunch of tenners. Sean remained in hiding, perhaps hoping that the matter of baby photography would be forgotten as soon as Tommy left Roxanne's flat.

After he'd gone, they curled up companionably on the sofa together. Sean was drinking wine, while Roxanne sipped chamomile tea – not because she enjoyed it especially but because it seemed like the right thing to do the night before a meeting with one's new boss. She rested her head on Sean's chest, once again picturing them together in her childhood village, with her showing him around, delighting him with its quaintness. After nine months together, it seemed important for him to understand where she was from, and get to know the place that helped to shape the person she was now. Plus, it would be fun to share a bottle of wine in the Red Lion, where she was occasionally allowed a Coke and a bag of crisps as a little girl. Sean would love its olde-worlde charm.

'So, what d'you think about that weekend in Yorkshire with me?' she ventured, turning to study his reaction.

'What's the date of the party again?' Sean asked.

'The ninth of June. Couple of weeks away.'

He nodded thoughtfully. 'I told you, darling – I'll have to check what's on. You know how crazy-busy it's been lately . . .' Of course, Sean was never merely busy, like a normal person; he was always *crazy-busy*.

'I'd just like to show Della some support, and I think it'd be fun,' Roxanne added, hating the pleading tone that had snuck into her voice.

'Sure, we can go away sometime. I'm just not quite sure about *this* time, okay?' He smiled and kissed her.

'Okay,' she said flatly, realising her suggestion was being treated in the same way as Tommy's request for a baby-on-fluffy-rug photo, in that it was clearly not something Sean wanted to do. She wondered then, as they settled in front of the TV to watch a late-night music show, whether their relationship would ever progress from how it was now. Of course, compared to Ned Tallow and the other reprobates, Sean was an absolute saint. Yet they still dated as if they were in that tentative early stage ('So, how are you fixed this week?'), their time together dotted in amongst their numerous other social engagements. Roxanne's evenings were often taken up with work-related events, and Sean was often shooting on location and didn't return until late. Around half the week, he stayed alone at his own sparsely furnished warehouse apartment with its bare-brick walls and enormous red fridge. But what more did she want, or expect from him?

Although she hadn't brought it up, she sensed that he

wasn't exactly itching to live with anyone. He had twice before, each time for a decade or so – first with a model (naturally!) called Lisa who had, by all accounts, left him broken-hearted when she had fallen in love with a fellow model on a shoot in the States. Then had come Chianna, a jewellery designer from whom he had simply 'grown apart'; she now lived in Devon with a brood of wild-haired children and a famous drummer. Sean had never been married, had no children and didn't seem saddened by the fact.

As for Roxanne, a few boyfriends had moved in with her for brief periods – although usually due to their own shaky financial circumstances rather than any real desire to cohabit with her. She had never had any yearnings for marriage and, obviously, children were out of the question now – which was *fine*. Yet, deep inside her – and it irritated her to even think this way – she needed to feel as if things were moving on. A few weeks ago, she had had the audacity to leave her spare toothbrush in the porcelain holder in Sean's bathroom, plus a small pot of night cream on his shelf. 'I think these are yours, Rox,' he remarked next time she'd stayed over, looking rather startled as he handed them to her, as if they were her false teeth. The more she felt he was keeping her at arm's length, the more commitment she craved. Roxanne had never felt so needy before, and she despised herself for it.

Later, at around 12.30 a.m., she found herself unable to sleep as they lay curled up in her bed together. He was spooning her, with one arm resting gently on the soft curve of her stomach. Roxanne stared at the glow of the street lamp through her cheap white Ikea curtains, failing to be soothed by Sean's rhythmic breathing.

This was happening more frequently: an inability to

drift off and, instead, a tendency to fixate on a whole raft of worries – such as, why had Henry found it necessary to call the fire brigade tonight? Which segued neatly into growing panic over the meeting with Marsha in a few hours' time – and the realisation that, really, the one person Roxanne wanted to talk to right now was her sister, up in Burley Bridge. Of course, she couldn't call Della now; it was the middle of the night. However, she fully intended not to just go to her party, but to spend time with her sister beforehand to help her prepare.

Would Marsha let her have some time off? she wondered. She would *have* to. Roxanne was still battling with residual guilt over the period leading up to her mother's death from cancer two years ago, and she was keen to make up for it. She knew she should have spent more time up in Yorkshire. Pretty much all of Kitty's care had fallen to Della. Della's ex-husband Mark had been useless; he had left her for another woman soon after Kitty's death, just as Sophie, their daughter, had flown the nest for art college. Roxanne was well aware that several Burley Bridge villagers assumed she had been flouncing from fashion show to fashion show whilst her mother had been dying in the hospice.

In truth, a lurking sense of ineptitude had kept Roxanne away. 'You need to get yourself up there,' Isabelle had chastised her, 'and help that poor sister of yours.' And so Roxanne had eventually driven north – but felt, just as she had as a child, that she was merely getting in the way.

One of her visits after Kitty's death had coincided with her brother Jeff and his wife Tamsin descending on Rosemary Cottage. As they had grabbed what they wanted from the house, so it had looked as if Roxanne, too, was only there to snatch her share of the pickings. She had taken an emerald felt hat with a short net veil, a string of

41

jet beads and the pretty rose-pattered tea sets, which until recently had resided in her unused oven – and that was all. She had watched, feeling faintly disgusted, as Tamsin breezed past with boxes piled high with silverware and, at one point, a vast fur coat. Roxanne hadn't wanted the coat – she never wore fur, and refused to feature it in the magazine. She had principles, although it hadn't seemed like that, as Jeff, Tamsin and their twin sons had swarmed like locusts all over the house, cramming their estate car with Kitty's possessions while Roxanne just stood there, feeling helpless.

'Can I do anything to help with the funeral, Dell?' she'd asked.

'No, it's all organised. There's nothing left to be done.' Her words had been delivered with a note of bitterness.

'Can't I make sandwiches, help with the food—'

'We're *fine* with the food, thank you!'

Well, her sister hadn't seemed fine. She had launched herself into scrubbing and packing up their mother's house, and announced that all she wanted was Kitty's vast collection of cookbooks. Even more startling, Della then decided to use them to stock a clapped-out old shop she had decided to rent, and subsequently bought, along with the flat above and then the vacant shop next door – how crazy was *that*? Not at all crazy, as it turned out. Eighteen months down the line, Della's bookshop had been featured in numerous magazines and even on TV. On the other hand, Jeff was still working in banking – and clearly despising it – while Roxanne had almost burnt down her flat and endured a stern ticking-off from a fireman who looked about nine years old.

Looking at it that way, she mused, still wide awake at 1.47 a.m., who ranked highest on the craziness scale?

Chapter Four

On a bright-skied Friday morning, Roxanne opened a bleary eye and watched as Sean pulled on his jeans. Even his back view was lovely. She took in the curve of his lightly tanned neck, his firm upper arms, the graceful lines of his shoulders. She yearned to touch him, to coax him back to bed just for a few more minutes. There was time; it was just 7.30. However, Sean's attentions were now directed elsewhere as his assistant, Louie, was already on the phone about some small drama concerning the party at Sean's studio that night.

'Foie gras canapés?' he exclaimed. 'Britt showed me the menu and they definitely weren't on it. Has she been running away with herself again?' There followed some urgent muttering. It was obvious to anyone who met Louie that he was clearly in awe of his employer, and Roxanne could picture the eager twenty-one-year-old's pale face flushing, his forehead beading with sweat. 'I don't care if they're on sticks – if they're *lollipops*,' Sean barked. 'I'm not having canapés made out of force-fed ducks or whatever the hell that stuff is. It's disgusting. Just cancel them, all right? Get onto Britt, say we've spoken. Okay, good. Catch you in a bit – and remember we need to be right on the nail with today's job. I want to be finished by five so the DJ can set up for tonight.' He finished the call, turned to Roxanne and rolled his eyes as if his fiftieth birthday party had been foisted upon him – which, in a sense, it had. 'It's a monster that's grown out of control,' he groaned. 'What's wrong with a big bowl of sour cream and onion Pringles?'

She laughed, slipping out of bed as he pulled on his white T-shirt. She knew the party really wasn't Sean's style, but that his agent had convinced him that this friends and contacts in the industry would love it. 'Why not make a big splash? You're only fifty once!' Britt had insisted, having breezed into his studio when he and Roxanne were in the midst of a shoot for her magazine a few months ago. He could afford it, of course. Sean was at the top of his game right now. Whilst magazine shoots were moderately paid, he could command thousands per day for an advertising job.

'Gotta go,' he said now, kissing Roxanne softly on the mouth. 'Cab's on its way. See you tonight, sweetheart.' There was the toot of a car horn in the street below, and he was off.

Roxanne showered quickly, reassuring herself that of course he meant to wish her good luck for the meeting; he'd just been in a hurry, that was all. Anyway, it was no big deal, and it would soon be over, and tonight she'd be clutching a glass of perfectly chilled Chablis (Britt would insist on the best of everything) at his party and having a little dance. Even aside from the fire brigade incident, it had been a long, hectic week, with problematic shoots to arrange, all under the watchful gaze of Marsha in her little glass cube at the end of the office. Roxanne needed to kick back and have some fun.

Dressed for work now, she surveyed her reflection in her dressing table mirror. With today's meeting in mind, she had chosen her favourite cream calico top with embroidery around the neckline, plus a knife-pleated black skirt, low patent heels that would also do for Sean's party, and a blue topaz necklace she had bought on holiday last summer with her friend Amanda. They had gone for four days to Ibiza together – Amanda's first trip without her daughters, who were then six and eight years old and had stayed at home with their dad.

Roxanne smiled at the memory, wishing she could spirit herself back there right now, instead of heading for her meeting with Marsha. It had been wonderful. They had chatted perpetually while sipping copious sangria in the quaint bars of the Old Town and swum in the clear turquoise sea. Amanda had been the unfailingly cheerful receptionist at Roxanne's first London office. Although Roxanne was five years older, they had become exceptionally close – and now she was godmother to Keira, Amanda's eldest daughter. Roxanne had reconciled herself with the fact that it was probably better to not be a mother herself than to have had children with any of the low-level lunatics she had involved herself with over the years. Imagine embarking on parenthood with a man who was incapable of heating up a ready meal! But then the brandy snap debacle shimmered back into her mind, so she banished all oven-related matters from her consciousness and concentrated instead on applying her make-up. To boost her morale, she applied a hideously expensive new primer called Blur which was supposed to, well, *blur* everything – but seemingly not sufficiently, she decided now.

Was she stressing too much over this meeting? she wondered. Marsha had already had one-to-one talks with the other department heads, and from what Roxanne had heard it was nothing to worry about. 'It was just an informal chat,' Zoe, the beauty director, had told her. Yet still Roxanne felt uneasy. Why had Marsha left their meeting until last, when fashion was by far the most prominent section of the magazine? 'I've cleared some time for us straight after yoga on Friday,' she had said with a brittle smile.

Pulling on her jacket now, Roxanne picked up her shoulder bag and sniffed the air in her living room. The burnt brandy snaps whiff still lingered, or was she imagining it now? Perhaps it had impregnated her curtains and sofa and she'd never be rid of it. Something else had been left behind, too – something of Sean's, but not in that I'll-just-pop-my-toothbrush-next-to-yours sort of way. There on her coffee table sat the signed Laurence Grier photography book.

After all her efforts, he had simply forgotten to take it.

Roxanne emerged from Leicester Square tube station and made her way through the crowds towards the nerve centre of women's magazines. She stopped to buy her coffee from her usual kiosk and quickened her pace through Soho, more through nervousness than because she was running late. Her stomach tightened as she glanced up at her publishing company's block. It was impressive from the outside, all blue-tinted mirrored glass, the kind of place a young wannabe might gaze up at and think, *Oh to work somewhere like that! Wouldn't that be so glamorous?* Imagining grandeur, visitors were often surprised at the scruffiness of Roxanne's magazine's office.

In she walked, greeting her colleagues, some of whom were already lounging on mats on the floor. Marsha, who was already arranged in a cross-legged position, gave her an inscrutable look, so Roxanne flashed her a tense smile. To be fair, it wasn't the actual yoga that most of the team objected to. It was having it foisted upon them every single weekday, in an environment that was hardly suited to it. Everyone was too crammed together on the stained, ancient carpet. This was a place for work, not for 'connecting with the breath'. The beige walls were scuffed, the tiny kitchen equipped with no more than a cheap toaster, a kettle and a rather sour-smelling fridge housing a half-empty bottle of Baileys that Roxanne suspected had been languishing there since the 90s. Six magazine teams were based in the building, ranging from the glossy *YourStyle* to mass-market titles in the diet and fitness markets. Roxanne regarded exercise in the same way as she viewed the kale in her fridge; in other words, she knew she should involve herself with it, but would prefer not to, if possible.

In the office loos, Roxanne changed reluctantly into her yoga kit. There were certain items of clothing she simply couldn't 'do'. Culottes and waterfall cardigans fell under this banner, as did the cheap leggings she'd bought, begrudgingly, for these morning classes, hence being unable to bring herself to wear them for the journey into work. Now appropriately attired, she hurried back into the main office and plonked herself down on the consistently last-to-be-taken mat next to Marsha's.

Throughout the class, she tried, unsuccessfully, to calm herself in readiness for her meeting. With Marsha twisting her skinny body into all manner of contortions a mere three feet away, it was virtually impossible. Perhaps Marsha had requested the 'chat' today just to establish her authority? If so, it really wasn't necessary; there was no doubt that she was boss now, although it never even occurred to Roxanne to pull rank with *her* team. Despite her senior position, she wasn't concerned about status at all. All she cared about was creating beautiful pictures and, alongside that, trying to keep her team happy and motivated so they could all work well together. *That* was what mattered.

After yoga, she changed back into her work outfit and touched up her make-up in the mirror above the basin. She was soon joined by Serena, her deputy, and Kate, the fashion junior.

'How long d'you think these classes are going to go on for?' Serena asked, leaning close to the mirror as she swept powder over her face.

'I'll ask Marsha,' Roxanne said dryly, 'when I have my meeting.'

Kate's dark eyes widened. 'Oh, is that today?'

Roxanne winced and nodded. 'Yep – in a few minutes in fact . . .'

'It'll be fine,' Serena assured her. 'Everyone knows Marsha doesn't have a clue about fashion. She totally needs you on board.' She snapped her powder compact shut. 'C'mon, cheer up – we're all off to Sean's party tonight. Looking forward to it?'

'Yes, of course.' She mustered a wide smile.

Serena grinned. 'Did he enjoy his brandy snaps?'

'Oh, God – things didn't exactly go to plan . . .'

Serena and Kate convulsed with laughter as Roxanne filled them in on last night's events, and by the time she stepped back into the office, their shared hilarity had dissipated her nerves a little. She slipped her bag over her shoulder – it was weighed down with the scrapbook she had brought in with her – and spotted Marsha in her little glass cube of an office, motioning for her to come in. Roxanne cleared her throat and strode towards her.

Marsha was out of her seat, all bared-teeth smiles whilst dispensing instructions to Jacqui, her PA, to bring them coffee. 'Sit down, Roxanne. How are you getting on with the yoga?'

'Oh, er . . . great!' She was conscious of her voice shooting up.

Marsha laughed. 'Before I came here I imagined you lot'd be a right bunch of yoga bunnies. You know, being fashion types, desperate to remain a size eight. But no! Everyone's really unfit!'

'Oh, I wouldn't say—' Roxanne started.

'Anyway – never mind that.' Marsha clasped her hands together as if in prayer. 'So, tell me. How's it all going with your team?'

'Great, thanks,' Roxanne said brightly, perching on the padded seat.

Marsha murmured her thanks as Jacqui glided in with two mugs of coffee. Her desk was completely bare, unlike Roxanne's, which at present was littered with magazines, books, tissues, packets of mints, a utility bill from home, a gift voucher, a cereal bar wrapper, a bottle of perfume and a tub of nail polish remover pads. 'Glad to hear that,' Marsha remarked. 'Serena and Kate are so keen, aren't they? That's great to see . . .'

'Oh yes, they're both amazingly creative and organised. I don't know what I'd do without—'

'So, what about you?' she interrupted again. 'Tell me all about your vision for the future.'

Roxanne frowned, and her nostrils flickered. Was that the burnt brandy snap smell she could detect? Had she

49

somehow brought it to work with her? Marsha sniffed audibly and twitched her tiny nose.

'Well, I know we're in challenging times,' Roxanne began, 'and glossy magazines are in decline. But women still enjoy them. They've just stopped buying a whole raft of titles and have whittled it down to just one, a firm favourite – the one they feel the most loyal to. I truly believe that, if we make ourselves stand out from the crowd, then that can be us.'

She swallowed hard, trying to drag her thoughts away from incinerated confectionery as she fished out her scrap-book from her bag and placed it on Marsha's desk.

'What's this?' she asked, crooking a brow.

'My ideas book. Would you like to see it?'

'Of course, yes!'

Roxanne felt the blood rushing to the tips of her ears as she flipped it open. Could the smell have clung to her top and/or skirt? Her French wardrobe was antique and the doors didn't fit too well. Perhaps the smoke had crept in through the gaps? Marsha's gaze had dropped to the scrapbook which Roxanne had opened randomly to show pages crammed with her own lively pen-and-ink sketches, plus pictures of outfits snipped from magazines.

'This all looks very . . . interesting,' Marsha said unconvincingly.

'Um, it's just the way I work,' Roxanne explained. 'It's how I gather my ideas together and plan the next few issues with the team . . .' She flipped the page to show more sketches, plus fabric swatches, scraps of denim and printed cotton and lace; the pages were bursting with ideas, annotated with Roxanne's beautiful looped hand-writing. 'People are always complaining that the clothes featured in glossy magazines are exclusively designer,' she added, showing Marsha page after page of her chaotic yet beautiful collages. 'Well, I think it's important to make our pages inspirational for *everyone*. We're not just reproducing top-to-toe designer looks. We're all about creating beautiful outfits that *any* woman can afford. Yes, we can use the odd designer piece, but we also bring in quality high-street buys, vintage finds, things we've customised ourselves . . .'

Roxanne paused for breath and glanced across the desk. Marsha's attention was waning, she could sense it. 'This all looks great,' she said briskly. 'It's so quaint and child-like – so old-school – to have a funny little scrapbook of ideas . . .'

A *funny little scrapbook*? 'Well, I do find it helpful to—'

'And I'm glad to see you're not fixated on blow-the-budget shoots,' she interrupted, 'insisting on flying everyone to Africa and hiring eighteen elephants as props . . .'

Roxanne smiled tightly. 'Er, no. We often shoot in London, the home counties or the south coast . . .'

'No elephants there,' Marsha quipped.

'. . . Unless you count zoos,' Roxanne said, ridiculously.

'Ha, yes, and I don't think they loan out their animals for fashion shoots, do they? Anyway,' she added, shutting the scrapbook firmly to indicate that she had seen quite enough, 'there's something else I need to discuss with you, while we're here.'

'Oh, really?' Roxanne's eyebrows shot up. Something solid and heavy seemed to have lodged itself in her gut.

Marsha's nose twitched again, like a mouse's. 'Yes. Don't look so alarmed. It's actually all good and I think you'll find it'll make your job much, much easier.' Roxanne shifted uneasily as Marsha picked up her mug and took an audible sip of her coffee. 'As I'm sure you're aware,

51

everyone's cost-cutting these days – making redundancies, culling whole departments . . .'

Oh, good lord. Here it comes – she was about to be given the heave-ho. Her job was about to become 'much, much easier' because soon she wouldn't have one at all.

' . . . And you'll be glad to hear I'm not about to do that. On the contrary, I'm investing in our brand, bringing in extra resources. I know our circulation has only dipped a little, but I'm here to reverse that trend before we find ourselves in real trouble.'

Roxanne nodded. 'What sort of resources do you have in mind?'

Marsha dispensed a quick, bright smile, the kind a nurse might give before plunging in the needle. 'Well, this is all terribly exciting and you're the first to know. I'm bringing in someone new, someone amazingly talented to take a fresh look at the whole magazine . . .'

'In which department?' Roxanne was trying to sound calm, as if Marsha had mooted the possibility of new chairs. She glanced down at her coffee. Jacqui had put milk in it, which Roxanne didn't take.

'She'll be my right-hand woman,' Marsha explained, 'helping me to implement all the changes I want to bring about. We've worked together before. She's brilliant, a real firecracker: I know you'll *love* her . . .'

The effort of trying to appear relaxed and non-defensive was making Roxanne feel quite light-headed. She focused hard on Marsha's mouth as she spoke. Her teeth were small and perfectly even, like a row of tiny chalks. While Roxanne had her own teeth professionally whitened – a faff, but sort of expected in fashion circles – Marsha's were obviously veneers. 'Who is it?' she asked, trying to keep her voice level.

'Tina Court. Have your paths ever crossed?'

'Um, yes, briefly, although we haven't worked together. I've seen her at plenty of events, she seems very, er . . .' She tailed off. What to say? Tina Court was fashion director on a mammoth-selling weekly and had a reputation for being utterly formidable.

'She thinks very highly of you,' Marsha added, widening her eyes alarmingly. 'She thinks it's amazing that you still want to create beautiful pictures when really, all anyone wants these days is twenty-five figure-fixing dresses crammed onto the page . . .'

Roxanne blanched. She detested the phrase 'figure-fixing', implying as it did that women's bodies were on a par with faulty guttering, and needed to be rectified. 'Er, that's good to know,' she muttered. 'So, have you worked together before?'

'Oh, lots of times. We're quite the team, the pair of us. We go way back . . .' She beamed, as if reflecting upon how *fabulous* they were together. 'So, she'll be working alongside you, offering lots of support as we move away from arty-farty shoots towards practical, *useful* fashion . . .'

A sense of dread was juddering up inside her. 'What sort of thing d'you mean?'

'Like, "Here are the hundred best knickers to squish in that nasty wobbly tum!"' Marsha beamed at her, as if astounded by her own genius. Roxanne started to speak, but Marsha charged on: 'That's what women want, and we might as well accept it. Big bottoms, porky thighs, saggy boobs, bingo wings, that hideous knee fat that sort of hangs down . . . we're all desperate to cover up our problem areas, aren't we?'

Roxanne shifted uneasily on her seat. 'Er, I'm just not sure about the message we'll be putting across—'

'Well, it's where we're going and Tina will be in charge of all that.'

For a moment, Roxanne just stared at her as this new information sank in. 'You mean Tina will be in charge of *all* of our fashion?' she asked carefully. 'Or just these figure-fixing pages you're planning to introduce?'

'Ha. Yes and no. Or, rather, yes and yes. From now on, *all* of our fashion will be body-correcting, using the cheapest brands available, and shot economically in a studio. So, no more arty outdoor shoots with your fancy photographers, okay?'

'But we're *known* for beautiful photography,' Roxanne said, aghast. 'It's what the magazine is all about . . .'

'Oh, no one gives a fig about that anymore. We're all about quantity and value now – and Tina's remit will be to oversee it all.'

What the hell will I be doing, then? Roxanne wanted to ask, although she couldn't quite manage to string the right words together. Almost thirty years she'd spent, creating gorgeous images. She adored her job and couldn't imagine doing anything else; only now, it seemed her skills were no longer required. 'So, uh . . . what will her job title actually be?' she managed to croak.

Marsha fixed her with a cool stare. 'She'll be fashion-director-in-chief.'

'Fashion-director-in-chief?' Roxanne repeated. 'I'm sorry, but what even *is* that?'

'It's the person who heads up the fashion department of course . . .'

'But I head up the fashion department!'

'Yes, and I think this'll be good for you,' Marsha said firmly, 'and your professional development. Tina's a power-house and we need that strong direction, the *clout* she'll bring us in the industry. I know you'll get along like a house on fire . . .'

Oh, will we? Roxanne opened her mouth to speak but no words came out.

'Please don't look so worried,' Marsha remarked.

Stop telling me how to arrange my face! 'It's just a bit of a shock,' she muttered, digging her nails into her palms now. 'I mean, if Tina's being brought in to do my job, then where will I fit in?'

'How d'you mean?' Marsha pulled a baffled look, and then – in an act that struck Roxanne as unspeakably disrespectful – bent to rummage in her leather satchel and pulled out a small, oil-stained paper bag from which she extracted a Danish pastry. As if Roxanne had ceased to exist, she took a large bite.

For a moment, all Roxanne could do was watch her, chomping. *Oh, sorry, was I interrupting your breakfast?* What was the etiquette here? It didn't feel right to question Marsha while she was cramming baked goods into her face, but then, weren't they supposed to be having a 'chat'?

'So,' she managed, her voice unsteady now, 'am I to understand that Tina will be managing my team and essentially doing my job?'

'Yes,' Marsha conceded, nodding emphatically whilst still chewing, 'but don't look at it like that. It's just a slight restructuring and you'll learn *so* much . . .'

'And when is she starting?'

Marsha swallowed and took another bite. 'On Monday,' she said, a flurry of crumbs shooting from her mouth.

Roxanne flinched. 'On *Monday*?'

Marsha nodded. 'Yes. I know her editor very well so I've managed to arrange for her to be released immediately. Time is of the essence here, I'm sure you understand . . .'

'Of yes, of course,' Roxanne said, wondering if she understood anything anymore. 'So, er, is that all?'

Marsha nodded, her cheeks bulging like a hamster's. 'Yes, thank you for your time . . .'

'Thank *you*,' Roxanne exclaimed, polite to the last and willing herself to hold it together as she sprang up from the seat and strode out of Marsha's glass box. *Thank you, thank you, thank you.* She would probably have expressed her gratitude if Marsha had kicked her in the teeth.

'Roxanne? You forgot this!' Marsha was standing up now, still chewing, bovine-like, waving her scrapbook and planting greasy fingerprints all over it. As Roxanne darted back to retrieve it, Marsha frowned and sniffed its appliquéd cover. 'Does this smell of *burning* to you?'

Chapter Five

All eyes were upon Roxanne as she made her way back to her desk with her stupid *old-school* scrapbook wedged under her arm. At least, it felt that way. In a decade of working here, Roxanne had always regarded the office as her second home, with its scruffy old swivel chairs and temperamental toaster and dog-eared magazines piled everywhere. In some ways she preferred it to her *real* home as all the team were here, the lovely people who cared about magazines as much as she did and who were like family, really. Ibiza jaunt with Amanda aside, she had never been one for holidays. If she did force herself to go away – alone, usually, on some kind of 'activity break' where you were pretty much guaranteed to meet other single people – she tended to spend the second half of the week sketching ideas for shoots and itching to return to work.

Not today, though. Right now, she'd have given anything *not* to be here – to be magically transported back to her flat, with the door firmly locked. She was aware of Jacqui's gaze following her as she lowered herself onto her chair back at her own desk. Zoe was staring openly, her mouth ajar. *Yes, I've just been told some awful news,* she wanted to announce, just to be done with it. *Someone's being brought in over my head, so I'm effectively demoted – but, hey, I'm fine with that because, apparently, I'm going to 'love' her!*

She glanced back at Marsha, insulated from the rest of the team in her glass office. Her predecessor, Cathy, had never used it, preferring to have a desk out here in the main space, in the thick of things. Marsha was on the phone now, stuffing more pastry into her pursed little mouth.

'Everything okay, Rox?' Serena murmured from her own desk, which faced Roxanne's.

'Yes, it's fine,' she said briskly, catching Kate giving her a quizzical look.

'Want to nip out?' Serena whispered. 'Get a coffee or something?'

'No thanks.' Avoiding eye contact, Roxanne shook her head.

'Are you sure? You look awfully pale. Was it something she—'

'I'm-fine-honestly,' she barked, causing Tristan to spin his head around from the art department. Roxanne started rummaging in her top desk drawer, not because she needed anything but to give herself something to do. Like the top of her desk, it was a terrible tip. She delved amongst staplers, rolls of Sellotape, parcel labels, bulldog clips, cans of hairspray, notebooks and lip balms in a cacophony of flavours, willing Serena to stop giving her sympathetic glances, and wishing everyone would just leave her be.

Roxanne wasn't sure she could handle anyone being kind to her right now. She thought again of that time with the fish slice, when her mother had smacked her upper arm: it wasn't the actual event itself that had triggered her tears. It had been later, when she'd run out of Rosemary Cottage and up into the hills by herself, and had happened to come across Len from the garage with his wife, Pat, and their two young children. They were out with their dogs and had beckoned her over to join them.

Hey, what's happened, Roxy? You look all upset!

People had called her 'Roxy' then. Not anymore; she had cast that off like an unwanted jacket when she'd moved to London. Pat had hugged her, and that's when the tears had flowed.

Roxanne shut her desk drawer, delved into her bag and pulled out the small notebook in which she wrote copious to-do lists. There was tons to get on with, and keeping busy would at least get her through the rest of the day. She had a shoot coming up and she needed to call in clothes and accessories from fashion PRs, as well as trawling her favourite vintage shops for quirkier pieces. She wanted to book a new model – a fresh face – rather than one of her regular girls, which meant arranging a casting. Plus, there were Kate and Serena's shoots to oversee, and a whole raft of product launches Roxanne should show her face at over the coming week.

She made a barrage of calls until lunchtime rolled around, at which point she grabbed her bag and darted out of the office before anyone could ask to join her.

On a bench in Golden Square, clutching a chicken sandwich she didn't want, she called Sean.

'Oh, darling,' he said, when she'd splurged what had happened. 'Tina Court! She's meant to be a bit of a terrier . . .'

'You know her?'

'Just in passing. We haven't worked together. So, what're you going to do?'

59

'Nothing. I mean, what can I do? Marsha's within her rights to bring in whoever she wants . . .'

Sean sighed. 'Just sit tight, darling, and see how things pan out.'

'Yes, I will. Sorry to land all of this on you. I know you're busy shooting today—'

'Hey, I'm okay for a couple of minutes,' he said gently.

She cleared her throat. 'Pringles all ready?'

'Huh?'

'For the party,' she prompted him.

'Oh. Haha – well, Louie's been onto the caterers. Foie gras lollipops! I don't *think* so . . .'

'Let me know if you need anything,' she added, before they finished the call – knowing, of course, that he wouldn't, and that this was hardly a casual flat party where one might expect friends to bring a bottle of wine. No, this was an extravaganza with waiting staff, a seafood bar and a budget of thousands, and right now she couldn't *wait* to slick on her red lipstick and get her hands on that first glass of wine.

The office announcement about Tina's arrival was brisk and to the point. Jacqui had rounded everyone up, in the manner of an eager sheepdog, and now the whole team stood around stiffly while Marsha, who was perched with exaggerated casualness on the edge of Jacqui's desk, enthused over Tina Court's imminent arrival.

'I know she's going to fit in so well here. You're all going to adore her. She's such a breath of fresh air . . .' Implying what? Roxanne mused. That they were currently *stale*? 'She'll shake everything up!' Marsha wittered on, seemingly oblivious to the cloud of gloom now hanging heavily above them as she babbled on about figure-fixing

60

fashion, page after page of cheap knickers that promised to squish in one's tum.

'How depressing,' Tristan mouthed at Roxanne, with a horrified look. She nodded and shrugged. At least her colleagues seemed to share her view. Roxanne had assumed a non-committal expression, and was trying to keep her gaze firmly on Marsha as she spoke. However, it was impossible not to register the quick looks of alarm and sympathy her colleagues were giving her. She knew what they were all thinking: *Poor Rox! How must she feel, being effectively demoted? Is this a sneaky way of trying to force her out?*

Then Marsha was thanking everyone for their time – 'We're heading into such an exciting new chapter!' she trilled – and everyone was trying to check out Roxanne's face as she scuttled back to her desk. Before anyone could accost her, she scooted out of the office and along the short corridor to the ladies' loo.

As she tried to collect her thoughts at the basins, Serena and Kate arrived in pursuit. 'My God, Rox, what's going on?' Serena exclaimed.

'You heard,' Roxanne replied with a grimace.

'Fashion-director-in-chief? We've never had one before. I've never even heard it used as a job title . . .'

'No, that's because Marsha probably made it up.'

Kate ran a hand through her short coppery hair. 'What does it mean?'

'It means she'll be running our department and changing the style of our pages beyond all recognition,' Roxanne muttered.

'But *why*?'

'Because that's what Marsha wants, and she and Tina go way back, apparently. They've worked together before. Marsha said they're quite the team . . .'

'Well, that's complete nepotism!' Kate gasped.

Roxanne murmured in agreement, once again visualising the chilled glass of wine she would soon be clutching at Sean's party. Usually she was happy to work late, but she was now experiencing a strong desire to escape from the building as soon as possible. 'Everyone hires people they know,' she said, trying to remain professional rather than letting rip with how she *really* felt. 'Cathy brought me in, remember? We'd worked together before too. It's natural to want people you trust.'

'Yes, but that's because you're the best,' Serena declared, 'and this is different. Tina's pages are a mess, more like a tatty old catalogue than proper fashion – and come on, we've all heard what she's like to work with. She's had her assistants and interns in tears. No one seems to last there more than a couple of months . . .'

'I've heard all that too,' Roxanne remarked, touched by her friends' loyalty, 'but we haven't actually worked with her ourselves. We should just keep an open mind . . .'

'Oh, stop being so *reasonable*!' Serena exclaimed. 'If it was me, I'd be having a complete meltdown.'

Roxanne forced a brave smile, pulling out her topknot and shaking her hair loose to signify that they had given the matter of Tina's imminent arrival quite enough of their attention for now. 'Don't worry,' she remarked dryly, 'I'm saving that for Sean's party so as many people as possible are there to witness it.'

And now she was extracting her make-up pouch from her bag, plus the original 60s black dress she had earmarked to wear tonight, and which was ideal for this kind of office-to-party scenario as it simply didn't crease, even after being scrunched in the bottom of a shoulder bag.

She turned to Kate and Serena, who were still looking

mournful in the wake of the day's news. 'Come on, you two,' Roxanne said briskly. 'Let's get ready and off to this party. Anyone would think we weren't desperate for a drink.'

Chapter Six

Sean's studio occupied the entire second floor of a canal-side warehouse close to King's Cross. All white-painted brickwork with a glossy concrete floor, tonight it had been filled with silver helium balloons which were bobbing up at the rafters. The biggest, tethered above the huge metal-framed windows, read SEAN50. When Roxanne, Serena and Kate arrived, the room was already bustling.

There was a pop-up bar, manned by almost laughably handsome young men. Roxanne recognised them as new faces at one of the model agencies she used regularly, and Serena and Kate scuttled over to say hello. Other fledgling male models patrolled the studio, joking and flirting and carrying trays laden with glasses of champagne. At the far end of the room, a DJ was playing mellow tracks.

'Hi, sweetheart,' Sean said, having made his way towards Roxanne and given her a heartfelt hug. 'Sorry about your awful day. Are you okay?'

'Oh, I'm fine – don't worry about that now. It's your party! It looks fantastic in here . . .'

He grinned. 'I'll give Louie his due, he pulled out all

64

the stops.' Sean paused and appraised Roxanne's appearance. 'You look drop-dead gorgeous tonight, babe—'

'Thanks, darling,' she said, glowing now as Serena strode over to greet him, followed by Kate. Soon a cluster of new arrivals were descending upon him too.

'Let me grab you girls some champagne,' he said.

'Oh, don't worry about us,' Roxanne said quickly, feeling buoyed up already by the jovial atmosphere. 'We can sort ourselves out, can't we, girls?'

'We sure can,' Kate chuckled, indicating the stunning young waiter who was gliding towards them.

'See you in a little while, birthday boy.' Roxanne kissed his cheek and stepped away, leaving him to welcome the stream of newcomers, and accepted a glass of champagne from the waiter gratefully. Naturally, Sean would be busy playing host tonight, which was fine by Roxanne; she was used to them each doing their own thing whenever they were at parties together. She could hold her own in social situations and had no desire to cling to him, limpet-like.

With Serena and Kate at her side, she milled around the studio in a flurry of kisses and hugs; Sean's crowd were an affectionate and demonstrative bunch, forever greeting each other with cries of delight. As Roxanne had expected, she knew almost everyone here. 'Daniella, hi! Sadie, hi, sweetheart! Angelo – so lovely to see you . . .'

'Oh, you look stunning, Roxanne,' enthused Jarek, a hairdresser she worked with regularly on shoots. 'What a fabulous dress! Is it vintage?'

'It is, yes . . .'

'You always find the most *perfect* thing . . .'

She thanked him and moved on. Make-up artists, hairdressers, models, photographers, stylists, PRs and agents . . . they were all out in force, filling the studio with chatter and boisterous laughter as the music grew louder and more champagne was swigged. It wasn't long before Roxanne began to feel quite light-headed. She was drinking too quickly, trying to shake off the stress of her meeting with Marsha. She really needed to slow down. One more glass wouldn't hurt, though, and she'd be sure to eat plenty and drink some water.

She took another glass of champagne from a tray and went in search of food to soak up the fizz. Bypassing the seafood bar, where piles of oysters glistened on ice, she made her way to the Indian street food stall where a glamorous young woman with her hair tucked into a crisp white hat was handing out paper cones of puffed rice. 'This is bhel puri,' she explained. 'Would you like some?'

'Ooh, yes please – it looks delicious.' Roxanne tucked into her cone with a wooden fork, noting that the light and spicy rice was proving especially pleasing to the fashion crowd, most of whom tended towards the determinedly skinny. Roxanne, who had settled at around a size twelve, feared for their bones sometimes. Sean's agent, Britt Jordan, looked as if she might snap. Even her back – which was entirely visible in a tiny grey sheath of a dress – looked starved, with all the nodules visible. You could actually *count* the vertebrae. Roxanne was sick to death of carb-avoiding these days. She tucked into a second cone of bhel puri and washed it down with her champagne. Who could blame her? It had been a *horrible* day, the sort that needs its rough edges smoothed by something chilled and delicious, and this particular vintage was doing the job extremely well.

'Hey, Rox, you're looking good, darling!' Britt had glided over towards her.

'Thanks, Britt. So are you. Isn't this great? I hear you had quite a hand in the organising . . .'

'Oh yes, I had to, or we'd have been sitting in the pub with a dish of dry-roasted nuts.' She laughed huskily. 'But he's loving it, isn't he?'

The two women glanced over to where Sean was holding court with a group of younger men and women by the DJ booth. Everyone was laughing and sipping champagne. 'I think he is,' Roxanne said with a smile, genuinely happy to see him enjoying himself.

Britt turned to her. 'All that not wanting a big fuss . . . it's all show, isn't it? Who wouldn't want a gorgeous party like this?'

'Yes, you're right,' Roxanne said, surprised that Britt was spending time with her. A notorious networker, she usually flitted from one potential client to another, eager to make contacts that might benefit her roster of fashion photographers. Roxanne booked Sean regularly, as she had before they were seeing each other, so there was no need for any schmoozing where she was concerned.

Britt's expression turned serious. 'Um, I hope you don't mind me saying, but I've just heard your news . . .' Roxanne frowned, uncomprehending for a moment. 'About Tina Court being brought in over you,' she clarified.

Oh, right, cheers for that! 'It's not really like that,' Roxanne said quickly, trying to take a sip from her glass before realising it was empty.

'Isn't it? Because Sean said—'

'No, it's just a sort of restructuring,' she explained, prickling at the fact that they had discussed it at all. Of course, they were friends; Britt had represented Sean for many years. But, still, Roxanne wasn't thrilled at the thought of being gossiped about.

'Really? Why are they doing that?'

'Erm, I guess Marsha wants to bring in someone with a strong fashion background as hers is more, er . . .' Roxanne trailed off. What was Marsha's area of expertise again? Diets. Celebrity diets, at that. All made up, of course; Roxanne knew from inter-office gossip that she used to harangue her interns into writing any old tosh. 'She's more health-focused,' she added carefully.

'But she has *you* to produce the fashion pages,' Britt was insisting now. 'Oh, it's awful, Roxanne. So insulting. Everyone's gutted for you—'

'Everyone?' Roxanne's face seemed to freeze as Louie, Sean's assistant, landed beside them clutching a large glass of red wine.

'Yeah, we can't believe it, Rox,' he said, glancing around as they were joined by Johnny, a make-up artist who was also clearly in the know.

'I admire you, I really do,' he announced, enveloping Roxanne in a hug.

'I don't know what for, Johnny,' she said with a tight laugh, disentangling herself and grabbing another glass of champagne as a waiter glided past.

'For putting on a brave face tonight,' he exclaimed.

'Oh, I'm not being brave – I'm fine, really. I'm having a *great* time—'

'We're all amazed you're here at all!' added Dinny, a fashion editor from another magazine who had popped up seemingly from nowhere. She clamped a hand around Roxanne's wrist. 'If it was me, I'd probably go into hiding . . .'

'Or throw myself off a bridge,' quipped Johnny.

What? 'Honestly, it's not a big deal,' Roxanne said, a shade too loudly as the DJ had misjudged the end of a track and the music stopped abruptly. 'And of course I'd be here for Sean's birthday.'

'Well, you're very stoical!' Louie gushed.

'You show them, Rox,' Britt added. 'You poor, *poor* thing. It's so demeaning for you . . .'

'Erm, would you excuse me for a minute?' Roxanne hoisted a rigid smile, still catching snippets of conversation as she strode away. She really had to escape from this group, before she drowned in a pool of pity.

'She should get her CV out pronto . . .'

'D'you think she'll resign, or what?'

'Christ – *I* would . . .'

And worst of all: 'I suppose she *has* been in that job a terribly long time . . .'

As Roxanne wended her way through the crowds, she tried to emit an aura of quiet dignity. She gulped her champagne and glanced around, looking for someone to talk to who wouldn't go on about Tina Court joining the team and her own career being truly up the spout. Perhaps, she thought bitterly, she could gather everyone around to decide which bridge exactly she should hurl herself off? If only her old friend Amanda was here – but then, this wasn't her sort of party at all. After her stint as a magazine publisher's receptionist Amanda had retrained as a primary school teacher; i.e., got herself a *proper* job. The parties she threw were casual affairs with bunting, sausage rolls and cheap prosecco in her kitchen or unruly back garden.

What was the big deal about Tina Court anyway? Amanda taught children to read and write – she helped to shape their futures – and here Roxanne was, despairing just because someone new was being brought in to oversee the fashion pages and drag them downmarket. She stood for a moment, sipping her now-lukewarm champagne, aware of an unpleasant tightening sensation in her chest.

Fashion Guilt, that's what it was. It had happened before when she was trying to pull together a cover shoot and a PR had sent the wrong fake fur jacket for the model to wear. Roxanne had been moaning to Kate in the office when a little voice in her head (the Fashion Guilt voice) hissed, '*You watched Syria being bombed on the news last night. And you're sitting there, nibbling your Pret a Manger sushi and drinking your coconut water and grumbling about a fluffy jacket?*

Wondering what to do with herself now, Roxanne found herself back at the Indian street food stall. She wolfed another cone of bhel puri, then regretted it immediately: all that puffed rice seemed to be swelling up inside her. Uncomfortably bloated, she stood tall and tried to hold in her stomach. No sign of Serena or Kate, and Sean appeared to be busy, still surrounded by friends, filling the studio with his wonderful infectious laugh which she had loved from the moment she first heard it. She would go over to join him soon, but right now it felt better to give him his space. She caught his eye, and he smiled. How handsome he looked tonight in a crisp white open-necked shirt and smart dark grey trousers. She didn't mind in the slightest that legions of younger women were perpetually clustered around him. That was what it was like, in this sort of world – just harmless flirting. Roxanne was overcome by a rush of pride in him, and almost wished she could fast-forward to the moment when they were home together, undressing and tumbling into his bed.

However, it was only 9 p.m., and there were *hours* to go yet. Aware of her tipsy state, Roxanne fixed her gaze on the area of floor in front of the DJ booth. She inhaled deeply, reassuring herself that she was perfectly capable of holding her own as she strode towards it and started to dance.

That felt good. She could sense any remaining tension floating out of her pores, dissipating into the fragrant air, as she started to move. Never mind yoga with its slow pace and emphasis on breathing; Roxanne had one of those restless minds, so was it any wonder she found it so hard to concentrate in eagle pose? This was *far* more her sort of thing. As the music filled her consciousness, she no longer cared about Marsha or whether Henry from the flat below would be banging on her door to tell her off again for the lingering burnt smell. Stuff all that, she thought, closing her eyes and swaying her body, barely aware that she was the only one on the floor.

Roxanne had always loved to dance, right from when she was a little girl; back then, no one had known as she'd done it in secret, in her bedroom, having put on one of her favourite records to mask yet another of her parents' monumental fights downstairs. As she'd twirled on her faded floral carpet, she had ceased to hear them at all.

An escape, that's what it had been back then in Rosemary Cottage – just as it was now. There was something magical about music, the way it could transport you to some other place. With her vast collection of crackly old jazz records, her neighbour Isabelle understood that too.

Roxanne caught the DJ's eye and he grinned at her. He had a full, bushy beard, as was mandatory amongst a certain breed of twenty-something males right now. What would happen when the fashion was over? she mused. Would the companies that made all the necessary beard oils, balms and pomades – she wasn't entirely sure how these products differed – go out of business?

71

The track ended, and she was seized by an urge to hear something from way back, something she had danced to as a little girl in her bedroom in the eaves.

Another track started but it wasn't right: all this music was all too esoteric. What the DJ needed to play was . . . *what* was it called again? Heck, it was her absolute favourite, she'd danced to it a billion times and now she'd forgotten it. She wobbled slightly on her black patent heels and pushed a slick of damp hair away from her face. Across the room, Serena waved and gave her an *everything-okay?* sort of smile, but Roxanne didn't really register it. She was too busy approaching the DJ, trying to explain over the pulsing music, 'D'you have, er . . .'

'Sorry, love? What was that?'

She frowned, trying to flick back through her mental Rolodex of songs that had meant so much to her as she was growing up. The DJ was peering at her in a bemused sort of way. 'I can sing it for you,' she yelled at him. 'Can you listen for a minute?'

'Aw, don't worry, darling,' he said with a patronising smile, as if she was an old lady who had just biffed him with her wheeled shopping trolley.

'No, no, I'll remember it if you let me sing the start. Could you turn your music down, please?'

He laughed and shook his head. 'Sorry . . .'

'I remember it now! *Dancing Queen* by Abba. D'you have it?'

The DJ sniggered again. 'No, love, it's not really my kind of—'

'You must have!' she begged. 'It can't be a party without *Dancing Queen* . . .'

'Oh, you reckon?' The young man grinned.

'Could you at least have a look?' She wobbled on her

72

heels and clung to the front of his booth as if it were a swaying ship.

'Off you go and dance,' he urged her. 'You're a great dancer. Pretty impressive moves, you've got there . . .'

She peered at him squiffily, wondering if there had been a trace of sarcasm in his voice. No, she was just being paranoid, and no wonder – it had been a terrible day, so of course she'd drunk too much and was feeling sensitive. But what the hell? She was tottering off now and dancing, still on her own, feeling happy and light and not caring that Sean had just thrown her a concerned look, and was shaking his head and muttering into someone's ear, or that she was one of the oldest women in the room.

Sean waggled his hand to beckon her over but Roxanne just laughed and turned away. How *boring* he was, never venturing onto the dance floor. Age didn't matter one bit! Britt was beside her now; skinny, sexy Britt, who Sean reckoned to be around forty, although no one was sure and she refused to divulge her age.

Roxanne glanced back at Sean and cried, 'C'mon, it's your party! Come and dance!' He just gave her an inscrutable look and disappeared back into the crowd.

Now more people had joined Roxanne and Britt on the dance floor: Johnny, Serena, Kate, Louie and a couple of new girls from Roxanne's preferred model agency. They were all dancing and whooping, hair flying, and nothing mattered to Roxanne anymore. Not until she glimpsed a new arrival who was looking around expectantly. Marsha! What was *she* doing there? Sean didn't even know her. Roxanne stopped dancing and stared, realising now that Marsha hadn't come alone, and that Tina Court was hovering at her side. Tina, who'd been hired as the new fashion-director-in-chief! Roxanne had seen her at enough

73

events to recognise her, even in dim light. She was a tiny woman, bird-like with pointy features and brows plucked to the point of near-invisibility. Her long, straight black hair hung in a glossy sheet, and her wincingly tight outfit comprised a shimmery cobalt blue dress with a silver belt and towering nude heels. Marsha was still wearing the same cream shirt and dark skirt she had had on all day. Now the two women were laughing together as if enjoying a particularly hilarious joke.

Roxanne glanced around wildly for Sean, seized by an urge to demand to know why they were here. Okay, so Britt had probably pulled together the guest list, but Sean must have been involved at some point. He'd have been happy to delegate responsibility for the bar staff, the DJ and drinks – but not who was coming. Maybe Britt had insisted Sean invited Marsha, with her being an editor of a glossy magazine now? Roxanne supposed that made sense. But why Tina – the one Roxanne was apparently being so brave and stoical about? Her blood seemed to pulse at her temples as she watched them accept drinks from a waiter and gaze around as if they were utterly entitled to be there.

'Okay, Rox?' That was Serena, gently touching her arm.

Roxanne flinched. 'Yes, I'm fine . . .' She tried to carry on dancing, realising how terribly drunk she was now, and aware of several glances in her direction. She needed water or more of that puffed rice. It was too hot in here, that was the trouble; lately, her internal thermostat seemed to have gone haywire. She tottered away and stepped outside, onto the red metal fire escape where she inhaled the evening air. From here, she took in the view of London; it was unusually warm, even for late May, verging on stuffy. Perhaps a storm was brewing.

74

Further down on the steps, a couple of models were smoking. Usually, Roxanne didn't mind the smell of cigarettes. She had been a smoker herself until she had finally managed to quit last year, after visiting Della and feeling like an idiot, puffing away on the pavement outside her bookshop with virtually every passer-by stopping to say hi. But now, as the girls' cigarette smoke plumed upwards, she felt queasy. She looked out again over the city she had loved with a passion since she had arrived here at eighteen years old, and felt nausea rise in her.

Back in the studio, she scanned the vicinity for Marsha and Tina, keen to avoid bumping into them. They were nowhere to be seen. A waiter glided towards her with a tray laden with more glasses of champagne. 'Thank you,' she murmured, knowing it was the last thing she needed, but since when was champagne about need?

As she took a sip, a familiar voice floated above the hubbub: 'Yep, Roxanne's definitely here. I spotted her dancing like a nutter a few minutes ago.' That was Marsha – and what did she mean by that? Roxanne whipped around to see her, still with Tina at her side, turned partly away and facing the seafood bar. A fresh wave of nausea rose in her stomach, and for a moment she feared she might be sick.

'I thought she might not turn up tonight after your big announcement,' Tina replied.

'Of course she has,' Marsha retorted. 'You do know she's seeing Sean, don't you?'

'You're kidding!' Tina gasped, still clearly not registering her presence.

'No – honestly, they're a couple. Everyone thought it'd just be a fling, 'cause you know what he's like . . .'

'Oh God, yeah,' Tina murmured.

75

'But *apparently* those days are over,' Marsha crowed. 'They've been together a while now . . .'

Roxanne's throat felt dry and sour. Fuzzy with booze, she felt incapable of confronting them or even wobbling over to talk to them and making any sort of sense. *What* was Sean like exactly? What the hell was she implying? Sure, he'd dated plenty of women during the lengthy periods between his serious relationships – but there was nothing wrong with that, and she'd never heard that he'd treated anyone badly. She frowned, trying to fathom out what Marsha and Tina had meant. Of course, the fashion business was rife with gossip, most of it widely overblown or patently untrue.

Roxanne sipped from her glass, feeling quite desolate now after having her dancing *and* her boyfriend criticised, virtually in a single breath. Kate was waving from the dance floor, trying to coax her to join them. However, Roxanne wasn't really registering her.

'I thought *everyone* knew about them,' Marsha added.

'Everyone apart from me, obviously,' Tina exclaimed with a high-pitched laugh. 'Always last with the gossip. God, though – Sean and Roxanne Cartwright? That's hysterical . . .'

Roxanne stood for a moment, clutching her glass which she might once have termed half-full but was now most definitely half-empty. She turned away and placed it on a windowsill. However, being made from uneven bricks, the windowsill was too wonky a surface for the glass to rest on without toppling. Topple it did, landing with a smash on the concrete floor, causing a momentary hush as Roxanne turned and ran out of the room.

Chapter Seven

Normally, Roxanne wouldn't have dreamed of making a 'French' exit, as a hasty departure from a social event was known in her circles. She would do the rounds, saying all her goodbyes; although it could easily add an extra half-hour to the night, to duck out of an event would seem rude. Tonight, though, she had just run out and was now clattering rather unsteadily down the concrete stairs and across the cobbled courtyard, pulling her phone from her bag only when she was safely out in the street.

She scrolled for Sean's number, reassuring herself that he'd be *fine*, all his friends were there, and he'd understand why she had left abruptly. Anyone would. Even aside from overhearing Marsha and Tina, how could she be expected to endure one more second of a party at which pretty much everyone felt sorry for her?

At the sound of his voicemail, she cleared her throat. *'Hi, darling, s'me. Look, I'm sorry but I'm going home early. You've probably realised. It was a lovely party but I'm just not in the right frame of mind and I don't want to be a wet, um . . . a wet blanket or a wet leek or what-ever it is, so I think it's best . . .'*

She glanced left and right, hoping to spy the yellow light of a taxi, but there was nothing.

'The other thing is, did you invite Marsha and Tina Court tonight? Oh, I know it's none of my business and it sounds horribly petty and maybe you didn't ask them and they just thought they'd come along anyway. But if you did, couldn't you have warned me, honey? I heard the two of them . . . blabbing on about us, about our thing, our relationship – can you believe their bloody cheek?'

Roxanne broke off and rubbed at an eye, past caring that she might be smudging her make-up. *'Anyway,'* she charged on, *'you know I've been feeling a bit wobbly about work and, well, I just couldn't face them tonight – is that ridiculous of me? A bit silly? It probably is and maybe I just need a break. I really want to see Della, hang out in the bookshop . . . d'you fancy that – coming to Yorkshire with me? Oh, I know I've gone on about that! Anyway, enjoy the rest of your party, darling. The seafood was amazing – actually I didn't have any but it looked amazing, all those gnarly little creatures all piled up. I had that puffed rice, that was good! And the little cones it was served in. So cute. Anyway, I'm going now. Happy birthday darling, I love y—'* With that, his voicemail cut off.

Roxanne exhaled forcefully and shoved her phone back into her bag. She'd have preferred to speak to Sean, rather than Sean's voicemail, but, on the plus side, at least she hadn't left a rambling message. Less happily, it had started to rain. She had somehow managed to leave the party without her jacket, and her left shoe was rubbing at her heel. On closer inspection, the heel appeared to have acquired a nasty abrasion and was all sticky and raw. A dancing injury – at her age! She was a fashion director, for goodness' sake. She should be capable of putting together an outfit that wouldn't injure her. Wincing now, and still glancing around for a cab, she started to limp towards Islington. She would find this funny one day, she tried to reassure herself. How the girls at work would chuckle over the time she ran out of Sean's party and hobbled home with a bleeding heel.

Halfway up Pentonville Road, she stopped and looked to see whether Sean had called to check on her welfare and she hadn't heard it ringing. No missed calls. But there was a text, from Serena: *Kate thinks you've gone home, are you ok?*

She replied: *Fine thanks just bit tired xx*.

Yearning for a friendly voice now – and since it was only 10.45 p.m. – she called Della.

'Rox, are you okay?' She sounded startled.

'Er, yes. Sorry. You weren't in bed, were you?'

'No, don't worry. So, um, how're things? What've you been up to tonight?'

'I've just been at Sean's fiftieth actually . . .'

'Oh! Was that fun?'

'Kind of,' she muttered.

'So, where are you now?'

'Um, I'm just going home,' Roxanne replied in her best sober voice. 'I've had quite a week and I need to go to bed.'

'Right. So, er . . . how are you getting home?'

Roxanne coughed and considered fibbing but wasn't sure she could pull it off. 'I'm walking but it's fine, I'm nearly there now.'

'You're walking home at *this* time, on your own?' Della gasped.

'Yes, but I told you, I'm nearly—'

'Rox, for God's sake, you're in London!'

'Yes, handily, because that's where I live.' Roxanne was striding along now, head bent against the rain. She was regretting calling Della because, of course, her sister was under the impression that you only had to pop out for milk in London and you were likely to be stabbed.

'Could you get a taxi, please?'

'Yes, I will – but listen, your party invitation's beautiful . . .'

'Thanks. Sophie drew it for me.'

'I thought she might have. How's art college going?'

'Loving it, as far as she tells me anything. So, d'you think you'll be able to come to the party?'

'Hope so,' Roxanne replied, 'but there's stuff going on, I have this new boss—'

'Oh, yes, you mentioned her. How's that working out?'

Roxanne pushed her damp hair from her face. 'I'll tell you when I see you. How's the lovely Frank?'

Della laughed at this reference to the man she'd been seeing for the past eighteen months. Secretly, Roxanne had never been terribly fond of her sister's ex-husband, Mark – a podiatrist who had refused to even treat his wife's feet, for crying out loud – even before it had come to light that he'd been having an affair with a patient, for whom he had left Della. In contrast, Frank really *was* lovely: an architect whose daughter, Becca, was at art college with Sophie in Leeds. It was their daughters' friendship that had brought them together. 'He's great,' Della replied. 'He sends his love. Look – *please* get a taxi, would you?'

'I told you, I'm nearly—'

'I don't like the idea of you tottering home drunk, all by yourself . . .'

'I'm *not* drunk. I'm fine!'

A pause hung between them. 'Okay, then. Just take care. I worry about you, Roxanne.'

'There's no need,' Roxanne said unconvincingly. As they said goodbye, she wondered if there would ever come a point when a phone conversation with Della didn't leave her feeling as if she was still fifteen years old.

It was almost midnight by the time Roxanne reached home. She was tired and sodden and Sean still hadn't called her back, not that she expected him to really. He'd be having too good a time to think of checking his phone, she decided. Maybe he hadn't even noticed she'd gone. That didn't seem quite so positive, but then, it was probably better than him being frantic with worry and searching for her. And he obviously *wasn't* worried, was he? Perhaps he had played her message and thought, 'Yes, I can totally understand why she wanted to leave', and gone back to enjoying his night.

At the main door into her block, Roxanne raked through her handbag for her keys. She really must become one of those sorted women who tidied their bag regularly and juiced kale.

No keys. They had to be in there somewhere. *Don't panic,* she murmured to herself. *Just be systematic.* Shivering, her wet dress clinging to her, she sat on the low brick wall that divided her block's tiny gravelled front garden from next door's. One by one, she started to remove items from her bag and set them on the wall beside her: her make-up pouch, a bunch of pens, loose tampons, a few opened packets of peppermint gum, a brush matted with hair, flyers for exhibitions, plus the party invitation from Della. Della never found herself drunk and keyless, at 11.35 on a rainy Friday night. Nothing so unseemly ever happened in Burley Bridge.

I worry about you, Roxanne. Wasn't that just a tiny bit patronising?

Now Roxanne's bag was empty apart from some loose coins and that irritating gritty stuff that works its way up your fingernails, plus something else that looked like Rice Krispies. How had they got there? Something was stuck to her hand, too – some kind of damp leaf. Roxanne shivered. It seemed the interior of her handbag was so disgusting that plants were growing in it.

She sniffed the leaf. It was sort of earthy – and slightly citrussy too.

'Coriander!' she said out loud. She must have accidentally tipped some of that bhel puri in there. But still no keys, which suggested, alarmingly, that they were either in a pocket of the jacket which was lying somewhere in Sean's studio, or she had left them in her flat this morning. Whenever she was in a hurry – which, being realistic, was most workday mornings – she just shut her flat door on the Yale behind her, without bothering to Chubb lock it. What did she have to steal anyway? That's how her reasoning went. It was incredible how little of value she had accumulated by the age of forty-seven. Really, it amounted to little more than a pot of Creme de la Mer, a few pieces of vintage Gucci and her antique French wardrobe – and who would try to manhandle that out of her flat? As for the main front door downstairs, that was just shut on the Yale lock too.

She looked at her block. It was entirely in darkness. Please, she willed her neighbours: someone either come home, or be going out, so she could at least be indoors, out of the rain – although she'd rather it wasn't Henry or Emma from the first floor. She couldn't face them right now, being all perfect, never burning their food or drinking too much or wearing ill-fitting shoes just because they had fallen in love with the style. *Emma's handbag would never have plant life in it,* she decided bitterly.

'Isabelle!' Roxanne called out in relief, waving as her living room light came on and her face appeared at the window. She frowned in surprise, then disappeared from view. Moments later she was at the front door in a fluffy peach dressing gown and rather glamorous mule-style slippers, which exposed burgundy-painted toenails. 'Roxanne!' she gasped. 'You're soaking. Come in. Whatever's happened to you?'

'I've lost my keys,' she said, realising how ridiculous this sounded – being the idiot neighbour for the second time in two days.

'Oh, you poor thing. Let's get you all warmed up . . .'

Minutes later, Roxanne was dressed in Isabelle's rose-patterned brushed cotton pyjamas, a pair of bobbly cashmere bedsocks and an embroidered cardigan, and drinking a mug of strong tea. Beneath the socks, a large plaster covered the raw, sticky patch on her heel. Isabelle sat beside her on the lumpen sofa, listening in sympathy as Roxanne explained what had happened at work, and at Sean's party. However, it wasn't the kind of sympathy that made her feel pathetic. It was the warm and comforting sort, and she wanted it all wrapped around her, like a blanket.

'You need a break from that office of yours,' Isabelle said, her dark eyes filled with concern.

'Yes, I probably do. I should call a locksmith too, let you get some sleep. I'm so sorry for keeping you up . . .'

'Don't be silly – I'm used to late nights and I was still

83

up. No point in calling someone now. You can stay here, sort things out in the morning . . . will you be all right on the sofa? The spare room's a bit—'

'Oh, I don't want to put you out, Isabelle.'

Her neighbour frowned. 'You're not. Just make yourself cosy. You look exhausted, dear . . .'

Roxanne eyed the squashy couch which, admittedly, did look inviting right now. She had glimpsed Isabelle's box room on previous visits, and seen the bed piled high with boxes of books, old jazz records and goodness knows what else. Isabelle was a hoarder, a collector of twinkly things and a lover of glamour, although everything bore an air of slight shabbiness.

'Okay, and thank you,' she said gratefully. 'The sofa will be fine, thank you.' As Isabelle padded off to fetch bedding, Roxanne sipped her tea, grateful for its sobering qualities, and glanced around the room. The centre light was an extravagant crystal chandelier with blue glass droplets – a fine cobweb dangled from it – and the two faded pink velvet armchairs were strewn with lushly embroidered silk cushions. An old-fashioned treadle-operated sewing machine sat on a small desk in a corner, and garments that appeared to be in various stages of construction were draped over a chair beside it. Roxanne got up to inspect one of the home-made dresses: a delicate thing in beaded black crepe with fluted sleeves and discreet ruffles at the hem. It was so lovely, she could just see it in one of her shoots.

'You really are an amazing dressmaker,' Roxanne murmured, replacing it on the chair when Isabelle reappeared.

'Oh, it's easy when you follow the pattern.'

Roxanne smiled. Despite her love of fashion, she could no more 'run up' a garment than operate on a human spleen; any customising required for her shoots was undertaken by Serena. 'Are they for anything special?' she asked, eyeing the beaded creations.

'Just a couple of gigs coming up.'

'Right.' She smiled. 'Where are you singing these days?'

'Oh, nowhere you'd know. Tawdry little places.' Isabelle chuckled throatily. 'Come on – let's get you all nice and cosy . . .'

As Roxanne lay down on the sofa, Isabelle covered her with a blanket and an old-fashioned eiderdown. The pillow she gave her smelt a little musty, but Roxanne sank her head onto it gratefully.

'I don't want to put you to any trouble,' she reiterated drowsily.

'You're *always* trouble,' Isabelle said with a smile.

'No, really. I mean, the fire brigade, and now this—'

'*Shhh.*' Isabelle hushed her and then, in an act that seemed so kind it caused Roxanne's eyes to mist, she brought her a glass of water and tucked her in, like a mother would. Only Roxanne couldn't recall that her own mother had ever done that.

Roxanne was woken by the trill of her mobile. Still bunched up in eiderdown, she scrabbled to retrieve it from the floor. 'Hello?'

'Rox? What on earth's going on?'

'Sean? Uh, nothing! What d'you mean?' She coughed to clear her throat. What time was it? She had no idea. It was daylight and there seemed to be some sort of clamp attached to her brain. More worryingly still, she didn't appear to be in her own bed. Isabelle's jumbled living room came slowly into focus: the chandelier, the cluttered shelves, the ancient record player. Roxanne spied her own black dress, having been spread out to dry on the radiator, and her shoes neatly paired beneath it.

'I mean, that was nice of you,' he remarked coldly.

She frowned. 'What, me leaving early? I'm sorry, darling. I did explain, in my message . . .'

'The message I only played about ten minutes ago,' he snapped.

Roxanne tried to process this. 'I'm sorry, okay? That's why I called you last night, to explain why—'

'You stormed off because Marsha and Tina Court turned up?' he asked incredulously.

'Yes. No! I didn't *storm*. I just – well, I didn't want to make a big deal out of it. I'd had a bit too much to drink and I thought—'

'Tell me about it,' he cut in scathingly.

Roxanne swallowed and rubbed at her eyes, noting that a smudge of last night's mascara had transferred itself onto her finger. Here it came: the great wave of hungover dread that must have been lurking just beneath the surface. 'I wasn't that bad,' she said quietly.

'Oh, *weren't* you?'

A hush settled between them, serving to crank up her morning-after paranoia several notches. 'I just had three or four glasses,' she added.

'Right, so that's why you were throwing yourself around on the dance floor like a lunatic and begging the DJ for Abba?'

Her heart seemed to clunk. 'I wasn't begging. I just asked politely . . .'

'D'you really think everyone wanted to hear *Dancing Queen*?'

'No, but does it matter? It was a party, Sean. I was just having fun—'

'Yes, and I spent most of it worried sick about you. Someone said you threw down a glass and marched out!'

'I didn't throw it – it just fell – and you weren't worried enough to phone me, were you?' She was trying to remain calm and not yell in her elderly friend's living room.

'No, because I'd lost my mobile. Only found it at the end of the party and by then it was out of charge—'

'Sean, why did you invite Tina Court?' she blurted out.

There was a stunned silence. 'Jesus, Rox. How old are you? Six?'

She wrapped Isabelle's eiderdown tighter around herself. 'Could you just tell me, please? I mean, I suppose I can understand why you asked Marsha. It would have seemed rude not to, seeing as the whole fashion department was there, but . . .'

'Britt sorted the guest list,' he said hotly. 'I trusted her girls to take care of pretty much everything . . .'

'You did get involved with the food, though, didn't you?'

'Huh?'

She eased herself off the sofa. 'You vetoed the foie gras lollipops.'

'Oh, for goodness' sake. Sure, I checked the guest list but only to make sure no one had been left out. She *is* my agent, I trust her with—'

'—Yes, with work stuff but not your social life, usually. You don't even *know* Tina. So why was she there?' Roxanne suspected she was being unreasonable now. After all, Marsha could just have brought her along as her plus-one. And, even if Britt *had* invited her personally, what was the big deal really?

Sean cleared his throat. 'Look, Rox . . . I, er, don't really know how to tell you this.'

Her stomach clenched. 'What?'

'I . . . well . . . Britt heard a week or so ago, just on the grapevine, about, um . . .'

Roxanne blinked, waiting for Sean to continue. '*What* did she hear?'

'That Tina might be joining your magazine in quite-a-high-up-senior-role-kinda-thing.' It came out all in a rush.

Roxanne took a moment to digest this. 'You mean, Britt knew Tina was being brought in above me?'

'Well, er, it sounded like that was a possibility . . .'

'So you knew too, obviously?'

He groaned. 'Rox, look – I *sort of* knew, but it might just have been hearsay, and what was the point of upsetting you if it was?'

'You still should have said something,' she exclaimed. 'I can't believe you didn't even mention it! When did you hear, exactly?'

'Uh, maybe a week ago?'

'A *week* ago?'

'Okay, I'm sorry. I was going to bring it up on Thursday night, but we were having such a nice time in the restaurant, and then there was all the drama about those burnt biscuits and the firemen and—'

'There were plenty of other times you could have told me,' she cut in. 'But no, instead you went and invited her to your party, just to get on her good side—'

'I told you. That was Britt . . .'

'—And neither of you cared that I'd be humiliated,' she charged on, shouting now, 'and you're giving *me* a hard time for having a few glasses of champagne? I don't know how you have the bloody nerve!'

A terse silence hung between them. Roxanne's heart was thumping, her eyes filling with furious tears.

'I think it's time you grew up,' Sean muttered.

'Don't patronise me! How could you listen to me telling you about my meeting with Marsha and pretend you didn't know a thing?'

'Look, I'm sorry, okay?' he thundered. 'I'm really sorry. Jesus – I didn't realise it'd be such an almighty deal . . .'

'Of course it's a big deal! How could you be so disloyal?'

'Okay,' he snapped. 'That's enough. Let's just stop this right now . . .'

'Yes,' she shot back. 'That's a very good idea. This conversation isn't getting us anywhere . . .'

'I mean,' Sean said carefully, 'let's stop this whole thing.'

Roxanne's heart seemed to jolt. She sat for a moment, her ear clammy now from being squished against her phone. Isabelle had appeared in the living room doorway, still wearing her peach dressing gown. Registering that Roxanne was on the phone, she quickly retreated.

'You mean, stop arguing?' Roxanne muttered.

'No, I mean *us*,' he said sternly. 'Me and you. I think we're done, Roxanne.'

The plumbing in Isabelle's antiquated bathroom clanked and growled. The interior of Roxanne's stomach seemed to be doing likewise. 'You really want us to finish?' she asked hollowly.

'Well, yes, I think that's best.'

'Fine, *okay*, if you really mean it,' she said, her voice wobbling, 'but you're probably just hungover, feeling all tired and poisoned and—'

'I'm *not* hungover,' he said sharply. 'I'm fine, actually. Some of us know when to stop.'

Her hackles rose and her eyes filled with more hot tears. How *dare* he lord it over her when he'd shown no loyalty to her whatsoever? And now they were breaking up

89

because of the party, because of Abba and the fact that she had had a little too much to drink. Well, bloody good luck to him, if that was what he wanted. She would be *fine* without him in her life. 'What about your book?' she asked coldly.

'What book?' he asked.

Her tears stopped, miraculously. She blotted her eyes with a sleeve of Isabelle's pyjamas.

'*Rox?*' he prompted her. 'What book?'

'Nothing,' she snapped. 'It's not important.' Roxanne cleared her throat, wiping her cheeks with the palms of her hands and trying to convince herself she'd be better off without him, when he was always too *crazy-busy* to spend more than one night at a time in her company and had already forgotten about the photography book she had trawled all over Paris to find. She pushed a clump of hair back from her clammy forehead, just wanting to finish the call and hide away in her own flat. 'But I have to tell you,' she added, 'it's not just me, you know. Lots of people love *Dancing Queen*.'

Chapter Eight

Roxanne gazed at the towering plateful of industrial white toast, plus lime marmalade and a fluted glass dish of tinned fruit cocktail, all set out by Isabelle at the table at her living room window. Despite the fact that she hardly felt like eating, Roxanne gushed her thanks and eyed the fruit cocktail, the likes of which she hadn't seen since she was a child. She forced it down, even the weirdly pinkish cherry and the syrup it was all lying in. Wishing not to offend Isabelle, and despite her hangover's protests, she followed it up with two slices of toast spread thinly with margarine and wondered if she had actually woken up in 1977.

'I really do think you need a break,' Isabelle remarked, perched on the opposite chair and having polished off her own bowl of fruit.

Roxanne nodded. She felt a little calmer now; stoical even. Tommy, the joiner, had been called, and was on his way round. 'Well, considering Sean and I have just finished, you're probably right.'

Isabelle's brows swooped down. 'No! Have you really?'

She shrugged. 'From what he said, it certainly seems like it.'

'What happened?

Roxanne sipped her tea, unable to face going into the whole Tina Court situation. 'A silly row that just escalated . . .'

'Oh, Roxanne, I *am* sorry.' Isabelle pressed her lips together. Even at just after 9 a.m., the older woman was wearing lipstick in a becoming soft pink, and her silver bob hung neatly at her chin. Roxanne was still wearing yesterday's make-up and had yet to de-matt her hair. 'Are you terribly upset?' she asked.

'I'm not sure *what* I am. I just need time to get my head around what's happening with work, with him . . .'

'Didn't you mention your sister sent you an invitation?'

'Yes,' Roxanne replied, deciding not to add that she had called Della, drunkenly, whilst tottering home last night. 'She's having a party to celebrate her new, expanded cookbook shop.'

'Well, couldn't you pop up there for a little recuperation?'

She managed to raise a smile. 'You mean, go into hiding in the country?'

'Just for a change of scene,' Isabelle added, getting up to put a jazz record on the turntable. 'I mean – it's not *quite* my thing but some people seem to think the countryside's good for the soul.' Her dark eyes glinted with amusement. 'Don't they?'

'Allegedly,' Roxanne said wryly, 'and I must admit, I'm tempted to stay for a bit longer than just a weekend . . .' She pictured herself pottering about in Della's cosy shop, straightening books on the shelves, indulging in a little light dusting. Compared to pulling together and directing fashion shoots – against a backdrop of everyone feeling *doubly* sorry for her now she and Sean had broken up – sitting behind a counter with soft music playing sounded blissful.

'Could you arrange some time off from the magazine?' Isabelle asked. 'London would always be here for you if the countryside got too much.'

Roxanne shrugged. 'I'm not sure. With Tina arriving, it's probably the worst time to ask. I'd better seem keen to do whatever they want, otherwise they might see it as an opportunity to shuffle me off . . .'

'They can't do that, surely?' Isabelle got up to turn over the record, blowing fluff from the needle before setting it back down.

'Oh, I don't know anymore,' Roxanne admitted, 'but . . . well, thanks for last night, and for listening to me.' She glanced towards the front window and saw a scuffed dark blue van pulling up outside. The driver's side door opened and Tommy jumped out. 'That's my joiner arrived – *again*,' she said, pulling a face. 'At least he's fitting my new door today, so it's all worked out for the best.'

'That's my girl,' Isabelle said with a chuckle. 'Putting a positive spin on locking yourself out.'

Roxanne laughed as she handed her her dress and shoes. 'Thank you *so* much, Isabelle. You're so kind.'

What she needed, Roxanne reflected as she hugged her neighbour, was a little calm in her life. In just two days she had been effectively demoted at work, embarrassed herself in front of her colleagues and now her relationship had ended. So here she was, apparently single again, and with Tina Court's smug face to look forward to at the office first thing on Monday morning. Her desire to run away and hide in a cosy rural bookshop was almost too much to bear.

*

Tommy had Roxanne's flat door forced open in less than a minute. If he was taken aback by the sight of her ensemble of floral pyjamas, cardigan and woolly socks, it didn't show on his face. In fact, his sole concern seemed to be the absence of Sean.

'He still hasn't texted me, you know,' he remarked, in the manner of a spurned lover.

'Really?' she asked. 'He's probably just been caught up in other things.' *Like humiliating me.*

Leaving Tommy to fetch the replacement door from his van, Roxanne darted off to brush her dishevelled hair and change into a more appropriate T-shirt and jeans. She kept out of his way, biding her time by constantly phone-checking to see if Sean had texted a grovelling apology, while Tommy fitted the door. There was nothing, and she certainly wasn't going to text *him*.

'We were going to arrange for your man to photograph Jessica,' Tommy explained, packing away his tools when the job was done. 'I told Molly, my girlfriend. We were getting all excited.'

Roxanne regarded this fresh-faced young man, feeling partly responsible for his disappointment. 'I'm really sorry. Sean is pretty busy right now.' *Busy sitting there on the moral high ground, crowing over my excessive drinking.*

Tommy shut his toolbox and pulled his phone from his jeans pocket to scroll through some pictures. 'I've got hundreds on here. I know it seems a bit sad. You probably don't get it, do you, unless you have one yourself?'

'Er no, I don't have any children . . .'

'Oh, she's not a *child*,' he said, brightening now and holding up his phone for her to see. 'Although I s'pose she is like our little baby really. This is Jessica.'

Roxanne peered at a photo of a small brown and white dog being held lovingly on a woman's lap. 'Oh, she's adorable,' she cooed. She was actually somewhat partial to dogs herself, and prone to sneaking them into fashion shoots whenever possible. *Another gratuitous pooch!* her old editor, Cathy, had often joked.

'She really is,' Tommy agreed proudly.

'And I *love* her outfit . . .' From a fashion director's perspective, Roxanne wasn't entirely sure about the teaming of tartan coat with pink neck bow, plus diamanté heart dangling at her studded collar – but then, she wasn't about to criticise anyone for over-accessorising. 'What breed is she?'

'A Cavalier King Charles spaniel,' Tommy replied. 'We love her to bits. That's why I want some proper professional photos done, so I can have one blown up massive for Molly's thirtieth birthday. D'you think he'll say yes?'

Roxanne hesitated. In terms of acts of revenge, pimping Sean as a willing snapper of pets probably rated as pretty feeble. She had heard of far more spectacular gestures. Tristan, the art director at work, had ordered thirty-five pineapple-topped pizzas from various takeaways to be delivered to the ad agency where his boyfriend worked, after an episode of infidelity had surfaced ('I bought them on his card,' he told Roxanne gleefully, 'but that's not what'll get him. He'll be mortified by the pineapple. Charles thinks people should be jailed for putting fruit on pizza'). Of course, Sean hadn't cheated, but he *had* lied by omission, and he deserved a little pestering by Tommy at the very least. Roxanne had known enough high-flying fashion photographers over the years to under-stand how pet photography was regarded. It was the kind of job your average high-street photographer, with a studio above Poundstretcher, would do for fifty quid.

'I'm sure he'll be delighted,' she said brightly, grabbing her mobile from her bag. 'I'll send you his number now.' She prodded at her phone. 'Here's his landline too, and agent's number in case you can't get hold of him. Her name's Britt Jordan. She can come across as a bit scary, but just tell her you're a personal friend of Sean's, and that he's promised to do this job for you.'

Tommy grinned at her. 'Wow. Are you sure that's okay?'

'Absolutely.'

'You're a star. Thanks so much. I've googled him, seen his work. He's pretty famous, isn't he?'

'Yes, I suppose he is.'

He blew out air. 'And he's going to photograph our little Jessica. Better get her to the groomer's!'

'I think you should,' she said, fetching her purse and pressing another wad of notes into Tommy's hand. He clattered off downstairs, leaving Roxanne with a palpable sense of delight. However, it soon dissipated as she wandered from room to room, wondering what to do with herself now with an entire, utterly empty weekend stretching bleakly ahead of her.

She perched on the sofa and picked at her fingernails – the polish needed retouching anyway – willing Sean to call, if only so they could end things on a less bitter note. Perhaps they could even meet up for a chat, have a spot of lunch somewhere and sort things out. It seemed ridiculous to miss him when they spent around half the week apart anyway. However, on Saturday mornings, as it was now, they generally enjoyed a few languid hours together in bed, either at his place or hers, drinking coffee and reading the papers and making love. They would then shower (together sometimes – they were still at that stage), then wander out to grab a sandwich at one of the dozens of alluring cafes and delis nearby.

Apparently, they wouldn't be doing any of those things anymore, a realisation that made Roxanne feel quite desolate. What would Saturday lunches consist of now? A single-serving can of mushroom soup? She checked her mobile, just in case Sean had called and she'd had it on silent accidentally. Of course he hadn't – but surely he *would*, in his own good time, when he had decided she'd suffered enough.

By midday she had managed to convince herself that of course they would manage to patch things up, once the cloud of ill-humour had dissipated. Maybe Sean simply hadn't wanted to be the bearer of bad news, regarding Tina joining Roxanne's magazine. If that sounded rather weedy, she knew he went out of his way to avoid upsetting people; it was yet another aspect of him that she loved. She had watched him take dozens of pictures of a certain model, even though it was clear that she just didn't 'have it', and that the client would only use the pictures of the other girls on the shoot. Sean would rather waste his time than risk the 'dud' model feeling rejected.

Roxanne leaned against her fridge, sipping a tepid coffee, trying to convince herself that they would soon be laughing about her middle-aged inability to hold her booze, and her over-fondness for a certain 70s floor-filler. In the meantime, she would try to enjoy a Saturday to herself, and prepare something sweetly forgiving to say – 'I guess we've both been a bit idiotic!' – when *he* finally called to apologise.

Having run herself a deep, hot bath, Roxanne marinated her aching body until her fingertips wrinkled. She dried off, pulled her slouchy jeans and grey sweater back on and curled up in an armchair with the Laurence Grier photography book. As she leafed through the pages, tears welled up again – about Sean, her job and the whole damn mess. It was ridiculous, the sheer volume of liquid that was falling out of her eyes. Tears were flooding her face, dripping onto the precious book that Sean hadn't wanted anyway, and making her cheeks sting with all the salt.

She set the book down on the coffee table, fetched a wad of loo roll to mop herself down, and inspected her throbbing heel. The plaster Isabelle had so kindly administered must have fallen off in the bath. Naturally, a woman who allowed her kale to rot in the salad drawer didn't have any fresh plasters in her flat. If she were more like Della, she would have a properly stocked first-aid box. The more she thought about Della, the more urgently she wanted to be with her: being comforted, being looked after, for once in her life. Was it okay to say that? At forty-seven years old she wanted to be all cosy in her big sister's flat above the bookshop, with a blanket around her and a plate of sugary biscuits on her lap. It wasn't that she was ungrateful for Isabelle's Del Monte fruit cocktail. Just that sometimes you really needed a bit of mothering, and when that wasn't going to happen you wanted the next best thing: some *sistering*. That was what she needed right now. But she couldn't call Della again yet; it would set her worrying – they tended to only speak a couple of times a week – and anyway, Saturdays were generally her busiest days in the shop.

Roxanne gathered herself up and spotted Isabelle through her living room window, crossing the street. She was wearing a chic purple skirt and a little fitted black jacket, all dolled up and looking like a woman on a mission, although she was probably just off on one of her random wanderings. 'It's heartbreaking really,' Emma from the first floor had remarked when she and Roxanne had met in the hallway recently. 'Poor, batty old lady, just wandering about, pretending to have this whole illustrious jazz thing going on . . .'

Was it really so sad? Roxanne had wondered. Okay, so Isabelle was alone, and seemed to be estranged from her son – but at least she did precisely what she wanted, and seemed pretty content. Was that such a bad way to live? Wasn't it far sadder, she thought now, to be married to a man who insisted on calling the fire brigade just because a batch of biscuits had been left in the oven?

The sound of her mobile ringing cut through the silence, and Roxanne grabbed at it and stared at the name on the display. It was just Amanda.

Just Amanda? Roxanne was appalled that she was even thinking that way. Amanda was her closest friend. What sort of person had she become?

'Hi, darling,' she said, trying to sound upbeat.

'Hey, Rox. Just checking you're okay for today?'

She frowned. What was she talking about? 'Er, I *think* so . . .'

A small pause hovered between them. 'Keira's birthday picnic?' Amanda prompted her.

'Oh! Oh, God, yes, of course it is . . .'

'Are you sure you're okay? Did you forget?'

'No, no, I'm fine, honestly. You know it was Sean's party last night. I'm just a bit fuzzy, just getting myself together . . .'

Amanda laughed. 'Well, we're not meeting till two. Still plenty of time to recuperate and I promise we'll be gentle with you. Remember we said by the bandstand in Highbury Fields?'

'Yes, of course.' She was sweating now. She actually *had* forgotten about her own god-daughter's birthday party.

'See you soon, then. Oh, and the main reason I was ringing – you know I hate blowing up balloons, but the girls insist on them? Ewan usually does it, but he hasn't got around to it this time. Can you believe he's having to stay at home with a sickness bug?'

'He's missing Keira's party?' This was unlike him; Amanda's husband usually threw himself into the proceedings, taking charge of the games, charming all the mums.

'At death's door, apparently,' she hissed, with uncharacteristic fury. 'Anyway – never mind. I can manage. You couldn't pick up one of those balloon blower-upper thingies though, could you, on your way? They sell them at that cute little toy shop by the Green.'

'No problem at all,' Roxanne replied, feeling like possibly the most despicable godmother on earth.

Chapter Nine

At least she had not only bought but *wrapped* Keira's birthday present. It was sitting on Roxanne's dressing table, so pretty in owl-patterned paper (Keira loved owls) next to the gift box she had made for Sean's brandy snaps. Roxanne changed her 'I am depressed' grey sweater for a perkier pink top – the sun had broken through, the sky had turned bluer – and inspected her face. Her cheeks looked lightly sanded and her eyes were veiny and swollen from all the crying; not the preferred look for a ninth birthday party. She splashed her face with cold water and made a mug of tea specifically for the purpose of preparing two wet teabags to place over her closed eyes, for de-puffing purposes. She lay on the sofa, trying to transform herself into godmother mode, as the PG Tips took effect.

It seemed to work – or at least, she looked marginally less frightening. She applied sufficient make-up to appear partyish, as opposed to looking like she was about to hurl herself off a bridge. With her tender heel padded with loo roll and Keira's present stashed in her bag, Roxanne pulled on lace-up pumps and set off on foot, grateful now for a reason to leave her flat. She had friends to see, things to do. She was not plummeting into a mushroom-soup sort of life. The air was warm, the shopfronts cheery, the streets busy with people out shopping and meeting for coffee, enjoying the day.

Oh, but she loved her local neighbourhood. Yes, it was insanely expensive now, and lots of people thought it too twee and smug, not 'edgy' enough – but who wanted edgy at forty-seven years old?

Roxanne had stretched herself to buy her minuscule flat twelve years ago – magazine journalists weren't paid nearly as much as people assumed – and never looked back. What was wrong with being able to visit a different cafe every day for a whole month, if you wanted to? There was the canal, the cinema, all the quirky boutiques, tons of welcoming pubs and green spaces, should you want them – like Highbury Fields, where she was now, picking her way between children kicking footballs about and adults sprawled out enjoying the sunshine. She spotted the birthday gathering in the distance and quickened her pace.

'Hey, gorgeous!' Amanda enveloped her in a warm hug, and she was soon besieged by Keira and her little sister Holly. The girls seemed to regard Roxanne as an exotic aunt. They were fascinated by her access to what seemed like the world's most beautiful clothing. Many of the child-friendly freebies that came Roxanne's way – jazzy scarves, feather boas and glittery face paint – were dispatched straight to her favourite girls.

'This is lovely,' Roxanne exclaimed, plonking herself down on one of the madras-checked throws, among the wicker baskets of party food and scattering of gifts. She gave Keira her present and was introduced by Amanda to the mothers she hadn't met at previous parties.

'Mum, look!' Keira yelled, ripping the paper from her gift. Roxanne had given her an extravagant jewellery-making set that she herself would have loved as a child. 'Can I make something now?'

'Another time, darling,' said Amanda. 'You'll lose all the little pieces in the grass.'

'We can do it together,' Roxanne added, 'next time I visit.'

'Yeah, you can help me.' Keira hugged her, and Roxanne reassured herself that perhaps she wasn't so awful after all, at least in godmotherly terms. When you didn't have children, people sometimes assumed you preferred not to be around them, that you found them noisy and unpredictable, but Roxanne enjoyed their company very much. She took Amanda's girls on outings to the zoo, the cinema and theatre and never forgot birthdays – well, *almost* never.

'Did you bring the balloon blower-upper, Roxanne?' asked Julie, one of the other mums whom she remembered from a previous gathering.

She clasped a hand to her face at the realisation that she had forgotten something else. 'Oh, I'm so sorry!'

Amanda smiled, and Roxanne tried to ignore a quick glance between a couple of the other women. 'Never mind. We can just blow them up ourselves . . .'

'But you said we'd have a blower thing,' Keira started to protest.

'Auntie Roxanne was at a party last night,' Amanda added, giving her a wink, as if that excused her omission. In order to redeem herself, Roxanne grabbed a handful of balloons and started to puff away.

Although rather light-headed by the time they had been

blown up, Roxanne felt her spirits lifting. She had always believed that there was very little in life that a beautiful spring day in London couldn't put right, and the gathering was already doing a sterling job of shaking off her Sean-related gloom. Initially rather reserved, as groups of mothers often were, the other women began to thaw as Roxanne quizzed them with genuine interest about their children.

'D'you have any kids?' asked a rosy-cheeked woman in a Breton top and black jeans.

'No, it didn't happen for me,' she said, with a quick smile: her stock response.

'Ah, right.' The woman paused. 'So that's why you look so young.'

'Oh, I don't think I do,' Roxanne replied with a quick shake of her head.

'But you don't have that knackered look,' another woman chipped in, 'like we all have.'

'Hey speak for yourself!' Amanda said, laughing and running a hand through her short dark hair.

'You can always tell a childless woman,' remarked the woman in the Breton top, 'because she has that youthful skin and no mum-line between the brows.'

Please stop overcompensating, Roxanne mused, noticing Amanda fidgeting uncomfortably now.

'You're supposed to say "child-free",' another woman added, at which point Amanda caught Roxanne's eye and grimaced.

'Anyway!' she announced, leaping up. 'Shall we have the hula-hoop contest now?'

'Great idea,' Roxanne said, thankful to have a role to play – i.e., dishing out hoops and encouraging the children, not to mention indulging in a little hula-hooping herself, despite still feeling slightly fragile. More games followed,

104

expertly marshalled by Amanda, and once again Roxanne experienced a wave of relief at being part of something on an otherwise lonely Saturday afternoon. The children's laughter and chatter continued until, gradually, mothers and daughters started to drift off home, leaving just Roxanne, Amanda and the girls lying on a blanket, eating ice creams they'd bought from a nearby van.

'Sorry about earlier,' Amanda murmured.

'What do you mean?' Roxanne asked.

'Come on, *you* know. All that "child-free" stuff. It's mortifying.' She shook her head.

Roxanne smiled. 'It's fine. I'm used to being pitied.'

'Oh, Rox, they *didn't* pity you . . .'

'I'm joking,' she laughed. 'Honestly.'

Amanda studied her face. 'They're just jealous because they know all about you and your fancy job.' She paused. 'So, how was Sean's party, anyway?'

'Uh, not so great, actually.' As they gathered up the picnic, and the girls ran off to fuss over a passing Labrador puppy, Amanda gently coaxed out the details of recent events. The fire brigade, the Tina announcement, the swigging of too much champagne, and Roxanne and Sean breaking up: as it all tumbled out, she was conscious of it all sounding so silly and juvenile. She looked at her friend. '*When* will I grow up?'

'You are grown up! Look at what you've achieved, how respected you are. I know loads of women who'd love your life. Who else could do your job like you do?'

Roxanne shrugged. 'Oh, I don't know. Plenty of people, probably. Who cares about all that stuff anyway?'

'You do,' Amanda said, squeezing her hand. 'Of course you do. Don't you?'

Roxanne opened her mouth to speak, but Holly

scampered back over and cut in: 'Auntie Roxanne, can we go to your flat, please? I need the loo.'

Amanda looked at Roxanne. 'Is that okay? I'm sure it's just an excuse. They love going to your place.'

'Mummy, I'm bursting,' Holly exclaimed, doing a little need-to-pee dance. So the picnic baskets and presents were loaded into Amanda's car, and onwards they walked to Roxanne's flat, where she made a pot of tea, apologising several times for the lack of orange juice or fizzy drinks. 'They're full of soft drinks anyway,' Amanda declared, as Roxanne found paper and pens for them to draw with. Soon she and the girls were sprawled on her living room rug, sketching fashion models in a myriad of outfits, while Amanda flopped out gratefully on the sofa.

'We've totally gatecrashed your day,' Amanda said when, much later, Roxanne phoned for pizzas.

'Not at all,' she insisted truthfully; although she couldn't bring herself to admit it, she still didn't want to be all by herself, and their presence had stopped her from checking her phone to see if Sean had texted. His photography book still sat, barely touched, on the coffee table. Sick of the sight of it now, she stashed it away on a shelf.

They ate pizza, watched TV and even played Monopoly until, finally, Amanda said they really should go. Roxanne was conscious of fixing on a stoical smile as she saw them downstairs and hugged each of them in turn. She stood on the doorstep, watching and waving as they wandered back towards Highbury Fields, a tired but happy little gang of three. And when Roxanne stepped back into her flat, and gathered up the pizza boxes, she realised her eyes were all wet again.

*

Roxanne spent much of the next day employing various strategies so as not to call Sean.

She stashed her mobile in the bottom of her favourite bag – which she had yet to clean out properly – in the hope that 'out of sight, out of mind' might work for her. When it didn't, she took herself out for a walk along Upper Street and deliberately left her phone at home. However, any pleasure she might have derived from stopping for coffee and reading the Sunday papers was marred by the fact that someone might be trying to contact her.

Sean, for example. Sean might have been calling to say he loved her and that he deeply regretted not tipping her off about Tina's appointment. She tried to savour her coffee from the window-side bench in a small and busy cafe, but she couldn't help imagining her mobile ringing and ringing in her flat. Now, in her mind's eye, her landline – that dusty old thing, a relic from a bygone era – was trilling too. Never mind that Sean was no more likely to call it than send her a telegram.

She sipped her muddy Americano, aware that she had played the whole business over in her head so many times she had lost any perspective on whether she had over-reacted – or perhaps *under*-reacted? – to the whole Tina Court business. As for that snippet of conversation she had overheard at the party – 'Everyone thought it'd just be a fling, 'cause you know what he's like' – she still hadn't fathomed out what *that* implied exactly. Yes, Sean was flirtatious – but then, in the fashion world, that was virtually the law.

Roxanne trooped home, meeting Henry and Emma on the stairs as they were heading out.

'No more burning incidents, Roxanne?' asked Henry with a snort.

'Nope, although I haven't tried to cook anything since then,' Roxanne replied with a terse smile.

'Hmm, that's probably for the best,' Emma remarked. 'So, what are you up to today?' She was all prominent front teeth and wide, trembling nostrils, faintly equine.

'Um, just having a quiet day,' Roxanne replied, and a distinct look of pity flickered between Emma and Henry. *Ah, poor lonely, middle-aged Roxanne.* 'I was at a party on Friday night,' she added quickly, 'and another one yesterday so I'm having a lazy Sunday . . .'

'Gosh,' Emma exclaimed. 'You have a far more exciting life than we do!' And off they trotted, leaving wafts of expensive fragrance in their wake as Roxanne stomped upstairs, jammed her new key into the lock and burst in to grab her phone and check it for missed calls.

There was just one – from an insurance company who'd called to tell her how to claim for an accident she had never had. She glared at her mobile, as if her current situation was all its fault. Whatever happened, she must *not* call Sean. After the way he'd treated her, she would not lower herself by getting in touch.

Now Roxanne was on her hands and knees, delving through the tatty old sideboard in her living room which acted as a sort of holding tank for everything that didn't have a proper place. As she burrowed into its depths, it struck her that this was yet another zone of disgustingness – like her favourite handbag, the bottom of her wardrobe and her desk drawer at work. At the back of the sideboard, her hand brushed unexpectedly against a clump of something soft and papery. She tugged it out and examined the small mound of shredded paper, trying to figure out why she might have put it there – then realising it hadn't been put there at all, but *made* there. It was a nest. So this was what things had come to; she was sharing her home with mice.

Still, at least she wasn't alone.

She continued to dig around in the sideboard, a little more cautiously now, finally finding what she'd been looking for: a block of fluorescent Post-it notes. DO NOT CALL SEAN, she wrote on the top one, tearing it off and sticking it to her phone. She wrote out a few more and plonked them on her fridge, bread bin, bathroom mirror and bedroom door: DO NOT CALL SEAN!!!

What would Della make of her behaviour now? She would think she had lost her mind – or at least reverted to being seventeen years old and in the throes of some crazed infatuation, which perhaps wasn't so far from the truth.

Would it count if she just called to hear his lovely, sexy Irish tones on his voicemail message? *Yes*, it would – as the real Sean might pick up. She paced from room to room, then spotted her laptop lying on her bed. For want of anything better to do, she perched beside it and logged onto Facebook, regretting it immediately as, naturally, the first thing she saw on her newsfeed was an album of photos of jolly, happy, smiling people having the time of their lives at Sean's party.

They were casual shots, taken by Louie. Roxanne hadn't even noticed him photographing anyone, possibly because she'd been fixated with Marsha and Tina and then too sozzled to notice what was going on. There were pictures of Britt with her skinny brown arms thrown around Sean. There was the whole crew of make-up artists and models, all raising glasses and grinning and seemingly not inebriated. Roxanne spotted Marsha, smirking in front of the DJ booth. There was even a picture of Tina, grinning malevolently in her skintight blue party dress. Roxanne studied each photo forensically. She didn't appear to be in any of them, which was something of a relief. At least she hadn't been snapped cavorting on the dance floor.

Ah – but *here* was one of her. She was standing alone by the Indian food stall, hair askew, with her mouth wide open as she tipped a cone of bhel phuri into it. Roxanne shut down the page, disgusted with herself, and with Facebook, for making it obligatory to post party pictures everywhere. *Hey, look at my fantastic life, everyone!*

Aware that she was becoming irrationally bitter, she snatched her phone. She would call Sean – just once. After nine months together it was ridiculous to finish so abruptly. They had to talk things through calmly, at the very least. Her heart seemed to stop as the phone rang and rang. Roxanne knew she should end the call, but she couldn't. She was incapable of rewiring her brain, or her heart or whatever it was, that caused her to be in love with him. Attempting to shut off those feelings was like trying to walk past her favourite shoe shop without at least peeking in. She was physically unable to do it. The day she had bought those heel-scouring shoes, she had been running late for her tooth-whitening appointment. Her dentist was terribly churlish if she wasn't on time, but even so, she had found herself being pulled into the shop by a powerful magnetic force, her own sandals removing themselves from her feet, seemingly without her having anything to do with it, and the delectable patent beauties being tried on and duly purchased.

With a jolt now, she realised Sean's voicemail message had finished. At a loss now of what she wanted to say, she hung up. Her instinct was to call his number again, just to hear his voice one more time – but no, this had to stop. She was a grown woman, for goodness' sake. Roxanne imagined her sister's face if she could see what she was doing now, moping over a boyfriend on a tragically empty Sunday afternoon. She pictured Della and Frank, and Frank's son Eddie, doing something wholesome like going for a country walk with Stanley, the rescue terrier Della has adopted a few months ago. How lovely to be with people who didn't judge you and find you lacking.

Hungry now, Roxanne peered into her fridge. There was a block of ageing feta, but she didn't have any bread or crackers to put it on, and nibbling it straight from the block seemed too sad, even for her. The kale was still sitting there too. Really it wasn't a salad drawer she had there, but a compost heap. Roxanne pulled out the bag of slimy leaves and stuffed it into her kitchen bin, along with the cream she had intended to whip up to fill those ill-fated brandy snaps. Perhaps it was just as well that she had never got to the filling part. She didn't own such a thing as a piping bag, and her plan to use a carrier bag with a hole cut in it would probably have resulted in a less than professional look.

Perhaps it was *also* just as well that she had got drunk and wobbled home in the rain and made Sean mad – because now she could see what a sanctimonious twerp he really was, not to mention a music snob, and who needed a ruddy great seafood bar anyway? It was a birthday party – not Selfridges food hall. Was half a mile of crustaceans really necessary? She suspected that the whole, 'Oh, I'd have been happy with a dish of Pringles' thing was just a smokescreen because he liked to play Mr-Down-to-Earth.

Stuff Sean – and stuff Tina Court. Tomorrow would be

a new start, Roxanne decided, knotting the bin bag tightly and lugging it downstairs to the wheelie bin at the back of her block. She would breeze into work, a model of poise and decorum and, if she didn't like the way things were going, she would . . . well, she wasn't quite sure what she would do. But she was sure she would think of something.

Chapter Ten

Monday morning, 8.47 a.m., and Marsha was already parading Tina from desk to desk to introduce her to the team. The new arrival was wearing a snug-fitting grey shift in a peculiar ruched fabric, with rather startling red heels. Her thick, straight hair hung in a curtain, as black and shiny as a patent handbag.

'I'm sure you'll love it here,' Jacqui was enthusing. 'Everyone's so thrilled about you joining us.'

Since Marsha's arrival, the office had split into two camps: Marsha and her loyal PA Jacqui – and everyone else. Still, everyone was doing a sterling job of fixing on smiles and saying all the right things: *We've heard so much about you . . . Anything I can help you with, just ask . . .*

'Hi Roxanne, lovely to meet you properly at last!' Tina had appeared at her desk, with Marsha lurking close by, like a minder. Roxanne jumped up as if stabbed with a fork.

'Hi, Tina. How nice to meet you too. Welcome to the team.' She beamed – the effort triggered a pain in her jaw – and shook her hand.

'Thanks. I'm so happy about being here.' Although Tina was smiling, her pale grey eyes remained flinty and her gaze kept flickering elsewhere.

'Such exciting times here . . .'

'Yep, the world of glossies is all new to me!'

'Oh, I'm sure you'll be fine,' Roxanne babbled nonsensically, as if she had been beamed into a factory at which a royal visit was taking place, and it was her turn to be confronted by Her Majesty.

'Shame you dashed off so quickly on Friday night, Roxanne,' Marsha remarked, stepping towards her.

'Friday night?' She frowned, feigning ignorance.

Tina bared her teeth. 'We were at Sean O'Carroll's party.'

'Oh, yes, of course! I thought I saw you. There was an awful lot of people, though.' Roxanne's cheeks burned. Why was she talking as if she was having difficulty with the English language?

'You looked like you were having fun on the dance floor,' Tina added with a smirk.

'Did I? Haha. The music was great, wasn't it? It was a really great night.' *Stop acting like you have never been to a party before, you goat . . .*

'It really was. I love seeing someone really letting go like that, not caring what anyone thinks.' Tina's eyes were glinting with devilment now.

'Haha, yes.' Roxanne glanced around in panic, sensing a fierce heat radiating from her face. 'I'd had a few wines. Maybe I was being a bit overenthusiastic . . .'

'Well, you certainly know how to have a good time!' Marsha crowed, clearly aware of the effect such a remark might have; i.e., causing the recipient to never venture out in public ever again, and perhaps consider fashioning a noose.

'Yes, I do, ha!' Roxanne stood there, laughing awkwardly, sweat prickling her underarms.

'Ready for yoga? Lily's arrived,' Marsha trilled, referring to the ridiculously lithe yoga instructor.

'Yes, of course,' Roxanne babbled.

'Are you joining us for yoga, Tina?' Serena asked pleasantly, looking up from her desk.

'Oh, no, I can't, unfortunately,' she replied. 'I have back problems.'

Ah, so perhaps it *was* optional after all.

Relieved to escape for a moment, Roxanne hurried to the ladies' loo to change into those wretched leggings and T-shirt. On her way out, she found Serena and Kate loitering in the corridor, ready to accost her.

'We were really worried about you on Friday night,' Serena exclaimed.

'Please don't go on about that. You heard – I've just had all that from Marsha and Tina . . .'

'No, not that. I mean, you disappearing without saying goodbye.'

'Oh, sorry. I did text you back . . .'

'Yes, but we were still concerned—'

'It was just so hot in there,' Roxanne said quickly, striding into the office now. From now on, she *wouldn't* be the last one to sit down and 'connect with the breath'.

'It *was* awfully stuffy,' Kate agreed.

'. . . So I went out on the fire escape for some air but that didn't help, so I snuck off home . . .' They all knew she was lying, but it didn't matter now as they arranged themselves cross-legged on their mats.

Across the room, Tina was already installed at a desk just outside Marsha's glass office. Her first day, and she was casually swinging on her swivel chair, twirling a Biro in the air absent-mindedly and yacking away on her phone: 'Yeah, so I'm here to basically oversee the fashion, steer it in a new direction . . .'

Class commenced, and Roxanne obediently followed Lily's instructions, working her way through the poses whilst trying to figure out how she might possibly handle working with this woman.

'Yep, any queries should come through me now,' Tina went on, seemingly unconcerned that class was in progress. 'Yes, and invitations too – send them to me. *I'm* your main point of contact now . . .'

Cat, cow, upward dog . . . Roxanne flipped about on her mat, on autopilot as a realisation began to build. She couldn't take this. She would not allow Marsha and Tina to take over as if she didn't exist; it felt imperative now to make it clear that she *mattered*. When she had started here, the magazine was regarded as being pretty low down in the fashion hierarchy. These days, they could access any photographer or model they wanted – and it was Roxanne who had built their reputation and garnered respect. Both Marsha and Tina needed her very much, and she needed to make that clear.

When yoga class finished, Roxanne changed back into her polka-dot wrap dress which always made her feel so right, so pulled together. Minutes later, she tapped on Marsha's glass door.

'Roxanne? Can I help you?' Marsha gave her a terse *I'm-rather-busy* frown.

'Yes, I wondered if we could have a quick chat, if you have time?'

'Oh. Yes, I suppose so. Come in, sit down . . .'

Roxanne bobbed down onto the chair and cleared her throat. Now she was here, her confidence had dwindled and she wasn't so sure about being invaluable after all. Besides, it wasn't in her nature to blab on about how 'needed' she was. Bigging herself up simply wasn't her style. 'Erm, I wondered if I could clarify a few things,' she began, 'about my role on the magazine, if that's okay?'

Marsha frowned again. 'Yes, of course. What do you mean exactly?'

'Well . . . it's just, obviously things are changing around here, and . . .' A tremor had crept into her voice . . . 'I think, I, er . . .' *Spit it out,* she willed herself. *You have every right to know what's happening to your job.* 'I'd like to know, do I still have a position here?'

Her editor's brows swooped down. 'Well, yes, of course you do! Why do you ask?'

'Because, as you explained last week, you've brought in Tina to head up the fashion department . . .' That was better. She sounded calmer now, more in control. 'Which sort of implies that I'm not needed . . .'

'Of course you are!' Marsha exclaimed. 'Gosh – I don't want you to feel that. Absolutely not. You're highly respected, Roxanne. Your name is synonymous with this magazine. No, Tina's role is to steer things in a new, more commercial direction . . .'

'Yes, but what will *I* do?' Roxanne cut in, all trace of nerves having evaporated now.

'You'll support her, of course.' Marsha's brow furrowed. 'Won't you?'

'Well, yes, as much as I can – of course I will. But on a practical level, I'm just not sure where I'll fit in day-to-day.'

For a moment, Marsha looked genuinely stuck for words. She scratched her head and shuffled a scattering of unopened mail into a tidy pile. 'Tina will have a huge job on her hands,' she said carefully, 'and she'll need you

117

working alongside her every step of the way. You're a *wonderful* asset . . .'

'Yes, well, that's great to hear, but I *do* need to know what I'll be doing.'

'Oh, I thought I just explained.' She fixed Roxanne with a cool stare. 'You'll be supporting Tina . . .'

So that's where they were: stuck in a 'support Tina' loop, with Roxanne still none the wiser about her position.

'Yes, but what will that actually entail?'

Marsha blinked at her. 'Well, I see you moving away from the creative aspect and more into an organisation role . . .'

Something heavy seemed to have lodged itself in Roxanne's gut. 'What does *that* mean?'

'Well, Tina will be incredibly busy managing the shoots,' she explained breezily, 'so she'll need you to keep tabs on the budget. Cutting costs is a big priority now, so you can be in charge of that.'

Roxanne realised her mouth was hanging ajar.

'. . . You're very experienced,' she went on. 'I'm sure you'll be able to come up with lots of ways we can save money . . .'

'Er, I don't think that's quite my—'

'. . . and competitions!' Marsha continued, seemingly unaware of Roxanne's growing dismay. 'You can set up loads of those. They bring the punters in . . .'

'Competitions?' This was the kind of thing the juniors and interns usually took care of.

'Yes, you know the kind of thing – ten pairs of jeans up for grabs, a lifetime's supply of tights. That kind of thing. You have amazing contacts, so I'm sure all the big companies will be falling over themselves to give us their stuff.'

Roxanne cleared her throat. 'Actually, Marsha, this isn't really what my job's all about.'

Marsha blinked at her. 'Yes, but it'll be good for you. Ten years is an awfully long time to be sitting there in the same old role. I see this as a career development for you. So, does that answer your question?'

Roxanne paused for a moment, allowing this new information to sink in. 'Yes, it does,' she remarked carefully. In fact, Marsha had answered a much bigger question – the one concerning Roxanne's future on the magazine.

'Well, I'm glad about that,' Marsha said with a brief smile.

'Yes, but it also means I can't work here anymore.' Roxanne regarded her new boss levelly across the immaculate desk. Although she hadn't planned to say it, it was the truth. Some people would be happy to manage a budget and figure out how to cut costs. But it wasn't Roxanne, and if she couldn't be fashion director here, then she would have to go elsewhere.

'You want to *leave*?' Marsha glared at her, as if Roxanne were a child who had just had a small tantrum.

'If that's what my job will be, then yes, I think I'll have to.'

'But you can't! I thought you'd be pleased to take a step back from the day-to-day running of things. I know how hard you work, always charging around . . .'

'Yes, but I love what I do,' she cut in.

'Isn't it exhausting for you, doing all these shoots?'

Now she was talking as if Roxanne was about ninety-seven. 'No, it's not!'

Marsha stared at her. '*Please* don't do anything rash. Your name's highly respected and you're very much needed here. Perhaps you just need some time away from the office – how does that sound? Just while Tina settles in?'

Roxanne eyed her suspiciously. As she had mentioned

to Isabelle, she did need a breather from the magazine. A full decade, she'd been here, with barely a break. Most years, she didn't even take her full quota of leave. 'You mean a holiday?' she asked cautiously.

'Well, perhaps a little longer than that. A sort of sabbatical . . . say, a couple of months?'

Roxanne frowned, confused now as to why Marsha wouldn't just accept that she wanted to resign. She couldn't regard her as important – not if she was happy to ship her off for two months. Perhaps it was just her name and contacts she valued? 'I don't really see how that would change anything,' Roxanne murmured.

'You're very important to us,' Marsha said, adopting an almost comically serious tone, as if she were trying to sell her a pre-paid funeral plan. 'We want you to be happy. We certainly don't want to lose you . . .' *Who's this mythical 'we'?* Roxanne thought dryly. 'You'd have full pay, of course,' Marsha continued, 'and you could keep in touch with the office as much or as little as you wanted to . . .'

Roxanne turned this over. Although it was tempting, the thought of returning to the office in this new role Marsha had dreamed up for her still filled her with dread. 'If I did take some leave,' she said hesitantly, 'would I still come back as the cost-cutting, competitions person?'

Marsha shook her head. 'I wouldn't dream of pushing you into a role you're not happy about, although naturally I do need you to work alongside Tina in a wholly positive way.' She speared her a sharp look. 'So perhaps, if you could use that time to think about what *you* want – bearing in mind Tina's position here . . .' She paused. 'In that case, I think a few weeks off would be time well spent. Don't you?'

Roxanne nodded. 'Erm, yes, I think it could be.'

'. . . You'd come back feeling restored, ready for anything,' Marsha added. 'I'm a great believer in work-life balance.'

'So am I,' Roxanne fibbed, because actually, she didn't fully understand the concept. Oh, the work bit was fine; that part she loved with a passion. It was just the life bit she had trouble with.

'So, does that sound like something we can work with?' Marsha smoothed back her rather lank chestnut hair.

Roxanne considered this. Why not? she thought. It was a pretty generous offer and, if the situation was dreadful when she returned, she could always hand in her notice then. She certainly wasn't trapped here forever. 'Yes, it does,' she replied, catching Tina's braying voice as she conducted another phone call.

'Excellent. Gosh – ten years you've been here, haven't you? You deserve a carriage clock at the very least!' She chuckled infuriatingly, and Roxanne smiled stiffly at the 'joke'. 'Excuse me a second,' Marsha added, jumping up and marching out into the main office space, where she proceeded to have a hurried exchange with Tina at her desk. The two of them returned to Marsha's glass box. 'I just wanted to tell Tina that you're taking a sabbatical,' she explained.

'*Amazing*,' Tina enthused. 'Have you any idea what you'd like to do with it?'

'Erm, I'm not sure exactly,' Roxanne replied, 'but I have been thinking recently that I'd like to spend some time in my sister's shop. She has a cookbook shop in the village we grew up in in Yorkshire . . .'

Marsha widened her eyes. 'A cookbook shop? You mean selling *only* cookbooks?'

'Yes, that's right.' Roxanne appraised her editor's bemused face, wondering what was so funny.

'How quaint and sweet,' she gushed. 'Oh, I can see the appeal of working somewhere like that. I mean, here we are, in these *incredible* jobs that most people would kill for, and don't you sometimes think, wouldn't it be so lovely to swap it all for a simple, down-to-earth sort of life?'

She was talking as if Della were a shepherd. 'Um, yes . . .'

'How about writing a blog for us while you're there?' Tina asked.

Roxanne peered at her. 'What sort of blog?'

'Oh, I don't know . . . something fashiony, for the digital edition? How about, "What our fashion director is wearing during her summer in the north" sort of idea? How does that grab you?'

Roxanne tried to wipe the startled look off her face. 'I'm not sure if—'

'I think it's a *fabulous* idea!' Marsha declared.

'We'd need photos of you, though, if that would be okay?' Tina added. 'The readers would want to see you striding out in the country in big boots, an anorak and a horribly unflattering hat . . .'

'Oh. If you really think—'

'This is exactly why I brought Tina to the magazine,' Marsha interrupted. 'I *love* this idea. It has humour, personality and a style angle—'

Tina turned to Marsha and grinned. 'We could have her out in the rain, drenched from head to foot, or standing in a field with one of her boots stuck in a cow pat . . .'

Roxanne realised her back teeth were jammed together.

'. . . Stuck in the middle of nowhere in all conditions,' Marsha continued, as if they were talking the northern reaches of Alaska and not merely a three-hour train journey from where they were sitting now, 'without access to decent clothes or even anywhere to get her hair done . . .'

122

Roxanne forced a tight smile. Perhaps writing a blog – and even being a figure of fun in terrible outfits – was a small price to pay for two whole months away from this double act. 'That sounds *great*,' she lied, 'if you think anyone would actually want to read it . . .'

'Of course they would,' Marsha insisted. 'D'you think you could rattle off a couple of posts a week and email them to me?'

'Er, yes, of course,' Roxanne said weakly. 'But won't you need to check with HR if it's okay for me to take this time off?'

'No – *I'm* saying it's okay. I've been brought in to make major changes here and Rufus has given me the green light to do whatever I feel is necessary to push things forward . . .'

'Er, that's great,' Roxanne murmured. 'So, when do you think I can go?'

'You may as well start your leave tomorrow,' Marsha replied briskly. 'Tina will be able to get stuck into making all the changes we need to implement without you being here.'

'Er, right! Well, um, thank you. . . .' She tried to look pleased; after all, she had just been awarded an extended holiday. However, as Roxanne left Marsha's office she couldn't ignore a niggle of unease, as she wondered if being utterly dispensable was really such a good thing after all.

Chapter Eleven

After an impromptu gathering in a favoured Soho pub with Serena, Kate and Tristan – 'Honestly,' Roxanne insisted, 'this isn't code for "I'm being sacked"' – she was grateful to make her way home. Although bolstered by everyone's heartfelt hugs and good wishes, she was keen to call Della to check if she would be happy with an extended visit. The evening was pleasantly sunny and warm, and Roxanne felt her Marsha-related tensions begin to float away as she let herself into her flat.

She kicked off her shoes, splayed out on her sofa and called her sister.

'Hi, Rox. How's it going?' Della sounded pleased to hear from her.

'Good, thanks . . .'

'Bet you didn't get a taxi home the other night, did you?'

'What, from Sean's party? That was three days ago! And yes – I did actually.' *I can't imagine why you might suspect I walked two miles in a drunken state with wet coriander in my handbag.* 'Um, can I ask you something?'

'Sure?'

'Is Sophie coming home for the summer?'

'Doesn't look like it. I've been trying to persuade her to pick up a few shifts at the pub, or even help me out in the shop – but, of course, it's far too dull around here and I'll be lucky if she drops by for the odd weekend. She's seeing this boy, did I tell you?'

'Yes, you mentioned him. Jamie, isn't it, from her course?'

'That's right. Term's finished already so they've gone Inter-railing. His parents have a place in Budapest – apparently it's amazingly cheap and brilliant fun out there. There are these places called Ruin Bars in derelict buildings . . .'

'Sounds terrifying,' Roxanne joked.

'It is. I'm a wreck, as you can imagine – a *ruin*, actually. But that's okay, that's my job as a mother . . .' She chuckled. 'So, you wanted to ask me something?'

'Er, yes.'

'It wasn't just about Sophie's plans for the summer, was it? C'mon, Rox – is something up? You *are* okay, aren't you?'

'Yes, I am, but I wondered . . .' Roxanne broke off, willing her sister to say yes. 'Erm, can I come up and see you, Dell? Would that be okay?'

'For the bookshop party? Sure – I was hoping you would.'

' . . . Or a bit sooner, maybe?' she ventured. 'If it's too much, I could always book a room at the Red Lion . . .'

'No, no, don't be crazy. There's always room for you here. When are you thinking of?'

Roxanne glanced at Holly and Keira's drawings, which were still strewn all over her coffee table. She liked the way the flat felt after they had been here; it was as if they had muddled up the stale air particles and made them dance.

'Stuff's been happening at work,' she said, aware now of a strong desire to leave London as quickly as possible. 'I told you we have a new editor, didn't I? Well, we had a chat today and I'm now officially on extended leave.'

'You mean she's sacked you?' Della gasped.

'Not exactly, but she thinks it'd be a good idea for me to have a couple of months off – and, well, I agree, actually. So I'm on a sort of sabbatical. How would you feel about me staying with you for a couple of months?'

She blinked, realising she was holding her breath. Della had gone terribly quiet. She hadn't expected the sound of champagne corks popping, or even, 'That's fantastic!' But she had anticipated *some* kind of reaction . . .

'A couple of months?' Della managed finally.

'Yes. I mean, with all the building work going on in your shop I thought you might appreciate an extra pair of hands. I know you might not think so, but I *can* be handy with a paintbrush, you know.'

'Well, er, we have a couple of men in, and Frank's been helping out, and we're sort of on schedule.' Della's reticence was palpable.

'Maybe I could help out in the shop, then?' Roxanne suggested, wondering how it had come to this: that she was virtually *begging* for shop work. 'I could man the till, stock shelves, sort through any new stock you've bought—'

'Oh, no, I need to do that really.'

'Well, I can do whatever you want . . .' *Please let me come. I need to be with you.*

'Look, Rox, I really don't think—'

'. . . And I won't overstay my welcome if it doesn't

126

work out,' Roxanne added, aware of desperation creeping into her voice. Ridiculously, she had almost convinced herself that Della would be grateful for some extra help.

Della cleared her throat. 'I just worry that you'd find it too sleepy around here, that's all.'

'I won't,' she said vehemently. 'I'd keep busy. I wouldn't *stop*—'

Della chuckled. 'Okay, we do get quite busy sometimes, and we are fitting out the new room so there's plenty going on. But it's still just a village bookshop, remember.'

'Yes, I know that.' Roxanne peeled a fleck of polish off her nail.

'I mean,' Della added, 'it's not at all glamorous. A lot of the day-to-day work is pretty mundane.'

'Trust me, mundane is exactly what I need right now.'

'Yes but . . .' An awkward hush settled between them. 'I didn't think you liked coming back here very much.'

Roxanne was aware of a sinking feeling in her stomach. 'Why d'you say that?'

'Come on – you know why. Remember how things were when Mum was ill?'

Roxanne's breath caught in her throat. Guilt prickled at her – not fashion guilt, but something darker and heavier. She had tried to bury it, but it was still lurking there: the feeling that she had let her sister down, and would never be able to make up for it. 'Dell, look – I know I wasn't there for you then, and I'm sorry.'

'Oh, I didn't mean that,' Della said briskly. 'I just meant . . . well, whenever you've been here, you've always seemed in a terrible hurry to get back to London. Are you *sure* this is what you want?'

Roxanne nodded, which was silly because Della couldn't see her; and so she found herself trying to explain how it had been when their mother was dying. 'I felt ashamed,' she murmured. 'You were so brilliant, so capable – and I felt as if I was getting in the way, just like when we were kids, you know? It was wrong. I was a coward. It was easier to stay in London and pretend to be too busy with deadlines and press day and dump it all on you. I'll never forgive myself for that—'

'Roxanne, stop.' Della's voice was firm. 'It's okay. I probably had to take charge of things – and look at all the good that's come out of it. I have Mum's cookbooks, and the bookshop, and I'm with Frank now . . .' She paused. 'Hey, how are things with Sean?'

'Um, that seems to be sort of over.'

'Rox, you should have said! Is that why you want to come up?'

'No. Well, sort of, I suppose. I don't know, Dell. I just need a change—'

'Fine, okay. So when are you thinking of coming?'

Roxanne hesitated, hoping her sister wouldn't think she had gone mad. 'Would, er . . . would tomorrow be okay?'

'*Tomorrow?*'

'I'm just not sure I can handle being here, by myself, with no job to go to.' Roxanne winced. How terribly feeble that sounded.

'Okay then,' Della said, in a softer tone. 'Let me know your arrival time and I'll meet you at Heathfield station.'

'Thanks so much . . .'

'That's all right. Look – of course I want you here, as long as you remember what the village is like and don't act all Londony.'

'When have I ever done that?' Roxanne retorted.

A pause hung in the air, and Della laughed. 'I'm teasing,

128

Rox. Come on – you're always welcome here, on one condition. *Promise* me you'll bring some sensible shoes.'

By the time she was ready for bed at 11.30, Roxanne had called Amanda to tell her of her plans ('You lucky thing!' she'd enthused), booked her train ticket and was almost ready to go. She far preferred to travel by train than driving these days, as it gave her the chance to watch the world go by. Roxanne's last car, a red Audi convertible, was bought in a flash of madness and frequently vandalised, then stolen and had never been replaced. 'Maybe next time,' her brother Jeff had remarked, 'you might choose a car that doesn't scream "I'm loaded" when you live in a dodgy area?' *Islington, a dodgy area?* she'd thought furiously. But then Jeff – like Della – was under the impression that pretty much every area in London, with perhaps the exception of Knightsbridge, was riddled with knife crime and guns.

Now she checked her suitcase, to ensure she had all she needed to see her through a summer in the country. This was always the best part of going away: the outfit planning. She had pulled together her bookshop look, for when she was helping out at the till, comprising a snug cardi worn over a soft cotton top with a knee-length bias-cut tweed skirt; rural librarian was the look she was going for. Flat shoes, of course. You didn't clop around a second-hand bookshop in heels, and you didn't over-accessorise either. Shame she didn't wear spectacles. Maybe she could buy some, with clear glass, just to lend herself a bookish air? She had also packed chunky sweaters for dog walking (it could still be chilly up there, even in summer), and several print dresses for trips to Heathfield on farmer's market days, when she would pick up some groceries for Della. Her sister would soon discover what an asset she was to have about the place. It felt terribly important to put things right once and for all.

She had just zipped up her suitcase when her mobile rang on her dressing table. Sean's name was displayed. She glared at it, steeling herself against answering it. For days, she had willed him to call, and now she was all set for Yorkshire – effectively running away – and didn't want to have to explain anything to him. Nor did she wish to delve into the whole Tina business again or even shift awkwardly into some kind of 'let's be friends'-type scenario. In her mind she was already the country bookshop lady, perhaps with her hair in a bun – nice touch, she decided – and now Sean was threatening to interrupt her soothing vision of herself happily pottering about, dusting the shelves.

The ringtone stopped, then immediately started again. But then again, what if he *needed* her? She snatched her phone. 'Sean, hi,' she said dryly, as if they were merely casually acquainted.

'Hey, Rox. Um, how's things?'

'I'm fine, thanks.' She didn't know what else to say. Whilst the sensible part of her brain was reminding her to feel cross with him, the very sound of his soft Dublin lilt was triggering all those physical reactions in her: a quickening of the heart. An overwhelming desire to *hurl herself into his arms.*

'You left your jacket at my party,' he continued. 'I noticed it when I popped in to check on the cleaners on Saturday.'

'Oh. Thanks.' So he was only calling about lost property matters. He, too, still had to collect the photography book he'd left at her flat.

Sean cleared his throat. 'So what are you up to tonight?'

'It's nearly midnight,' she said curtly. 'I'm sitting here in my PJs and going to bed in a minute.'

'Ah, right.' He coughed awkwardly. 'It's just, I heard a little rumour that you're taking some time off work, is that right?'

Roxanne frowned. 'Uh-huh. That news travelled quick. Who told you?'

'Oh, er, Britt heard through Serena, I think. It just came up . . .'

'Right.' She pressed her lips together. In her industry, gossip spread with impressive speed. 'So, um, I'm leaving tomorrow.'

'Wow, so soon! So, what's that all about?'

'I just fancied a break,' she said briskly. 'Marsha suggested it and, with Tina starting, it seemed like a good idea to just let them get on with things.' No need to tell him she'd tried to quit, she decided. 'Look, Sean,' she added, 'I thought we were finished?'

He exhaled heavily. 'Oh, Rox. Look . . . I'm sorry about Saturday morning. I think I overreacted a bit. I was just, you know . . .' She waited for him to finish. 'You weren't actually that bad,' he added, which surely ranked alongside *You certainly know how to have a good time!* in terms of cringeworthy post-party feedback.

'Well, that's good to hear,' she muttered.

'And I'm sorry about Tina showing up like that. Honestly – I should have paid better attention and not just left the organising to Britt. You know how I am with these things . . .' He tailed off. 'It was really insensitive of me,' he added. 'I guess I screwed up.'

'I'm glad you feel that way,' she murmured, 'because I wouldn't have wanted us to finish on such bad terms.' Without warning, her eyes filled with tears.

131

'Rox, we're not finished,' Sean exclaimed. 'That is, unless you really want us to be?'

She blinked rapidly in order to clear her vision. How she missed him. What she'd give, right now, not to be going to bed alone but having him here with her, in her arms. 'I don't know,' she said quietly.

'Oh, sweetheart. Can I come over?'

No, Mr Sanctimonious of Moral High Ground, you absolutely can-bloody-not.

'Yes, okay.'

'I'll call a cab now. Darling, I'm so sorry. I didn't mean to upset you. Christ, I know I can be such an idiot sometimes.'

They finished the call and, despite everything, she felt her spirits lifting as she made a pot of tea. Perhaps it wasn't ideal that she was about to leave for Burley Bridge, if she and Sean were about to try to fix things. But then, Yorkshire wasn't far. He could visit, and they could spend time together up there, perhaps booking into a hotel for a couple of nights. It could be the making of them, Roxanne decided, even moving things on to a new level. She pictured them strolling, hand in hand, as she showed him all her childhood haunts.

As she waited for Sean, she texted Della her arrival time at Heathfield tomorrow afternoon, then realised she had forgotten to leave Isabelle a spare key. Throwing on a sweater over her PJ top, she padded downstairs, checking first that music was still playing in her neighbour's flat. She tapped on the door, and Isabelle opened it.

'I'm so pleased for you,' Isabelle enthused, when Roxanne had filled her in on the day's events. 'They'll fall apart without you. Make them realise what they're missing!'

Roxanne smiled, touched by her loyalty. 'Thanks,

Isabelle. It will feel strange, though, not being there for two months. I mean, the magazine's my whole life—'

'Then maybe you need more going on in your life?' Isabelle asked, not unkindly.

Roxanne smiled. 'You're probably right. Oh, and on that note – Sean's coming over in a minute. Looks like we're not finished after all.'

'Oh, really?' Isabelle raised a brow. 'So what happens now?'

'Who knows?' She laughed dryly. 'Anyway, thanks for keeping an eye on my place. Lunch is on me, as soon as I'm home.'

Roxanne hugged her neighbour farewell and returned to her flat. She was attempting to zip up her overstuffed toiletry bag when Sean arrived, looking contrite and smelling deliciously freshly-showered. How good it felt to be in his arms again; she stood for a moment, feeling the warmth of him as he held her close.

'Hey, darling. I'm so sorry,' he murmured.

'Oh, me too,' she said. 'I didn't mean to embarrass you, I'm so sorry—'

'Shush, babe. It doesn't matter.' His smile seemed to illuminate his face as he stood back and looked at her, and she sensed a twang of missing him already. 'So, you're off tomorrow,' he added as she handed him a mug of tea in the kitchen. 'No hanging around.'

She shrugged. 'I sort of wish I wasn't going so soon, but then, if I'm not at work, I don't really want to just hang about here . . .'

Sean kissed her softly on the lips. 'You may as well get going.'

'Yes, I guess so.' She glanced at him, willing him to try to persuade her to stay.

133

'The change of scene'll be good for you,' he suggested gently.

Roxanne nodded. 'Well, I need to spend time with Della, if nothing else.'

'Yes, I think that's a great idea.'

She glanced up at those clear green eyes that made her heart turn over, hating the neediness that was welling up inside her now. 'You seem pretty keen for me to go.'

He frowned in bafflement. 'You want me to cling to your ankles, weeping and begging, "Don't go"?'

'No, of course not! It's just—'

'I think you need some time and space away from everything,' he cut in. 'It's only a few weeks and it'll go in a flash. Most people would give their right arm for the whole summer off, knowing they still had their job to come back to at the end of it.'

He was right; she had a charmed life. Fashion guilt niggled at her once more.

'Yes, I know.' She paused and looked at him. Something else still bothered her; as she didn't know when she would see him next, she was seized by an urge to bring it up now. 'Can I ask you about something? About something I overheard at your party?'

Sean's eyes met hers, full of concern. ''Course you can. What was it?'

Roxanne sensed her cheeks reddening as she sipped her tea. 'It was Marsha and Tina. They were gossiping about us, and Marsha said something like, "Oh, everyone thought it'd just be a fling." Between me and you, I mean . . .'

'Jesus, Rox—' He exhaled loudly.

'"Because you know what he's like." *That's* what Marsha said . . .'

'What the hell did she mean by that?'

'I have no idea!' she exclaimed.

He stepped away from her and stood at the kitchen window, glaring out to the street below. 'And Marsha knows me, does she? For God's sake, I hope you don't think—'

'No, I don't,' she said quickly. 'Of course I don't . . .'

He turned back to her and wrapped his arms around her. 'I'm glad to hear that, baby. You know what it's like – how people love gossip and, when there isn't any, how they like to speculate or just make things up.'

She smiled and nodded. 'Yes, I do.'

Then they were kissing and tumbling, still entwined, into her bedroom. As they undressed and fell into her bed, Roxanne pushed any lingering concerns from her mind. He was right; there was nothing to worry about and, of course, people in their industry would always have something to say. It was a side of working in fashion that she deplored sometimes – the love of gossip, the superficiality. Lying in his arms now, she refused to give anyone else's opinions another second's thought.

At around 2 a.m., Roxanne studied Sean's face as he slept. Such a finely honed, handsome face, she thought. She wanted to photograph him with her phone, so she could take the picture with her to Burley Bridge, but feared that he might wake up. She would just have to hold the image in her mind.

Later that morning, as she boarded her train at King's Cross, Roxanne could still feel him close as if they were still entangled together. He hadn't been able to see her off, but that was fine; he'd had a job to rush off to, an important client who'd been keen to kick off at 9 a.m. sharp. And now Roxanne was stashing her unwieldy suitcase in the luggage area in the carriage, then waiting patiently as the woman sitting at the window begrudgingly moved her tartan rucksack from Roxanne's seat.

She sat down and sipped from her bottle of water, still not quite comprehending that she wouldn't be going to work for two whole months. The concept seemed both thrilling and faintly terrifying. Her job had always been pretty much everything to her – but perhaps, as Isabelle had suggested, that wasn't such a healthy state of affairs.

As the train started to move, her phone bleeped with a text. *Love you beautiful,* Sean had written.

She blinked, sensing a sharp pang of missing him already. *Love you too,* she replied.

Chapter Twelve

There was something about the way Della drove, Roxanne noticed. It was that rural politeness – 'After you', 'No, after *you*' – and it struck her every time she was a passenger in her sister's ancient navy blue Punto. Even a manoeuvre as simple as exiting a car park necessitated a myriad of encouraging gestures before, finally, someone edged forward first amidst mouthed thank yous ('No, thank *you*!').

'Sorry if the shop's in a bit of a state at the moment,' Della was telling Roxanne as they made their way along Heathfield High Street. 'Knocking through to next door sounded so simple when I bought the place.' Della glanced at her sister and grinned. '*Knocking through* – like, a few taps with a hammer and we'd be done.'

Roxanne chuckled. 'Well, I'm here to help, okay? We can get stuck in together. Just ask me to do whatever you need . . .'

'Oh, the guys are taking care of everything,' Della said briskly. 'The fitting out, the electrics – it's all in hand and, amazingly, we've managed to stay open while all that's been going on.'

'What about painting?' Roxanne asked.

Della threw her a quick glance.

'What?'

'Nothing,' Della said with a smirk.

Roxanne could sense herself bristling already, mere minutes since she had stepped off the train. 'Dell, I *can* paint, you know. I'm capable of moving a roller in an up and down motion without ruining your property or maiming myself.'

'I'm sure you are,' Della said, insincerely, as if Roxanne were a child asking to 'help' with an electric carving knife. 'But you don't want to get paint all over that lovely cardigan.'

Roxanne scoffed and looked down at the soft pink cashmere. 'This old thing?'

'It doesn't look old to me.'

'Oh, it is,' she fibbed, 'and I have brought other clothes with me, you know.' Roxanne glanced at her sister. Della was clearly tickled by the idea of Roxanne involving herself in anything practical, or indeed deigning to wear an outfit suitable for manual work. That was one aspect of her job that Roxanne didn't enjoy so much: the assumption, by her siblings mainly, that she was permanently kitted out in designer attire. In reality, often entire weekends were spent in her comfiest old jeans and any old washed-out top.

'Anyway,' Della continued, 'you don't want to spend your time here up to your neck in DIY. Aren't you here for a bit of headspace away from the hectic whirl?'

Roxanne hesitated. 'We've been through all that, Dell. I'm not planning to drift around aimlessly. I can serve customers, keep the shop tidy, categorise new books . . .'

'Oh, Frank and I tend to do all the categorising,' Della said quickly.

'Well, couldn't I help?'

'It *is* quite complicated,' Della murmured, eyes fixed on the road ahead.

'What's complicated about it?'

'Just my categorising system.'

Roxanne couldn't help smiling at this. *Categorising system?* It was just cookbooks, not the entire catalogue of the British Library. 'But you let Frank dabble with your "categorising system",' Roxanne teased, and Della laughed.

'Only under my watchful eye and, even then, I double-check everything afterwards.'

Roxanne chuckled, feeling grateful now to be here as Della drove slowly through the thriving market town. Understandably, the period leading up to and following their mother's death had been difficult, their brother Jeff cranking up the discomfort with his perpetual criticisms and put-downs. However, right now, he was at home in Manchester – or, more likely, in the global bank head-quarters where he worked – and it was just the two sisters together, a rare occurrence indeed. Roxanne finally allowed herself to believe that it might bring them closer, and hoped Della was genuinely happy that she was here, rather than feeling obligated to have her.

Della turned on the car radio. They were out in open countryside now, surrounded by softly rolling hills.

'So, how are things with Frank?' Roxanne ventured.

'Great,' Della replied. 'He's . . . well, you know Frank. He's lovely. He makes me very happy. I still fancy him like crazy and we're best friends, if that doesn't sound too disgustingly smug.'

'Of course it doesn't. I think it's brilliant.' Roxanne glanced at her. In fact, she hadn't even needed to ask. Before the cookbook shop endeavour, when Della had still been married to philandering Mark, Roxanne had always thought her sister seemed rather put-upon. Lacklustre is the word she might have used: *lacking in lustre*. Nothing seemed to be lacking now, she noted. Della's wavy chestnut hair shone – she was wearing it longer these days, and it suited her – and there was barely a line on her make-up-free face. At fifty-one, she could pass for a decade younger. Roxanne knew for a fact that her sister's skincare routine consisted of soap, water and a brisk flannel rub; meanwhile Roxanne, who was frequently disappointed by the frankly outrageous promises spouted by premium skincare brands, had noticed recently how jaded her own face looked. She had to concede that country air might be more beneficial than anything that came out of a pot.

'I'm so glad you're happy,' Roxanne added, 'after everything you've been through.' She paused. 'Had much contact with Mark lately?'

'No, thank God,' Della said vehemently. 'It would've been different if Sophie was still at home but, as it is, she sees me, she sees her dad – and she tells me little snippets about his *lady-love* . . .' Della gave Roxanne a quick, amused look. 'I know it's naughty but she can't resist.'

'They're still together, then?'

'Yes, just about, although I get the impression that Mark hasn't quite turned out to be the fabulous catch Polly thought he might be.' Polly was the patient Mark had treated at his podiatry practice; a younger woman in expensively tailored dresses, and the reason for his countless lies and golfing alibis.

Roxanne crooked a brow. 'Oh, really? Why's that?'

'Reading between the lines, it was more exciting for her when he was just nipping round to see her whenever he got the chance. He wasn't criticising her home decor then. He wasn't suggesting that her cerise bedroom was rather tacky, or that she might have her yellow kitchen repainted in Farrow and Ball's Skimming Stone.'

The two sisters chuckled. 'He always loved a neutral tone,' Roxanne remarked, turning to Della. 'So, d'you think you'll move in with Frank? I mean, d'you ever talk about that?'

'Well, he's suggested I live with him and Eddie, but . . .' She shrugged as they took the twisting lane that led them to Burley Bridge, nestling down in the valley. 'Oh, I don't know, Rox. We love spending time together, but we each have our own thing, you know? Eddie's only nine; Frank's still in the midst of the dad thing. Becca's away at college but she still needs her father when she's home in the holidays. And then there's his work. Being a self-employed architect isn't the easiest thing. Sometimes it's manic, and other times it's scarily quiet.'

'And you have your life too,' Roxanne pointed out.

Della nodded. 'I do, yes, and I love being right in the village . . .'

'In the thick of things.'

Della smiled. 'Yeah. In the heart of the thriving metropolis! No, seriously – it's so handy being above the shop. Frank's place is gorgeous but it is out in the wilds – and maybe I'm just keen to hang onto my independence, after what happened with Mark.'

'That's just natural,' Roxanne conceded.

Della looked at her. 'I'm sorry about you and Sean, Rox. I know it must be really hard for you.'

Roxanne exhaled. 'Maybe there's nothing to be sorry about. He called me yesterday and came over, and well . . .' She shrugged. 'All seems fine. Hopefully he'll come up, spend some time with me here – if that's okay with you,' she added.

'Er, yes, of course it is,' Della said lightly, a trace of uncertainty in her voice.

Roxanne glanced out of the window as the village came into view, deciding not to quiz Della on whether she might have a problem with Sean visiting. Perhaps any reservations were simply due to wanting as much time as possible together, just the two of them. Roxanne hoped so.

Burley Bridge looked so pretty today, so quaintly old-fashioned and well-tended. Perhaps it took a lengthy period away from the place to fully appreciate it. Stone terraced cottages hugged the edge of the road that led to the centre. On this bright and breezy Tuesday afternoon – the last day in May – window boxes and hanging baskets were already bursting with blues, pinks, yellows. Roxanne's horticultural experience amounted to caring for a small cactus, the only present she could recall Ned Tallow ever giving her, and which she later discovered he had shoplifted from a garden centre as a joke (at forty-three years old. What a hoot!).

They turned into Rosemary Lane, the narrow street of shops and small businesses that formed the very heart of the village. Roxanne gazed out in wonder. Of course, it hadn't always been as picturesque. The whole village looked brighter these days, as if it had been given a good hosing down. There were more people around than Roxanne ever remembered seeing – wandering in and out of the shops and gallery and giving the impression that they were visitors rather than locals. She spotted a couple of familiar villagers too; Nicola the hairdresser, and Len, the owner of the garage, whom her mother had once accused of putting the wrong sort of oil in her car, chatting on the forecourt. That was one thing that hadn't changed. Len still dispensed petrol himself; if you stopped here for fuel you might be forgiven for thinking it was 1979. Irene Bagshott, who ran the general store and had been kind enough to take home-made chicken-and-leek pies to Roxanne and Della's elderly mother, marched down the street laden with shopping and a huge bunch of cut flowers. Roxanne's London friends would go crazy for this place – at least, in a weekend holiday-cottage sort of way.

'Oh, there's a new greengrocer's,' Roxanne remarked.

'Yes, and it's doing pretty well, I think. Remember when the only lettuce you could buy around here was iceberg?'

'I do,' she smiled. 'Ooh, and that boutique's so cute!'

'I knew you'd spot that. Yes, they opened last month . . .'

'There's a bakery, too. That looks lovely . . .'

'Beautiful, isn't it?' Della agreed.

'It really is. Like something out of a children's book!' She peered out at the homely-looking shop with its red-and-white striped awning and windows filled with cakes and jaunty bunting. Terracotta pots of geraniums were clustered around its entrance. A vintage bicycle, its front basket cascading with pink blooms, was propped – clearly just for decoration – against the wall.

'He opened last year,' Della explained, 'but you probably didn't even notice. It's only recently that he's had the sign painted and it's looked this inviting. You must try their soda bread. It's the best . . .'

'Soda bread in Burley?' Roxanne gasped.

'Yes – and *amazing* focaccia and feta and black olive plaits. We've got it all here now,' Della said with a trace of pride. 'In fact, I think there's a sourdough workshop happening soon. Maybe you'd like to go to that?'

Roxanne spluttered. She would be no more likely to take up Morris dancing. 'That's not quite my thing, Dell.'

'Well, there's loads of other stuff going on in the village these days. A film club, belly dancing classes, book groups, a choir—'

'Della . . .'

'I've been having a look around,' she added quickly, 'to find out what's happening, see if there's anything you'd enjoy . . .'

'Thanks, but I'm happy just to help you with the shop.' Roxanne exhaled slowly, wishing Della wouldn't regard her as she might a small child who needed to be kept occupied at all times. She could see Rosemary Cottage in the distance now, the house they grew up in, huddled down its single-track lane. It had been freshly white-washed, and the garden looked neatly tended. After their mother died, Della had overseen the sprucing up and selling of the house. Roxanne knew from Della that a young family had moved in, and that the house and garden were filled with children again. Roxanne hoped the atmosphere was somewhat happier than when she had been a young girl.

'A sourdough workshop,' Roxanne murmured with a smile. 'Don't tell me it's gone all poncey around here. We don't want things too posh, do we?'

'Of course not,' Della said firmly. 'It's still the same old Burley Bridge. But people do say my shop helped to revitalise things, and encouraged other people to try new things here . . .'

'You're incredible,' Roxanne said, as Della pulled up in front of the bookshop. 'You made all this happen. I'm so proud of you.'

'Oh, don't be crazy. I just gave things a little kick-start, that's all.'

'Come on, no need to be so modest. Look at what you've done here . . .'

'I look at it every day,' Della laughed as they climbed out of the car. She hauled Roxanne's enormous suitcase from the boot, and the sisters stood side by side for a moment outside the shop.

The sign, which read simply *The Bookshop on Rosemary Lane*, was hand-painted in gleaming gold against bright cobalt blue. The window of the shop next door, which would soon be part of Della's emporium, was obscured by newspaper to conceal the activity happening within. However, the existing shop's window was an utter delight. Silvery fairy lights twinkled, and tissue paper flowers were suspended on fine gold threads. The display of vintage cookbooks looked so enticing, it would lure in someone who wouldn't even know a potato rosti if it hit them in the face.

Roxanne glanced at Della, who was smiling at her and understanding, perhaps, how much she needed to be there. It wasn't to learn to make bread, join a choir or take up belly dancing. It was just to *be*. Della opened the narrow door beside the shop, which led to a tiny hallway and the steep flight of stairs to the flat above.

'C'mon, Rox,' she said gently. 'Let's have some tea then you can tell me what's really going on.'

Chapter Thirteen

Roxanne tried to explain about Marsha's new regime and the shock appointment of Tina. However, while she was clearly trying to be sympathetic, Della didn't seem to grasp why this was so catastrophic.

'Are the yoga classes free?' she asked as they sat at her kitchen table with slices of perfectly moist apple cake and mugs of tea.

'Yes, but that's not the point.' Roxanne caught herself before she could continue. Here she was, bemoaning a practice that was being offered to benefit her mental and physical wellbeing. How spoilt that sounded, Roxanne realised as she bent to stroke Stanley, Della's mottled grey terrier who was curled up at her feet. 'It's more about what's happening to the magazine,' she added, explaining that her remit was no longer to produce beautiful shoots with top photographers. 'She wants to fill the mag with stuff like "the fifty best knickers to hold your wobbly stomach in".'

'But wouldn't that be quite . . . useful?' Della ventured, sipping her tea.

Oh, God, how to explain without sounding like a ridiculous fashion ponce? 'It's not really about usefulness. Magazines are more about luxury, a treat, and beautiful pictures . . .'

'Are there really fifty types of stomach-flattening knickers?' Della cut in.

Roxanne looked at her sister and laughed. 'There are probably more, actually.'

'I could do with a pair . . .'

'Don't be crazy, Dell. You look great. It's good to see you looking so happy. Honestly – you're actually glowing.'

Della smiled. 'I do love being back here, you know. When I was still in Heathfield, I never imagined I'd ever want to live somewhere like this – I mean any village, let alone the one we grew up in. But now it feels like just the right place to be.'

Roxanne nodded, sensing a twinge of something. Regret, perhaps, that she had never quite managed to find a place where she truly belonged. Yes, she loved London, her local neighbourhood especially, but she had never felt truly at home anywhere. Her flat was just a place to sleep, really. Apart from the French wardrobe, and Isabelle downstairs, there was little to love about it. For most of her adult life she had waited patiently for the nesting instinct to kick in – to suddenly become excited about choosing cushions – but so far it hadn't happened. On the other hand, Della clearly adored her little flat above the shop. The kitchen was cosy and homely, its shelves filled with mismatched crockery and brightly coloured storage jars. Vintage curtains, printed with a jaunty coffee pot design, hung at the window that overlooked the fields to the rear of the high street.

'You will still have a job when you go back, won't you?' Della asked, frowning.

'Oh, yes,' Roxanne replied. 'I realise I'll have to either accept that Tina's my boss, and that my job is changing beyond all recognition – or try and find work somewhere else.' She drained the last of her tea. 'Oh – and they're asking me to write a blog about my "summer in the country" for the digital edition of the mag.'

Della smiled. 'That sounds fun – as long as *I'm* not in it . . .'

'Don't worry. They just want pictures of me out in the rain, wading through dung or herding sheep, that kind of thing . . .'

'I'm sure that can be arranged,' Della said, laughing now as she got up and glanced at the kitchen clock. 'I'd better get down to the shop. I told Faye she could leave at four today.'

'So you have some help these days?' Roxanne was struck by how little she knew about the workings of her sister's business.

Della nodded. 'Yes, Faye does a few hours a week, fitting around her college work and her other job in the pub. She's a great girl – a friend of Sophie's from school . . .'

'And where's Sophie now?'

'In Vienna, just about to leave for Budapest – as far as I know. Dashing from city to city with no itinerary.'

'God.'

'I know. It's terrifying.' Della smirked. 'And wonderful too. Oh, I'm just jealous really. It's so tempting to jump on a train and tail them all through Europe, wreck their whole experience . . .'

Roxanne laughed. 'But, luckily for them, you have a shop to run. Anything I can do to help while you're working?'

'Oh, no – why don't you just settle in and chill out? Watch some TV, run a bath if you like . . .'

As if Roxanne wanted to spend the rest of her afternoon in the flat alone. She had quite enough of that at home. 'How about I take Stanley for a walk?' she suggested.

'Are you sure? You've only just got here, Rox.'

'I'd love to, honestly,' Roxanne said firmly. 'I need a leg stretch after the journey and if you won't let me help to categorise your books, then I'd better find some other way to make myself useful.'

As Roxanne got up to pull on her jacket, Della wrapped her arms around her. 'Oh, Rox. You're worrying too much. Please, just relax and enjoy being here.'

'I will, I promise.' Roxanne pulled back and studied her sister's face, taken aback by the surge of emotion that had welled up in her. However, she knew what had triggered it. Roxanne couldn't remember any other time when Della had hugged her like that.

If the shop looked impressive from the street, Roxanne found it even more delightful inside, and cookbooks weren't even *remotely* her kind of thing. She had seen it before, of course, but on each visit there was always something new to admire: the framed artwork, created from old Parisian café menus, and Della's younger customers' crayoned pictures made into a montage hanging behind the till. Della had insisted on Roxanne popping in before she took Stanley out on his walk, and Roxanne could see why. The squashy velvet sofas and glowing lamps made it the kind of place you could easily while away an afternoon. It smelt wonderful, too: of coffee, but also of old books, of pages turned and pored over. A chalkboard announced the upcoming party, featuring a retro cocktail demonstration and tasting. Soft music was playing – one of those crackly jazz ladies, the kind Isabelle loved – and half a dozen customers were browsing the shelves.

'It'll be amazing when the extension's ready,' Faye was saying, after she and Roxanne were introduced, indicating the opening where a plastic curtain hung to conceal the work going on next door. 'We'll be able to do more events, readings, demos, that kind of thing. We manage now but it can be a bit of a squeeze if it's a popular event.'

'It's looking wonderful, though,' Roxanne enthused, scanning the different sections of books – parties, picnics, preserving – while Stanley pottered about at her side. Another customer had just come in and was quizzing Della about a particular book he was looking for.

'I think it's the first book ever published about rustic fermented breads,' he explained.

'Yes, I do know of it. I can picture the cover, black and red, drawing of a lady with a mixing bowl . . .'

'That's the one!'

Roxanne smiled, impressed by her sister's passion for her specialist subject. The customer was a tall, slim man, with small wire-rimmed spectacles and neatly trimmed dark hair flecked with silvery grey. He had a soft southern accent, was wearing black jeans and a plain grey T-shirt, and looked in his late forties, at a guess. Roxanne wondered if the book was for him, or a present for someone, and indeed, what a fermented bread might be – did it have *beer* in it? It still amazed her how keen people could be about cooking when there were shops, delis and restaurants, all staffed by fully-trained people who could sell you delicious things to eat, without you having to stress yourself.

150

Della was checking the relevant shelf. 'Ah, sorry – I was pretty sure we had a copy in stock. I guess you've looked online?'

'Yep, no luck . . .'

'I'm due to pick up some new collections soon. I'll keep a careful lookout, if you like?'

'That would be fantastic,' the man said enthusiastically, looking around the shop now. 'I loved that Almanac of Grains you found me last week.'

'Oh yes, that's unputdownable . . .'

Roxanne's mouth twitched as she imagined Serena and Kate – or, in fact, Sean – listening in on this, and she had to turn away to hide her amusement.

'I might just have a little browse now,' the man added. 'I've left Jude in charge of the shop and he should be able to cope without me.'

'Browse away,' Della said warmly. 'D'you fancy a coffee while you're looking, Michael? Faye's just made a pot . . .'

'That would be lovely, thank you.'

Della turned to pour a cup from the percolator that sat behind the counter. 'Rox, would you like one too?'

'No thanks, I'm heading off in a second—'

'This is my sister, Roxanne,' Della told the Grain Almanac man. 'She's just arrived from London – she's staying with me for a few weeks.' She turned to Roxanne. 'Michael owns the new bakery down the road. He runs it single-handedly—'

'My son and daughter help,' he said quickly. 'I can't take all the credit . . .'

'Oh, I saw it when I arrived,' Roxanne enthused. 'It's *beautiful*. It's about time we had decent bread around here . . .'

'Well, do pop in sometime,' he said with a smile.

Roxanne noticed his striking light blue eyes as he accepted the mug of coffee from Della. 'I will,' she replied.

'Roxanne might be interested in your sourdough workshop,' Della added with a sly grin.

'Really? Oh, that's great!'

'Erm, I have to say I'm not really a baker . . .' *The emergency services tend to be involved . . .*

'Don't worry,' Michael said warmly, selecting a book from the shelf. 'No prior experience required.'

Roxanne's expression set as Stanley whined and strained for the door. 'Um, hopefully I'll make it along, then. But we'd better get going . . .'

'Enjoy your walk,' Michael said, adding, 'I think it might rain, though. Don't you have a coat?'

Roxanne couldn't help smiling as she glanced down at her fine-knit cardi and knee-length cotton skirt. Although she had brought a couple of perfectly serviceable jackets, the sun was shining and she really didn't require guidance on how to dress herself. 'I'm sure I'll be fine,' she said. 'It's such a beautiful afternoon.'

Della glanced out of the window and frowned. 'The sky's looking darker now, Rox. I'd definitely put on something waterproof if I were you.'

'Honestly, Dell, I'll be—'

'I'd take an umbrella at least,' Michael cut in, apparently fascinated now by her silver leather ballet flats.

'You're not wearing *those,* are you?' Della exclaimed, also staring at Roxanne's feet, as if she was wearing ridiculous clown shoes. Her unremarkable footwear had become quite the spectacle – but then, nothing much happened in Burley Bridge.

'Yes, it looks like I am,' Roxanne laughed, 'but don't worry – I have my phone, and if I'm not back by midnight you have my permission to send out a search party.' She caught Michael's eye, and he grinned.

'Don't you have some wellies she could wear, Della?' Faye called out. Now even the teenager present was concerned about her attire!

'Yes, I do. Rox – go back upstairs and change,' Della commanded. 'They're sitting in the hallway. Take the red ones, not the green – they're Frank's . . .'

Roxanne looked around at all these people who were gazing at her, seemingly of the opinion that her delicate London skin might dissolve at the first contact with moisture (and anyway, it *definitely* wasn't going to rain). 'I'll wear them next time,' Roxanne said, to appease her sister.

'And I have waterproof trousers,' Della added. 'They'll fit you fine. They're in that trunk in the hallway.'

'That's really kind of you, but no. I'm only going for a little walk, not traversing the Siberian tundra on a dog-sled.'

Michael spluttered into his coffee. 'All the same, don't forget your whistle and torch,' he added with a smile.

Roxanne laughed and patted her small leather shoulder bag, which was probably equally unsuitable for country walking – should she have an enormous backpack, like a Sherpa? – and contained nothing but her mobile, purse and Stanley's poo bags. 'All present and correct,' she said.

'I thought we'd have dinner in the pub tonight,' Della added, her voice softening.

'I'll look forward to that – if I make it back alive.' Roxanne turned to Faye with a chuckle. 'So this is what it's going to be like, Faye. Della's reverted to big sisterly mode. I've offered to help with categorising new stock but she's obviously worried that I might put a fondue book into the entertaining section instead of on the party food shelf.'

Faye laughed as, with Stanley whining and rapidly losing patience now, Roxanne allowed him to pull her towards the door.

'I'd put fondues in the *retro* section,' Michael remarked as she left the shop.

It was a relief to escape, which didn't bode well for Roxanne's entire summer here; she had been back in Burley for less than two hours. However, she was determined to remain positive. She strolled through the village, deciding now that she would *force* Della to let her help out in the shop, now she had been reminded how alluring it was. The idea of whiling away pleasant afternoons with mellow jazz playing was becoming more attractive by the minute. For one thing, Della kept the shop cosy and now Roxanne *was* rather chilly, being jacketless on what had turned into a blustery afternoon.

She stopped outside the bakery. So this belonged to Michael, who appeared to be a fan of umbrellas (Roxanne couldn't abide them. Poky, dripping and frequently flipping inside out – wasn't it time a more *dignified* alternative was invented?). She looked up at the sign which, like the book-shop's, was hand-painted, as seemed to be the style around here these days. *The Little Bakery on Rosemary Lane*. Hmm. A slight copy of Della's, perhaps, but then, this *was* Rosemary Lane, and it had a welcoming ring to it.

Roxanne glanced in and saw that the shop was being manned by a tall and skinny young man – presumably Michael's son – who was sweeping the floor in front of the counter. Now shivering a little, she did fancy a coffee, but at 5 p.m. the place was clearly about to close. Looping Stanley's lead around the metal hook embedded into the stone wall, Della decided to try her luck, and stepped in. 'Hi, could you possibly do me a takeaway coffee?'

The young man peered at her through shaggy dark hair that was dangling into his blue eyes. 'A coffee?'

'Yes, please.' She eyed the perfectly serviceable-looking coffee machine behind him, along from the wicker baskets containing a small selection of remaining loaves.

'Uh, sure. What would you like?'

'Could you do me an Americano?'

Now he, too, was staring down at her silver leather ballet flats, before muttering something unintelligible and setting the machine into action. 'That's a pound, please,' he said, handing the carton to her.

'Is that all?' she exclaimed, then caught herself. Was this what Della had meant by 'acting all Londony'? Yet her morning coffee from the kiosk near work cost nearly three times as much and, as she discovered as she left the shop and took her first taste, this was even better.

Roxanne sipped it as she and an excitable Stanley made their way along the lane. Clearly knowing the way, he tugged her towards the unmade track that led out of the village and up into the hills, where there was only the occasional farmhouse or cottage.

Roxanne finished her coffee, dropping the carton into the last litter bin before they left the village behind. She didn't hold with the 'no coffee after noon' rule that so many of her colleagues abided by. Caffeine was her fuel, and discovering that the new bakery did takeaways suggested that she would be able to survive here after all.

However, she would have to come up with a strategy to stop Della from bombarding her with suggestions for activities to fill her time (what was the etiquette about not attending a sourdough workshop you'd been invited to? Roxanne wondered). At least there was Stanley to take out. He was certainly delighted to be out in the wilds now, his little body quivering with excitement at the sights and smells around him. Roxanne had always been fond of dogs and begged for one of her own as a child, but her mother wouldn't allow it. Too demanding and needy, Kitty had always insisted, making them sound like the sort of boyfriend one would do well to avoid. In London, of course, with Roxanne living in a tiny flat and being out at work all day, it was out of the question.

She climbed the path that would take her steeply up into the hills, stopping now and again to look back and take in the dramatic scoop of the valley and the village nestling in its folds. It was beautiful here – all soft, mellow contours as far as the eye could see. The pockets of woodland looked from here like the tiny lichen-like trees Jeff used to stick on the terrain for his model railway when they were children.

Roxanne breathed in deeply. Already, the stresses of recent events had all but faded away. Locking herself out of her flat, the post-party row with Sean and being reprimanded by a child in a fireman's uniform now seemed like distant memories. Even her angst over Marsha and Tina had given way to a 'let's just see what happens' approach. No point in fretting constantly – and anyway, wasn't the whole point of coming up here to have a proper break from all of that?

At least here, the only thing she was likely to be hassled for was her refusal to dress like a North Sea fisherman. Perhaps next time, just to appease the entire population of Burley Bridge, she would deign to wear wellies, as it was becoming pretty muddy underfoot – although she might have to buy her own. She had glimpsed Della's glittery red ones in the hallway and wasn't sure she could go there quite yet. A nice smart pair of Hunters could act as her *gateway* wellies, easing her gently into the realm of wet weather attire; she could even write about them for her 'fashion director stranded in the country' blog. If she was to return to work on good terms with Marsha, she would have to find *something* to write about.

Without her properly noticing, an hour had passed, and she and Stanley were now at the top of the hill. Her mobile rang. Expecting Della to be checking up on her welfare, Roxanne pulled it from her bag.

'Sean! Hi, darling.'

'Hey, babe, how's it going?'

Her heart seemed to soar at the sound of his voice. She perched on a rather wobbly drystone wall, overcome by a surge of missing him. 'Well, so far I've had Della, her assistant and customer all convinced I'm improperly dressed for the weather conditions – but apart from that, it's all good.'

Sean chuckled. 'Don't tell me you're wearing those black heels from brandy snap night?'

'No, of course not!'

'So, where are you now?'

'Out on a walk,' she said with a trace of pride. 'I'm with Stanley – remember I showed you pictures of Dell's little rescue dog?'

'Oh, yeah. So, what *are* you wearing?'

'I'm wearing entirely appropriate clothing for the geographical conditions,' she replied with a smile.

He chuckled, and she could picture his beautiful green eyes crinkling. 'Liar.'

'I am! Of *course* I am. I did grow up here, you know. I do know what the countryside's like – unlike some people . . .'

157

'Hey, I do visit the countryside now and again, I'll have you know.'

'Like, when?' she teased him.

'I shot that wedding dress story for *Modern Brides* on Hampstead Heath the other week.'

'Hampstead Heath's not the country,' she retorted. 'It's NW3 . . .'

'It might as well be. It's grassy and muddy and at certain points you can hardly see London at all. Louie was worried I might have a panic attack.'

'Yes, but it's still *in* London, darling . . .'

'And remember we did that winter tartans shoot together on Clapham Common?'

'You can't say Clapham Common's the country either. You're insane!'

They were laughing now, and she gazed across the vast expanse of unspoilt beauty, wishing he was here to see it too.

'Anyway,' she added, 'I'm wearing my pale pink cashmere cardi with a camisole underneath, and my navy cotton skirt, and I'm *fine*.'

'Hmm. Well, be careful out there. Don't try to climb any electrified fences, and remember livestock can get territorial and charge you.'

She chuckled. 'Thank you, sweetheart. You've obviously been watching *Countryfile*.'

'Happy to help.'

Roxanne smiled. 'So, how was your shoot today?'

'Great. All warm and toasty in the studio, thanks. In fact, my client's still here – I'd better finish up . . .'

'I'll let you go, then.' Something twisted in her. *Why* wasn't he desperate to set up a date to come up and see her?

'Have a fun evening,' he added. 'Hitting the bright lights tonight, are you?'

'Thanks. Actually, we're going for dinner in the Red Lion. It's such a cosy, old-fashioned pub. You'd love it.' She paused and chewed at a fingernail. 'You know you're welcome here any time, don't you?'

'Yes, of course—'

'Della has room. Or we could take a little trip somewhere, find a snug hotel to stay in for a night or two . . .'

She sensed his hesitation. 'I'll see how things go, okay?'

What did *that* mean? Stanley pulled on the lead, and she glanced down. 'Yes, all right – but if you're nervous about the rural aspect, I'm sure there's a crash course in survival skills you could take.' A splash of rain landed on her face. The sky had darkened dramatically, as if suddenly flooded with murky grey ink.

'I'll bear that in mind. Sorry, darling, really gotta dash—'

'Okay. Bye, honey,' she said, before slipping her phone back into her bag just as the heavens opened and good old Yorkshire rain began to fall.

Chapter Fourteen

As she tramped down the hill towards the village, it struck Roxanne that this was happening too often, this finding herself out in the rain, improperly dressed, as if she had missed one of the fundamental lessons of being a grown-up (i.e., the one entitled Always Take a Coat). But the night of Sean's party hadn't been anything like this. London rain rarely was; in fact, she couldn't remember a downpour this heavy, this *wetting,* in years. Within seconds she was drenched, with no hope of shelter and no alternative but to hurry back to Della's with Stanley trotting along beside her, rather sulkily, it seemed to Roxanne.

'I'm in for a right old lecture,' she told him gravely, 'for not wearing the red wellies.' She looked down at him. Her first day here and already she was talking to a terrier. Actually, that didn't seem so bad. At home, in the absence of pets, she had sometimes found herself chatting to that stolen cactus.

'Oh dear, looks like you've been caught out!' a voice called out to her. Roxanne glanced round to see a figure almost entirely shrouded in a padded moss green jacket, their face hidden deep inside the funnel of an enormous hood, stomping out of the woodland towards her. An ancient chocolate Labrador lumbered along at their side.

'Yes, I sort of misjudged it a bit,' Roxanne replied, something of an understatement as her hair was plastered to her head and rivulets were running down her cheeks. It was even raining into her *eyes*, requiring an awful lot of dabbing with her wet cardigan sleeve, as if she were crying.

'I heard you were coming, Roxanne. Lovely to see you back here.'

Pushing her hair from her face, Roxanne realised it was Irene Bagshott, a hardy woman who was still referred to around Burley Bridge as 'the postmistress'. Normally Roxanne would be happy to stop and chat, but right now, with her freezing, sock-less feet slithering in her silver leather ballet flats, she was just desperate to hurry back to Della's. 'Thanks,' she murmured. 'It's lovely to be here.'

'Not right now, though, eh?' Irene boomed. 'Imagine, coming out in this weather without a coat! What were you *thinking*?'

Roxanne forced a joyless smile as they started to make their way back down the path together. 'Yes, I know. Aren't I an idiot? They shouldn't let me out!'

Irene guffawed. 'Not used to our weather, are you?' she added, as if Roxanne were more accustomed to Caribbean climes. 'You've been down south too long, going to all your parties . . .'

Roxanne laughed tightly as Sean's party flashed into her mind. Bad dancing, drunkenness and belly-bloating rice: what a success *that* had been.

'Very exciting about the bookshop, isn't it?' Irene went on. 'The expansion plans, I mean. Della was ever so brave buying that clapped-out old place next door.'

'Yes, and she's already done amazing things with the shop. It's looking fantastic.'

Irene wiped a droplet of rain from the tip of her own nose. 'You'll be working with her, I'd imagine? Getting the paintbrushes out and mucking in? *Rolling up your sleeves?*'

Roxanne prickled, wondering if that might be a sneaky reference to the fact that she had hardly been on hand when Kitty, their mother, was sick with cancer. 'If I'm allowed to,' she replied, keeping her tone light. 'I'm not sure Della trusts me, to be honest.'

She nodded. 'I suppose it's her baby and she's very proud of it.'

'Yes, quite rightly so.'

Irene was staring pointedly at Roxanne's bare, muddied legs. 'You'll remember to wear trousers next time?'

'I'll try my best, Irene,' Roxanne replied with forced jollity.

As they trudged on, Roxanne started to wonder if she had craved a life in London not due to a love of fashion after all – but because everywhere was properly paved and didn't become impossibly slippy at the first drop of rain. Funny how she was capable of pulling together a fashion shoot with a budget of thousands, booking the photographer, models, hair, make-up and being involved in every aspect from finding the perfect location to the choosing of earrings (readers of her magazine didn't realise it, but every shoot required hundreds of decisions to be made). Yet here she was, in the midst of a colossal fashion malfunction, drenched right through to her underwear.

Perhaps it had been a rash move to come here; an overreaction to Tina's appointment. Now she feared she had landed in totally the wrong habitat.

Irene was studying Roxanne's sodden ballet flats as they

made their way down the marshy path. 'Can't see them recovering, Roxanne,' she remarked.

'Oh, I'm sure a quick wipe down and they'll be fine.' *And if they're not, I'll no doubt appear in the* Heathfield Gazette: *Fashion director's inappropriately chosen silver leather pumps RUINED!*

At the foot of the hill, as they parted company, Roxanne tried to figure out how to sneak up to Della's flat with minimal interaction with anyone else. The best-case scenario was that Della would be still fully occupied in the shop, even though it would have closed. That way, Roxanne could nip in through the side door and hurtle upstairs without being spotted. She knew Della never locked the door to her flat when she was in the shop. She'd heard it so many times around here – the 'We never lock our front door!' thing – and it never failed to amaze her that such a level of trust still existed. Roxanne *did* lock her door. Of course she did, she lived in Islington – and when things went awry, London's noble fire brigade smashed it down.

This was ridiculous, she decided as the bookshop came into view. There was something about being back in her childhood village which seemed to propel her back to being a teenager. Here she was, at forty-seven, trying to figure out how she might 'sneak in'! It was as if she was sixteen again and wobbling home to Rosemary Cottage after a few illicit Pernod-and-blacks and Marlboro Lights at her friend Gabby's down the road.

She glanced in through the bookshop window, hoping the rain might have somehow rendered her invisible. Della was sitting cross-legged on the multicoloured rug in the middle of the bright and inviting shop, with books piled up all around her. Absorbed in sorting out stock, she looked the picture of contentment. Plus, she was *dry*. If

163

Della had ventured out in the rain she would, of course, have been appropriately attired, being a fully-functioning woman who had raised a daughter to adulthood, breezed through a divorce, launched and made a success of a seemingly barking-mad business, found herself a lovely and attentive partner who would *never* sneer at her musical tastes and was, Roxanne decided now, the most together person she knew.

Roxanne was aware that she should move on and stop staring, and that it was actually quite weird to gawp at your sister as if she were an exhibit in a gallery entitled 'A Study in Being a Proper Grown-up'. But despite the rain dribbling down her face, Roxanne couldn't tear herself away.

Would *she* ever be a bona fide adult like this, with a well-stocked fridge and nothing untoward lurking at the bottom of her handbag? Not according to her brother: 'What kind of person buys a flat because they fall in love with the wardrobe in it?' Jeff had crowed when Roxanne told him, fizzling with excitement, about putting in an offer on the Islington place. Perhaps that was why she was really here – to learn the fine art of being truly mature so she would never again fill her flat with disgusting fumes or lock herself out.

Slowly, as Roxanne stood there staring through the bookshop window, an idea began to form. She could see now precisely *why* she needed to be here. Not for the opportunity to wear an ugly anorak, but to make fundamental changes to how she lived her life. She would *reinvent* herself here, using Della as her mentor. After all, most people would have crumbled after being left by their spouse – yet her sister had flourished. What better example could she find of a woman who had turned her life around?

Never mind Roxanne's professional life in London and

all the so-called successes that had brought her. None of that really mattered if she couldn't live a proper grown-up life. What was so great about garnering awards and acclaim, and having a diary packed with events to attend, if you went home at night too exhausted to do anything more taxing than make a sandwich, and delved into your bread bin to find one hard crust, fuzzed with mould?

'Rox!'

Roxanne flinched.

Della was scrambling up from the rug and hurrying towards her, still clutching a copy of *The Joy of Fondue* as she threw open the shop door. 'My God. Look at the state of you . . .'

'I'm *fine*!' Roxanne forced a tight smile as she gripped Stanley's lead.

'How can you say that? Oh, you poor thing – what did I say about the weather? Come in . . .'

In her motherly fashion, Della bundled Roxanne into the warmth of the bookshop. While Roxanne stood there, dripping and shivering, her sister ran off to fetch a towel from the minuscule bathroom at the back. She tried not to dwell upon the fact that it was her, and not Stanley, who was getting a rub down: as if *she* were the drenched pet.

'Here, dry your hair,' Della commanded. Roxanne took the towel and obediently dabbed at her head. 'Look at your shoes!' They both stared down.

'Oh, they don't matter,' Roxanne insisted. 'They were just cheap.'

'How much?'

£149 if I remember rightly . . . 'About twenty quid,' she fibbed with a shrug.

'Take them off, let me see if they're rescuable.'

Obediently, Roxanne peeled them off and handed them to Della, who peered at the labels inside. 'These are LK Bennett! They weren't cheap . . .'

'They're old though. *Years* old.'

'Oh, come on . . .'

'. . . *And* they were in the sale . . .'

'Rox, you wore LK Bennett shoes to walk Stanley up the hill?'

The two sisters stared at each other. Roxanne was all too aware that, to Della, LK Bennett was an eye-wateringly expensive brand that had probably never before been sighted in Burley Bridge. And to Roxanne, it was . . . well, she might as well be honest. It was just ordinary.

She was conscious of Della's unwavering stare as she bent to unclip Stanley's sodden lead. As she stood up, she knew that now was the time to take the first step towards her new incarnation as a bona fide adult. This being treated like a child; it would have to stop. She had been patronised enough lately: first by Marsha at work – 'It's so quaint, so *old-school* to have a funny little scrapbook of ideas!' – and now her own sister was telling her off as if she had run through a puddle in her best party shoes.

'Dell, please don't speak to me like that,' she said quietly. Della frowned. 'Like what? What d'you mean?'

'I mean, about my choice of footwear. Okay, maybe they weren't ideal for a dog walk. But I *am* an adult, and I'm capable of dressing myself and dealing with the consequences. I mean, even if I decided to take Stanley out in an Agent Provocateur corset dress and six-inch Jimmy Choos, then that would entirely be my decision.' She took her limp, wet shoes from Della and jammed them back onto her feet.

'Er, of course,' Della said in a hollow voice. 'It might

not be the *wisest* choice, but it would be completely up to you.'

Water was still dripping from Roxanne's hair onto her cheeks. She gave herself another blot with the towel. 'What I mean is, I know I might not seem terribly sensible sometimes. But I do have a decent job, and I've earned my own living since I was eighteen years old without having to ask for a penny from anyone – not from Mum and Dad or a husband or anyone else.' She paused and swallowed.

'Yes, I know that,' Della said faintly.

'So please just remember that I've managed to run my life, on my own, without too many disasters along the way.' Roxanne cleared her throat, trying to ignore the fact that even her *bra* was soaking wet.

'Oh, Rox. I'm so sorry.' Della reached out to touch her arm, but Roxanne shrank back.

'There's something else,' she muttered, meeting her sister's steady gaze.

Della frowned. 'What?'

'I get the feeling I'm just getting under your feet by being here . . .'

'Of course you're not! What makes you think that?'

'Well, you don't want me to help out in the shop, do you?'

'It's not that. It's just—'

'It *is* that, Dell. Just be honest with me. You're absolutely against it and I can't understand why. D'you think I'll try to take over, or are you worried I'll make a mess of things here?' *It's only a little village bookshop!* she wanted to add, frustration bubbling up in her now. *How hard can it be?*

Concern flickered in Della's dark eyes. 'I just think you might not enjoy it . . .'

'You mean I'm not passionate about it like you are.

167

That I might put things on the wrong shelves and wouldn't know where to find books about fermented breads.'

Della tried for a smile. 'Well, yes, just like you wouldn't expect me to know how to pull together a fashion shoot for a magazine . . .'

Roxanne exhaled. 'Okay, I get that. Your customers expect *you* to be here – an expert on braising and hors d'oeuvres and suet, not just any old random person manning the till . . .'

Della nodded.

'But you have Faye helping out—'

'Yes, and she's excellent – but she's only here because Frank convinced me I needed help and I finally gave in. I mean, we were never seeing each other, apart from in the shop. I was working crazily long hours, six days a week, often late into the night. Our idea of a date was to order takeaway pizzas and eat them right here on the floor, surrounded by books and bubble-wrap, while we packaged up orders together.' Pink patches had sprung up on Della's cheeks. To Roxanne, that kind of date sounded impossibly romantic.

'Well, if Faye can man the place for a few hours,' she said carefully, 'don't you think I can too?'

'Yes, I suppose so,' Della muttered.

'Or d'you think I'd put people off with my fancy London ways?' She pushed back a strand of wet hair and smiled.

'No! No, of course not.'

'So . . . can you please let me help out? Not categorising books, or being an expert on tinned peach desserts or doing anything terribly complicated but . . .' She broke off and looked around the shop. 'Just sitting here, manning the till and being pleasant to people? Can't I at least do that?'

Della's eyes shone out at hers. 'Yes, of course you can.'

'Okay, great. And another thing . . .' Roxanne looked over at Stanley. He had taken himself off to his wicker basket by the Cooking for Pets shelf. 'How often is he being walked these days?'

'He's walked plenty,' Della replied defensively.

'But how on earth d'you find the time?'

'Well, he has a quick walk first thing, and then he'll sit around in the shop and we nip out at lunchtime. And I walk him again in the evening.'

Roxanne looked at her. 'Not many long walks, then?'

'It's hard to fit those in,' Della admitted, 'except for Sundays . . .'

'So, how about I take him out on a long walk every day?'

'Are you sure?'

'Yes – I'd like to. It'd be good for me, and it's something I can do to make up for—' She stopped.

'Rox, honestly, you don't have to make up for anything.' Della looked down at the books, as if avoiding eye contact, then glanced around at Stanley. 'Actually, I'm not so sure he'll want to go out with you again.'

Roxanne frowned. 'Why not?'

'Oh, it's not your fault. He just hates the rain. Honestly – he's a complete wuss about it. If he's taken out and gets a soaking, he holds a grudge for ages.'

Roxanne laughed in disbelief. 'Don't worry, I've worked with models who've thrown a strop because the sun was shining too brightly or there was a *teeny* bit of wind. I'm sure I can win him round.'

'Okay,' Della said with a smile. 'Good luck with that. You can take charge of his walks – on one condition.'

'What's that?' Roxanne handed her the damp towel.

'Look, I hear what you're saying about being perfectly capable of dressing yourself. Of *course* you are – but can

169

I at least dig you out some proper outdoor gear?' Roxanne blinked at her. 'Don't look so appalled,' Della added. 'You're not in Islington now.'

'What d'you have in mind?' she asked nervously.

'Well, waterproof trousers for one thing, for when it's raining . . .'

'Oh, for goodness' sake. I have jeans and I *will* wear your wellies, okay? I was only joking about the Agent Provocateur corset dress.'

'C'mon, Rox, this is the *country* . . .'

'Waterproof trousers are disgusting!'

'No, honestly – they're brilliant. You don't know until you've tried them.'

Roxanne spluttered. 'I'm not a child, refusing to eat sprouts.'

'I'm just saying give them a go,' Della insisted.

'Remember Mum said that to us when she wanted us to try one of her new recipes? Like that time she made that terrible salmon mousse?'

'God, yes – that pink hillock on an oval plate the size of a boat . . .'

Roxanne chuckled. 'And she got terribly angry with Jeff when he refused her ham in aspic . . .'

'"You don't know until you've tried it,"' Della mimicked, and Roxanne sensed the knot of tension unravelling in her stomach as they laughed. 'Will you at least try a pair on?' she added.

Roxanne sighed. 'Yes, all right. My editor wants me to write that style-in-the-country blog. I suppose waterproof trousers can be my debut post.'

Della smiled broadly and patted her arm. 'Great. Now, off you go for a hot shower and *please* stop dripping all over my shop.'

Chapter Fifteen

Della's boyfriend Frank had bagged them a table at the Red Lion. The only pub in the village, it had managed to modernise and bring in new, passing-through clientele, whilst losing none of its faded charm. Frank's face literally lit up when he spotted Della, as if someone had turned up his brightness. Roxanne never realised that actually happened to people, especially when they had been together for eighteen months, as Della and Frank had. From Roxanne's perspective, this ranked as virtually a lifetime together. Sean aside, most of her liaisons had petered out after a few weeks.

He hugged each of the sisters in turn. 'Hey, Rox! Great to see you. I see you've dried off.'

She laughed in disbelief. 'Yes, Frank. So word's got around. Did you see it on the news?'

'I did.' He nodded gravely. 'Something about a London fashion editor being caught in a downpour in an inappropriately thin cardigan and what could only be described as slippers.'

Roxanne chuckled. Although she had only met Frank

a handful of times, he was one of those people who made you feel instantly at ease.

'Fashion *director*, actually,' Della corrected him.

'Oh, sorry!' He pulled a mock-alarmed face. 'Can I make it up to you with a drink, Rox?'

'A white wine would be lovely, thanks.'

He turned to Della. 'Same for you, angel?'

He called her *angel*. What a sweetheart Frank was, Roxanne thought as he headed for the bar.

'Yes please,' Della replied, glancing to the door. 'Oh – Michael's just arrived.' She waved over and glanced back at Roxanne. 'Hope you don't mind that I asked him to join us. Remember he popped into the shop today?'

'The Almanac of Grains man? Of course I don't mind – as long as he doesn't try to rope me into going to that sourdough workshop.' Roxanne glanced over to see that Frank and Michael had fallen into conversation at the bar.

'You should give it a try,' Della cajoled. 'Be open-minded. It's only *baking,* nothing to be scared of really . . .'

'You don't know until you've tried it,' Roxanne quipped, and they both laughed.

The men arrived at the table and set down their drinks. 'So, how was the walk?' Michael asked, taking the seat beside her and stretching out his long, jeans-clad legs.

'Not so great actually . . .'

'I did say to take a whistle and torch.' He chuckled, and Roxanne found herself smiling too.

'News of my near-drowning has travelled fast then,' she added.

'It's that kind of place,' Frank remarked. 'You know what it's like around here.'

Roxanne murmured that she did, and turned back to

Michael. 'You're not from around here, are you? How come you ended up setting up a bakery in Burley Bridge?'

He paused and sipped his beer. Behind the wire-rimmed glasses, his kind, light blue eyes were edged with long dark lashes and undeniably attractive. In his chunky grey sweater he looked like an active sort – a keen gardener, maybe, or a hill walker, *always* correctly attired.

'I'm from Canterbury originally,' he explained. 'I moved up this way – to York – to take up a new teaching post about ten years ago.' He smiled briefly. 'I was a chemistry teacher in a previous life.'

'Wow, that's a bit of a jump to running a bakery, isn't it?'

'Mum used to say baking was all about chemistry,' Della remarked.

Michael paused, as if wondering how best to explain it. 'It was my ex-wife's idea actually.' He glanced briefly at Della and took another sip from his tall glass. 'And it's all because of your sister, really – or, rather, her shop. Suzy, my ex, and I were driving through the village on our way to see relatives. She spotted the bookshop and we decided to stop. And that was it – she fell in love with it, and with the whole village when we had a wander around. She couldn't get it out of her head. She was determined that we should live here, and perhaps even set up a small business of our own.' He smiled at Della. 'Bought up half your stock, didn't she?'

Della nodded. 'Yep – most of the baking section, if I remember.'

'She was working in the council's press office back then,' Michael went on, 'and pretty much hating every minute, and she'd always loved to bake. Redundancies were on the horizon so she started studying baking, huddling over

173

all these vintage books, memorising methods, getting to grips with the science behind it all . . .'

'Wow,' Roxanne murmured.

'. . . She started baking for friends – celebration cakes, breads, that kind of thing, then supplying a local deli and selling at farmers' markets. Unbeknown to me, she was also keeping an eye out for properties, and then the perfect place came up on Rosemary Lane . . .'

'What was it before?' Roxanne asked, delicately side-stepping the ex-wife issue, as she figured that they could barely have launched their business before splitting up. In fact, she genuinely couldn't remember what the shop had been prior to its incarnation as a bakery. Until Della had moved back here, when Roxanne had returned only occasionally to visit their mother, everything had sort of merged together in a sprawl of dismal grey stone.

'A hardware shop.' Michael chuckled. 'We breezed in, like you do when you haven't a clue about the nightmare you're about to launch into—'

'Nightmare?' Roxanne cut in, unable to rein in her curiosity.

However, Michael's story was cut short when Nicola Crowther, the hairdresser whom Roxanne knew from way back in primary school, hurried over to join them. 'I thought it was you. You look amazing, Roxy! I *love* your dress . . .'

'Thanks, Nicola,' Roxanne replied. 'So, how are things with you?'

'Where's it from?' Nicola asked, ignoring her question. 'Designer, I expect?'

'No, er, Oasis actually . . .' How ironic, Roxanne thought, that she worked on a fashion magazine yet had never had her clothing scrutinised as much as it was here. 'So, how are *you*?' She tried again.

'Oh, just the same, you know how it is around here . . .' Nicola gazed some more at Roxanne's blue and white spotted shift dress, then turned and beckoned to her companion at the bar. 'Bev? Remember Roxy Cartwright?'

'Yes, of course! Always won the art prize at school . . .' The other woman hurried over to join them.

'You won't remember my sister,' Nicola said.

'Of course I remember Bev . . .' Roxanne said truthfully, recalling her being something of an athletic champion back in the day.

'You never age, do you, Roxanne?' Bev exclaimed. 'I swear – not a day. I don't know how you do it.'

'That's so kind,' Roxanne blustered. 'You're both looking great . . .'

The sisters beamed at Roxanne, and Roxanne caught Della, Frank and Michael exchanging bemused expressions over the table. Although Nicola and Bev knew Della too, they had barely given her a cursory greeting.

'Look who's up from London!' Nicola trilled, and another woman – Penny Rattan, who ran a garden centre just outside the village – hurried over to join them. Roxanne squirmed in her seat, wondering if this was how it felt to be a minor celebrity.

'How long are you here for?' Penny asked.

'Erm, a couple of months, I think,' Roxanne replied. She remembered Penny from primary school too; a terribly popular girl who was always given the much-coveted role of Mary in the nativity whilst Roxanne never progressed from being a lowly shepherd. It amazed her how many familiar faces were still here.

'A couple of months? Gosh, that's a long time to be away. Has something happened?'

175

'No, uh, I'm just having a break from work. A sort of sabbatical.'

Penny frowned. 'Oh, I see.' *So you're in the throes of some kind of breakdown,* her tone suggested.

Possibly in an attempt to rescue her, Michael passed Roxanne a menu. 'The fish and chips are supposed to be the best in Yorkshire,' he remarked. 'They've just brought in a new chef here.'

'I might just go for that.' *Fish and chips.* What could be more delicious? she thought, picturing the look of alarm this would provoke on her colleagues' faces back at the office. Zoe, the beauty director, once confided to Roxanne that she hadn't had a chip for fifteen years. Although her mind was made up, Roxanne continued to study the menu in the hope that her hovering audience – who were all standing up, looming over her – might drift away.

'So, how's life in the big smoke?' Bev asked.

'It's great. Really great.' Roxanne forced a wide smile.

'I spotted you briefly at Kitty's funeral, swanning about looking gorgeous, of course, but we didn't get the chance to chat.' Did the whole world think she had just 'swanned about' at her mother's funeral? 'Still working in fashion?' Bev quizzed her.

'Yes, just about hanging on in there,' she replied. A young waitress with her dark hair in skinny plaits came over, and they all ordered. Even now, Nicola, Bev and Penny remained clustered around her.

'Bet it's exciting,' Penny remarked, pushing her black-rimmed spectacles up her nose. 'So, d'you have any kids?'

'No, that's never happened for me,' Roxanne replied, for the second time in a week.

Bev raised a brow. 'Are you married?'

Roxanne baulked at the woman's directness. 'Er, nope, that hasn't happened either . . .'

Nicola grinned. 'They must be mad, those men in London!'

'Oh, they are. Every single one of them.' Roxanne smiled stiffly, catching her sister's bemused glance across the table and wondering whether that might be the end of the interrogation for now. *I do actually have a boyfriend!* she wanted to announce, like a fifteen-year-old desperate for kudos. *I mean, someone desires me. Okay, he did finish with me on Saturday but by Monday it was all back on . . .*

She'd forgotten what it was like here; how every little thing became everyone's business. For almost three decades she had lived fairly contentedly, a tiny speckle in the vastness of London, in which anonymity was pretty much guaranteed, and where you could pop out to the shops in a top hat and a pair of marabou-feathered hot pants if you so desired, and no one would even give you a second look. Perhaps the anonymity aspect wasn't quite so ideal if you collapsed in your flat and lay there, slowly bleeding to death and being nibbled by mice. But in the general scheme of things it suited her just fine.

Finally, Nicola, Bev and Penny said their goodbyes and wandered off to the bar. Pinging impertinent questions was clearly thirsty work – or had they merely been expressing a friendly interest? Perhaps Roxanne just wasn't used to that northern directness anymore.

As the talk turned to Frank's architectural work, Roxanne waited for an opportunity to steer the conversation back to Michael's bakery. He had piqued her interest. If his ex-wife had driven the whole project from the start, then why wasn't she still around, up to her elbows in flour and yeast and God knows what else?

'Frank's just completed an amazing glass-and-oak house in Hestlebridge,' Della was saying proudly as platefuls of cod and chips arrived. The portions were enormous, the great mounds of chips the most enticing thing Roxanne had laid eyes on since that bowlful of creamy carbonara at the little Italian place near her flat.

'That's brilliant, Frank,' she said, vigorously sprinkling her plateful with malt vinegar. 'So, is business pretty healthy at the moment?'

'It's not bad,' Frank replied with a self-deprecating smile, 'but for every one of those kind of projects there are twenty-five garage conversions.'

'D'you mind that?' Roxanne asked. 'The less exciting jobs, I mean?'

'Not a bit. It's all work, and obviously, I have Becca to see through the rest of college, and Eddie to think about too. Whatever the scale of the job, I just try to do it as well as I possibly can.'

Roxanne nodded. 'I like your attitude – that sort of getting-on-with-things approach.'

Frank smiled and shrugged. 'What else would I do?'

They tucked into their cod and chips, and when their plates were finally cleared by the cheerful young waitress, Frank wrapped an arm around Della's shoulders. Roxanne couldn't help but notice again the way he looked at her sister, as if, even now, he could hardly believe his luck to have found her. Would anyone ever look at her that way, she wondered? She couldn't recall that Sean ever had – and he certainly wasn't one for an affectionate arm-draped-around-shoulders scenario in the pub. Her mobile rang, and she pulled it from her bag. It was Sean – twice in one day, which was most unlike him – just as he'd popped into her mind.

'Sorry, I'd better take this,' she said quickly, jumping up from the table and stepping towards the wood-panelled wall as she took the call. 'Hi, darling,' she said. 'This is a nice surprise . . .'

'Hi,' he said brusquely. 'It sounds noisy there. Where are you?'

'In the Red Lion. We've just had dinner. Frank's here, and Michael, he runs the local bakery—'

'Rox, can I ask you something?' Sean cut in abruptly.

She frowned. 'Of course.'

'Did you give Tommy my phone numbers?'

'Tommy?' she repeated.

'The joiner. That guy who fixed your door. He's been calling me constantly about doing that job for him.'

Roxanne sensed her cheeks blazing. 'Oh God, I'm sorry. He asked again, he seemed so keen – and you did say you'd photograph Jessica, remember?'

'Yes, but only to get him off my back. *You* knew that. I had no intention of actually contacting him, and I didn't realise she was a bloody dog!'

Roxanne glanced over her shoulder. Della and the others were in earshot. She hated conducting phone conversations in social situations; it seemed so rude. Michael's gaze caught hers, and she mouthed 'sorry' and flapped her hand about. Still clutching her phone, she edged her way past convivial groups in the bustling pub and stepped out into the cool evening. 'I didn't think for a minute that he'd start bothering you,' she murmured.

'Stalking, more like! And it's hardly what I do, is it? Pictures of pets on fluffy rugs? Christ!'

A small chill ran through her. Back home in London,

179

Sean's rant might have sounded perfectly reasonable. Yet here, standing outside the impossibly picturesque pub in her childhood village, his response to Tommy's pretty innocuous request seemed ridiculous. He'd been asked to photograph a puppy, for goodness' sake, not clean a petrol station lavatory with his tongue. 'Oh, come on,' she muttered. 'Just do him a favour. You were all mate-this, mate-that when you met, laughing about all the inept women you'd both known . . .'

'I was just being friendly,' he insisted. 'So, anyway, what d'you suggest I do now? He's called my mobile *four times*. He's tried my landline too. For God's sake – I'm being hounded!'

'"Hounded",' she repeated, trying to lighten the mood. 'Very appropriate . . .'

Sean sighed heavily. Roxanne waited for him to ask how the rest of her first day here had been, and how Della was – the usual questions one might expect from a caring boyfriend who was far away. She waited for him to add that he was planning to come up to see her, as soon as humanly possible – it was only two hundred miles north, for goodness' sake, hardly the Arctic Circle. But Sean said nothing.

Roxanne inhaled a lungful of cool evening air. 'Just tell him you're too busy,' she murmured to break the silence.

'Yeah, that's what I said.'

'Good. Oh, come on, honey. I'm sure you'll figure something out. Do we have to end the day on this note?'

'Well, *I* don't want to,' he huffed.

'Neither do I,' she said, stepping back into the pub and glimpsing Della, Frank and Michael all chatting animatedly at the corner table. At this moment, rejoining them was

180

a far more appealing proposition than appeasing a fifty-year-old man about a dog.

'I'll see what I can do,' he conceded.

'Okay, darling,' she said quickly. 'I miss you. Bye for now.'

'Bye for now, babe. Miss you too.'

She hung up and made her way back to the others.

Michael turned to her. 'Everything okay?'

'Er, yes – just some mini crisis at home.'

Della frowned. 'Something at your flat?'

No, that was last week . . . 'I, er, met this joiner guy who wants his dog photographed – you know, a pet portrait kind of thing. So I gave him Sean's numbers.' She looked around the table. Three bewildered faces peered at her.

'Rox's boyfriend's a photographer,' Della told Michael, before turning back to her sister. 'I don't understand why this is an issue, though. This dog thing, I mean . . .'

Roxanne shrugged, wondering how to explain it without sounding quite mad. She glanced at Michael, who was regarding her intently, and realised how reluctant she was to go into this now. 'Well, it's not really Sean's thing,' she started to explain. 'I suppose, where photography's concerned – or anything creative, really – some jobs are more prestigious than others. He's sort of reached a certain level, and it would be bad for his profile to do anything below that.'

She glanced at Frank, an architect who was as willing to draw up plans for simple garage extensions as he was to design a stunning glass-and-oak home. It was all *work*, after all. It paid the bills and enabled him to support his children, and wasn't there something honest and admirable about that?

'Sean shoots for all the big fashion magazines,' she continued, sweat prickling at her underarms now. 'He does major ad campaigns. You'll have seen his work on billboards.' She paused, waiting for someone – any one of them – to look impressed. She was still met with bemused looks. 'Honestly,' she went on, 'he's at the stage where he can pick and choose his jobs and so, the way he looks at it, he doesn't want to lower himself to shooting some joiner's dog.'

She stopped and laughed. 'Poor choice of phrasing,' Michael chuckled.

'You know what I mean.'

He was peering at her now, amusement glinting in those clear blue eyes. 'Is the dog terribly unattractive?'

'No,' she exclaimed. 'She's a very cute Cavalier King Charles spaniel, from what I saw on her owner's phone . . .'

'Ah, a pedigree. We just have a mutt – your typical fifty-seven varieties . . .'

'But the breed isn't the point,' she added, aware of how petty and silly the whole episode sounded. 'I mean, *any* dog he'd have a problem with . . .'

'Or in fact any pet at all?' Michael suggested, raising a brow.

'Yes!'

'Like a hamster or gerbil?'

Roxanne nodded, and wondered if he was gently teasing her now.

'It's what the actual assignment might do to his reputation,' he added.

'Yes, that's it exactly.' She drained her glass, excused herself and made her way to the ladies', irritated at Sean for interrupting her evening with this whole ridiculous business. She had been enjoying talking to Michael, getting to know someone new who wasn't involved with magazines or fashion. But of course, Sean had just wanted to offload to her, which was understandable. She reminded herself now that he wasn't really pretentious, and that they really did have the best times together – plus she fancied him terribly. She was still prone to sitting up in bed of a morning, taking in the glorious sight of him as he wandered naked around her bedroom, casually stretching and tugging on his clothes.

Roxanne washed her hands unnecessarily – she didn't actually need the loo – torn between bubbling annoyance and a fierce desire to see Sean right now and jump into bed with him. It had felt good to be here tonight, until he'd called – now it seemed as if her two lives had slammed together, awkwardly, and thrown her off course.

Back out in the pub, she made her way to their table. She recognised a few faces and briefly said hi, but kept on moving through the crowd. It was busy for a Tuesday night – but then, the village had a feeling of having been woken up and revitalised, and that had all started when Della's shop had put Burley Bridge on the map. Without the bookshop, there would be no bakery, no boutique, no gift shop or art gallery, and even the Red Lion would have been pretty dead on a week night a few years ago. When she considered what Della had done for the village, Roxanne's own achievements seemed rather paltry.

She registered a male voice – Michael's voice – floating above the general chatter. 'I know what you're up to, Della. Bit of matchmaking, wasn't it? You couldn't resist!'

Roxanne froze as Della laughed awkwardly. None of them had noticed that she had stopped by the old-fashioned jukebox; the one that had sat there, glowing gaudily, for as long as she could remember. A song finished, and the inner workings clicked and whirred as another was selected.

'I just thought you'd get along,' Della said lightly, a trace of defensiveness in her voice now.

'Yes, but she's seeing someone, isn't she?' Michael retorted. 'You conveniently forgot to mention that part.'

Chapter Sixteen

And from then on, of course, it was excruciating sitting with Michael. He was no longer just the man from the bakery down the road; he was a potential set-up. Perhaps that was why Della had suggested dinner at the Red Lion in the first place – as an opportunity to engineer the two of them spending some time together. As Michael himself had suggested, she seemed to have forgotten that Roxanne was in a relationship – a rare situation, perhaps, and maybe Sean fell short of Frank's exemplary standards, but still, she was *going out with someone*, to use an inappropriately teenage phrase. Roxanne had a boyfriend, even if that made her sound nineteen years old. Lately, the word 'partner' had slipped from favour in her circles, the b-word having been reclaimed (Roxanne liked the breezy playfulness of it, even if it did sound rather juvenile; she was certain she would never be anyone's 'other half').

The conversation around the table had turned to everyone's offspring, and Roxanne tried to fix on an expression of rapt interest. Normally, she didn't mind child-related talk; after all, Sophie was her niece, and Roxanne had always been keenly interested in what she was up to. She had eleven-year-old twin nephews too – her brother Jeff's children – and she tried to be an attentive auntie, as much as distance allowed. However, now she just felt rattled. She glanced at Frank, whose nine-year-old, Eddie, was with his mother tonight. Naturally, Frank would be party to Della's little matchmaking project too.

'How old are your kids, Michael?' Roxanne felt uncomfortable sitting there mutely, even though she was hardly in the mood for small talk now.

'Elsa's sixteen and Jude's nineteen,' he replied.

'Would it have been Jude who made me a coffee just before closing time today?'

Michael smiled. 'Yep, that was my boy . . .'

'Your kids must be a big help to you,' she added.

'Well, yes – Jude seems to have no plans for any sort of alternative career at the moment, so it's kind of convenient that there's a ready-made job for him.'

'What an obliging dad you are,' Della said with a smile.

Amusement glinted in Michael's eyes. 'Yeah. Funnily enough, most days he forgets to thank me.' He turned back to Roxanne. 'I'm kidding. They're both pretty good really. The sourdough workshop was Elsa's idea, so please try to come, won't you?'

'Oh, um – I'll do my best . . .' As if her schedule here was jam-packed.

'Elsa thinks we need to give things a big push,' Michael went on. 'She's always on at me to put on events in the shop, be more active on social media, anything we can do to drum up publicity . . .' He broke off. 'She's just about stopping short of finding a giant loaf costume and making me dance down Rosemary Lane in it.'

'Maybe that could work,' Roxanne remarked, chuckling.

186

'You think Burley Bridge could handle that?'

'I mean the publicity side,' she said, feeling more relaxed again now. As Michael clearly wasn't making a big issue of Della's matchmaking endeavour, so Roxanne felt able to shrug it off too. 'You wouldn't believe how seemingly ordinary businesses have taken off,' she added, 'just because a journalist has mentioned it in their magazine . . .'

'You think we're ordinary?' He raised a brow and smirked.

'No! Oh, you know what I'm saying.'

Michael nodded. 'Yes, I do. You work on a glossy magazine, don't you? Della mentioned it . . .'

'Yes, that's right,' she said, glancing at her sister who was now deep in conversation with Frank. So, she had given him some background info. What else had she said? she wondered.

'I'm not sure I understand anything about that world,' Michael added.'

'Most people don't,' Roxanne said with a smile. 'It's a peculiar industry and it doesn't really have much bearing on reality, although I've always loved it . . .' She paused and drained her glass. After the earlier quizzings from Bev and the others, she was keener to find out more about Michael's working life than talk about her own. 'So,' she started, 'how's it been, setting up your bakery in a place like this?'

He sipped his beer. 'It's still early days but we're getting somewhere, I think. At the moment I'm still focusing on getting things right in the shop – like, making bread that people will come back for again and again.'

'It's the best for miles around,' chipped in Della.

'Glad you think so.' He smiled and turned back to Roxanne. 'We've only been going for six months and it's taken a lot of experimenting and tweaking.'

'Hence you buying all those vintage books from us,' Della remarked. 'To study traditional methods . . .'

'Yep, that's the plan – and we're almost there, I think.'

Having offered to fetch a final round, Frank went to the bar and returned with more wine and beers. If she hadn't discovered that Della was trying to set them up, Roxanne might have tried to ascertain when Michael and his wife split up, and what his situation was now. The way he'd been speaking about her, there didn't seem to be any particular animosity between them – but perhaps he was just a decent sort who preferred to live his life without bitterness. Anyway, it didn't feel right to ask him about anything too personal now.

They left the pub at ten-thirty and stopped to part company as they reached the bakery.

'Thanks for a lovely evening,' Michael said.

'Hope we didn't keep you out too late,' Della remarked with a smile, turning to Roxanne. 'Michael's up at five to start baking every morning.'

'That still counts as night time,' Roxanne said, now keen to flop into bed herself in Della's cosy spare room.

'Occupational hazard,' Michael remarked. 'So, see you around the village?'

'Bound to,' she replied with a smile. As she, Della and Frank wandered further down the lane, past all the shut-up shops with their window boxes and prettily painted signs, Roxanne reflected upon what a bizarre evening it had been. It was only her first night, and already she had been grilled about her marital and child-free status and unwittingly steered into a sort of blind date.

Della let them into her flat. 'Anyone like a pot of tea?' she asked brightly.

'No thanks – I'm done in,' Frank replied. He turned to

Roxanne. 'Night, Rox. Early start for me too so I'll probably be gone by the time you're awake.'

'Oh, I'll be up at the crack of dawn to walk Stanley,' Roxanne insisted, keen to show she was planning to launch herself into country life.

As Frank disappeared into Della's bedroom, Roxanne strode to the kitchen and filled the kettle. Della wandered in after her and set out two mugs. 'Please don't ever do that to me again,' Roxanne murmured.

Della frowned. 'Do *what* again?'

'Try to set me up.'

Della's face fell. She glanced at Stanley, who was curled up on a matted tartan blanket in his basket. 'What? I mean, how did you—'

'I heard Michael,' Roxanne said quietly, keen for Frank not to overhear, 'when I came out of the ladies'.'

Della pressed a hand at the side of her face. 'Oh God, I'm sorry. I just thought . . .' She broke off. As if sensing Della's discomfort, Stanley eased himself out of his basket and pottered towards her, plonking himself down at her feet with a small thud. 'I just thought you'd get along. That it would be a nice thing for both of you, and you could enjoy each other's company while you're here . . .'

'Well, it was just a bit awkward.'

'I know, but just—'

'D'you know what, Dell?' Roxanne cut in. 'I'm actually a little bit tired of people thinking on my behalf, making assumptions about me. You know, like – "Oh, funny Roxanne and her London ways, heading out in the pouring rain in her LK Bennetts" and, "Oh, there's poor Roxanne – d'you know she hasn't managed to find herself a husband or have any children? And now of course it's far too late!"'

She stopped. To her horror, tears had flooded her eyes.

189

'Rox, I'm *so* sorry.' Della looked aghast.

Roxanne wiped her eyes on her sleeve. 'Also, whether you like the sound of him or not, I'm seeing Sean, so I'm really not in the market for meeting anyone else right now.'

'No, I realise that, and he sounds like a great person, he really does.' Of course, Roxanne knew Della didn't really believe that. From her perspective, he had failed to see Roxanne safely into a taxi after his party, and he seemed to have an irrational aversion to the photographing of small pedigree dogs.

Roxanne turned away to make tea, trying to calm herself with slow, deep yogic breathing. *Everything starts with the breath,* Lily, the office yoga teacher, always said – whatever that meant. Yet thinking about the office made her feel anything *but* calm. She pictured Marsha, cramming that Danish pastry into her mouth, and Tina suggesting – probably just to humiliate her – that she blogged about style in the country. Well, that's what Roxanne would give her – starting from tomorrow. Had Tina cooked up the blog idea just to humiliate her? It occurred to her now that that was a distinct possibility. Well, if that was the case, Roxanne would show she was game; just because she had worked in fashion all her adult life didn't mean she couldn't laugh at herself. She would appear on the online edition of a top fashion magazine, clad in hideous wet weather gear if that was what was required of her. She would gambol across the fields in a wretched cagoule and Della's glittery red wellies. What did it matter if she looked deranged? She was past caring what anyone thought of her anyway.

'Rox? Are you okay?' Della placed a hand on her shoulder. 'I'm sorry. It was silly and badly judged of me.

I just thought, Michael's such a lovely person, all on his own, working his fingers to the bone and—'

'It's all right,' Roxanne interrupted, mustering a faint smile now. 'You thought you'd put two tragic, lonely souls together.'

'No!' Della exclaimed.

'I'm joking – and it's okay.' She placed the crocheted tea cosy over the pot, poured two mugfuls and handed one to Della. 'It's just a bit embarrassing, and of course, now I'm going to be running into the poor man every time I leave the flat . . .' She broke off. 'What happened with him and his wife, anyway? From what he was saying, the bakery had been all her idea.'

Della nodded. 'Yes, it was – and now he's stuck with it, having to make a go of it as all their money went into buying the shop and the flat above it.'

'So, why did they break up?' Roxanne blew across her mug of tea.

'Michael was doing some supply teaching to keep the money coming in while Suzy supervised the conversion into a bakery. Only, she'd been supervising more closely than anyone realised because she and the twenty-eight-year-old kitchen fitter . . .' Roxanne raised a brow. 'That's who she's with now. She left Michael for him – a man twenty years younger than her.'

'Wow,' Roxanne breathed.

'So, really, is it any wonder he doesn't completely love being in the bakery all hours, surrounded by the ovens, worktops and shelving his wife's new boyfriend installed?'

Roxanne shook her head. 'I'd want to rip the place to pieces. I certainly wouldn't want to be up at five every morning making loaves.'

'Why doesn't he just sell it and go back to teaching?'

191

'I'm not sure,' Della replied. 'You'll have to ask him. Maybe it's a pride thing – I mean, he's achieved such a lot already, but there must have been times when he just wanted to give up. But the kids are into it – Elsa especially. I suspect he's kept on going for them . . .'

'Do they see much of their mum?' Roxanne asked.

'A little, I think, but from what he's said they're still pretty angry with her.'

Roxanne sipped her tea. 'And you wanted to cheer him up,' she added with a smile. 'You said, "Oh, you should meet my sister".'

Della's cheeks flushed. 'I might have said something like that. So, d'you forgive me?'

'I'll think about it,' Roxanne said, hugging her good-night, before carrying her mug of tea off to bed.

She pulled off her clothes and slipped on her cosiest pyjamas, the pink and white spotty ones Amanda had bought her for her last birthday, which felt so soft and were never worn when Sean was staying over. On those nights, it was the black lacy slip, or similar – if anything at all. Enticing, but hardly snug.

Roxanne stretched out on top of the bed, just for a moment, to collect herself. The bed was covered by a beautiful blanket of crocheted squares – 'granny squares', as they are now known – made by her mother from scraps of wool. Kitty had been a frugal sort, unravelling old sweaters once worn by her three children, in order to reuse the wool.

Closing her eyes momentarily, Roxanne could almost smell her childhood. Perhaps Della's heart had been in the right place, she reflected, when she had had the bright idea of trying to set her up with Michael. Bringing them together like that now seemed like an act of kindness, rather than meddling. However, she still wished Della had simply invited him along, without any 'You should meet my sister!' agenda.

Roxanne clicked off the bedside lamp, and was snuggling down beneath the duvet when her phone bleeped with a text. Sleepily, she groped on the floor to retrieve it.

Darling, it read, *so sorry was such a grump on phone about Tommy's dog. Just been working too hard lately. Why do you put up with me? I love you and miss you. Are you okay up there? Are you stomping across the fields, talking to yourself yet? Are there more than three channels on TV? Do they still dance to Abba up there? (Joke!) Hope you're behaving yourself sweetheart. All my love, Sean xx.*

She smiled, trying to think of a suitably witty reply. But sleep was already folding over her like a blanket – was it always this exhausting, being in the country? – and she drifted off with her phone still clutched in her hand.

Chapter Seventeen

Then, somehow, eleven hours later, it was morning.

Eleven hours! Roxanne blinked awake, aware that the air was different. It wasn't London air. It was fresher, sharper, and this wasn't her bedroom with the flamboyant French wardrobe or the tumble of clothes strewn all over the spindly chair. Of course, she was back in Burley Bridge.

She sat up, pushed back her mussed-up fair hair and looked around the simply-furnished, white-painted room. How had she managed to sleep so long? Perhaps it was due to this wonderful bed, with not a pancake-flat duvet like the one she had at home, but a gorgeously thick one, puffy as a cloud, and the plumpest pillows she had ever encountered. Or maybe it was due to devouring a cod the size of a Viking longboat last night, and three large white wines? Of course, the quietness here was all-enveloping. Back home, although she was well used to constant, round-the-clock noise – evidence that London simply never shut down – sudden sounds outside would often wake her. Here, there was absolute silence.

Roxanne slid out of bed, picked up her phone and

re-read Sean's text, just to remind herself that he had actually sent it. *Love you too,* she texted, rather belatedly, but never mind.

Della had hung a white towelling dressing gown on the hook on the door, and Roxanne pulled it on, luxuriating for a moment in the feeling of waking up somewhere that wasn't home. She wasn't about to be confronted by her dismal fridge containing the small carton of skimmed milk that was teetering on the edge of sourness. She didn't have to go to work. She was free to do exactly as she pleased.

Roxanne noticed knitted slippers paired up at the foot of the chest of drawers, and smiled. Her sister had made the room all ready for her, and yesterday she had just dumped her suitcase in here and not even noticed. She hadn't even unpacked or hung anything up in the wardrobe. Della was trying to look after her, she realised – and yesterday she had berated her, simply for being concerned about her getting drenched in the rain. Roxanne glanced at the window – yet more rain, streaming down the glass in rivulets – and tried to quell a niggle of guilt. Pulling on the dressing gown, she stepped into the hallway.

'Dell?' she called out.

No response.

Of course, it was almost ten-thirty so Della would have been manning the shop for at least an hour. Frank had obviously gone too. Only Stanley was here, eyeing her dolefully in the hallway. She showered quickly and pulled on jeans and a sweater, then called for him, which he failed to respond to. In the kitchen, she found him apparently dozing in his basket.

'We're going for a walk,' she told him. Stanley eyed her briefly, as if she had suggested a trip to the vet's, and turned away. 'A walk!' she repeated, lifting his red leather lead from the back of a chair and dangling it. Still no signs of enthusiasm. Roxanne frowned. Della would have taken him out for a quick pee first thing – but weren't dogs supposed to jump at any opportunity for proper exercise? Surely he wasn't aware of the rain outside from his current location of his basket . . .

Roxanne turned her attention to a small pile of clothing laid out on the kitchen table, with a small scribbled note placed beside it. PLEASE WEAR!! Della had written. Frowning, and with rain patting insistently against the window, Roxanne examined each item in turn.

There was an anorak, of the thick, waxy type, in a particularly dismal shade of murky brown. This is the country, Roxanne reminded herself. It really didn't matter what you looked like. The navy blue waterproof trousers were more troubling. Were they really necessary? Imagining Della's mouth set in a firm, faintly disapproving line, she pulled them on over her skinny jeans. *You don't know until you've tried them!* Well, she was trying them now and they were, Della would be satisfied to note, as hideous as Roxanne had expected. Roxanne pictured Sean creasing up with laughter, thankful at this moment that he was two hundred miles away.

Next to the kitchen table sat a pair of stout walking boots. Clearly, these had been put out for her too, lest she should consider venturing out in her LK Bennetts again and cause a national furore. She put them on – each one seemed to weigh roughly a tonne – and grabbed a wodge of poo bags from the gingham holder on the back of the door.

In the hall mirror she glimpsed herself in the terrible ensemble, her face devoid of make-up and not even treated to its usual skincare routine as, in her haste to pack, she had left her Creme de la Mer sitting on her dressing table at home. She peered more closely, pushing her hair back from her forehead to confirm that, yes, the Botox she'd had six months ago had now worn off. As she'd suspected at the time, a 'teeny shot' would only open the floodgates to her wanting more, like a child being told she could take just one chocolate finger at a party spread. 'A gateway treatment,' Amanda had remarked dryly, batting off Roxanne's protestations that she had only succumbed when she had happened to meet Sebastian, a renowned practitioner in media circles who was famous for his non-frozen 'Botox-lite' approach. The deciding factor was that he had offered the entire staff free treatments in exchange for a small mention in the magazine.

Anyway, the vertical crease between Roxanne's brows had returned – but never mind that now. It was still raining. Amazingly, while the anorak possessed many seemingly pointless dangly cords with plastic toggles, it did not seem to have a hood.

In the hallway, she rummaged through a wicker basket stuffed with all manner of outdoor accessories: hats, gloves, scarves, goggles, balaclavas, a couple of snoods (were snoods still a thing around here?) and, ah, here was a thing Roxanne hadn't seen since her youth: one of those transparent plastic rain hoods you wore like a headscarf, the kind that folds up really tiny. She had assumed such items had simply ceased to exist, without anyone noticing their decline – like video rental shops. But, no, here it was – perhaps the last one in existence.

Oh, stuff it, Roxanne decided, opening up the rain hood, plonking it over her head and tying the strings under her chin. No one was going to see her and even if they did, at least she wouldn't be told off for wearing the wrong clothing.

197

She clipped on Stanley's lead. As if coaxing a child to the dentist's, she led the reluctant terrier downstairs, pausing to wave through the glass panel in the side door to the shop. Della looked up, registered Roxanne's unlikely headwear and laughed.

Roxanne stepped into the shop. Low music was playing – she recognised the Ella Fitzgerald track as one of Isabelle's favourites – and Della was still creasing up.

'Look at you! What would your workmates say now?'

She grinned and touched the plastic hat. 'I know. I've only been here twenty-four hours and this has happened. Yours, I take it?'

Della chuckled. 'A customer left it and I stuffed it in the basket just in case I'd ever be so desperate as to need one. But so far, that hasn't happened.' Her gaze dropped to Stanley. '*He* looks keen to go out.'

'I know. He's obviously holding a grudge, like you said.' Roxanne patted his wiry fur. 'C'mon, little man. You're a dog. This is supposed to be the highlight of your day.'

Off they set, with Roxanne gently tugging a still-reluctant Stanley along beside her. They made their way along Rosemary Lane, past the gift shop with spindly white trees hand-painted on its window, and the small art gallery, a selection of delicate silver jewellery arranged in the window display, its walls adorned with watercolour paintings of village scenes. Burley Bridge really had prettied itself up.

When she came to the bakery, Roxanne paused and glimpsed her reflection in the glass door. If her aim today had been to look quite deranged, then she had pulled it off remarkably well. Just a few minutes ago she had been momentarily perturbed by the vertical crease between her brows when, in fact, perhaps she should have been more concerned about looking like a crazy person pretending to be the queen. She looked beyond her reflection, into the shop, where Michael was setting out something on the glass-topped counter. He glanced up, registering her presence and gave her a bemused look and a wave. Roxanne waved back quickly and strode onwards, keen to escape to the hills before anyone else spotted her.

Now she was 'properly' dressed, the rain was less of a problem than the fact that Stanley clearly didn't want to be out at all. Time and time again, he refused to continue without a gentle tug. It reminded Roxanne of being out on Hampstead Heath with Amanda and her girls, when they were small and seemingly allergic to walking, requiring the two women to offer shoulder rides. However, Roxanne was not prepared to *carry* Stanley; this was supposed to be his daily exercise.

Heading up to the hills now, she let him off his lead, hoping that would improve his mood. He stopped and sniffed a clump of dandelions. For Roxanne, who was used to pelting about everywhere, this was tortuous.

Someone was striding towards her; a girl in a black beanie hat, with tracksuit bottoms tucked into mud-splattered navy blue wellies and a red waterproof jacket hugging her tiny frame. A small rucksack hung low on her back and a rather dishevelled dog, its fur a mix of greys and browns, was trotting happily ahead of her. The dog bounded towards Roxanne and jumped up at her.

'Down, Bob!' the girl yelled. She grimaced at Roxanne. 'Sorry. He's muddied your jacket. He can be a bit too friendly sometimes.'

'Oh, it's okay,' Roxanne said. 'I wish Stanley was as keen to be out as he is. I swear, he's in a huff because he got soaked yesterday.' She looked at the girl and laughed.

'Am I being mad? Do dogs really have huffs? I don't really know how they operate. He's not mine . . .'

The girl grinned. 'I know Stanley. My dad goes to Della's bookshop all the time. We own the bakery.'

'Oh, I've met your dad. I'm Roxanne . . .'

'I'm Elsa. Nice to meet you.'

Roxanne smiled as Elsa bobbed down to make a fuss of Stanley. From her jacket pocket, she produced a small brown seed-covered object; it looked like the kind of snack Serena often picked at her desk – the sort that was sweetened with dates instead of sugar and could never, to Roxanne's mind, come anywhere near the pleasure of a proper biscuit.

'C'mon, Stanley. Look – Bob's here. We can all go for a walk together.' Elsa held out her hand and Stanley wolfed the snack. 'Good boy! Is that better? Are you going to stop sulking now?' Miraculously, Stanley started to trot ahead, with Bob pottering alongside him.

Roxanne glanced at her new companion. She was used to being around teenage girls; many of the models she worked with were only eighteen or nineteen years old. Yet they were knowing and worldly and seemed so much older than their years. It struck Roxanne how unaffected Elsa was; a delightfully normal sixteen-year-old who loved to walk her dog. Perhaps Roxanne had lost touch with what *non*-model girls were like.

Stanley turned and ran back to Elsa, jumping up and nudging his nose at the jacket pocket where her snacks were apparently stored. She gave him another as they made their way further up the hill.

'So, what are you doing in Burley?' Elsa asked.

'I'm Della's sister. I'm sort of having a break from work and I thought I'd come up and help her out for a while.'

'Oh, Della's mentioned you,' Elsa said with a smile. 'You work on a magazine, don't you?' She slipped the rucksack off her back and pulled out a camera case.

'Yes, that's right – it's called *YourStyle*. Have you seen it?'

'Yeah, 'course I have!' Elsa pulled a Nikon camera out of the case, looped its strap around her neck, and stuffed the case back into her rucksack. 'What d'you do there?'

'I'm the fashion director. I put together all the fashion pages, set up and direct all the shoots, that sort of thing . . .' *At least, that's what I used to do,* Roxanne thought wryly.

'What an amazing job!'

Roxanne smiled. She thought so, too, until recently. 'So, what about you? Are you still at school?'

'Yeah.' Elsa gave her a rueful look. 'Well, not today, obviously. I am sick – honest.'

She chuckled. 'You're just having a walk for medicinal purposes. I'm sure that's what a doctor would recommend.'

Elsa grinned and called for Bob, who had disappeared into a patch of woodland and leapt out immediately at the sound of her voice. She took a series of pictures as he darted about.

'You like photographing Bob?'

'Yeah – it's mad, though. I have hundreds of shots of him already but he's a pretty good subject.' She paused. 'I like taking pictures of nature as well. It's great for that around here.'

Roxanne nodded. 'You like living here?'

Was it okay to ask? she wondered, as soon as the words had left her mouth. After all, it had been Elsa's mother's idea to set up a bakery in the village, and now she was living with another man.

'Yeah, I do. Jude moans about it. He's my big brother – says it's boring here. And Dad finds it hard, you know, with the long hours and running the shop . . .' She stopped, as if unsure how much information to share.

'I imagine you're a huge help, though?'

Elsa shrugged again and thrust her hands into the pockets of her tracksuit bottoms. 'I try to be but I'm not really into baking, to be honest. Biscuits are fine, dog treats are easy, but bread and cakes . . .' She shook her head. 'I've had too many disasters.'

Roxanne chuckled as the girl stopped and took some shots of the dramatic scoop of the valley below. 'I know that feeling,' she said. Then, because she couldn't resist, Roxanne told Elsa about her brandy snaps disaster and resulting visit from the fire services.

'Oh, my God,' Elsa laughed. 'I haven't done anything like that, but I do leave most of the baking to Dad. I tend to do the background stuff, the cleaning and washing up, the packaging – I'm the sort of making-things-look-good person. He doesn't have a clue about any of that.'

'What kind of things d'you do?' Roxanne asked, catching her breath now from the exertion of climbing the hill. Already, her thigh muscles were protesting. Still, that was good, she decided; with daily vigorous walks she would return to London a newly-honed version of herself. She looked forward to Sean's reaction.

'I planned the whole look of the bakery,' Elsa explained. 'I mean, Dad's great, he really is. It was meant to be his and Mum's joint thing – their business together – and, uh, when that didn't work out he's just had to get on with it and learn to make the most amazing breads.' She paused. 'So I chose the colours and designed all the labels and packaging, and the main shop sign outside . . .'

202

'You painted that?' Roxanne gasped.

'No, we got a proper sign painter but I drew it out first. The shop was awfully quiet when we first opened so I designed flyers to put all around the village, and I made Dad put out baskets of samples of breads and cakes for people to try . . .'

'What brilliant ideas,' Roxanne exclaimed, genuinely impressed.

Elsa shrugged. 'Well, it's helped, I think. Things are a *little* bit better.'

Roxanne looked at her. From Elsa's tone of voice, she deduced that perhaps business wasn't quite as healthy as she would like. 'The baked dog treats were my idea too,' Elsa added with a note of pride.

'Really?'

'Yeah – they're easy to make and need a low heat, so I make them once the morning bake's finished and the oven's still warm. I'm trying to persuade Dad to have a basket of them on the counter. I mean, virtually everyone has a dog around here, don't they? But he's not convinced they'd sell . . .'

'You're very enterprising,' Roxanne remarked, hoping that hadn't sounded patronising. 'Honestly – I'm so impressed.'

Elsa smiled broadly. She had a fresh, pretty face and clear blue eyes edged by dark lashes, like her father's.

'Well, I just do what I can and occasionally he lets me have a day off school. Actually,' she added quickly, clearly worried about making her father sound irresponsible, 'I think he gets worn out with me asking, so sometimes he just gives in – like today.' Roxanne caught Elsa glancing at her rain hat. 'Erm, I hope this doesn't sound rude, but that's not the kind of thing I'd have thought a fashion director would wear.'

Roxanne laughed. 'Della gave me such a hard time for getting soaked yesterday, I thought I might as well go the whole hog.'

'Suits you, though,' Elsa added with a snigger.

'I think so too,' Roxanne replied. 'I should put them in the magazine, try to start a trend. Actually, I'm supposed to be doing a blog for my magazine about style in the country and I haven't even thought about what I'm going to write.'

Elsa beamed, her lovely bright smile reaching her eyes. 'With that hat, you've got your look right there.'

'That's what I was thinking. You wouldn't take a couple of pictures of me looking like an idiot, would you?'

'D'you mean they'll be published in the magazine?' Elsa exclaimed.

'Yes – at least, in the digital edition. They'll be much better quality on your camera than anything I could do on my phone . . .'

'Sure,' she replied. 'Mum bought me this camera before she, uh . . .' She tailed off. Clearly, recent family events still hurt. While Roxanne could never claim to know how it felt to be a mother, she couldn't imagine falling for anyone so hard that it would cause her to walk out on her own children.

'It looks really professional,' Roxanne offered.

Elsa nodded. 'I'm finding my way around it, getting used to all the settings. I'm thinking of doing a photography course so it'll be good practice for me.'

And that's how a forty-seven-year-old fashion director ended up being photographed pulling a range of expressions, from horror to mock delight, all caught on camera by a sixteen-year-old girl whom she had only met half an hour ago. Elsa took dozens of shots, and then suggested that Roxanne cavort about without the rain hat: 'So we can focus on the waterproof trousers – will they be right for your blog?'

'They'll be perfect,' Roxanne enthused. 'I think I know what I'm going to do now. I'll make it an anti-style blog and send myself up. It'll be a "terrified London fashion person having to brave the elements in the Yorkshire countryside" kind of thing. Does that make sense?'

Elsa laughed. 'I think so. Magazines can be too serious sometimes. I mean it's only fashion . . .' She caught herself. 'Sorry, I didn't mean—'

'No, you're absolutely right. It *is* only fashion and it's good to have a break from all of that.' An image flashed into her mind of a recent shoot; the model couldn't stop crying, due to boyfriend problems – models were *always* having boyfriend problems. Ever the calming influence, Roxanne had spent the entire shoot placating the exasperated photographer, and dispensing hugs and relationship advice to the girl (like she was any kind of expert on matters of the heart).

'I'll dig out all my sister's wet weather gear,' Roxanne added. 'She has plenty more.'

'And I'm happy to do all your photos. I can take time off school.'

'Ah, no. *Out* of school hours only. I don't want to upset your dad.'

Elsa tutted and smiled, apparently realising there was no point in arguing. They took yet more photos, and Elsa made a note of Roxanne's email address on her phone, with a promise to send her the pictures as soon as she had selected the best. How bizarre this seemed, Roxanne reflected as they made their way back to the village – yet how comfortable too. Back home, she hung out with a seventy-five-year-old lady, so why not befriend a sixteen-year-old girl here in Burley Bridge? Did age really matter at all?

The sky was bright blue now, the air fresh and invigorating after so much rain. As the dogs scampered ahead, Roxanne inhaled deeply, took in the sweeping beauty all around her and felt her spirits soar.

Chapter Eighteen

After the walk and impromptu shoot with Elsa, Roxanne had made the bold decision to transfer her clothes from her suitcase into the wardrobe and chest of drawers in Della's spare room. Unwittingly, she had been holding back from making such a commitment – in the way that Sean had so far not left so much as a pair of boxers at her place, lest it might be interpreted as signifying that he might wish to move their relationship on a notch. However, after the day's successes she had been filled with a new sense of optimism and contentment.

And now, on her third day here, Roxanne was tackling a little light sprucing in the bookshop – under Della's watchful eye, as if she needed close supervision in order to operate a feather duster.

Behind the heavy plastic curtain that divided the shop from the new room next door, the whir of an electric screwdriver indicated that shelving was being fitted. Although the mellow music and aroma of freshly brewed coffee were helping to retain the bookshop mood, Della clearly felt the need to apologise to her customers. 'This'll all be over soon,' she reassured a woman who was buying an entire series of 1950s housekeeping manuals – *'A must for every new wife!'* read the text on the cover. Books like this made Roxanne smile and marvel at the fact that, not so very long ago, the image of idyllic domestic life involved an immaculately-coiffed woman in a pinny presenting dinner to her husband on his return from work. Yet, although outmoded, such cookbooks still possessed a certain charm, and many were beautiful in their own right.

As the morning progressed, Roxanne began to fully understand why the shop was such a success. It was a little oasis, a haven in which you could browse and potter undisturbed. However, lots of bookshops offered that. What this one could do was transport you back to simpler times: an era of kitchens filled with the aroma of home-baked scones, and dining rooms alive with the laughter and clinking glasses of convivial dinner parties. Della had decided – wisely, Roxanne thought – not to have customer Wi-Fi. Step inside, and it was as if the modern world had simply ceased to exist. Even the cash till was a fully-working antique model in polished wood.

'I hope this new extension won't alter the character of the shop,' remarked an elderly man as he perused the world cuisine section.

'Not at all,' Della reassured him. 'There'll just be more space – and hundreds more books, of course. We'll be able to put on lots more events too. You will be coming to our opening party, won't you, Mr Sinclair?'

'Yes, of course,' he enthused.

Meanwhile, Roxanne continued to dust and tidy, in between flitting back and forth like an efficient waitress with coffees for the electrician and joiner. Only when lunchtime rolled around did she manage to persuade Della that she could man the shop without trapping her hand in the till, and shoo her out of the door for a short break. When an extremely posh and glamorous young woman came in, saying she needed advice on the best kind of gravy to make for roast lamb, Roxanne managed to locate *200 Classic Sauces and Gravies for Every Occasion*. The woman was thrilled.

'It's my first Sunday lunch for my fiancé's parents,' she said with a tinkly laugh, 'and I'm petrified. Bet you wouldn't be fazed by that.'

'Oh, it's always pretty stressful with the prospective in-laws,' Roxanne said, omitting to mention that she had never *had* any in-laws, and the only gravy she had ever made – when she had been round at Amanda's, trying to be 'useful' while her friend prepared a huge roast dinner – was an unappetising grey, and no one wanted any. 'Erm, I hope you don't mind me asking,' Roxanne added, as she slipped the woman's purchase into a brown paper bag, 'but did you try looking for a recipe online?' Her eyes flicked to the door in case Della had reappeared. To mention such an option seemed treacherous – yet Roxanne was genuinely curious. Although she had never dived into such waters herself, she was pretty certain the internet would be awash with gravy recipes.

The woman laughed. 'My mother-in-law's an incredible cook, and they like everything done *properly,* in the traditional way. And she'll be so impressed if she sees this book lying about.' That was the crux of it, Roxanne decided: these retro books harked back to a more leisurely time, before speedy bish-bosh cooking, or simply grabbing something from the supermarket chill cabinet to sling on a plate. The woman thanked Roxanne profusely as she left.

Della returned, seemingly relieved that the shop had suffered no visible damage in her absence, and shooed Roxanne off for her own break.

Upstairs, at Della's kitchen table, Roxanne settled at her laptop. Elsa had sent her the pictures via a file transfer service, which struck Roxanne as impressively professional. She pinged off an enthusiastic thank-you email and clicked through the images, pleasantly surprised by what she saw. Of course, she looked unhinged in the ridiculous garb, but that was the whole point. On a positive note, since Sean's party, a few pictures of her dance floor cavorting had reared up on Facebook ('Still got it, Rox!' someone had jeered), and Elsa's rain hood photos were certainly less harrowing than those.

Roxanne made a sandwich and settled down to tackle her first two blog posts. Her plan was to choose one piece of clothing in turn – 'the rain hood that folds up teeny-tiny', 'the nylon trousers of doom' – and write a brief and hopefully amusing account of how it felt to wear said items in public.

Despite the fact she didn't consider herself a writer – being more of a visual person – the words sort of tumbled out, perhaps because she had decided to just relax and not stress about it too much. All her adult life, Roxanne had been reverential about fashion, yet there was something wonderfully liberating about poking fun at clothes and, indeed, at herself for caring so much about them.

What can I say about this ghastly garment? she wrote. *Wearing a double layer of trouser feels quite wrong. However, I can say from personal experience that it's preferable to becoming so drenched in a downpour that your freezing wet pants are stuck to your bottom. Available in black, navy and, for the particularly adventurous, mud brown and slime green. Suitable for: a country hike if you are unlikely to bump into anyone you know. Unsuitable for: a first date.*

She rattled off a similar post about the rain hood: *If you can imagine wrapping your hair in cling film you are part-way there. However, on the plus side, what other accessory folds up to the size of a piece of chewing gum? Just for fun, you can experiment with wearing it in various styles (turban, bandana, etc). It can also be handy for wrapping your sandwiches or dressing a freshly-administered tattoo . . .*

Having quickly re-read her efforts, she emailed her posts to Marsha with an accompanying note:

Hi Marsha,

Hope all's good with everyone. My first two blog posts and pictures are attached. I hope they're the kind of thing you had in mind. Would you mind crediting the photographer? Her name is Elsa . . . Roxanne paused to check the name on the file transfer . . . *Bramley. It would mean a real lot to her.*

Many thanks,

Roxanne

Feeling pleased with herself for having had such a productive day so far, she now had an urge to call Sean but, as he would probably be shooting, made do with texting him instead: *Missing you sweetie. Give me a call when you're free? xx.*

That afternoon, she set off for Heathfield, the lively market town where Della had lived before returning to Burley Bridge. Roxanne was keen to do a grocery shop for her sister – to be as useful as possible – and she also wanted to pick up a small present to thank Elsa for the photos. Burley Bridge had its gift shop and gallery, but she hadn't spotted anything that would be particularly enticing to a sixteen-year-old girl.

Having managed to convince Della that she was indeed capable of navigating country roads safely, Roxanne had borrowed Della's car. She drove over the hills with the window open, relishing the solitude for once. Although she was enjoying the novelty of being back in her childhood village, it was, admittedly, pleasing to escape it for a few hours.

She passed the golf course that Mark, Della's ex, had used as his alibi whilst conducting his affair with Polly Fisher. There had been another, even more startling discovery at around the same time Mark's infidelity had come to light – that Della had been the result of their mother's affair with Rafael, a Mallorcan artist. It had become known when Della had discovered an affectionate pencilled note from Rafael in one of their mother's vintage cookbooks. However, although Della and Rafael met up occasionally, and got along pretty well, Roxanne knew that he would never be regarded as Della's dad in any real sense. That would always be the quiet and unassuming William Cartwright, who passed away a decade ago.

The afternoon had turned mellow and golden by the time Roxanne parked near the medieval Heathfield Castle, where Della used to work in the gift shop. Having also borrowed her sister's wicker shopping basket – a pleasing accessory, Roxanne noted approvingly – she browsed the cheery independent shops clustered around the town centre, and wandered into a cookware store with the intention of choosing something for Della. However, it was Elsa who sprung to mind when her eyes fell upon a net bag of dog-themed cookie cutters. There were dogs of various breeds, plus a bone and a kennel – ideal for cutting out home-baked treats. She also selected a gift box of mugs for Della, each featuring the cover of a classic cookbook, making them perfect for the shop.

Onwards then to buy rolls of cellophane and ribbons in an array of jewel-bright shades, which Roxanne felt would be ideal for packaging up the canine cookies and, hopefully, convince Michael to let his enterprising daughter have a go at selling them in the bakery. Was she muscling in? Roxanne wondered. She hoped her contribution wouldn't be viewed that way. She merely wanted to encourage Elsa and thank her for helping out with the blog photos.

Roxanne's phone bleeped, and she paused to read a rather belated reply to her text to Sean – but then, he wasn't really the texting type. *Hey darling,* it read, *miss you, crazy busy here, what you up to? Sxx.* With a shrug, she slipped her phone back into her bag. No point in regaling him now with her adventures in Heathfield's quaint cookware shop or stationery store. Instead, she made her way to the supermarket, where she ticked off everything from the list Della had given her, adding some treats from the deli section and a bottle of wine for a casual supper for the two of them. Della had tried to foist a wad of tenners on her, but Roxanne had refused. It felt important to contribute during her stay.

On her arrival back at Burley Bridge, Roxanne decided to stop at the bakery before it shut for the afternoon to surprise Elsa with the cookie cutters. She loved to choose and give presents, hence her having gone to great lengths to choose the perfect birthday offering for Sean, several months before the actual event. That lavish photography book was still sitting there, barely touched in her flat, she reflected as she parked at the bookshop and strode towards

213

the bakery. 'These are perfect!' Elsa exclaimed, setting out the cutters reverentially on the counter. 'Thank you so much.' She was still in school uniform – white shirt, navy pleated skirt and striped tie worn ultra-short – with her light brown hair pulled into a ponytail. 'I'll make some tomorrow,' she added. 'Dad, you don't mind if I stay off school to—'

'I *do* mind actually,' he called out, striding through from the kitchen in his navy blue stripy apron worn over a black T-shirt and jeans. 'See what I have to put up with?' he added with a chuckle.

His daughter pulled a face, and Roxanne laughed. 'So, how're you doing?' he asked. 'Managing to readjust to country life without too much trouble?' Michael's eyes met Roxanne's and he smiled.

'You know, I really am,' she replied. 'Only three days here and I feel like a different person already.'

'That's good to hear,' he said warmly.

'Dad – look what Roxanne's bought me,' Elsa exclaimed, and Michael's gaze dropped to the array of cutters.

'Hey, that was sweet of you . . .'

'Just a little thank you,' she said. 'Elsa was kind enough to take photos for my blog . . .'

'Yes, she mentioned that,' he said with a bemused glance.

Roxanne looked around at the beautifully calligraphed cards that had been placed on the shelves to denote the various bread varieties. Walnut sourdough, sesame and poppy seed cobbler, wholemeal plait . . . she could still hardly believe such speciality loaves were baked right here in Burley Bridge. 'Did you write those labels?' she asked, turning to Elsa.

'Yeah.' Elsa grinned.

'Well, you obviously have a real flair. Maybe you could

bake more treats and pipe designs on them with some kind of dog-friendly icing?'

Her face lit up. 'I'd love to do that . . .'

'And perhaps you could wrap them with this?' Roxanne added, hoping she wasn't overstepping the mark now as Michael looked a little nonplussed. She pulled the roll of clear cellophane from her bag, plus reels of fine satin ribbon.

'They'll look so pretty,' Elsa enthused, turning to her father. 'If they work out okay, can we start selling them in the shop? What d'you think, Dad?'

He mustered a smile but it didn't quite reach his eyes. Perhaps he was just tired, Roxanne mused. All those 5 a.m. starts must take their toll. 'Let's get the sourdough workshop out of the way first,' Michael added, 'and then we can think about new lines to stock. I just don't have the headspace right now.' He glanced at Roxanne and frowned. 'To be honest, I'm not sure this is such a great idea . . .'

'The dog treats?' She glanced at Elsa, whose disappointment was apparent. 'Oh, I'm sorry – I didn't mean to interfere—'

'No, no – this workshop . . .'

'But that's next week, Dad,' Elsa reminded him. 'There's loads of time to get ready . . .'

He shook his head distractedly. 'Yes, but that's not the point. I mean, I know Della has all kinds of events at the shop – but it's the kind of place people want to hang out in. It's like someone's living room. We'll just be cramming a few people into our kitchen . . .'

'Our kitchen's *fine*, Dad,' Elsa protested.

'It's still just a kitchen, though, isn't it? We've invited the whole village to spend the evening staring at our oven, Els. Does that seem like a sensible thing to you?'

215

'They won't be staring at the oven!' his daughter exclaimed, while Roxanne shifted uncomfortably, caught as she was in a small father–daughter dispute. 'They'll be watching *you*,' she added, 'showing them the right way to knead, and then they'll have a go themselves . . .'

He shrugged, looking genuinely perplexed. 'But does anyone really want to see that?'

'I do,' Roxanne declared, as convincingly as she could muster.

'Dad,' Elsa asserted, '*everyone* wants to know how to bake . . .'

'Do they, though, when they can buy perfectly good bread from a shop? And if they do start making their own, turning out perfectly decent sourdough every day – because it's ridiculously easy actually – then what'll be the point of us?' Although he clearly meant it as a joke, it missed its mark as Elsa's face fell. He set about gathering up the paper linings from the empty bread baskets.

Roxanne stepped quietly towards the door. 'I'll let you get on then,' she murmured, casting Michael a glance and thinking, *Talk about quashing your daughter's enthusiasm. Was there really any need for that?* Their goodbyes were a little lukewarm as she left the bakery.

However, as she strolled down Rosemary Lane, Roxanne started to wonder whether Michael's reticence was understandable. While Elsa's gung-ho nature seemed endearing, perhaps it was a different matter to be subjected to it every day. Clearly, she had cajoled her dad into hosting a workshop he didn't want to have – in the very kitchen his wife's new boyfriend had fitted. Roxanne had the impression now that Michael would be far happier being left alone to bake his loaves in peace. It was too easy to judge a person, she decided, and what did she know about

216

raising teenagers anyway, let alone those whose mum had made a shocking departure from their lives?

Roxanne's own mother had certainly been far from perfect. She had conducted an affair, been somewhat slap-happy with a fish slice, and perhaps too frequently attached to a clinking glass of gin. But at least she had been *there*.

She stopped and glanced back. What a thing Michael had been through, she reflected: being persuaded to move to a village and set up a business, and then left in the lurch to graft away at all hours to try to make it work. Would it freak him out to ask him out on a dog walk, just as friends? she wondered. Della had mentioned that he popped into the bookshop regularly while Jude took care of the bakery, so perhaps he'd appreciate a stroll in the hills. He had certainly given the impression that he could do with the odd break now and then.

Roxanne paused, then strode back to the bakery and pushed open the door. She glimpsed him in the kitchen, sweeping the floor.

'Michael, hi!' she called out.

'Oh! Roxanne . . .'

'Sorry, didn't mean to creep back in like that . . .'

'Everything okay?' He looked a little taken aback.

'Yes, uh . . . I just wondered . . .' She was fidgeting awkwardly now, like a teenager, as he came towards her. How ridiculous. People met up for walks together constantly in Burley Bridge; if yoga classes were mandatory in London, then dog ownership was here. It was just what people *did*. 'It was lovely having Elsa's company on my walk yesterday,' she continued. 'I've sort of taken on walking Stanley duties, you see. Della's so busy with the shop, she doesn't really have time . . .' She paused, realising she was babbling. 'Erm, I don't suppose you'd like to join me sometime and bring Bob too?'

'Oh, er . . .' Michael looked surprised, but not entirely horrified. 'Yes, that'd be lovely.'

She beamed at him. 'How about tomorrow? I imagine your mornings are terribly busy but—'

'I could do late morning,' he said, 'about eleven-ish?'

'Yes, perfect.' She grinned. 'I'll call for you, then. If that doesn't make us sound about ten years old?'

Michael laughed, his eyes crinkling, the warmth having returned to his smile. 'I'll look forward to it,' he said.

And so, Roxanne realised, would she – very much.

Chapter Nineteen

Next day, Roxanne was delighted to be greeted by an overcast but mercifully dry morning, which meant that no hideous waterproof clothing was required. It wasn't that she minded terribly what she looked like here. Indeed, her make-up bag had barely been unzipped since she arrived. However, where Della's nylon trousers were concerned, Roxanne could now safely say that she had at least 'tried' them and, like their mother's rather sinister-looking salmon mousse, once had been quite enough.

'So, are you glad you decided to come up here?' Michael asked her as the two dogs ran ahead, with the diminutive Stanley gamely trying to keep up with the rangier, long-legged Bob.

Roxanne glanced at him. 'Yes, I really am. It's funny – I'm friendly with this elderly lady back home who lives downstairs in my block. Isabelle's a real Londoner through and through. When I was talking to her about possibly coming up here, she said, "London will always be here for you if the countryside gets too much", as if I might suddenly snap and run, screaming, onto a King's Cross-bound train . . .'

Michael laughed. 'Maybe she forgot you grew up here.'

'Yep, I think so.' Roxanne nodded. 'I was an indoor sort of girl really, always drawing and reading and dreaming, but I did appreciate being able to go out and wander from a very young age, and no one ever worried where I was.' She omitted to mention that, along with turning up her music and dancing alone in her bedroom, it was one of the tactics she used to escape when her parents were in the midst of a row.

'What about when you were a teenager?' he asked.

'Oh, I was desperate to get away then,' she said quickly.

'I can understand that. Even all this beauty and peacefulness can become a bit too much sometimes.'

'D'you find that?' She wasn't sure whether he was joking or not.

'Sure,' Michael replied. 'I mean, I grew up in Canterbury. It's hardly London but, you know, there was always plenty going on . . .'

'And then you moved to York?' she prompted him.

'Yes, I was teaching at a big comprehensive there.'

She nodded, burning with questions now. 'How d'you really find it, living here in the village?'

He seemed to be mulling this over as they strode onwards. 'It's taken some adjustment,' he ventured, and immediately, Roxanne decided it was a subject best left alone. However, he continued, 'But it wasn't all Suzy's doing – setting up the bakery, I mean . . .'

'You wanted to do it too?' she asked hesitantly.

'Not exactly – I mean, it's not what I'd have chosen for myself. It was very much her idea, her driving the whole thing. But then, I didn't want to stand in her way either. I'd been in teaching a long time – since I was twenty-three and just qualified, and I'm almost fifty now . . .'

'That's a very long time,' she agreed.

He nodded gravely. 'Yep, I'm ancient.'

'Oh, me too. I'm forty-seven, and in magazine terms that's basically antique.' They both chuckled.

'I wouldn't say that,' he added.

Roxanne grinned. 'Yes, but it's a very strange world. The women who buy our magazine are in their thirties and forties but the models we use have an average age of nineteen.'

Michael looked baffled by this. 'Why *is* that?'

'It's just the way it is,' she replied. 'Once they're all made up, they no longer look as if they're barely out of school. They're proper grown-up women then, but with the skin of peaches . . .'

He laughed in disbelief. 'It's really skewed, isn't it?'

'It's completely bonkers,' she agreed. 'So, you said you'd been teaching for years . . .'

'Oh, yes – and to be fair to Suzy I was absolutely up for something new, you know? Teaching is great, but the way it's gone in recent years, you're ploughing through the curriculum and even though you try your best, you sometimes wonder if you're really making a difference, in a way that matters.'

She nodded, remembering her own favourite teacher: Miss Smith, with the wispy voice, bobbly cardigans and seven cats, who headed up the art department. 'So you started off wanting to be that inspirational teacher who changed kids' lives?'

'Yeah.' His smile crinkled his clear blue eyes. 'Ever the idealist.'

'I bet you were a great teacher. You're a very approachable person . . .'

'Well, thank you,' he said, laughing bashfully. 'But

221

anyway, I scaled it down to a bit of supply teaching while we set up the bakery and, well . . . here I am.'

'And you don't regret it?' Roxanne ventured, at which Michael shook his head.

'Occasionally, as it's damn hard work, but most of the time . . .' He shrugged. 'Not at all. I know it seems rash and a little crazy to throw everything we had at this project, which we knew virtually nothing about . . .'

'Just like Della did,' Roxanne observed, and Michael nodded.

'Exactly.'

'It was a sort of leap of faith?'

'Yes, it was, and you know what's funny? I'm actually immensely proud of what the kids and I have managed to do here, from what seemed at first like a totally disastrous situation.'

Roxanne nodded, flattered that he was being so open, and suspecting that he rarely found the opportunity to talk about what had happened to his family.

' . . . And if none of it had happened,' he added, 'and I hadn't had to teach myself to bake properly . . .' He smiled wryly. 'Well, I'd have stayed in my nice safe teaching post, probably until retirement. And how boring is that?'

'It sounds perfectly reasonable to me,' she remarked.

'But hardly adventurous, right?'

'Well, no, perhaps not,' she conceded, reflecting now how glad she was that she had asked him to join her today. They fell into a comfortable silence as they reached the top of the hill, where the dogs sniffed around in the ferns. How natural this felt, Roxanne reflected, walking together and getting to know Michael a little better. Perhaps Della had been astute in plotting for them to meet, that first night at the Red Lion. Had she been single,

222

Roxanne may have been interested – a minor detail that her sister seemed to have overlooked, and which made Roxanne's mouth twitch with amusement now.

'Something's funny?' Michael caught her eye and smiled.

'Oh, it's nothing really. I'm just enjoying this, um . . . *being out in nature* thing.' She laughed. 'I never thought I'd hear myself say that.'

'I was the same,' Michael offered. 'I mean, I could see the appeal of the countryside, to visit . . . *briefly* . . .' He looked at her again and they chuckled in recognition. 'But I was always quite happy to leave it behind again. It really is quite entrancing, though, isn't it? Once you've adjusted to the gentler pace of life, and stopped wishing you could just pop out to the cinema . . .'

Roxanne considered this for a moment. 'Even at home, I probably get to the cinema about twice a year.' She smiled ruefully.

'So, what *did* bring you here?' Michael asked as they started to make their way back down to the village. And so she told him about the developments on the magazine, and her job changing beyond all recognition – which sounded quite petty and ridiculous, just as it had when she'd poured out all her woes to Della. She omitted to mention Sean, and the recent drama surrounding his party. That, too, seemed silly and insignificant now, and in the company of this engaging – and, yes, undeniably eye-pleasing – man, she realised she had no desire to mention her boyfriend at all.

'I think it was a smart move, coming to stay with your sister,' Michael observed.

She glanced at him in surprise. 'Really? Why d'you say that?'

He shrugged. 'Sometimes you need a change of scene to see things in a different light.'

'Yes, I think you're right.' It was true; Roxanne was no longer of the opinion that her life was effectively over just because Marsha had tried to put her in charge of cost cutting and competitions.

'Will you stay on the magazine, d'you think?'

'Oh, I really don't know what'll happen. I'll deal with all of that when I go home.' She glanced at him, grateful for his company and his willingness to listen. 'Right now,' she added, clipping on Stanley's lead as the road leading into Burley Bridge came into view, 'I'm just taking things one day at a time.' She paused. 'Thanks for walking with me. I've really enjoyed it . . .'

'My pleasure,' Michael said, 'and I have too.'

They parted company at the bakery and, as she headed back to the bookshop, sunshine broke through a chink in the clouds, beaming warmth onto Roxanne's face. As she strode into the shop, and greeted the customers who were sipping coffee and browsing, she knew in her heart that right now, there was nowhere else she would rather be.

Meanwhile, in the offices of Britain's best-loved fashion magazine on a muggy Friday morning, Roxanne was being missed far more than Marsha had anticipated – and she had only been gone for four days.

This was ridiculous. Marsha had a mind to call her right now, summonsing her back from her sister's, up in God-knows-where, and admitting she'd made an error of judgement in effectively packing her fashion director off to the country for two months.

Two months! How on earth were they going to manage without such a crucial member of the team? Marsha had thought it would be easier to revamp the mag without

Roxanne being around, insisting on everything being tasteful and beautiful; but how wrong she had been.

There had been a disastrous meeting between Tina and a prestigious fashion house that would never have happened if Roxanne had been here, being her usual charming and diplomatic self. In other ways, too, Roxanne's presence was being sorely missed. Her team seemed jaded and lacklustre, as if they were merely going through the motions of what Tina had asked them to do. When Tina had presented her ideas to Marsha for the next issue's fashion pages, they had been, to put it mildly, disappointing.

'I thought we could do something on vests?' Tina had suggested.

'What kind of angle did you have in mind?' Marsha had asked, a question which had apparently befuddled Tina. 'I mean, are we talking the essential vests? Or the sexiest? Or *what*? I'm sorry if vests are a *thing* right now, but maybe you can be a bit more specific . . .'

Tina had merely frowned and looked confused. 'I just thought it'd be quite useful.'

'Right, so, what am I to put on the cover?' Marsha had barked. '"Here's a bunch of vests"? Can't see that boosting sales!' Although she and Tina had worked together before, Marsha had never been Tina's direct boss. She now wondered if she had been a little hasty in bringing her onto the magazine.

To make matters worse, several influential fashion PRs had been on the phone to Marsha, demanding to know why Roxanne had been sacked – and intimating that they would be loath to lend clothes for shoots if she was no longer heading up the fashion department. A notoriously ferocious model agent had called Marsha and ranted in her ear for twenty-five minutes without listening to a word

225

she was trying to say. All of which had required an almighty amount of cajoling and placating, and now, quite frankly, Marsha needed a stiff drink. Hell, she would call Rufus and *demand* that he wangle some excuse to get away from his wife and out for a few hours, and she would make him buy a bottle of crazily expensive champagne, which she would proceed to neck.

First, though, she'd phone Roxanne – just to keep a connection going and remain on her good side. Marsha had been pleasantly surprised by Roxanne's rather batty and eccentric blog posts and accompanying photos. Who'd have thought someone of her standing in the industry would willingly send herself up in a plastic rain hood? Thanking her was just the excuse Marsha needed to call her.

'Hello?' Roxanne answered immediately.

'Roxanne? It's Marsha. Hope you're having a good time up there?'

'Yes, thanks. It's doing me good, actually.'

'That's great to hear. Any fun things planned?'

'Er, well, I'm going to a sourdough workshop next week, would you believe . . .'

'Sourdough?' Marsha repeated incredulously.

'It's a kind of bread,' Roxanne explained.

'Yes, ha, I do know that. So you're doing cookery classes. How sweet!'

'Uh, it's not exactly—'

'Well, I guess you've got to find something to amuse yourself on a Friday night in the country!'

'Ha, yes.' They both laughed stiffly.

'Um, anyway,' Marsha went on, 'just wanted to say, your blogs are excellent – very funny! So unusual to see a fashion person being willing to laugh at themselves . . .'

226

'Oh, thank you. I'm so glad you—'

'And those pictures,' Marsha went on, 'in those dreadful plastic trousers or whatever the heck they are! Good on you, Roxanne, for not giving a fig about what people think of you. Who did you find to take them?'

'Just a local photographer,' Roxanne replied.

'Elsa something? You mentioned in your email . . .'

'Yes, that's right. Her name's Elsa Bramley.'

'Well, she's very good. I hope you don't mind me saying, but I was expecting rubbishy selfies taken on your phone . . .'

'No, there *are* actually some proper photographers up here,' Roxanne said breezily. 'So, er, we will be able to pay her, won't we?'

'Gosh, yes, of course. Get her tied up to shoot the whole series and we'll sort out a fee . . .' Now Tina was hovering at Marsha's office door, sipping from a chipped mug. Marsha had requested a chat at her earliest convenience. 'Better go. Thanks again for those *fantastic* posts,' she gushed. 'It really is excellent work.'

She finished the call and beckoned a nervous-looking Tina in.

'Sit down,' she said sharply, extracting a strawberry yogurt from her bag and tearing off its foil lid.

Tina bobbed down into the chair.

Marsha glared at her across her desk. 'So, I gather your breakfast meeting with the Pierre Moreau lot didn't go too well?' Tina had explained this already but Marsha needed to hear it again, just to get her head around the fact that one of their biggest clients – a fashion house that spent hundreds of thousands of pounds a year on advertising – had just announced that they were pulling out with immediate effect.

'I suppose it could have gone better,' Tina replied, staring down at her lap.

Marsha took a plastic spoon from her drawer and started to devour the yogurt. Perpetually on a strict diet, her method for remaining stick-thin was to consume only doll-sized portions at proper mealtimes – with the result that she was permanently ravenous and teetering on the brink of a psychotic mood. Hence the perpetual at-desk snacking, which wasn't quite part of the diet plan – but she adhered to the theory that, if it wasn't eaten off a plate, then it didn't count. 'So, how did you put it to them? I mean, what did you say that horrified them so much? Tell me exactly what happened . . .'

Tina glanced through the glass wall into the main office, as if wishing to spirit herself through it. She gnawed a fingernail and flicked her straight black hair back from her face. 'Well, I did my presentation, just as we'd discussed. I explained that we were stopping the arty-farty shoots that Roxanne's being churning out for years, with all the top models looking gorgeous and whatnot. I said, people were sick of all that – and instead we'll be featuring masses of cheap, disposable high-street pieces, with the emphasis on figure-fixing.'

Marsha stared at her. 'Tell me you didn't actually put it like that to one of our top advertisers.'

'Well, isn't that what we're planning to do?' Tina threw her a confused look.

'Yes' – Marsha jettisoned the now-empty yogurt pot into the waste-paper bin – 'but we don't say that. We don't say, "Oh, you know all that stunning photography you love so much, that we're famous for? Well, we're stopping all that and filling the pages with cheap tat from the low-end high-street stores you despise because, let's face it, they can rip off what they see in your shows and get it in their stores within two weeks. Sure, the quality's crap, and it all falls apart if anyone so much as breathes on it – but it's a tenth of the price so who's caring, eh?"'

Marsha stopped abruptly, aware that she had been shouting. Tina was scratching at a patch of flaky skin on her hand. Marsha found herself fixating on it, wondering how many flakes were coming off with each scratch. Thousands? *Millions?* While she frequently left a scattering of pastry crumbs in her wake, she had a strong aversion to the idea of being in close proximity to particles of someone else's epidermis.

'So, what should I have said?' Tina asked in a small voice.

Marsha gave her a withering stare. 'You could have said we're refreshing the brand, making a few subtle changes that they're going to love . . .' She inhaled deeply, trying to suppress the urge to go right round there and shove Tina off her chair. Hadn't she listened to a word she'd said during their pre-meeting meeting yesterday? *Be careful with these people,* Marsha had warned her. *Treat them like royalty because that's pretty much what they are. Whatever you do, don't scare them, or they'll pull their advertising and then we're stuffed. We need these big fashion houses in order to survive – do you understand?* Yes, Tina understood, or so she had said.

'The thing is,' Tina said, sounding more emboldened now, 'they'll know soon enough when they see the magazine . . .'

'Yes, and by then our sales'll be rocketing so they won't mind a bit.'

Tina hesitated. 'D'you think it's absolutely right, what we're doing?'

Marsha's nostrils seemed to enlarge as if air had gusted through them. 'Of course I do. It's why Rufus brought me in to do the job . . .' She broke off. Had that been a flicker of something in Tina's eyes, or was she just being paranoid? No one knew about her and Rufus, did they? Marsha cleared her throat. 'Anyway, the damage is done now. All I can do is arrange another meeting with Pierre Moreau – *if* they'll see me – and butter them up, try to unpick the damage . . .' Marsha shot another quick glance at Tina, still rattled by the possibility that she might have an inkling about her affair with the company's big cheese. 'Okay, no point in going over and over this now. Not in a hurry to rush off for lunch, are you?'

Marsha saw Tina's pale grey eyes flicker towards the clock on the wall. She had heard her braying about her lunchtime plans earlier. It was her boyfriend's birthday, and apparently she had booked somewhere amazing way across town where *no one* could ever get a table – but apparently they would need it back by two, and it was already almost noon. 'See what happens when you can say, "I'm fashion-director-in-chef on *YourStyle*!"' Tina had crowed. Well, it looked as if no one was going out for a fancy Friday lunch now.

'Well, er, I was planning to meet Darius,' she muttered. 'It's his birthday . . .'

'Aw, that's a shame.' Marsha gave her a flinty look, then turned her gaze to her own computer. 'It's just, Roxanne's sent me her first style-in-the-country blog posts and pictures and they're excellent. D'you know, she's even found a photographer up there in the middle of nowhere? Fast work, huh?'

'Amazing,' Tina growled.

'Okay, so I'm just going to email them over to you now.

Choose one, give it a look over – because grammar's not her forte – but don't worry too much because it's hilarious as it is, and I don't want to lose any of her personality or spirit, all right?' She paused and stared at Tina.

'Could I do this after lunch?'

'Nope, sorry – I want you to get it up on the site within the hour. No time like the present. You *can* manage that, I assume?'

Tina's cheeks blazed as she gave her hand a final clawing, brushed the lap of her skirt and stood up to leave Marsha's office. 'Yes, of course I can manage.'

'Great.' Marsha smiled tartly, extracted a Kit Kat from her drawer and ripped off its foil aggressively. 'Christ,' she growled, snapping the chocolate fingers, 'at least *one* thing's gone right today.'

Chapter Twenty

On Saturday morning, Della headed for Heathfield to distribute jaunty posters for the forthcoming bookshop party. Her plan was to do the rounds of all the shops and cafes, handing them out to anyone who would agree to display one. The shops in Burley Bridge already had them up in their windows; Roxanne had even spotted one Blu-tacked to the glass door of Nicola's hair salon. However, worried now that the 'grand opening' of her new-improved bookshop might be something of a damp squib, Della had decided that word must be spread further afield.

With Faye unavailable, this meant she really had no option but to leave Roxanne to man the shop for the entire day. Despite the fact that Roxanne had already managed to operate the till without causing harm to either herself or others, Della had insisted on demonstrating yet again how it worked. It was a relief to Roxanne when her sister had finally picked up her box of posters and driven away.

In fact, Roxanne was delighted to be left in charge. She had dressed the part especially in a neat lemon cardi and knee-length denim skirt, 'teamed' – such a fashion word, that – with black pumps and her simple Ibiza necklace. After all the tramping about in dog-walking attire, it made a pleasant change to spruce up, with hair freshly washed and even a slick of mascara and lipstick on.

'So *this* is the real you,' Michael joked when he popped into the bookshop just after lunchtime.

'Not really,' she laughed, omitting to remind him that he had already seen her dressed smartly, that first night in the Red Lion. 'I feel like I'm playing at being shop lady to be honest,' she admitted, 'but it *is* quite fun . . .'

'You're obviously very good at it,' he observed, glancing around the shop, in which several customers were chatting and browsing while their children were happily amused with crayons and paper at the small table in the corner.

'Glad you think so,' Roxanne said, hesitating to say it was easy. However, without wishing to belittle her sister's achievements, it was, after all, just a shop, and Roxanne found herself able to make customers feel welcome and well attended to. Whenever they praised the shop and quizzed her about it – as happened several times during the day – she was quick to explain that it was all her sister's doing. Roxanne could see now why the bookshop had been featured in so many newspapers and magazines, and why Della was often called upon as an expert in historical food writing. There literally wasn't anywhere else quite like it.

'Well, I'd better get back,' Michael said after a coffee, at which Roxanne detected a trace of reluctance. 'See you again soon for another dog walk?' he added.

'Yes, I'd like that,' Roxanne replied. 'We were up at the top of the hill at seven this morning and I'm sure Stanley missed Bob.'

'Let's get them together then,' he said with a smile, and she wondered if there might have been a hint of something else there: of wanting to spend more time together, and not just because of the dogs. She found herself watching him leave, and realised she had barely thought about Sean since she had received his last text, when she'd been shopping in Heathfield yesterday.

With a steady flow of customers throughout the rest of the afternoon, there wasn't time to call him anyway. She'd leave him be for now, Roxanne decided as what looked like a coach party of elderly ladies all poured in. She'd been spending far too much time fixating on his moods anyway lately, and if he had decided he was too *crazy-busy* to nip up and see her, then so be it. She was having a perfectly pleasant time in Burley Bridge without him.

There was another aspect to working in the bookshop that Roxanne was enjoying. Without a man around, there was no one to manhandle her out of the way in order to establish himself as Chief Friend of Tradesmen. She was allowed to interact directly with Matt and Chris, who were busily fitting out the shop's new room, although Roxanne could never remember who was who, necessitating a lot of, 'Would you like some coffee . . . *guys*?' They flirted with her – praising her outfit and calling her darlin' – and made her laugh. It was all terribly un-PC but, although she hesitated to admit it, actually quite fun; a world away from how men and women interacted in the fashion world.

Della returned just as Roxanne was closing the shop for the day. 'Everything okay?' she asked, peering around in the manner of an anxious parent who had left her small charge in the care of a babysitter for the first time.

'It's been more than okay,' Roxanne replied proudly. 'It's been great. How about you get on with other jobs on Monday and let me look after things here?'

Della blinked and pulled a mock-aghast face. 'Give you an inch and you're taking over!'

'Come on,' Roxanne said, grinning. 'I've so enjoyed myself and surely there are lots of other things you've been meaning to tackle that you can get on with, now I'm here?'

'My sister, the rescuer,' she said with a fond smile. 'Yes, actually – there's an order of books over in Scarborough that I'm due to pick up. I just haven't had a moment and I really need them all in place for when the new room's finished.'

'There you are then,' Roxanne said, beaming. 'You can go off and do your thing, and I promise I won't scare off any of your customers with my fancy London ways.'

On Sunday morning Roxanne and Elsa headed off, with Stanley and Bob in tow, to shoot more pictures for the blog. Up on the hill, Roxanne modelled Della's mammoth walking boots, something called a 'base layer' (i.e., an unattractive long-sleeved top) and fat, hairy socks. She was looking more and more like someone from a rambling club, and she didn't care. She now had her shop lady persona and her dog walking attire and could flip quite easily between the two.

'I saw my pictures up on the website,' Elsa said proudly.

'Were you pleased with them?' Roxanne asked as they made their way back down to the village.

'Yeah, of course!'

Roxanne looked at her and smiled. 'I'm sorry your first assignment wasn't a little more glamorous . . .'

Elsa smirked. 'I don't care about that. My name was actually on it, and someone called Jacqui, I think, sent me an email about payment . . .'

'Of course you should be paid,' Roxanne remarked. 'You're a professional now.'

'No I'm not,' Elsa blustered, flushing now. 'I'm just—'

'Please,' Roxanne cut in, 'never say you're just anything.'

Elsa beamed and thanked her profusely as they said goodbye at the bakery, despite Roxanne insisting that she should be thanking her. Although the shop was closed, being a Sunday, Michael was busily cleaning the inside of the windows, and waved as he caught Roxanne's eye.

I seem to be seeing a lot of him, she mused with a smile as she made her way back to Della's. But then, Burley Bridge was that sort of place.

Next morning, Roxanne had walked Stanley, written up her blog posts, pinged them off to Marsha and was now opening up the bookshop – all by 9.30 a.m. 'It's as if you owned the place,' Della teased her before setting off for Scarborough in a hired van with Frank; the cookbook collection was a bumper haul, apparently. Alone in the shop now, Roxanne made a pot of coffee and took a few minutes to enjoy her first mugful of the day.

It felt good to be here, she decided. She allowed herself to fantasise for a moment staying here, as her sister's trusty sidekick, instead of returning to her job on the magazine. No Marsha or Tina, no temperamental make-up artists or models . . . would it be possible to say goodbye to all that? It was a ludicrous idea, but tempting. After all, she enjoyed chatting with customers, offering them coffee, and occasionally keeping younger visitors entertained with crayons and paper while their parents enjoyed some uninterrupted browsing. That morning, one apparently exhausted mother even dozed off on the velvet sofa over a book about carved vegetable garnishes.

Gaining confidence now, and becoming familiar with Della's sometimes eccentric categorising system, Roxanne found she could easily locate a rare tome on 1950s farmhouse cookery, and had started to prove herself adept at suggesting appropriate books for gifts.

Later that day, when Della returned demanding a full report on her sister's day at the helm, it seemed to amaze her that Roxanne had breezed through numerous food-related exchanges with customers without making a fool of herself.

'You look different, being here,' Della observed as, in pyjamas now, the sisters curled up on her sofa with mugs of tea.

'In what way?' Roxanne asked.

Della shrugged. 'Sort of . . . more relaxed. Maybe it's just being away from London, and your job, all that stuff going on with your new editor . . .'

'That's probably it,' Roxanne agreed, knowing now that something else was happening too. She felt needed here and, much as she loved to direct her shoots, what she was doing here felt actually useful in a very different way. Okay, so it really amounted to walking a terrier, doing a few errands and looking after a shop from time to time. But all of those things seemed very necessary, which in turn made Roxanne needed, and that was why it seemed so very right to be here, right now.

Chapter Twenty-One

The Bookshop on Rosemary Lane is about to get bigger,
better, brighter . . .
Come and celebrate the opening of our new-improved shop!
Double the size, hundreds more books to browse!
Join us for drinks and nibbles
Retro cocktail (and mocktail) demonstration and tasting
The Bookshop on Rosemary Lane,
27 Rosemary Lane, Burley Bridge
Friday June 9, 6.30 pm
Children welcome

By Tuesday afternoon, Matt and Chris were packing up
their tools in their van for the final time. The plastic
curtain had been removed and the two rooms flowed
together beautifully, the deep raspberry paintwork lending
the shop an exotic air. The shelving and counter were
complete, the floorboards sanded – thankfully this had
been undertaken in the evenings, when the shop was closed
– and a cheerful chequerboard rug laid down. There was
a central island for events, and the existing kitchen at the

back had been upgraded to enable Della to use it if she was giving a demonstration. She had chosen elegant table lamps, plus strings of fairy lights for the children's section. It looked wonderful, and Roxanne and Della gazed around in awe.

'Not bad, is it?' Della said, flushing with pride.

'Not at all,' Roxanne replied, hugging her. 'I'm so proud of you, Dell.'

Della looked at her and laughed. 'Oh, stop it.'

'C'mon, are you really taking in what you've done here? Look!' Della gazed around, and Roxanne did too. As they closed the shop for the evening, the sisters conceded that, considering this had been a bonkers idea, all based on Kitty's old books that no one in their right mind would *ever* want to buy, even their rather formidable mother would be proud if she could see her own cookbooks displayed so beautifully today.

'I think I'll walk Stanley,' Roxanne said. 'It looks like it's brightening up out there.'

'It does,' Della agreed, glancing out of the shop window, 'now the rain's just about stopped. Why not see if Michael wants to join you?'

Roxanne caught her sister's eye and laughed as they made their way upstairs to the flat. 'Don't start that again . . .'

'I'm not starting anything! But I'm sure he'll be pleased. He seems to enjoy being around you.'

Roxanne considered this. She enjoyed being around him too, she reflected. While she still felt as if she should tread a little carefully around him, there was something about him that intrigued her. It was his determination, she decided: how he had soldiered on and was well on his way to making the bakery flourish. She couldn't help admiring him for that. 'You don't think he'll find it a bit

239

much,' she ventured, 'with me spending time with Elsa, and then dropping by . . .'

'Of course not,' Della retorted as they stepped into the flat, where she called Stanley immediately and clipped on his lead – which apparently settled the matter.

As Della had predicted, he was delighted to join her, and soon they were gazing in wonder at the perfect rainbow which hung, as if placed there just for their delight, over the valley in which Burley Bridge nestled.

'Isn't that stunning?' she gasped, whipping out her phone to photograph it.

'It's rare you see one so vivid,' he agreed.

She took photo after photo but, of course, her pictures didn't do any justice to the real thing.

'I wonder why that happens?' she asked, showing him the screen. 'Why it loses its brightness like that?'

'I guess it's one of those things you need to experience for real,' he said. 'Like, um . . .'

'The Northern Lights?' she suggested.

'Yeah.' Michael smiled. 'Suzy and I went on a sort of pilgrimage to see them, actually, about twenty years ago now. One of those trips-of-a-lifetime type things . . .'

'Where did you go?' she asked.

'Northern Lapland. We stayed in a glass tree house – it was a big family thing to mark her dad's sixtieth. Suzy's parents had always wanted to see the lights . . .'

Roxanne called for Stanley as they strolled through the area of woodland just off the main path. 'That sounds pretty impressive,' she remarked.

'Oh, it was. Where we were staying, they're meant to appear pretty much every second night, but of course, when you've travelled thousands of miles and built your-self up for the whole experience – well, you wait for days and days and nothing happens . . .' He laughed.

'And then you come out on an ordinary dog walk and see that!' Roxanne said with a smile. They had emerged from the woods to see the rainbow still there, shimmering. It was perfect. 'There are two,' she exclaimed suddenly. 'It's a *double* rainbow. Isn't that magical?'

'It's beautiful,' he agreed.

Roxanne breathed in deeply, filling her lungs with fresh Yorkshire air.

Michael turned to her. 'Feels good being up here, doesn't it?'

'It does. I really love it. It's funny, but I hardly ever came up here as a kid . . .'

Just for a moment, their eyes met, and something remarkable seemed to happen to Roxanne. It didn't matter that she had never appreciated how beautiful this place was, because she was here now, with a man she had only met a handful of times, and who she didn't know – not really – yet she felt utterly right being here.

Michael smiled at her, as if reading her thoughts. Flustered now, she glanced quickly away at the dogs, who were snuffling around the still-damp undergrowth, and when she looked back at Michael his smile triggered something, like a shoal of tiny fish, in her stomach. *Butterflies*, that's what they were. She was experiencing a flurry of butterflies over being in close proximity to the bakery man. Had he looked at her in a certain way? Or had she just imagined it? She scolded herself, and tried to think of Sean, back in London.

'So, um, did you ever see the Northern Lights?' she asked, flustered now.

'Yes, on the very last day of our trip,' he replied.

'Was it amazing?'

He was looking at her, with a bemused look on his face now. 'D'you know, it wasn't actually as amazing as this.'

She blinked at him, then laughed in realisation at what he meant. 'And you haven't had to travel all the way to northern Lapland to see it.' Her phone rang in her jeans pocket, and she flinched.

'It's fine, take it,' Michael said lightly.

Roxanne winced apologetically as she pulled it from her pocket and looked at the screen. Sean.

'Sorry. I guess I'd better.' Roxanne accepted the call. 'Sean? Everything all right?'

'Yeah,' Sean replied. 'Well, no – not really, to be honest. I had another call . . .'

She frowned. 'Who from?'

'From Tommy, your joiner mate.'

'Oh, not again. What happened this time?'

Michael had called for the dogs and set off a little way ahead as they began to make their way back to the village.

Sean sighed audibly. 'Okay, so *this* time he says he really needs the pictures doing soon as possible because it's his girlfriend's birthday coming up and he'll need to get them framed. I said, sorry, I don't have time – as I explained very clearly last time we spoke. I told him to contact a high-street photographer, there'd be someone local who'd be delighted to do the job . . .'

'Good advice,' she murmured, carefully sidestepping a patch of mud.

'But no, he wants *me* to do the pictures. Jessica's worthy of a top photographer, is what he says. Won a commended at Crufts two years in a row . . .'

'Oh, how awkward for you. Well, I suppose it's flattering . . .'

'Huh? I can hardly hear you . . .'

'Probably the signal,' she fibbed, realising she had been keeping her voice low deliberately. She didn't really want Michael to overhear her part of the exchange.

'. . . and it turns out he's googled where I work from,' Sean went on, 'and he was standing right there, outside my bloody studio!'

Roxanne spluttered, and Michael looked back and gave her a quizzical look. 'You mean, he'd turned up with his dog?'

'Yeah!'

'What did you do? Did you let him in?'

'Well, I didn't have much choice, did I? I just thought, well, I have nothing else on this afternoon apart from the *hundreds* of things I should have been doing, of course – and this'll get him off my back once and for all. So I'd said, "Okay, this is totally irregular, I never do this for anyone, I don't even take my own bookings normally. Britt handles all that . . ."'

'What happened?' Impatience had crept into Roxanne's voice. She glanced up at the rainbow and saw it fading before her very eyes.

'So, in they come, Tommy and his little dog – I mean, he'd just taken her to the groomer's, he'd gone to that trouble, so she was all freshly washed with a pink bow in her fringe, if dogs have fringes . . .' Michael was striding further ahead now, the dogs scampering at his side, and Roxanne quickened her pace to keep up '. . . I told Louie to set up a plain white background and some lights. We'd keep it nice and simple so, in theory, it should all be over in half an hour . . .' He paused for breath. 'We even found an old rug in a cupboard, not too shabby – but would Jessica sit there and pose nicely?'

'Er, I guess not?' she suggested. 'Shame you didn't have

any treats to bribe her with. I met this lovely girl from the village. She bakes these home-made dog cookies—'

'Charging about, she was,' Sean cut in, as if she hadn't spoken, 'crouching down by my light stands, has a pee . . .'

'No! Really?'

'. . . then another pee on a socket board so the damn thing's fused, and it'll probably stink forever . . .'

'*Oh*, Sean.'

'. . . and only then does she finally sit on the rug – no, it's not *sitting*, it's more of a squat, and she does a sh—'

'No!' she gasped, gripping her phone. Michael glanced back again briefly, and she fell silent.

'Rox?' Sean snapped.

She continued to plod down the hill, picturing his face, his mouth set firm, jaw clenched, puddles of wee all over the floor. 'That's terrible,' she muttered, a bubble of mirth starting to build in her now as Michael rounded a corner, out of sight. 'But, come on – don't you find it a *little* bit funny?'

Silence. The effort of displaying no emotion whatsoever was giving her a pain in the side of her head.

'Well,' she added, when no response was forthcoming, 'at least that's him out of your hair once and for all. That's good, isn't it?'

'Yeah, I guess you could look at it that way. So, thanks for that, Rox. Thanks for dishing out my number when, actually, I could have spent the afternoon prepping for tomorrow's shoot instead of having my studio used like a giant dog toilet.'

And with that, he ended the call.

Roxanne frowned and thrust her phone back into her pocket, wondering whether she had deserved that telling off. Seemingly, yes. In giving out his phone numbers, she had chalked up yet another misdemeanor – along with burning his birthday biscuits, guzzling too much champagne at his party and haranguing the DJ for 70s pop.

Trying to shrug off her unease, she hurried after Michael and the dogs, and by the time she caught up with them they were nearing the end of the path. 'Sorry about that,' she said, clipping Stanley's lead onto his red leather collar.

Michael flashed a quick smile as they made their way along the roadside towards the village centre. 'Oh, it's no problem – really.'

She grimaced. 'That was Sean. Dog trouble again.'

'So I gathered,' he said, amusement flickering in those light blue eyes.

'It went on a bit longer than I'd imagined. The call, I mean.'

He nodded and smiled briefly. 'Really, it's fine. I'd better get back, though. Jude'll be wondering where I am, complaining about child exploitation at nineteen years old . . .' He paused. 'Are you coming to the sourdough workshop at the bakery tomorrow?'

'Oh, yes, of course,' she said quickly, adding, 'It'll be fine, you know. But I realise Elsa's sort of pushed you into it . . .'

He grinned. 'And I'm pushing you into coming, aren't I? I imagine it's not *quite* your thing . . .'

'Maybe it could be,' she said, hoping she sounded convincing as they said goodbye.

Roxanne stood for a moment, watching as Michael and Bob crossed the road and disappeared into the bakery. She *did* want to show her support at the bakery tomorrow. However, Sean's tetchy call had somehow knocked the wind out of her, and when she glanced back up at the sky, there was just a wash of pale grey and the rainbow had gone.

Chapter Twenty-Two

The following evening, soon after the bakery had closed for the day, Michael was demonstrating how to make a sourdough loaf. The workshop was taking place at the back of the bakery, a gleaming space fitted out with immaculate stainless-steel ovens, marble worktops and sleek beechwood shelving holding fat glass jars of ingredients and pots of utensils. Rows of wooden chairs had been set out, borrowed from the Red Lion – everyone was always helping each other out around here – and bowls of various doughs placed on the worktop. There were far too many chairs, it turned out, as only Roxanne, Della and Frank – plus Frank's son Eddie, Irene Bagshott and Joan and Vincent from the gallery – had turned up.

'I think the weather must've put people off,' Frank murmured, at which Roxanne nodded. An hour earlier, the heavens had opened and the torrential rain hadn't stopped yet.

Roxanne glanced at Michael, who had thanked everyone warmly for braving the rain and was now announcing, 'Okay. I should start by explaining that this kind of bread-making takes an entire day.' It was already 6.30 p.m. Did that mean they would all be sitting here, heads nodding at one a.m. with Eddie, a nine-year-old, in their midst?

Thankfully, that wasn't the case. Michael had prepared doughs at various key stages of the process – a 'here's one I made earlier' sort of approach. It reminded Roxanne of *Blue Peter*, only the host here was rather more attractive in his fresh white T-shirt, striped apron and slim dark jeans than any of the presenters she remembered.

Anyway, never mind Michael's eye-pleasing qualities. Roxanne had only decided to attend as a supportive friend; and now she was doing her best to make up for the poor attendance by giving his demonstration her unwavering attention. In fact, as she was discovering, the chemistry behind bread-making was really quite fascinating. Who knew that, instead of a handy little sachet of yeast, which cost – well, Roxanne had no idea how much it was, she had never had occasion to buy such a thing – you could make your own sourdough 'starter'?

'It's also called the mother,' Michael explained, wafting a jar of evil-looking bubbling stuff in front of everyone, 'and it's a natural raising agent. In other words, it's what makes the magic happen.'

'What *is* that stuff?' Irene asked, wrinkling her nose.

Michael smiled. 'It's made from water I boiled potatoes in, and I've added flour, sugar and salt. Flour contains natural yeast and microorganisms, and when it comes into contact with the water, then it starts to metabolise and amazing things begin to happen.'

'Like what?' Eddie asked eagerly.

'Carbon dioxide is produced,' Michael explained, 'which creates bubbles. It'll start to bubble away and smell a bit

247

beery until, in around three days, you'll see fermentation starting to happen . . .'

'Cool,' Eddie muttered.

Roxanne leaned forward, genuinely amazed. This wasn't like cooking. This was a scientific experiment. She had no idea this kind of thing could happen in a kitchen.

'When I'm making a loaf,' Michael continued in his soft southern tones, 'I take a bit of my starter out of the jar and chuck in more flour to feed it, to keep the process going. And that's all you do. It just goes on and on, indefinitely really. This mother's about nine months old . . .'

Nine months? That made her rotting kale look positively juvenile! 'You invented this?' Roxanne asked.

'Oh, no,' he said with a wide, disarming smile, 'it's an ancient process . . .'

'I just thought, with you being a chemistry teacher . . .'

'Well, yes, I am attracted to that side of baking. The simple reactions, the release of carbon dioxide causing all those bubbles. Really, if you just follow the process, it's pretty much idiot-proof.'

Roxanne glanced at Della and Frank, who were holding hands, she noted. Eddie seemed completely relaxed about this, and was now watching Michael with interest. He was a handsome boy with a mop of wavy light brown hair and a smattering of freckles over his nose and cheeks.

She turned her attention back to the demonstration, wondering what Sean would say if he could see her now. Now Michael had taken a dollop of starter and was mixing it with his hands into a bowl of flour until it all gunked together. It was oddly attractive, all this vigorous squishing and squeezing and clearly not minding about getting all messed up. Sean flickered into Roxanne's mind once more, hectoring her about Jessica peeing on his socket board, and she quickly pushed the thought away.

'Now here's one that's been rising all day,' Michael added, turning his attentions to another bowl of dough. 'I'm going to show you how to knock it down, then give it a little light kneading . . .'

It was all so casually done, as if it were effortless.

Now everyone was invited up to the counter and given their own lump of dough to knead, whilst Elsa lifted a freshly baked loaf from the oven. There were others, too, which had been baked earlier and were flavoured with tomato, fresh basil and pumpkin seeds, sitting there all tempting in a wicker basket.

'Am I doing this properly?' Roxanne asked, surprised at how much she was enjoying herself.

'That's perfect,' Michael replied.

She laughed. 'It's so easy. I always thought you had to be terribly macho with bread, and pummel the hell out of it . . .' She dropped the dough into a tin with a satisfying thud.

Meanwhile, as everyone's loaves were put in the oven to bake, Elsa and her brother Jude offered around glasses of wine and soft drinks. Michael sliced the ready-made breads into bite-sized chunks. Elsa set an extravagant cheeseboard on the worktop, and everyone started to tuck in.

'Oh, these are delicious,' Roxanne enthused. 'You've made it look so simple!'

'Well, it is really,' Michael replied. 'You could get a loaf started before you set out to work in the morning, you know . . .'

She smiled, deciding not to mention that she was usually charging about, trying to find keys, purse and unladdered tights. Instead, she allowed herself the luxury of snacking on more bread and cheese.

'So, d'you think you'll turn into a baker now, Rox?' Della teased her.

'I'll have a go,' she replied, 'as long as Michael can guarantee that starter stuff doesn't get out of control and start bubbling up and flooding over.' Roxanne sipped her white wine and turned to him. 'I have these terribly fussy neighbours below me. I can't imagine they'd be too impressed if it escaped from its jar and started dripping down through the cracks in the floor.' She looked at Michael, and he laughed.

Elsa went around refilling everyone's glasses and soon, their own batch of loaves was ready. Jude obligingly took them from the oven, placed them on the cooling rack and, as soon as they were ready to handle, wrapped them in crinkly brown paper for everyone to take home.

As Michael busied himself with clearing up, Roxanne was aware now that perhaps they were overstaying their welcome. After all, he had been up since five.

Perhaps sensing a mood change too, Della and Frank drained their glasses and pulled on their jackets, and Irene, Joan and Vincent were already making their way out.

'We'll leave you in peace,' Della said, thanking Michael warmly. 'C'mon, Eddie, you're staying at mine tonight.'

'On the camp bed in the living room?' His green eyes shone with delight.

'Yes, of course, darling.' She took his hand.

'Could you stay a minute, Roxanne?' Elsa asked. 'I have something to show you.'

Roxanne paused and glanced at Michael, who was gathering up plates. 'Is that okay, Michael?'

250

'Yes, of course,' he said as Della, Frank and Eddie said their goodbyes. 'She's been desperate to show you.'

Elsa opened a cupboard and lifted out a Tupperware box, removing the lid with a flourish. 'What d'you think?'

Roxanne gazed at the canine-friendly cookies decorated with finely piped eyes, mouths and collars. 'These are amazing,' she gasped. 'So professional. Honestly, did you really make them yourself?'

'Yes, of course – the icing's just cream cheese and a little bit of tapioca.' She glanced at her father. 'Dad suggested that.'

Michael smiled and raked back his hair with his hand. 'They've worked out pretty well. I reckon we can package them up like you suggested and start selling them in the shop.'

'I'll write a blog post about them,' Roxanne added. 'It's supposed to be about style in the country and, well, these are pretty stylish, I'd say.' If Elsa seemed delighted by that, she was a little less thrilled when Michael handed her a floor brush. Unsurprisingly, she soon scampered off upstairs, with the excuse that she needed to check the *YourStyle* website to see her pictures online. Jude had long since disappeared.

'I'll help you clear up,' Roxanne offered, keen to assist as everyone else had gone home. 'This is beautiful,' she added. 'The whole place, I mean. You should be so proud of what you've done here . . .' She broke off, her cheeks blazing. What a stupid thing to say. Michael's wife's new boyfriend had built this kitchen.

She glanced at him as he started to load the dishwasher, wondering if the heat had suddenly intensified in here.

'I can't believe I made a loaf tonight,' she continued, more to break the awkward silence than anything else.

'At least, I did the kneading part, and it's actually turned into something I'd want to eat. Amazing!' She tailed off, feeling foolish now, and unsure whether Michael was even listening. Had they really shared that lovely moment with the rainbow, up on the hill?

'It reminded me of those anti-cellulite mitts we had in the nineties,' she rambled on, grabbing a cloth from the kitchen and wiping a dough splodge off a chair. 'They were a craze in my office, all the women kneading away at their thighs, and nothing happened, of course, apart from a few bruises . . .' She beamed at him. 'You don't realise how lucky you are to be a man!'

He smiled briefly and muttered something she didn't catch, and started to sweep the floor. She stood there, gripping a plastic spatula, wondering what to do next. 'I liked the way you explained it all tonight,' she struggled on, 'about feeding the starter with a spoonful of flour, like a pet . . .' She paused, conscious that she was *going on a bit* now. She hadn't reached the ripe old age of forty-seven without becoming aware of some of her less appealing character traits, like babbling when she was uncomfortable. 'D'you ever name it?' she asked.

'Sorry?' Michael gripped the floor brush and blinked at her.

'Your sourdough starter. You were saying you feed it, and I wondered if . . .' She stopped. 'Oh, never mind.' She looked at him, and their eyes met for a moment. 'Can I help with anything else?' she asked.

'Er, no thanks – I think we're fine here.'

Hmmm. Clearly they weren't. 'Um, are you okay, Michael?' she ventured tentatively as he recommenced sweeping. She looked around the kitchen, overcome by a wave of sadness for him. All that effort he'd put in for tonight, and for what – seven people to turn up, and one of those to put her foot in it?

He turned back to face her. 'I suppose I'm just a bit disappointed, that's all.'

'Oh, it was *fascinating*, though . . .'

'Thank you, but I was only making bread.' A beat's silence hung between them. 'Anyway, thanks again for helping,' he added, which Roxanne interpreted as, *And could you leave now, please?*

'You're welcome,' she said, feeling rather hurt as she picked up her paper-wrapped loaf, relieved now to say goodnight.

The rain had stopped, and the air felt clammy and damp. She should have learned from last time, she decided now; the brandy snap fiasco should have taught her a lesson. Something was telling her loud and clear that she and the fine art of baking would never be a perfect match.

Chapter Twenty-Three

As Roxanne strolled back to Della's down Rosemary Lane, she became aware that something else didn't feel right. The whole Sean thing, that's what it was; the Jessica-pooing debacle. She wouldn't call him back, though. She would leave it for now. All Roxanne really wanted, as she let herself into Della's flat, was to curl up in that pristine guest bed.

Instead, she tried to settle down to watch TV with Della, Frank and Eddie. Keen to get to know Eddie a little, she gently quizzed him about what he liked doing – playing football, or computer games? – all the while conscious of behaving like the slightly awkward child-free visitor.

'Eddie, Roxanne asked you a question,' Frank prompted him, arm slung around Della, who was snuggled close to him on the sofa.

'Oh, er . . .' He reddened.

'I'm sorry. I'm acting like I'm interviewing you,' Roxanne said quickly, mustering a wide smile. Eddie smiled too, and seemed to relax a little. But really, you could tell he just wanted to watch TV in peace – it was some comedy box set which was clearly a favourite among the three of them. And so, Roxanne made her excuses and retired to bed, at 9 p.m. – in other words, earlier than the nine-year-old in the house.

She undressed quickly and climbed under the sheets, but she couldn't relax. She couldn't stop thinking that the distance really *wasn't* doing her and Sean any good – but then, if they couldn't survive her spending a little time with her sister, then what hope was there, really?

She reached for her phone, dithering over whether to call back, to apologise for . . . what exactly? Giving Tommy his number? She had already said sorry for that. For laughing, then, like any normal human being? Irritated now, she placed her phone on the bedside table. She got up to fetch her laptop, and started to write a blog post about Elsa's doggie treats, but that didn't flow easily either. Instead, she emailed Amanda, detailing all that had happened since she arrived here – the dog walk soaking, the foldable rain hat, the unsettling incident of Della trying to set her up with the village baker, and the enjoyable walks they'd had together since. Roxanne didn't mention that moment with the rainbow. She had yet to try to make any kind of sense of it herself.

It felt good, though, to get most of it down – almost like talking. Roxanne signed off her email to Amanda with a flurry of kisses and turned off her light. Soon the TV was turned off, and Eddie's chatter subsided. The velvety silence – the kind you only ever noticed in the country – seemed to settle over her, bringing sleep.

A little way down Rosemary Lane, Michael was sitting at the small, wobbly desk in the corner of his bedroom, trying to write a short, succinct note. He was aware that it might seem odd, and wasn't sure this was the right way to go about things. However it was better, he felt, to put his feelings down this way, as he wasn't brilliant at explaining things face to face either.

Dear Roxanne, he wrote on the blue lined notepad. *I think I owe you an apology for tonight.*

He stopped, unsure as to how to proceed. His confidence had taken quite a bashing after Suzy had left him for that cocky little shit, Rory King – or 'His Royal Asshole', as he thought of him privately. Six foot four, gym-honed, with an infuriating swagger and a lazy cockney accent that Michael suspected was fake, or at least exaggerated for effect. *Are you happy with the tiling, mate? Pretty neat, innit, mate?* It was all mate-this, mate-that. *Some people, they get in a tiler 'cause they think it's fiddly and boring but not me, mate. I find it therapeutic.* It transpired that tiling wasn't the only activity he found therapeutic – not that Rory had been entirely to blame, of course. Suzy had been a more than willing participant. In fact, she had broken it to Michael that the stud kitchen fitter was 'the love of her life'.

She and Michael had just 'run out of steam', she'd told him, and hadn't he noticed? Well, yes, he had – sort of. However, he'd assumed they'd been chugging along fine, and if things weren't as thrilling and sparkly as they had been at the start – well, perhaps that was something to do with the fact that twenty-four years had passed, during which they had raised two teenagers and sunk all their money into a little hardware shop which, Suzy kept insisting, 'will make such a darling little bakery'. Michael had supported her idea; encouraged her, even: Christ, when you had tried to teach first-year science for the twenty-sixth year, and someone found it hilarious to direct the bunsen burner at someone's bum . . . well, he'd conceded that perhaps he and Suzy were ready to start a new life. Then she had hotfooted it before the bakery had even opened.

Even now, six months on, the very thought of the home-wrecking tradesman made Michael's blood bubble up like his undeniably active sourdough starter. Perhaps his insides were fermenting too, because something pretty awful seemed to be happening to him. The teenage stud – okay, he was twenty-eight, but that was galling enough: he was born in the 80s for crying out loud – had stepped into their lives, recommended by a friend of Suzy's, and in one fell swoop destroyed his family. Before all of this, Michael had never been a bitter or vengeful man. Now, on a particularly off day, he could quite easily take a hammer to those cripplingly expensive shelves Suzy reckoned they just had to have.

The kids had taken it reasonably well, amazingly – at least, Jude seemed to be no surlier than when Suzy had been here, nagging him to have his hair cut and worrying about his asthma. Recently they had even started to visit their mother from time to time, at the home she had set up with Rory King in Ormskirk in Lancashire; a situation which Michael conceded was probably healthier than wanting to incinerate any photos that featured her. Despite everything, he didn't want his kids to hate their mum. And Elsa had . . . well, she had *rallied,* was the only way he could put it – urging him to give his all to the business, starting with choosing the right paint colours to make the place look fresh and inviting, as opposed to announcing 'The owner of this bakery is severely depressed!' to passers-by.

Quite frankly, without Elsa being all-round brilliant (apart from her aversion to housework, but then no one was perfect), he didn't know how he'd have coped. He padded through to the kitchen, poured himself a glass of wine and sat back down at the desk in his bedroom.

The thing is, he wrote in his neat rather old-fashioned handwriting, *I was sort of embarrassed when so few people turned up for the workshop tonight. With you being there and, I don't know, bringing something new and different to this little village of ours, it seemed important that it went well. I was glad you were there, once I got things started. You were very kind and seemed so engaged and interested. I hope it was genuine, that you did enjoy yourself (I'm sure it's not your usual sort of evening entertainment!). If you didn't, then you played the part extremely well.*

He stopped and sipped his wine. Was he fawning? Did it sound overly formal? He hoped not. He pictured her lovely face, her light blue eyes and bright, unguarded smile, and remembered the first time Della had mentioned her sister's imminent arrival in Burley Bridge. 'Just come and meet her,' Della had said. 'As friends, I mean. She's been having a tough time at work and I know she'd love to meet you.' As friends, indeed. 'Well,' Della had said, laughing, 'why not just be open-minded and have a fun evening, see what happens? What is there to lose?' Conveniently, she had omitted to mention that Roxanne had a boyfriend back in London – some hotshot photographer by all accounts. So why on earth was he sitting here writing to her now?

But there had been that moment, when they'd been out walking the dogs. The way she'd looked at him, when they'd seen the rainbow – had he imagined it? He'd wanted to kiss her then. How ridiculous, he thought now. A moment of madness; just as well she'd had that phone call from her boyfriend, the one who seemed obsessed about small dogs.

258

Fortifying himself with more wine, he continued: *So, and I hope this isn't presumptuous of me, I was wondering if you might like to come over for lunch one day, just so I can sort of apologise for being so offish before you left tonight, and to say thank you?*

He signed it, added his mobile number, and frowned. To thank her for what? He re-read his words, wondering again if it did sound too gushing, or as if he was asking her on a proper date – which he absolutely was not. This was crazy. It now felt less like a chatty note and more of a terribly stressful homework assignment. Perhaps he was worrying too much over what was really just an invitation to a casual lunch? Yet he so wanted to get it right. He hardly knew her but, for the first time since Suzy had left him for Rory King, something had happened to him. He *wanted* to get to know Roxanne – how could he not, when she was so lovely and unaffected and had asked him if he *named* his sourdough starter? Yet his faltering attempt at a friendly note seemed quite ridiculous now. He couldn't possibly drop it through the bookshop letter box. He'd look like an idiot and it would be so uncomfortable if she replied saying thank you, but no. That was the thing with living in a village like Burley Bridge. The downside of all the beauty and tranquillity was the fact that you ran into everyone pretty much every day; there was literally no escape.

Michael scrunched up the note and pinged it in the general direction of the waste-paper basket. Draining the last of his wine, he bent to pat Bob, who had sidled up beside him, and wondered what on earth he was going to do with the rest of his life.

Chapter Twenty-Four

Come Thursday – the day before the party – the newly arrived books had all been allocated to their correct sections on the new shelves. A new burgundy velvet sofa had been sourced on Gumtree, and vases filled with fresh spring flowers were dotted all around. It all looked immensely cheery. There were even jars of old-fashioned sweets and lollipops for younger customers.

For the actual party there would be drinks and retro snacks – a modern take on vol-au-vents, cheese straws and even things on sticks, just for fun. Michael was taking care of the edibles and had nipped in to go over the menu. Leo, the Red Lion's landlord, knew a local band, and there would be competitions to win limited editions of classic vintage books.

'But the main focus,' Della said to Roxanne as she switched the sign on the front door to 'Closed' – it was 5.30 p.m. – 'will be the retro cocktail demonstration.' She paused and grimaced. 'Hopefully we won't see a repeat of—'

'Michael's workshop?' Roxanne sighed. 'I'm sure we

won't. Look how many regular customers you have. Everyone's been talking about the party all week.'

Della rubbed at her eyes. 'It still feels like there's so much to do, though. I can't believe I've left it so late.'

'Yes, but we have all of tomorrow, don't we? The party doesn't kick off till six so I can run around picking up any last minute bits and pieces during the day. Just give me a list and I'll help.'

Della looked at her and smiled. 'You know what, Rox? I don't know what I would have done without you . . .' She broke off to retrieve her ringing mobile from the counter. 'Slow down, darling,' she said, frowning. 'I can hardly hear you. Take a deep breath and tell me again what's happened . . .'

Roxanne busied herself with pinning up bunting along the tops of the shelves.

Della was pacing back and forth behind the counter, phone clasped to her ear. 'Sophie, love, it'll be okay. Don't panic . . . Okay, listen to me please, darling,' she said firmly. 'I'll call my bank and see if there's any way to transfer money if you have no ID. There must be some way to do it . . .'

She broke off, glancing at Roxanne with an alarmed face. Sophie was still talking. Roxanne could hear her niece's voice, frantic yet distant, a nineteen-year-old young woman now, but sounding like a frightened little girl.

'Soph,' Della cut in, 'listen to me, *please* – of course you'll be able to get back home. We'll figure out the money situation, but what you need to do is report it to the police, okay? Have you done that yet?' Small pause. 'Okay, well, that's important. You have to do that. Then you'll need to go to the British embassy and they'll be able to help you. They'll probably give you a temporary passport – I can

261

look online for you, see what happens? Honey, please don't cry. It happens to lots of people. I just wish you'd put your valuables in the hotel's safe, like I said—' Sophie's voice rattled tinnily from the phone. 'Okay!' Della exclaimed. 'Okay, sweetheart. No need to shout. I'm sorry. I know there's no point in saying that now . . .' She tried to placate Sophie some more, then finished the call with a loud groan and slumped into the chair behind the counter.

'What's happened?' Roxanne exclaimed. 'Is she okay?'

Della rubbed her hands all over her face. 'Christ, Rox, the thing is with being a parent, it never stops. The worrying, I mean, the stress of it all . . .'

'She's not hurt, is she?'

She shook her head. 'No, thank God. Well, not in that way, not in a physical sense . . .' Della emitted another low moan of despair. 'She's travelling with Jamie, right? This boyfriend from her course, who's supposedly wonderful? They're in Berlin now and things were getting a bit tetchy, she said. They weren't getting along. I'm not sure about the details – just that he was panicking over every little thing and she . . . well, you know what Sophie's like. She just takes things as they come.'

Roxanne nodded.

'Then last night they had a row, and he just stormed off and left her. Left her alone in the hostel which was okay-*ish*; she thought he'd be back, that he'd call at least when he'd got over himself – but he didn't. And in the morning she woke up to find her bag had gone from under her bed. Someone had come in and nicked it – wallet, passport, tickets, her decent camera, the lot. The only reason she still has her phone is because she'd been texting Jamie in bed and fell asleep and it must have fallen under her sheets . . .' Della shook her head.

'That's so awful. So, you've told her to go to the police, and then the embassy . . .'

'Yeah. I just wish I could be there. That's what it's like, Rox. When something happens . . .' She broke off as tears filled her eyes. Roxanne kneeled beside her and held her close. 'When something happens to your children,' Della added, 'all you want is to be there. Does that sound silly? I know she's a grown-up . . .'

'But she's still your girl.' Roxanne pulled back and looked at her. 'So, Jamie hasn't come back?'

'Nope – he just texted her to say he was going home and that was that.'

Roxanne shook her head in disbelief. Of course, she didn't know how her sister felt exactly; she didn't have a child thousands of miles away, stranded with no money or means of travelling home. However, she couldn't remember seeing Della looking so distressed – not even after all the Mark stuff: finding out about Polly Fisher in her fancy detached house.

They moved to the sofa and just sat together, quiet for a while and then going over what Sophie could do, and venting their anger at Jamie – what had he been thinking, abandoning her like that in a city she didn't know? He was supposed to love her!

'I just feel like a terrible mum because I'm not with her,' Della added. 'I feel helpless, Rox.'

'I'm sure you do, but come on – she'll do the things you said, and you can find out how to send some money over, and she'll be fine . . .'

'She has literally not one euro on her!'

Roxanne nodded, aware that it wasn't enough to just sit here, listening, trying to reassure her. 'Could Mark help in any way?' she ventured cautiously.

'Oh, he's completely useless,' Della exclaimed. 'He pays his share of her rent, as we agreed, and slings her the odd bit of birthday and Christmas money. But apart from his financial contribution, he doesn't seem to want to be involved at all. He hasn't bothered to go and see her in months. Sophie and I think he's sulking because she's not terribly enamoured with the idea of going to stay with him at Polly's.'

'That's not so surprising.' She paused. 'Could *I* go, then?'

Della stared at her. 'What – to Berlin?'

'Yes, of course.'

'But . . . I couldn't ask you to do that!'

Roxanne frowned at her. 'Why not? I could take her some money, help her to sort out a passport – I'd just be *there* for her . . .'

Della rubbed at her eyes with her sweater sleeve. 'It just feels like too much.'

'*Why* is it too much? I travel for work, it's not a big deal, Dell. Come on, one of us should go . . .' She broke off. 'Would you rather go?'

'Yes, I would,' she said softly. 'I really want to see her, make sure she's okay – but it's the party tomorrow. What a mess, Rox. What bloody awful timing . . .'

'Does that really matter, though? I know you've worked so hard to get to this point. But the main thing is, the shop's all ready and it looks fantastic . . .'

Della picked at a nail. 'I suppose I could just cancel the party and get a flight tomorrow. I could put a notice in the window, apologising, for when people turn up . . .'

'Or *I* could do it,' Roxanne suggested. 'Take care of the party, I mean. Be a sort of surrogate you.'

Della gave Roxanne an incredulous look. 'I couldn't ask you to do that either. That's ridiculous—'

'You're not asking – I'm offering,' she said firmly.

Della pondered this for a moment. 'But . . . d'you think you could cope?'

'Yes, of course!'

'Oh, I don't know, Rox.' Now Della was eyeing her as if she were a seven-year-old who had just wandered in and asked if she could play shops.

'What are you worried about exactly?' Roxanne asked, losing patience now. 'Come on, you must admit, you're surprised how well I've managed in here these past few days . . .'

'You *have* been quite a help,' Della conceded.

Roxanne smiled. 'So, can't you trust me to hand a few vol-au-vents around?'

Della was still studying her, almost suspiciously, for goodness' sake. Roxanne inhaled deeply, knowing she had to tread carefully. 'I know you'd hate to miss your own party,' she added.

'It's not that,' Della murmured. 'It's more important that I see Sophie . . .'

'Just go then,' Roxanne urged her, 'and remember it won't just be me all by myself. Faye will be here, and I'm sure Frank will help out.'

'Yes, but—'

' . . . And maybe Elsa and Jude wouldn't mind handing out drinks. And then there's Michael . . .'

'Oh, yes, I'm sure everyone'll pitch in . . .' Della bit her lip. 'But what about my cocktail demo?'

'That might be a bit beyond my capabilities,' Roxanne conceded, 'but we'll think of something – if we need a demonstration at all. Isn't it really about welcoming your customers to the new shop? There'll be plenty going on.'

Della looked a little calmer now. 'Yes, I guess there will

be. Okay, so I'll try to fly back early Saturday morning in time for the shop opening . . .'

'Why?' Roxanne exclaimed. 'I can look after things here.'

'Yes, but after the party it might be too much—'

'Dell, listen to me, please. I'm *not* ninety-five years old and it won't be too much. We're talking a party in a bookshop – not an all-night rave . . .' She stopped and smiled. 'Do people even go to those anymore?'

'No idea,' Della said, a hint of a smile on her lips.

'Well, anyway, I can take care of Saturday so please don't worry.'

Della exhaled. 'Okay, I *will* go, even if I have to fly from Heathrow. I'll tell Sophie now.' She picked up her phone from the coffee table and started to text. 'Thanks, Rox,' she added. 'Thank you so much.'

Roxanne swallowed. 'Well, I sort of owe you.' Their eyes met, and Della put her arms around her and hugged her tightly.

'You don't owe me anything – truly. Are you really sure about this?'

'Absolutely,' Roxanne said. 'Now, off you go and see if you can book a flight.'

Chapter Twenty-Five

Of course Michael would pitch in.

'I'm going to be there anyway, aren't I?' he said, handing Roxanne a coffee over the bakery counter. He had just opened up on Friday morning and a delicious aroma filled the bakery; warm and comforting, it was like being enveloped in a hug. After their curt conversation after the baking demonstration, Roxanne was pleased that things seemed to be back to normal between them.

'Yes, I know,' she said, 'but this is a bit different. You won't just be milling about, drinking and eating and chatting to people. You'll be sort of . . . *on duty.*'

He feigned alarm. 'Not juggling or fire eating or anything like that?'

'No, that won't be needed,' she said with a chuckle.

'Then I'm very happy to report for duty. What should I wear?'

She blinked at him. 'Er, just your normal clothes are fine . . .'

'Not a waiter's outfit or anything?' His blue eyes were glinting playfully now.

'No,' she said, laughing, 'that won't be necessary either.' She paused. 'I just mean handing out drinks, maybe giving me a hand with the raffle, that kind of thing . . .'

'Well, that doesn't sound too arduous.'

She smiled. 'Thanks so much, Michael.'

'Ah, that's okay.' He looked away and started to straighten the baskets on the shelves.

It was a bright, sunny morning, and the shop was already filled with freshly baked breads, cakes and pastries. On the counter sat a shallow wicker basket filled with Elsa's cellophane-wrapped packets of dog treats, iced and labelled 'Doggie Bites – home-baked, all natural and delicious'. It didn't look as if any had gone.

'How are these doing?' Roxanne asked tentatively.

'Like hot cakes, actually.'

'Really?'

'Yep – I had to refill the basket twice yesterday. Elsa's been toiling away, cutting them out and icing them, doing all the wrapping – she's even had to rope Jude in to help. We had a guy in asking if we can do an order of fifty packets for him to sell at Heathfield farmer's market yesterday.'

'That's amazing!' she gasped. 'Will you do it?'

'Will Elsa do it, is more the question.' Michael smiled. 'Could be a nice little earner for her. So, when's Della off, then?'

'She's already gone. Managed to catch a flight from Manchester at seven this morning . . .'

He raised a brow. 'And you're really okay with it? Manning the fort, I mean?'

Of course, Michael knew how protective Della was about her shop.

'I'm fine,' she replied firmly. 'My only worry is that

Stanley will start pining for Dell. They're literally never apart for more than a few hours.'

Michael grimaced and handed her a packet of doggie bites. 'Take these. Take as many as you think he'll need to keep him happy while she's away. So, when's she coming home?'

'She was planning to just stay tonight and come back first thing on Saturday, but I told her I could easily look after things at the shop, and we're closed on Sundays anyway . . .'

'*We're* closed,' he repeated with a smile.

Roxanne laughed. 'You see what's happened? She let me onto the till, then reluctantly agreed that I could put out new books on the shelves – and now I'm starting to think of it as my shop too. I'd better not talk like that in front of Della.'

Michael grinned. 'You Londoners, coming up here, taking over the place . . .'

'By the time she comes home on Sunday night I'll have had the whole shop redecorated to my own personal taste.' She looked at him and smiled. 'Anyway, I'd better get back to open up.'

'Good luck, then,' he said, 'and remember, anything you need – just shout.'

She thanked him warmly as she left the bakery, re-assuring herself that she could manage without Della for a few days. After all, her sister had pretty much pulled everything together, and Roxanne's proper job was significantly more complex than organising the last few details of a gathering in a village bookshop. Party organiser: that had been her ex Ned Tallow's job, allegedly. However, she didn't recall him ever writing any to-do lists, or involving himself with any actual planning for that matter. The Ned

Tallow brand of party organising had merely involved booking some clapped-out venue which reeked of damp, then phoning his mates to do the real hard work – the sound, lighting, security and bar. The 'parties' he organised involved cramming lots of people into a sweaty, dilapidated building in some dingy corner of South East London, and ensuring that the necessary drug dealers were present. There were invariably police raids, arrests, spaced-out girls crying in toilets and the odd minor injury. Roxanne had gone to some of these parties and hung around in the shadows, declining the offer of drugs and sipping dreadful wine out of plastic cups, feeling like everyone's rather concerned aunt. She was confident that a gathering in a bookshop would be somewhat less stressful.

Roxanne opened the shop, put on a Nina Simone album and considered what she still had to do. Della had ordered in glasses and crockery, so all Roxanne had to do was blow up balloons – she had remembered to buy a pump this time, from Irene's general store – and set everything out once the shop closed for business at the end of the afternoon. However, the cocktail demo aspect was troubling her. Even if she had the necessary knowledge, there were still too many ingredients to amass, recipes to get her head around and plenty of potential for disaster. Faye was popping in at lunchtime to give her a break, but it still seemed too much to pull together. She just wanted to focus on ensuring everyone was having a good time, but she knew some kind of demonstration would be fun – perhaps something for the children would be easier? Della was always keen to emphasise that hers was a child-friendly bookshop – hence the supply of paper and crayons, and the selection of toys kept in a box under the counter. Kids loved to bake fairy cakes, and Michael was the obvious person to help her – but she was concerned that asking him would seem rather insensitive after his own, ill-attended workshop. She couldn't possibly do it herself – not after her brandy snaps episode. Did it have to be cakes, though, she wondered now? She knew from hours spent in Amanda's kitchen that children basically loved the mixing part, the stamping out shapes with a cutter, and decorating with icing.

That was it. She would ask Elsa to share her Doggie Bites recipe, and perhaps even run the show – or, if she wasn't prepared to do that, at least hover around in an assistant's role.

Roxanne grinned, a flurry of excitement growing inside her now. A Doggie Bites workshop! It was a little mad, perhaps, and she wasn't entirely sure it was what Della would want. Plus, Elsa would be at school right now – at least, she should be on a Friday morning – but there was no harm in texting to ask if she would help. She found her mobile number on the email she'd sent and fired off her request. Minutes later, Elsa replied with a ton of smiley emoticons which Roxanne interpreted as a resounding yes.

At lunchtime, while Faye looked after the shop, Roxanne took Stanley for a short walk over the hills. She had grown to love their hikes together. They helped to clear her head, worked her thighs and there was something wonderfully freeing about setting out in a disgusting murky green fleece – a future style blog subject – and her old jeans, with not a scrap of make-up on her face and her long fair hair pulled back into a ponytail.

Already it seemed unhinged to spend more than £100 on a moisturiser, or to go to a man in a tiny Covent Garden clinic to have Botox injected into her forehead.

In her office, pretty much everyone – even Tristan – had had injectables, plus dermabrasion, chemical peels and, in certain cases, a touch of lip plumping. It was unremarkable to see someone come back from lunch with their face all red and angry-looking, as if it had been scoured vigorously with a Brillo pad. Here, out in the wilds with a small, scruffy terrier, Roxanne's age wasn't even an issue – whereas at work, with pretty much everyone else at least a decade younger (*two* decades, in many cases) she was conscious of it pretty much all of the time.

Roxanne didn't know the programmes they watched, or listen to the music they liked – but pretended she did. Secretly – as there was no way she'd admit this at work – she was a bit of a jazz fan. Although she was certainly no expert, through time spent with Isabelle she had grown to love Ella Fitzgerald, Sarah Vaughan and Billie Holiday, those ladies whose voices could break your heart. Sometimes, she and Isabelle just sat quietly together and listened to an entire side of an album (all of Isabelle's music was on vinyl; Roxanne had never glimpsed a CD in her flat, and the idea of downloading music was, to Isabelle's mind, ridiculous).

Back at the bookshop now, Roxanne unclipped Stanley's lead and took over from Faye at the till. Della texted to let Roxanne know she had arrived safely, and that Sophie was fine; well, fine-*ish* – in one piece at least. They had a 'fun' afternoon planned of going to a police station – which Sophie hadn't managed to find yet – followed by a visit to the British embassy.

Glad to hear all okay, give my love to S and don't worry for one second about anything here, Roxanne replied.

Perhaps triggered by the word 'worry', Della fired back: *Anything you're worried about tonight, I mean ANYTHING AT ALL – please phone me anytime. And good luck!!*

Roxanne smiled at her sister's concern and replied with a smiley face and a thumbs up; not her usual style, but preferable to batting back more reassurances when she had customers to look after. By now, she was switching easily into the role she had found herself in. She had never imagined she would enjoy working in a shop quite so much. It wasn't that she thought it was beneath her; more that, since she had landed her first magazine job at eighteen years old, she had never considered doing anything else.

The early afternoon was busy, with a mixture of customers: locals who popped in regularly, people who were driving through the village, spotted the shop and just had to stop out of curiosity, and others who had made a trip here specially. When a customer was looking for a specific cookbook that wasn't in stock, Roxanne searched for it online and ordered it for them. Della had explained that there was no real profit in this – she only added on a tiny mark-up – but felt that it was a service she should offer.

By around 4 p.m., things had quietened down, allowing Roxanne time to check that everything was looking just so for the party. Wine and beers were put to chill in the fridge, vases of flowers refreshed, the music selected and all the bookshelves given a speedy once-over to ensure that nothing was looking untidy after the customers' browsings during the day. She unpacked glasses and plates and set them all out on the island unit, and arranged the raffle prizes of beautiful vintage crockery, which Della had gleaned on her travels while picking up new collections of cookbooks, and bottles of champagne.

Although Della had bought the various components, she hadn't got around to assembling the star prize of a lavish hamper, and so Roxanne set to work, arranging the bottles and jars on a bed of scrunched tissue paper and wrapping the entire basket in clear cellophane, tied with a lavish red bow. She blew up the balloons and hung them up around the shop.

When everything was done, she decided, she would call Sean – just to fill him in on recent events. The silence between them had stretched for long enough. While she understood that Tommy's surprise arrival had been inconvenient and awkward, his response seemed rather extreme. Roxanne wondered now if it was for the best that he wasn't coming to the party. Given his recent huffy behaviour, and the fact that she was hosting the do, she wasn't sure she had time for any more dramas or sulks.

Something had happened to her, in this short time she had been back in Burley Bridge. With all those walks in the hills, and the headspace they had given her, she had started to worry less, about . . . *stuff*. She served a cluster of customers, and when they had left she called Sean.

'Hello?' His voice was abrupt.

'Hi, darling. Sorry, you're probably in the middle of—'

'No, no, it's okay. I'm okay at the moment. Everything all right?'

Roxanne frowned. Now two elderly ladies had come in, and were enthusing over the display of 1950s dinner party books that Della had set out, along with a selection of dinnerware from the period, on the table.

'Yes, I'm good. So, um, how are things?' *By which I mean, have you recovered from photographing a sweet little dog yet?*

'I'm fine, Rox. How about you?'

'I'm fine too.'

Silence. Great. So, they were to slip into an *I'm-fine* loop now, were they? Already, she prickled with irritation

274

at having called him. From the hubbub in the background it sounded as if he was out somewhere, rather than in his studio. 'Okay, sorry if I've called at a bad time . . .'

'No, look, er – *I* wanted to say sorry.' His voice softened. 'Sorry about the other day. With the dog thing, I mean. It wasn't your fault. Well, it was, sort of . . .' He chuckled softly, and something snagged at her heart. 'But I forgive you.'

She considered this for a moment, keen to wrap up the call now. At least they were on speaking terms. However, she was taking her bookshop duties seriously and didn't feel comfortable being on the phone. 'That's good to hear. So, where are you now?'

'Just in a cafe.'

'Oh, where?'

'Uh, nowhere you know.'

She made eye contact with one of the women, and said, 'Okay, I'm looking after the shop right now, maybe speak later?'

'Yep, that'd be good.'

And for now, that was that. She would tell him about Della hotfooting it to Berlin some other time. The women bought seven cookbooks between them – 'We're kind of addicted!' they'd said, giggling – and as they were leaving, Michael and Jude arrived brandishing enormous, foil-covered trays of party food.

'Where shall we put them?' Jude asked.

'Oh, here please, on the counter.' She smiled at Michael. 'Can I look?'

'Yes, of course!' he said, laughing. 'I hope they're what you – well, what Della had in mind . . .'

Roxanne lifted a corner of foil and gasped at the array of exquisite canapés. A world apart from the unwieldy vol-au-vents her mother served at drinks parties, these were miniature beauties, a mere mouthful of perfectly golden puff pastry with some kind of creamy filling, garnished with fresh herbs.

'These are perfect,' she enthused.

'Thanks.' Michael grinned at her. 'I should run a bakery really . . .'

'You'd be excellent.' Unable to resist, she popped one into her mouth. 'Oh, these are so good . . .'

Jude disappeared, returning a few minutes later with more trays, this time bearing tiny quiches and bite-size poppy-seed-speckled sausage rolls.

'There's more to come,' Michael explained. 'Elsa's on her way.'

She looked at him, hoping she hadn't overstepped the mark by asking his daughter to pitch in with the demonstration. 'So, she's bringing all the doggie bites ingredients too?'

'It's all in hand,' he said cheerfully. 'She was thrilled you asked her, actually. You do realise she regards you as her glamorous new friend?'

Roxanne laughed and flushed. 'That's very flattering.'

'Hey, she's not wrong either.'

She laughed awkwardly, sensing herself reddening even further. *Why* was he having this effect on her? 'Thanks, Michael – but I feel far from glamorous right now.' She hesitated. 'Erm, I hate to ask, but . . .'

His eyes met hers. How kind they were, and reassuring. She was so glad he was here.

'D'you need me to do anything? Come on – ask away . . .'

'If I shut the shop now, would you mind hanging around here, just in case anyone turns up early? I'd love a few minutes to get ready.'

'Of course,' he said firmly. 'Off you go and prepare to greet your public.'

'Thank you,' she said, and with that she flipped the shop sign to closed and ran upstairs.

Up in the flat, she showered and wondered what on earth to wear for hosting a party in a bookshop. The truth was, she had never hosted a party of her own before. Her flat wasn't really conducive to it; on the few occasions when she had cranked up her music, either Henry or Emma had given their ceiling a brisk bang, presumably with a broom handle. She had never felt confident enough in her catering skills either. A flashy do like Sean's with three miles of crustaceans on ice wasn't to her taste or budget, yet the people she knew – apart from Amanda and Isabelle – weren't the types to arrive at a party and expect to be presented with nothing but a dish of Kettle Chips.

So really, she thought as she stood in Della's spare room, this was the best sort of party – because, strictly speaking, *it wasn't hers*.

Wrapped up in Della's spare dressing gown, she opened the wardrobe and assessed the possibilities hanging before her. She had no worries about appearing too flash for a Burley Bridge gathering because even back in London most of her clothes had been gleaned from second-hand shops, market stalls on holidays, and the mid-to-cheaper end of the high street. The designer pieces she owned were mainly vintage; of course, she had bought the odd new piece, when caught up in the pressurised atmosphere of the shows in London, Paris and Milan. After all, occupying the front row required a certain dress code. 'I love your skirt,' fellow fashion editors would gush, as they took their seats. 'Who's it *by*?' It was never, 'Where's it from?'

However, wearing such pieces tended to create no small degree of stress. Nothing was more likely to guarantee a coffee spillage than a brand new Stella McCartney chambray shirt.

She chose a simple pale grey dress, black tights and flat black sandals, adding the topaz necklace from her Ibiza trip with Amanda – just for luck. There was no full-length mirror in Della's flat, so she made do with the one on the hall wall. She looked relaxed and comfortable, rather than glamorous. That would have to do.

Taking a deep breath, she reminded herself the party wasn't really about her anyway. She was merely there to do Della proud, and she was determined to do her best tonight, for her sister, and for the wonderful shop that had grown and blossomed from the seed of a crazy idea.

It'll be okay, she reassured herself. She wouldn't be handling this alone. Michael, Elsa and Frank would be there to help her; Jude and Eddie too. It seemed she had made herself some new friends in the village she'd once been so keen to escape from.

She slicked on a little pinky-brown lipstick and dabbed some powder, which would have to do for make-up.

'Stanley!' she called out, and he scuttled towards her. 'Come on, little man. We're going to a party tonight, and you can be my plus-one.'

Chapter Twenty-Six

Before Roxanne had even walked into the shop, she could see through the glass door panel that the place was full already, milling with faces both familiar and unfamiliar, with every age group accounted for, from the impressively ancient to small children, whirling around.

It was just gone six o'clock.

This *never* happened in London. If a party was due to start at eight there really wasn't much point in showing up before nine, because who wanted to be that first guest, looking all stranded and lonesome, giving off the overly eager, delighted-to-be-invited vibe? At Ned's parties, some of the guests didn't turn up until it was *getting light*. Here, though, the party had been officially open for four – no, *three* – minutes and the whole world and his dog had seemingly piled in. While Roxanne was applying her lipstick upstairs, a vol-au-vent stampede had been going on. She glanced down at Stanley who was looking up at her. 'C'mon then,' she murmured, pushing open the door. 'Looks like we're already late.'

She fixed on what she hoped was a confident smile as

she greeted Nicola the hairdresser, Len from the garage, and Irene who had been so concerned about her traumatised LK Bennett pumps. Naturally, with new businesses having sprouted up in the village, she didn't know everyone – a fact that Michael seemed to pick up on instantly, as he proceeded to whisk her round for introductions.

'This new extension is wonderful,' said Loretta, who owned the greengrocer's. 'It's the most gorgeous bookshop – so welcoming and inspiring. Truly, you should be very proud . . .'

'Thank you. Of course, it's all Della's work – you do know she's had to go away, don't you?'

'Oh, we all know about Berlin,' chipped in Nicola. 'Thank goodness you're here, Roxy, saving the day!'

Her smile set at Nicola's insistence on using her childhood nickname. 'I'm just sort of manning the fort,' she said, then quickly made her excuses and, tailed by Stanley, went to greet Elsa, who was setting out her utensils and ingredients on the island unit.

And then the band, an amiable and ramshackle bunch in tatty jeans and checked flannel shirts, arrived. Roxanne didn't even know what sort of music they played. It now felt as if everything had just sort of happened, and somehow the party had all come together – but then, Della had been planning it for weeks.

A slightly awkward-looking Jude glided by with a tray of wine glasses, and she took one gratefully.

Still more guests were arriving, the chatter and laughter now filling the entire two rooms of the shop; the newly acquired space merged beautifully with the existing room, as if they had always been one.

The band started, and Roxanne was relieved to discover that they were an acoustic, country-type outfit, enhancing the atmosphere rather than dominating the proceedings.

'Hey, looks like you're coping okay,' a voice called from behind her.

She turned to see Frank standing beside her. 'So far so good,' she said, hugging him.

'So, what d'you think about Della's mercy dash?'

'She had to do it, I guess.'

He nodded and sipped his beer from the bottle. 'Shame for her – but this all looks fantastic . . .' He nodded towards a family who had just wandered in. 'Come and meet the Wilsons. They bought your old house . . .'

'Really?' Roxanne turned to the new arrivals.

'This is Lucinda and Ivan,' Frank announced, 'and their children are, um . . .'

'Marnie and Sam,' Lucinda said quickly, meeting Roxanne's gaze with a bright, clear smile.

'Lovely to meet you,' Roxanne said. 'I actually grew up in Rosemary Cottage.'

'Oh, did you?' she exclaimed. 'We love it, don't we, Ivan?'

A red-headed man in a crumpled white T-shirt and navy corduroys turned and smiled. 'Yes, it's wonderful. Brilliant garden for the kids, and the house itself – well, you know it. So characterful and unique.'

'It is, yes,' Roxanne replied. 'I'm really glad you're happy there.'

Then she was called away by Michael to alert her that Elsa wanted to run through the proceedings for the doggie bites workshop.

As she made her way through the crowds, the singer from the band – a man who was easily well into his late sixties – caught her eye and winked suggestively.

Roxanne laughed and quickly went to Elsa.

'How d'you want to do this?' she asked.

'I was thinking I'll make up a batch of mixture,' Elsa explained, 'and get the kids to help with stirring, rolling and cutting out, and then we'll bake them. Does that sound okay?'

'That sounds perfect.' Roxanne wanted to hug her but held back. She wasn't with her huggy magazine crowd now.

'The oven's on, heating up,' she added.

'Oh – I didn't even think of that!'

Elsa beamed at her. 'It's fine. Stop panicking. They only take twenty minutes to cook so we should be fine – the children can take them home with them. And I've brought a batch I made earlier for the kids to decorate, because they won't be able to ice their own biscuits until they've cooled down.'

Roxanne laughed in amazement. 'I can't believe how brilliant you are, Elsa. You really think of everything. How d'you know how to do all this?'

Elsa pulled a face and laughed. 'I think you're forgetting something. I do work in a bakery, you know.'

The band finished a song to enthusiastic applause, and Roxanne made a brief announcement to thank them, and to introduce Elsa. 'There's been a slight change of plan,' she explained to the assembled crowd. 'I think everyone knows that Della, who owns this wonderful shop, has had to dash off to Germany on a sort of family emergency. So, as I lack my sister's flair with a seventies cocktail shaker' – there was a ripple of laughter – 'we have changed our demo today from cocktails to making the most delightful doggie treats – and here, to show us exactly how to do that, is the brilliant Elsa from the Bakery on Rosemary Lane.'

There was more applause, and all the children gathered

around as Elsa started to explain what to do. As promised, Roxanne hovered nearby, handing Elsa utensils, greasing a tray for baking, ready to assist when needed. In fact, she wasn't needed, which gave her an opportunity to take in what was actually happening, for the first time tonight.

She gazed around the new-and-improved shop, with its balloons and streamers and fairy lights, a grotto of treats filled with Della's friends, neighbours and loyal customers. The swell of support for her sister's venture was quite moving, and she experienced a sharp pang of regret that Della wasn't here to see it.

Roxanne skimmed the room, filled with so many faces she remembered from her childhood, much older now, obviously, but still comfortingly familiar. Then she saw another face in amongst the crowd, smiling at her but holding back, as if trying to be inconspicuous. It wasn't a face from her life here – but from London, from her life now. Sean was standing right there, clutching a glass of red wine and a plate of canapés, in the middle of her sister's shop.

At first, a crazy part of her brain told her it *couldn't* be him; it was just someone who looked very like him, and her mind was playing some kind of trick, just to stress her out. But it was Sean, and he'd raised his hand in greeting. Her heart seemed to lurch as she smiled stiffly. Elsa's workshop was still in progress, and she didn't want to interrupt the proceedings by dashing to his side. Her gaze skimmed the room, then back to Sean. Even in the short time she'd been here she had almost forgotten how strikingly handsome he was; tall and slim and lightly tanned, with that flirtatious smile, his dark brown hair curling over his neck. But she wished he'd called to tell her he was coming.

Why hadn't he warned her?

Elsa's demonstration ended, and as the shop filled with applause, Roxanne made her way through the crowds to greet him.

'Hey, baby!' He kissed her lightly on the lips.

'Darling . . .' She was stuck for words for a moment. 'What are you doing here?'

He pulled a mock-confused face. 'Er, maybe I've come to see you? Could that be it, d'you think?'

She laughed and shook her head. The sheer audacity of the man. Why couldn't he just do things in a normal, predictable way?

'When you called me this afternoon I was halfway here,' he added.

'You were driving?'

'No, I'd stopped at a service station for a coffee. That was the cafe I meant – a Moto service station on the M1.'

'But why didn't you just say?'

'I wanted to surprise you, baby!' He flung an arm around her shoulders and gazed around in wonderment. 'Look at this amazing shop – this party. It's so much more, I don't know . . . *professional* than I'd expected. All that wonderful food . . .'

'Yes, Michael from the local bakery made everything—'

'Honestly,' he cut in, 'I had no idea this place was so impressive. I'd imagined a dingy little shop with a few mouldering second-hand books. So, where's Della?'

Roxanne grimaced. 'She's gone to Berlin to rescue Sophie . . .'

'Sophie?' He frowned.

'Her *daughter*, remember?'

'Oh, yes, of course!'

'She was travelling around Europe and split up with her boyfriend, then her money and passport were stolen . . .'

284

'Della just upped and left on the day of her party?'

'Yesterday actually – but it's fine. It's all gone amazingly well so far . . .'

'That's good. Clever you.' He looked around the room. 'So, um, are you going to introduce me to your new friends?'

Roxanne laughed awkwardly and sensed herself flushing. Michael was standing nearby. Although she knew she was being ridiculous, and there was no reason whatsoever that they shouldn't meet, that moment with the rainbow still shimmered in her mind. She cleared her throat and she found herself introducing him first to Frank and Eddie, then Nicola, Irene and a whole bunch of other villagers and regular customers, until she caught Michael's quizzical glance and took Sean over to meet him.

'Erm Michael – this is Sean. He's just come up from London . . .'

'Hi, good to meet you.' Michael shot out an arm and shook Sean's hand.

'Good to meet you too. Decided to drive up and surprise her.' Sean chortled. 'Maybe that wasn't the best idea, huh, darling?' He turned to Roxanne. 'I have to say, you didn't exactly look delighted to see me . . .'

'It was just a bit of a shock,' she said, reddening again. 'Um, Michael owns the village bakery. He's been a huge help with the party . . .'

'Oh, we just put together a few nibbles,' Michael said.

'*Nibbles*.' Sean smiled. 'How quaint.'

'Michael's daughter did the demo,' Roxanne added, prickling with awkwardness for the first time since the party had started. Why had he said 'nibbles' in that faintly patronising way when he reckoned he'd have been happy with Pringles at his own do?

285

'That was sweet of her,' Sean said vaguely. After a little more small talk, during which Roxanne was conscious of jamming her back teeth together, Michael excused himself to track down Jude, and Roxanne continued her tour of the shop with Sean. She was aware of a flurry of interest around this rather striking new arrival, who clearly wasn't from around here. If Roxanne had felt a little like a minor celebrity that night in the Red Lion, then she imagined Sean must be experiencing this tenfold right now.

'You're a photographer?' Len exclaimed, clutching a glass of white wine. 'What kind of stuff d'you do?'

Sean told him, affecting the slightly humble voice he used when encountering non-media people, but stressing the 'advertising and editorial mainly' angle, presumably so as to discourage Len from asking him to photograph his cat.

'Met anyone famous?' Len wanted to know.

'No, not really.' That was a lie – countless celebs had posed in Sean's studio – but, understandably perhaps, he didn't want to go into that right now. Roxanne had heard him being quizzed before. Give someone a smidgeon of celebrity gossip and it opens the floodgates for a whole tidal wave of probing questions.

The band started playing again, and during a break between songs Roxanne enlisted Elsa to help her to announce the raffle winners. Len scooped the hamper, and when Frank won a bottle of champagne he insisted on opening it and divvying it up to share out.

It was almost 10 p.m. when the party finally started to wind down. Roxanne did the rounds, saying her goodbyes, keeping a lookout for Michael so she could make a point of thanking him.

'I think Dad must have gone home,' Elsa said with a shrug. 'D'you need me to stay and help clear up?'

286

'No, not at all,' Roxanne said quickly. 'Thanks, but Sean can help me with that.' She tried to shake off a snag of disappointment that Michael had snuck off without saying goodbye. Had she upset him in some way, or had he felt awkward too, when she had introduced him to Sean? She hoped he realised how much she appreciated his help.

And so the final guests drifted out into the night, leaving a curious stillness behind them.

'Well, that seemed like a success,' Sean remarked as they started to gather up glasses and plates.

Roxanne nodded. 'Della would have been pleased. I've taken loads of photos with my phone – and Elsa has too . . .' She stopped, conscious of him studying her as she collected the empty wine bottles.

'Is *was* okay for me to come up, wasn't it?' he asked hesitantly.

'Yes, of course it was,' she exclaimed.

'It's just, you did seem a bit taken aback . . .'

She smiled as he wound an arm around her waist. 'No, honestly – but it's great, darling. I'm just a bit done in, that's all. There's been a lot going on . . .'

'It all happens in the country,' he teased, and Roxanne laughed.

'You'd be surprised – and it's been quite a night.'

He nodded and kissed her forehead. 'Well, you were brilliant, flitting about the place, charming everyone.'

Roxanne smiled. 'I did my best.'

'I'm proud of you,' he added.

'Thanks,' she said, pleasantly surprised by the compliment as she turned her attentions back to tidying the shop. Saturdays were generally the busiest day of the week, and it needed to be spick and span for the morning – but how would Sean amuse himself while she was manning the place? She caught herself fretting that he'd be bored here, just as Della had tried to foist belly dancing classes upon her. Of *course* he'd be fine. She was just worrying too much as, despite the party going brilliantly, everything felt a little out of kilter now. She could only put it down to two different compartments of her life being slammed together, and everything muddling up.

It was gone eleven by the time Elsa arrived back at the bakery. While she was delighted at how well her demonstration had gone, her dad seemed subdued when she found him stretched out on the sofa, watching TV, remote in hand, and she couldn't understand why. Oh, there were plenty of possible reasons – she knew he'd found it difficult to socialise since her mum had left – but why tonight particularly? The party had been wonderful, and Roxanne had obviously appreciated him being there.

'I'll give Bob his night walk,' he said when she came in, getting up from the sofa and fixing the red leather lead onto their dog's collar.

'Okay, Dad. I'm just going to wrap Mitzie's birthday present for her party tomorrow.'

Michael nodded. 'See you in a few minutes. Put the kettle on, would you, love?'

'Sure.' Alone now – Jude had retreated to his room – Elsa filled the kettle and clicked it on, then wandered through to her father's bedroom in search of Sellotape. She was always taking things from his room – pens, phone chargers, the occasional book – and she knew it annoyed him. However, she only wanted to wrap her best friend's gift, and she'd put it back as soon as she'd finished.

She opened his desk drawer and spotted a roll of tape.

As she made her way out of the room, her foot caught the waste-paper basket and it toppled over. Elsa picked it up and dropped the discarded newspapers back into it, and reached for a crumpled sheet of blue notepaper that was lying on the floor.

Frowning, she stopped and studied it. It was covered with her dad's funny old-fashioned handwriting. Curious now, she smoothed it out on his desk, realising it was a letter he'd written – to Roxanne.

Why was he writing to her? Ridiculously, she panicked that it was something about her. Had the two of them been discussing her aversion to school, or something? Elsa suspected she was being irrational, but since her mother had walked out she had been prone to bouts of anxiety that kept her awake at night with a racing heart and too many convoluted thoughts tumbling through her head.

Elsa knew she shouldn't read it. She'd go mad if she ever discovered that her dad had read anything private of hers – not that he ever would – yet she simply couldn't help herself. It was as if she had lost all control of her eyes. He'd obviously found it difficult to write; there were a couple of crossings out, and her heart twisted for him. Her funny old dad, always trying to do things properly; who even bothered to write letters anymore? But he was like that: sort of old-school. His mobile was a tragic brick phone and he'd no more have a Facebook page than a tattoo. He always said he had no time in his life for social media, and she conceded that he had a point. Her father worked harder than anyone else she knew.

She perched on the chair at his desk and read the letter quickly. So he was apologising for being a bit of a grump after the sourdough workshop and inviting her to lunch. It was a sweet letter, a little awkward, perhaps – a bit like him really. It just made him sound endearing. Funny, she thought, smiling now, how you can sense shyness coming off a page.

Anyway, Roxanne had a boyfriend – that tall, confident man from London who had showed up tonight – so this suggested lunch date was obviously just meant to be a friendship thing.

She hesitated, wondering if she should actually be dabbling in her dad's life at all. It had been awful at first, when the whole thing about her mum had come out – although in a weird way, it had been a relief too, because Elsa had known about it before anyone else had. She had been over at Mitzie's one night – she lived in Larksop, a village about five miles away – and Mitzie's mum had driven Elsa home. It was just after 10 p.m. when she had pulled up, let Elsa out of her car and drove away.

Elsa had stood in shock on the pavement outside the shop that would soon be a bakery. At first, she wondered if she had made a mistake and it was the wrong shop. But no – it was definitely where she lived. Through the open interior door that led to the back room, she could see her mum, although she couldn't quite believe what she was doing. In the room that would soon be the bakery kitchen, she was kissing a man.

At first, Elsa couldn't figure out who he was, but she knew he wasn't her dad. For one thing, this man was much younger. And for *another* thing, her father was hundreds of miles away, staying at his mum and dad's.

Her mum and this man were locked in an embrace in front of the new stainless-steel oven. When they pulled apart, Elsa realised he was that builder – the one who was doing all the work in the shop, and always flirting with her mum in the most awful, cringeworthy way. Elsa felt sick. She almost vomited up Mitzie's mum's lasagne right there on the pavement. There was only one way up to the flat, and that was through the shop – so she made a point of waggling the door handle and taking her time to step into the shop, giving them a chance to separate and make out they were just hanging out and chatting.

'Hey, Else,' her mum called through from the back, 'have a good time at Mitzie's?'

'Yeah, great, thanks.' She was already halfway up the stairs.

'I'll be up soon, darling,' she trilled. 'We're just discussing tiles . . .'

Oh, was *that* what you called it? Her mum must have thought she was an idiot. People often did, just because she struggled with maths and English at school – not the reading part but the interpreting of texts. It baffled her. What she loved was drawing and taking photos. Elsa's dad – and now Roxanne, this fascinating woman who had just arrived out of nowhere and become her friend – were the only people who had ever encouraged her to believe that she might be a real photographer one day.

For weeks after seeing her mum kissing that man, Elsa had kept the secret close to her heart. Telling Mitzie would have meant going over and over it, so she decided not to say a word. She hadn't even told Jude; she knew he'd have freaked out and gone straight to their dad and all hell would have broken loose. Although it had been a proper snog – there was no mistaking that – as time went on she worried that she had somehow misinterpreted it, and they'd just been messing around. Perhaps they'd been drunk, or she'd somehow imagined it? She tried, unsuccessfully, to force herself not to think about it at all.

Now Elsa stood for a moment, remembering how devastated her dad had been when it had all come out about that awful man. She had been distraught, too – but there had also been a certain amount of relief, as now the secret was out.

She dropped her gaze to the letter. Why had he thrown it away? she wondered. Perhaps he'd lost his nerve or worried that Roxanne wouldn't want to come over for lunch. However, Elsa was sure she would. They seemed to get along well, and it was good to see him looking happier.

She heard movement downstairs, and the sound of the front door being locked. Her dad was talking to Bob. 'C'mon, old fella. Good boy . . .' Footsteps were approaching now, her father's heavy ones, accompanied by the scuffle of Bob's paws on the stone stairs. Elsa's heart was racing as she stuffed the letter into the back pocket of her jeans.

Chapter Twenty-Seven

Before Roxanne was even fully awake, she was aware of soft, slow breathing and the warmth of Sean lying beside her. For a moment, she assumed they were in her bed in London, which suggested that the bookshop, the party and country-style band had just been one happy, retro-themed dream. But no – Sean was here, in Burley Bridge. He had attended a party at her sister's bookshop where sausage rolls and vol-au-vents had been served. A party with a raffle – and a doggie bites demonstration. The very idea made her smile.

Now he was awake too, blinking in the pale morning light and kissing her gently on the cheek. 'What time is it?' he murmured.

She glanced at the small clock on the bedside table. 'Only seven-thirty. No need to get up just yet. I'll have to work in the shop today, I'm afraid, but we don't open until nine-thirty.'

'Oh, I'm wide awake,' Sean announced, stretching now, then rolling straight out of bed.

'Must be the country air,' she teased. 'You'll be suggesting we go on a hike next.'

He smirked. 'That might be bit extreme, darling. I was thinking more a wander through to the kitchen. I assume there's decent coffee here?'

'Of course there is,' she scoffed. 'Believe it or not, they're not limited to Nescafe up here. I mean, there's the real stuff. Della even has a cafetiére.'

'Whoo!' He laughed.

How bizarre, she mused, to see her boyfriend wandering nakedly around her sister's spare room, now retrieving his black stretchy boxers from the chair and pulling them on. He was in particularly good shape at the moment, she noticed. His stomach was taut, his bottom nicely shaped and, actually, pretty pert for fifty – or for any age, in fact. A little light running, and a couple of gym sessions every week, seemed to be keeping everything in check.

She watched him as he pottered around bare-footed, picking up his jeans and a T-shirt from his bag. He had terribly attractive feet, she reflected. Terribly attractive everything, really: those impish green eyes still did things to her, and he only had to smile for her to melt a little.

He went to stand at the window, with his back to her. At first she thought he was admiring the view – Della's guest room looked out onto the fields at the back – but then she realised he was poking at his phone.

'Come back to bed,' she urged him.

He turned to her and grimaced. 'Look, Rox—'

'Sorry I'm having to work today,' she added. 'I'll see if Faye can do a shift, but I doubt it at such short notice. But never mind. You can hang out with me in the shop . . .'

'Erm, I don't think . . .'

'And we can have dinner tonight at the Red Lion. Does that sound good to you?'

He was pulling on his jeans now, doing up his favourite

worn brown leather belt, and then tugging on the T-shirt. 'It does, darling. It really does.' He blinked at her.

'It's much better than you might think,' she added. 'I mean, it used to be all greasy chicken in a basket but now they have this new chef, and the cod and chips, oh my God . . .' She pulled an ecstatic face, which melted away rapidly when she noticed the oddly strained look on Sean's face. 'You like that kind of place, don't you?' she added. 'Nice, simple, un-mucked-around food. No slates,' she added, with a feeble laugh.

Sean came over and sat heavily on the edge of the bed beside her, causing it to dip a little. 'Sweetheart, it's not about the pub or the food. It's – oh, God, I'm so sorry, darling. I was hoping we could at least have today together, and I'd head back tomorrow night. But I'm going to have to set off now . . .'

'Now?' she gasped, staring at him. 'What d'you mean?'

He pursed his lips in exasperation and shook his head. 'Louie's been texting me.'

Roxanne frowned. 'What about, at this time on a Saturday morning?'

'Just a really complicated shoot tomorrow,' Sean muttered, up on his feet again now, and pacing back and forth. 'Seems like I can't trust him to put it together . . .'

'Put what together? I mean, what needs to be done that can't be handled here, with a few calls?' She exhaled loudly. 'And anyway, you don't usually shoot on Sunday . . .'

'Yes, I do.' He turned and stared at her.

'Well, not very often . . .'

'Honey,' he said, adopting a patronising tone now, 'I'm freelance. It's an occupational hazard, having to work weekends. I hadn't planned to – Christ, if I'd known I wouldn't have driven all this way just for one night . . .'

295

'Oh, wouldn't you?' she said witheringly.

Sean's face crumpled. 'Please don't be like that.'

'Sorry,' she murmured. 'I'm just a bit disappointed – but it's fine. Of course it is. And I'm really glad you came.'

His expression softened, and he kissed her, then gathered together his few possessions and strolled through to Della's kitchen while Roxanne showered and dressed. By the time she joined him, he had poured two mugs of coffee.

'You will have something to eat before you go, won't you?' she asked, flinging open the cupboard, and listing the cereals – 'Rice Krispies, Shredded Wheat, Alpen' – as if he were nine.

'Don't worry, babe. I'll pick up something at a service station on the way home.' Catching the look on her face, he added, 'I'm really bloody annoyed about this. Maybe I should find myself an assistant who can just get on with things rather than needing to be babied?'

'You're not thinking of getting rid of Louie, are you?' She frowned. 'He worships the ground you walk on.'

Sean chuckled wryly. 'Maybe he should concentrate more on using his initiative. Anyway,' he added, shrugging, 'I'll see you soon, darling, I promise, and I'll stay for longer next time.'

'Great,' she murmured.

He glanced at his watch. 'Okay, love, I'm going to head off now . . .' He hugged her tightly, protesting that she didn't need to come outside to see him off.

'I'm coming,' she insisted, clipping on Stanley's lead.

Minutes later, she and the little terrier watched as, without having even showered or drunk his coffee, Sean climbed into his slightly mud-dappled black BMW and drove away.

*

In the shop that day, despite a steady flow of customers, Roxanne couldn't shake the feeling of flatness that seemed to have settled over her.

'Yes, it was a brilliant night,' she said for the umpteenth time as another villager complimented her on the party. 'Oh, yes, I was thrilled by how many people turned up. It's a shame Della had to miss it . . .' She felt rather phoney, claiming any credit whatsoever as all she'd had to do was be there, basically, and enlist Elsa's help with the doggie bites – a masterstroke of delegation.

Then Della herself was on the phone, thanking her again. 'I really owe you for this,' she said.

'You don't owe me anything,' Roxanne told her.

'Well, I'm just so glad you were there. Oh, Frank called – told me Sean showed up, out of the blue!'

'Yeah – that was a bit of a shocker. He's already gone back to London – had some shoot to set up. It was hardly worth him coming . . .'

'He was obviously missing you madly,' Della said with a chuckle.

'Hmm. I'm not sure, actually – but it was lovely to see him. So, how's everything with you and Soph?'

'Oh, great – it's amazing here. So vast! She's going mad for all the vintage stores and flea markets. It's lovely, actually, having some time together. A kind of bonus I hadn't expected.' She paused. 'So, what're you up to tonight?'

'Um, I'm just about to shut up the shop. I think I'll just chill out, watch some TV . . .'

'I should have asked Frank to meet you for a drink,' Della remarked.

Roxanne laughed. Her voice was a little hoarse after all the chatting last night, and she coughed to clear her throat. 'Honestly – I have no inclination at all to go out tonight.'

'Well, I guess it's a bit boring with only the Red Lion on offer . . .'

'Dell,' she said firmly, 'please don't think that. I'm really enjoying being here, honestly.'

'Oh, but I just thought, with it being Saturday night—'

'I hardly ever go out on Saturday nights,' Roxanne cut in, truthfully. 'Please don't worry about me at all. Me and Stanley have planned a cosy night in.'

By the time they finished the call Roxanne had managed to persuade Dell that she was perfectly happy in her own company. She was used to it, after all.

Roxanne locked up the shop and headed upstairs to the flat, grateful, in fact, for some time to herself. Sean had texted to say he'd arrived home, and she had sent a brief reply, but she felt no real urge to speak to him now. All too often these days, their phone conversations ended in tetchiness.

She was prowling around in the kitchen, plundering Della's cupboards in order to assemble herself a makeshift supper, when her phone bleeped with a text.

It was from Della, and had a photo attached – her and Sophie in a fabulously glamorous revolving restaurant in Berlin, the city visible through the huge window behind them, a haze of sparkling lights against an inky sky. The message read: *Us last night, love you xx*. Roxanne smiled. In some ways, although the timing had been rather off, it was probably doing Della the world of good to spend time away with her daughter. After all, Frank was often around these days, and although Sophie approved of him wholeheartedly, Roxanne was sure she would appreciate some time with her mum alone. She studied the photo, the two of them all bright, wide smiles, the restaurant decor fabulously futuristic in a 1960s sort of way, aware of a small stab of . . . what exactly? Envy? They just looked so happy together.

Roxanne pulled her hair up into a messy bun, put on a pot of linguine to simmer, and checked her emails from the past couple of days. There was nothing of note: just reams and reams of junk mail and impersonal press releases, invites to product launches and fashion-related events, most of which should have gone to her work email but often seemed to wing their way to her personal account too. No, she wasn't interested in attending a lunch to celebrate the launch of un-snaggable fishnet tights or a new kind of pair of jeans that somehow managed to shrink your bottom. She couldn't care less about a brand of frankly hideous diamanté-encrusted T-shirts or 3-D stickers for nails, or exercise wear in Barbie pink that claimed to boost the number of calories burned. It was all tosh, a load of fake promises playing on women's insecurities. At the very least, it was stuff nobody needed. Although Roxanne loved fashion, she was patently aware that the world would not cease to turn if no new collections were created ever again, and everyone just had to make do with what they had. They could mend things, the way her mother used to, granted rather badly – cursing as the needle stabbed at her finger. Of course, if there was no new fashion, there would be no fashion director's post because her magazine wouldn't exist. But would that be so terrible?

Roxanne continued to scroll through her emails, flagging up a couple she would need to reply to, and quickly reading another brief, praising missive from Marsha, thanking her for her latest blog post. Her editor was being far more responsive than she had expected, considering when they were in the office together, she had barely acknowledged Roxanne's existence unless they were having an actual meeting.

She closed her laptop, devoured her linguine and watched a little TV. Just before 10 p.m., she went to draw Della's living room curtains. As she looked down to the street, she spotted a young woman and a dog striding along towards the bookshop. A moment later and she could see it was Elsa with Bob. Perhaps Michael had asked her to do his last walk of the day. Odd, she thought: it struck her that he was the kind of dad who'd prefer to do that himself, rather than sending his daughter out late at night. But then, this was Burley Bridge, not London. It was hardly riddled with crime.

Now Elsa had stopped, presumably to look into the bookshop window. But no – she seemed to be extracting something from her jeans pocket, which she quickly posted through the letter box before turning and marching back home.

How odd, Roxanne thought. Unable to quell her curiosity, she hurried down to the shop to retrieve it. It was a slightly crumpled letter, not from Elsa herself, but her father. Elsa, she realised as she came back upstairs, had just been the delivery girl.

Dear Roxanne, she read, *I think I owe you an apology for tonight . . .*

She stepped back into the flat and frowned. Did he write this last night, and was referring to the way he'd snuck out of the party without saying goodbye? There was no need to apologise for that. She read on: *. . . I was sort of embarrassed when so few people turned up for my sourdough thing tonight . . .* Ah, he was talking about Wednesday evening. That was strange too. Why was it

300

only delivered tonight? . . . *You were very kind and seemed so engaged and interested. I hope it was genuine, that you did enjoy yourself (I'm sure it's not your usual sort of evening entertainment!).*

Roxanne smiled at his rather formal, hesitant tone.

If you didn't, then you played the part extremely well . . . So, and I hope this isn't presumptuous of me, I was wondering if you might like to come over for lunch one day, just so I can sort of apologise for being so offish before you left tonight, and to say thank you?

She re-read his words, flattered to be asked, yet somewhat confused.

Seeing that he had included his mobile number, she picked up her phone and texted him:

Hi Michael, Roxanne here. Thanks so much for your lovely note. You have nothing whatsoever to apologise for! In fact, it's me who should be treating you to lunch after your help at the party. Your food was lovely and it really helped knowing you were there. But yes, if you'd still like lunch together I'd be delighted. How about tomorrow seeing as it's both of our days off? Thanks again, Roxanne

With that, she pressed send. By the time she had taken Stanley out for his night walk and returned to the flat, Michael's reply had appeared.

Roxanne – Lovely to hear from you and you're very welcome about last night. Sorry to dash off the way I did (here I am, apologising again!). Must have seemed a bit rude, I realise now. But you looked busy and happy and I didn't want to interrupt. Yes, tomorrow is good for me. Shall we say one o'clock? If the weather's decent we could eat in my terribly neglected garden! Looking forward very much, Michael.

Chapter Twenty-Eight

On Sunday, late morning, Roxanne found herself taking rather more care than was perhaps strictly necessary for a lunch date.

No, not a date – it was just lunch, to say sorry. Or thank you. She was no longer quite sure why Michael had asked her, other than to be kind and sweet – yes, that was it, she assured herself as she blow-dried her hair. He was just being neighbourly. This was the kind of thing people did around here. It was nothing whatsoever to do with the fact that Della had made a rather clumsy attempt to set them up, on her first night back in the village, or that moment between them, which she had now decided she'd imagined, up on the hill. Anyway, Michael knew she had a boyfriend, and now he'd even met him – ouch, she thought to herself, *that* had been rather uncomfortable – so there was not the slightest hint that this was anything but a friendly invitation.

Roxanne took in her reflection at the dressing table mirror in her bedroom here, noticing now that her hair seemed to have acquired a pronounced shine and bounce that had been lacking recently. Was it all this wholesome country air, or the fact that she hadn't bothered with a single hair product – bar shampoo and conditioner – since she'd left London? Some mornings she hadn't even blow-dried it. She had just rubbed it briskly with a towel, then headed off into the hills with Stanley without a second thought. After sporting a plastic rain hood and waterproof trousers, venturing out with her hair a damp tangle hardly seemed worth fretting about. She realised now, as she pulled on a pretty blue and white floral-print cotton dress, that so much of her supposedly spare time back home was taken up with appearance-related matters.

Really, compared to many of her fellow fashion direc-tors on other magazines, Roxanne had always considered herself to be pretty low-maintenance. However, she real-ised now that a ridiculous number of her lunch breaks seemed to be swallowed up by appointments for mani-cures, pedicures and various waxings – not to mention the occasional electrolysis treatment to zap the odd hair that sprouted out of her chin. In the fashion world, allowing a facial hair to waft about unfettered would be considered as slovenly as giving up on washing, or the brushing of teeth.

She applied light make-up, pulled on a lilac lambswool cardigan and a pair of blue canvas lace-ups. She was satisfied that she looked smart enough, but not too overly done. It was a fine balance. She didn't want to alarm the man by turning up too glam.

Roxanne glanced out of the kitchen window and noted that she sky was a cloudless blue, the sun was shining, and the day seemed filled with promise. Della would be back from Berlin tonight, and Roxanne could happily report that all had gone well in her absence. She pictured herself telling Della about her lunch with Michael, her sister raising a brow and grinning, and Roxanne stressing that they were just friends. She *wanted* to be friends, very much, and hoped they would stay in touch once she had returned to London. Naturally, she would always make a point of seeing him whenever she visited Della from now on.

Roxanne picked up her bag and gave her face one last check in the mirror. She looked younger, somehow. Less lined, less weary of life. Well, that was good, she decided with a smile, stepping towards the door now. That's precisely what was required on the day she was having lunch with an admittedly attractive and personable man.

Stanley had already been walked, and she was just saying goodbye to him – yes, she had started talking to him, like a housemate – when her mobile rang.

Isabelle's name was displayed. Roxanne's heart jolted. 'Hi, Isabelle. How are things?'

'Roxanne, I'm so sorry to call. I didn't know if . . . I mean I wasn't sure if I should, but I thought, surely you wouldn't mind—'

'Please, tell me what's happened?'

'Oh, it's okay. Everything's fine now. It really is.' The tremor in her voice made it clear that it wasn't. 'The police have been,' she charged on. 'Gave me a right old lecture, of course – just like that fireman did with you. Who do they think they are, these youngsters in uniforms, being so patronising to people like us? They've barely lived!'

'Isabelle, what's *happened*?'

'It was my fault,' she continued. 'I fully accept that. What an idiot I am, Roxanne. A stupid old woman . . .'

'You are *not* stupid . . .'

304

'Can't believe I did it. I mustn't have clicked the main front door shut behind me . . .'

A chill ran through her as her mind jumped to a conclusion as to why Isabelle was calling her. 'Have I been burgled?'

'I'm sorry, I should've—'

'Please,' Roxanne cut in, 'if someone's broken into my place, then it's not the end of the world. I mean, yes, it's horrible to think someone's been there – but really, there's very little to take . . .' It struck her how little emotion she felt about her own home.

'Oh, it's not *your* flat,' Isabelle exclaimed. 'Yours is fine. It's mine. They came in and kicked the door in. Just one shove was all it'd have taken, the policeman said. It was that flimsy . . .'

'Isabelle, that's terrible! Are you okay? Have they taken anything?'

'Not much – not really – so I don't know why I'm making such a fuss. They've just . . .' Her voice cracked. 'They've just made a terrible mess, Roxanne. I mean, broken so many things of mine . . .' She was crying now, properly crying, making her words difficult to decipher. In the twelve years she had known her, Roxanne had never seen her shed so much as a single tear.

'Oh, Isabelle. What sort of things?' Roxanne asked, enraged by the thought that anyone could do something like this to an old woman living alone.

'Just my ornaments, pictures, vases, nothing valuable. None of it is. It's just a load of junk really. And my records . . .'

'They broke your records?' she gasped.

'They opened my living room window and threw them out into the street, like frisbees – can you believe it?

305

They're still lying out there all over the place. That's what makes the police think they were kids, teenagers – just people on drugs or drunk, doing it for the hell of it . . .'

She was crying so much now, Roxanne could barely understand her at all. 'Is there anyone who can be with you right now?' she ventured.

'Don't like to bother people . . .'

'But you *need* someone with you. Things like this are really traumatic. It's a violation, Isabelle – it's not about having things broken or stolen. It's about not feeling safe in your own home . . .' She hesitated, wondering whether to suggest what had popped into her mind. 'What about your son? I'm sorry, I don't know anything about your situation. But if you need someone with you—'

'*He* won't be with me,' she blurted out, sounding almost angry now. 'I can't call him. He's made sure I don't even know where he is . . .'

Roxanne blinked, and the silence stretched between them. She glanced down at Stanley who seemed to have interpreted her putting on shoes and readying herself for leaving the flat as an indication that he was coming too.

Of course, she could take him to Michael's with her – she was certain he wouldn't mind, as the two dogs got along fine. Only she wasn't going for lunch now. She couldn't possibly go. 'I'm coming home,' she announced. 'I'll just have to make a few calls to sort out things here . . .'

'No, please, that's not why I called—'

'It's fine, Isabelle. I'll need to find someone to walk Stanley later, that's all. Della's back tonight.'

'But I just wanted someone to talk to! You *can't* come back.'

'Well, I can't stay here,' Roxanne said firmly, 'so please

don't worry. Just sit tight and try to be calm, and I'll be with you as soon as I can.'

It might have surprised Roxanne to know this, but the fact that Michael owned a bakery didn't mean that he was an excellent cook. Oh, he could bake all right, of course. He'd always been a reasonably competent bread maker but now he'd had to up his game dramatically, and was confident that pretty much any kind of loaf, cake or biscuit he made would turn out all right. Okay – *better* than all right. He was proud of everything he offered in the bakery now. However, making lunch today was seriously challenging him. He had wanted to make something light and summery – it was a beautiful day, and he planned for them to eat in the garden at the back of the shop. Perhaps he should bake something? He was aware that some people feared pastry but it was a sort of security blanket for him. Such fuss was made about having cold hands and rubbing in the fat with a light hand, but it was really very simple. And then, once you had your pastry right, your finished dish was pretty much guaranteed to be delicious. He decided on a light and summery roast vegetable tart.

Michael kept his cookbooks rather messily stacked on a shelf in the kitchen in the flat. It had been Suzy who had been into collecting them – hence her demanding he stopped the car when they drove through Burley Bridge that first time. 'Stop!' she'd yelled, as if he could screech to a halt with another car right behind him. He'd pulled over by the Red Lion and they had walked back to the shop.

If that hadn't happened, Suzy wouldn't have fallen in love with Della's bookshop, and emerged laden with books about yeast cookery, biscuits and party cakes. She would never have launched herself into a baking project which kicked off with her making speciality brownies to order for her friends, and culminated in the purchase of the old hardware shop with its foul-smelling drain and rising damp, which all had to be sorted at exorbitant cost. And if *that* hadn't happened, she wouldn't have hired that home wrecker Rory-sodding-King to create the perfect professional kitchen, ensuring she was on hand at all times to supervise operations.

'The thing with tradesmen,' she'd said, 'is that you have to keep a close eye otherwise there's no quality control.' How cunning to appoint herself as project manager, specifically to 'keep an eye' on more than the work-in-progress, as it later transpired. Meanwhile, she had encouraged Michael to take on as much supply teaching work as he could handle, 'to keep the cash rolling in until we're up and running'. He hadn't imagined the 'running' part would entail Suzy leaving not just him, but Elsa and Jude (and Bob! What about Bob, whom she had insisted they adopt when she had seen him on a rescue site's Facebook page?) in order to set up home in a small rented cottage in Ormskirk.

When Suzy had announced that she and Rory were in love, Michael had had no idea, not the slightest suspicion. And the thing that bothered him most was the fact that they had used their bed.

Understandably, most of their mutual friends had leapt to his aid with so many visits and hugs, great carloads of wine and casseroles and Tupperware boxes of chilli and curry and God knows what else. However, Michael didn't want to be consoled or fussed over; he knew it made him seem ungrateful, but he couldn't help it. Nor did he want a freezer stuffed with what he could only think of as 'pity food'. For weeks, he could barely stomach a thing – he only made a half-hearted effort to at least partly consume a meal in order to put on a 'we're-coping' front for Jude and Elsa.

Six months on, he was over her now – truly, not in a brave-and-stoical sort of way. Yes, he still felt angry and down sometimes, but then, didn't everyone? Recently, he'd enjoyed a myriad of compliments about his breads, and that had helped to restore his self-esteem, reassuring him that he was doing something well, for his family. He felt proud of what they'd achieved here and realised, almost as an aside, that, whilst being left for someone else was no picnic, it *was* something you might be able to recover from. He certainly had.

While Michael wasn't one to blow his own trumpet, he was proving himself to be more capable than he could have imagined at running his family alone. The business was ticking along, he had learned to enjoy the whole process of baking, of making something so simple and delicious with little more than flour and yeast, or his famous bubbling sourdough starter – the one he should 'name'.

The very fact that he had invited Roxanne for lunch – albeit just as a friendly thing, certainly not as a date – felt like yet another extremely positive and, admittedly, rather *thrilling* step. Okay, so he'd chickened out and hadn't planned to deliver the note; it was Elsa who had taken matters into her own hands. The audacity! he thought now, smiling. But of course he forgave her because now he had lunch with Roxanne to look forward to, entirely thanks to his daughter's meddling ways.

When he knocked his mobile phone off the worktop

and its screen smashed on the hard slate floor, he realised that perhaps he was far more nervous than he was prepared to admit to himself. But no matter. Phones could be replaced – it was ancient anyway, Elsa was always making fun of it – and in just a couple of hours' time, Roxanne would be here. He stuffed his dead phone into a drawer and swept up the tiny shards of glass from its cracked screen. Checking his watch, he called out goodbye to Jude and Elsa who, in an extremely rare gesture, were taking the bus into Heathfield together to see a movie.

And now he turned his attentions to his tart as he lifted it from the oven. It looked perfect, he decided: its filling soft and wobbly, its crust golden. It boded well for the rest of this beautiful summer's day.

Chapter Twenty-Nine

Roxanne flopped, gasping and panting, onto the seat on the train. She had caught it with ninety seconds to spare. She had forgotten how difficult it was to do anything spontaneously in Burley Bridge – like call a taxi to Heathfield station. Of course, it wasn't really a proper taxi company with multiple cars all waiting to be booked. It was just Bill Swinley and his Vauxhall Astra and he wasn't geared up for mercy dashes to catch the next London-bound train. 'I'm just having my lunch,' he'd explained, when she'd called. What was it with country people and their lack of urgency?

There had also been Stanley to sort out, as Della wasn't due back until late and he would need his dinner and an afternoon walk. Luckily, Frank was around and had driven over with Eddie to collect him. As Bill the taxi driver seemed to be still eating his lunch – perhaps pasta, piece by piece? – Roxanne had called back to cancel her booking, as Frank had insisted on driving her to Heathfield himself.

'You'll be fine,' he'd assured her, speeding along the country roads with Eddie in the back seat and Stanley looking rather perplexed in his basket beside him.

Roxanne felt terrible about not showing up at Michael's for lunch. However, he'd have understood when he'd listened to the apologetic rambling messages she'd left, not just on his mobile voicemail but on the shop landline answerphone too. She had hastily googled the bakery, hoping the real Michael would pick up the phone, as he wasn't answering his mobile. But no luck. It niggled her now that what she *should* have done was leg it round to the bakery and tell him, face to face – but then she would have missed this train, and on a Sunday there wasn't another for three hours.

Roxanne tried to steady her breathing to something resembling normal. The grey-haired man sitting opposite, wearing silver-rimmed specs and tapping at his laptop, kept throwing her startled looks. Next to her, at the window seat, a woman in a matted brown sweater was tucking into an extensive array of smelly home-made tuna sandwiches, their crinkled foil wrappers scattered all over the table.

Roxanne exhaled forcefully and pushed her hair roughly back from her face. She really was a lunatic for doing this, when she was supposed to be on a restorative break and had only just persuaded her sister that she was capable of operating a till. Surely Isabelle must have someone else she could call?

What about Henry and Emma from the first floor – couldn't they have stepped in and spent some time with her? They were terribly proactive when a faint whiff of burning brandy snaps could be detected; clearly, less so when a seventy-five-year-old lady had had her flat burgled and needed help.

Less than ten minutes out of Heathfield station and already the man opposite was barking into his phone. 'Yes, well, tell Casper Jollip that we expect a *seriously* impressive turnaround by Thursday . . .'

Roxanne fixed her gaze on the flat horizon. As the day progressed, the sky had turned from a cheering blue to a washed-out grey, and rain now streaked diagonally across the window.

She picked up her mobile from the table and scrolled through her contacts to find Sean's number, poised to call him, to let him know she was on her way. But did she really want to speak to him now? She decided to assess the damage at Isabelle's, and help to tidy up her flat, and when that was done she would go over to his place to surprise him. Instead, she texted Della, giving a brief résumé of events and hoping she wouldn't be cross or upset at Roxanne lurching off like this with no warning. At least Della would be back to open up the shop tomorrow.

She bought a chicken salad sandwich in the buffet car and nibbled at it without any pleasure whatsoever, trying to quell another prickle of unease about Michael and wondering if she should try calling him again. Her phone bleeped with a text, and she snatched it, expecting it to be him. *I think it's wonderful you're doing this,* Della had written, *but come back soon! xx*

Would she? There was no reason why not, as long as Isabelle was okay – although right now, she couldn't even think that far ahead. But perhaps she should go back to work early and forget all about this break? Would Marsha even allow her back so soon? And, if she did, Roxanne considered with a sinking feeling: what on earth would she do there, now her fashion director role had effectively been erased?

It was almost 4 p.m. when she arrived in London and dragged her wheeled case across the station concourse towards the taxi rank. She tried calling Isabelle from the cab, just to say she'd be home soon – but there was no answer. That was hardly unusual. Although Isabelle had a mobile, in some bizarre act of protest she rarely switched the thing on – and even her landline handset was often left lying around her flat in unlikely locations, out of charge.

Through the taxi window, Roxanne watched the hustle and bustle of traffic all around her. She had been away for less than two weeks, yet London seemed busier than she had ever remembered it. Usually, when she came home from a holiday, she was relieved to be back in the city she loved, the place where she belonged; perhaps because she often went away alone. She didn't feel that way on this damp and grey afternoon.

The taxi pulled up in front of her block, and she thanked and paid the driver, glancing around in horror as he drove away. Records were scattered all over the road. Parking her wheelie case at the front door, she quickly gathered up as many as she could. Some were still in their sleeves, all of which were wet and scuffed, but perhaps the actual vinyl inside would still be playable. Others, however, had clearly been run over, and most of the albums weren't even in their sleeves at all. 'They threw them out like frisbees,' Isabelle had said. Roxanne could tell just with a glance that any without sleeves were damaged beyond repair, but she still collected as many as she could. All the jazz ladies that she and Isabelle had listened to so many times: she wasn't prepared to just leave them lying out there in the road.

With an armful of records clasped to her chest, Roxanne let herself into the block, dragging her case into the hallway. She knocked on Isabelle's door, just out of courtesy really as the woodwork around the lock was cracked and splintered, presumably from where the burglar had forced entry into the flat, and it hung ajar.

'Oh, you're here,' Isabelle said as she came to meet Roxanne, hugging her and taking the albums from her. 'You picked them all up for me!'

'Well, as many as I could find. There might be more lying about out there, I can have another look later.'

'Thank you. I couldn't face it.' Isabelle's dark eyes watered as she beckoned her into the living room.

As Roxanne glanced around, taking in the terrible sight, she realised she had done the right thing in rushing home. The room was all but destroyed. The floor was covered with smashed crockery, books and magazines. There was broken glass everywhere. Isabelle's record player lay in the middle of the room, its lid cracked – possibly stamped on – its arm clearly broken.

'Oh, Isabelle,' Roxanne gasped, 'this is just awful. It's so disgustingly mean. Why would anyone do this to someone's home?' Tears had filled her own eyes, and she wiped them away hastily with her hand. The last thing Isabelle needed was her crying over the mess.

'I've absolutely no idea,' she said. 'But, like I said on the phone, the police reckoned they were probably on something . . .'

Roxanne shook her head in disgust. Glancing through to the kitchen, she could see that a great pile of cutlery and kitchen implements had been thrown all over the floor and were lying in a pool of what looked like milk. Most of the living room shelves were bare, suggesting that someone had swept a hand along them, knocking off all the ornaments and knick-knacks that Isabelle treasured. Roxanne doubted if anything was valuable, but the point was, they mattered to Isabelle, very much. In the corner of the living room, the sewing machine lay on its side, and fabric and clothes were strewn around as if a small child had tired of a game of dressing up, and run off to play. However, the most shocking aspect was the living room walls, which had been sprayed liberally with aerosol cans – not in any legible way, just a mass of random scribblings in angry red and black over the numerous framed photographs and paintings.

Roxanne couldn't bear to just stand there, staring, so she clicked into action and started to pick up shards of glass and crockery, placing them on a sheet of newspaper. 'When did it happen exactly?'

'This morning, when I went out for a walk,' Isabelle replied. 'I was only gone an hour.'

'So, what else did the police say? Do they think there's any chance of catching them?'

Isabelle perched on the edge of the sofa and stared down at the floor. 'Not really. They told me I'd need to get my door fixed as soon as possible, like I didn't realise that: as if I was planning to leave it wide open so I could be burgled again.' She stopped, catching herself. 'Oh, I suppose they were kind enough. They gave me a number of an emergency joiner and he's on his way now.'

No sooner had she spoken than the joiner turned up: not Tommy, thankfully, as Roxanne didn't feel up to discussing Jessica-the-spaniel's debut photo shoot right now, but a short, stocky man of very few words named Gary, who got straight down to work at Isabelle's front door.

'The police also said I was lucky,' Isabelle added wryly, 'that nothing valuable was taken. I mean, I don't even have a TV, do I? Or a computer or a proper camera. Hardly any of my jewellery's valuable and the pieces that are – gold necklaces, earrings, a ruby ring – they didn't find . . .'

Roxanne picked up a broken table lamp, its ceramic base cracked, its pink paper shade dented, and surveyed the room again. 'That's not the point, though, is it? Your things are important to you. It's not about how much they're worth, money-wise. This is your home, you've lived here for forty-five years and you should feel safe.'

Isabelle nodded mutely, her lips pressed tightly together, then bent to reach for a small silver photo frame. Its glass was cracked, obscuring whoever the couple were in the tiny black-and-white photo behind it. It wasn't a photo Roxanne recalled seeing before. 'You know what I feel really dreadful about?' Isabelle remarked.

Roxanne sat beside her on the sofa and put an arm around her shoulders. 'Someone being in your home, I'd imagine. It's such an awful feeling – like being violated.'

'Well, yes, there is that. But I feel bad about you, too, coming all the way back here just for me . . .'

'Isabelle, it's not a big deal,' Roxanne murmured, squeezing her hand. 'I'm glad you called me, truly—'

'Well, Henry and Emma are away, and I wouldn't want them here anyway, lecturing me about how I should've been more careful . . .'

Roxanne turned and looked at her. 'You left the front door ajar. It's easily done – and the burglars just went for

317

the first flat door they came to. After nearly burning my own place down I'm the last person to judge you.'

Isabelle's eyes shone with tears. 'I'm so glad you're here.'

'So am I.' Roxanne stood up and made her way through to the kitchen. 'D'you mind if I carry on clearing up? I think it might make you feel better . . .'

'Yes, I suppose we should get stuck in . . .'

'I can do it,' she added quickly. 'You can just tell me what you'd like me to do. I'll make us some tea first . . .' She stepped over the milk lake, filled the kettle and glanced back to the living room. 'D'you have any bin bags?'

'Cupboard under the sink,' Isabelle replied. Roxanne fished some out, plus some old cloths to mop up the spillage.

They drank their tea black – Roxanne always did anyway – and then Roxanne began to tackle the mess.

'I'm not sitting here watching you working,' Isabelle retorted, and she joined in.

Within an hour, the floor had been cleared of broken possessions, and any remaining fragments of glass and crockery had been hoovered up. Any books and unbroken knick-knacks had been put back in their rightful places on the shelves. While the record player appeared to be beyond repair, the sewing machine seemed to have survived its rough treatment. The flat still looked dreadful with the sprayed walls, but at least there was a sense of order again with the carpet visible.

Roxanne stopped, pushed back her hair and checked the time on her phone. 'It's almost seven. We should eat something. How about coming up to mine for a bit of supper?'

'Oh, I don't expect you to cook. Not when you've been on a train for hours and hours . . .'

318

'Well, *three* hours,' Roxanne said with a smile. That was the thing about Londoners like Isabelle and Sean: they had this idea that Yorkshire was somewhere near Greenland, with permafrost. 'It'll only be something from the cupboard like a bowl of soup,' she added. 'I'll just go up and get myself sorted, then I'll rustle up something for us.'

As Isabelle thanked her, Roxanne felt gratified to see her looking brighter already. Perhaps it did feel right to be back in London. Burley Bridge would always be there for her and, now she had settled into the everyday workings of the bookshop, she felt confident that she could visit at any time and actually have a part to play there. Any awkwardness about returning to her childhood village seemed to have disappeared.

Roxanne hauled her suitcase upstairs and let herself into her own flat, flinching as a mouse scooted across the living room floor. Well, at least she wouldn't be here alone tonight. She wandered into her kitchen. Of course the fridge would be as empty as she'd left it, having assumed that she would be away for several weeks – but no harm in checking, in case it had magically self-filled with all sorts of tempting delicacies. It was bare apart from a small green puddle at the bottom (kale seepage).

Her food cupboard was only marginally less depressing in that it did at least have food in it: non-perishables, the kind of tins an elderly couple might keep in their static caravan in Whitley Bay (sardines, sweetcorn, kidney beans – but no soup), plus rice, dried noodles and muesli. Clearly, she wasn't going to be 'rustling up' anything for supper tonight.

Feeling grubby after her journey, she showered quickly and wrapped herself in a scratchy bath towel. In her bedroom now, she stood naked and looked down at her pale body, noticing for the first time that she was a little more toned than when she had set off for Yorkshire. Of course, she had been hoofing up that hill every morning, with Stanley, whereas in London, leisurely strolls with Isabelle were pretty much the only exercise she involved herself in.

A little blast of the countryside had done her good.

Della would be home from Berlin now, Roxanne realised. She hoped Michael had played her message and wasn't too cross with her. As for Sean: she needed to stay with Isabelle, so she wouldn't be going around tonight. How would he react to her surprise early return? she wondered. Surely he'd be delighted; after all, he had driven all the way to Burley Bridge, just to be with her for one night. Yet these days, she could never quite predict what sort of mood he'd be in. What a fuss he'd made over a trickle of dog pee on a socket board. Meanwhile, two floors down lived a seventy-five-year-old lady whose flat had been trashed, and whose lifelong record collection had been slung out into the street like old junk – and she was doing her damnedest to be stoical about it.

They wouldn't eat here tonight, Roxanne decided. Her flat felt as if it had been lying empty for months, and even sitting there eating takeaway pizza would be depressing. No, she would treat Isabelle to an Italian tonight. Roxanne pulled on jeans, a jauntily striped lambswool sweater and her silver LK Bennetts – which *had* survived the battering they'd received, thank you very much, Irene Bagshott – and set off to take her friend out to dinner.

They strolled arm in arm, down the steps to the towpath and along the canal, to the little Italian where Roxanne had first been with Isabelle, then with Sean on his fiftieth birthday.

While the two women tucked into what they agreed was the best spaghetti carbonara they had ever tasted, two hundred miles north, Michael Bramley was eyeing the half-eaten tart that was sitting on his kitchen table. The first time he had cooked for a woman who wasn't his wife since – well, it felt like medieval times – and she hadn't turned up. As well as the tart, he had also planned to serve a green salad and new potatoes with fresh mint. He'd kept checking his watch, calculating how late Roxanne was now and reassuring himself that the food didn't need to be piping hot; in fact it would be nicer served warm. The new potatoes were a little more time-sensitive, but they only took minutes and he wouldn't put them on to boil until Roxanne had arrived.

So Michael waited and waited. By 1.30 p.m. the tart was tepid, and by 2 p.m., rather worried now, he had nipped down the road to the bookshop and buzzed the door to Della's flat above. No answer. Perhaps she had forgotten, or something more enticing had come up? Whatever had happened, Michael had to face the fact that he would be eating that tart alone – not that he'd managed much of it. Being stood up tended to be a bit of an appe-tite quasher. He and the kids had had another slice for dinner – by which point he was heartily sick of the thing. He gave up and offered the rest of it to Bob, which trig-gered an episode of canine flatulence.

It wasn't until 5 a.m. on Monday morning, as Michael pulled on a clean stripy apron in preparation for a morn-ing's baking, that he noticed the red answerphone light winking at him. Elsa was always getting onto him about that – about not checking the phone in the bakery: 'Dad, you have to listen to the messages. What if someone wants some catering done? Or a massive order? We could be really missing out!'

He smiled, wondering when exactly their roles had switched like that; when had she become the eye-rolling one, keeping him in check. He didn't mind it; in fact, he rather liked it. His daughter's concern was somehow comforting and sweet.

He pressed 'play'.

Michael? Hi, it's Roxanne here. I am so sorry. I've tried calling your mobile but maybe it's switched off? I'd have come round to tell you in person but I've had trouble getting a cab to Heathfield and there's no time now, you know what Sunday travel's like, it's a nightmare with trains – so Frank's coming over and I need to be ready and it's such a rush. Sorry, I'm babbling on here . . .

She wasn't half. What on earth had happened?

What I should have said right at the start is that I have a neighbour, Isabelle, lovely old lady – bit eccentric, says she's a jazz singer but I've never found any evidence of that. Anyway, we're friends. She lives two floors below me and we go for coffee or lunch sometimes. She likes to wander around, discovering new places, and she called me just now – well, half an hour ago. I'm so sorry. I do hope you didn't go to too much trouble . . .

Michael shook his head in bewilderment. Would she ever get to the point?

. . . So, she was burgled and phoned me and I'm on my way to catch a train to London in a minute because she really doesn't have anyone else.

Pause.

Can you believe that, Michael? That something so

322

terrible could happen to an elderly lady, and there was no one else she could call? I do hope you'll understand. It's been lovely getting to know you and I'm sorry about, er – what I mean is, I know Della sort of . . .

Tried to set us up, that night in the Red Lion? Was that what she was referring to? He shuffled uncomfortably and twiddled with his apron strings.

Anyway, never mind all that, she added, in that rather scatty but lovely way she had of speaking, *I really would have loved to have had lunch with you today.*

And that was it. Michael tried to take comfort in the fact that Roxanne had called and not simply stood him up. But he still couldn't shake off the rather desolate thought that he didn't know when, or even if, Roxanne Cartwright would be coming back to Burley Bridge.

Chapter Thirty

It was late morning on Monday when Roxanne contacted Sean. She knew he would probably be in the midst of a shoot, so a quick text would suffice for now: *Hey love, how's things? What are you up to tonight? A* slightly odd thing to ask, she realised, but she needed to know if he'd be around later.

Just a quiet night in once this shoot's finished, he replied. *Need you back here to liven things up. Hope all's good babe xx.*

She smiled and slipped the Laurence Grier photography book first into a soft cotton pillowcase to protect it from knocks, then into her biggest leather shoulder bag. She looped the bag, experimentally, over her shoulder. The book weighed around the same as a small filing cabinet – and she was planning to lug it around all day. The things she did for love. Her plan was to deliver it to Sean personally – but she had important business to attend to first.

'You're back already?' Marsha had exclaimed when she called. 'But your blog's already pretty popular! How can we have "our fashion director trapped in the country" if you're in town?'

Roxanne had leaned against her fridge, accidentally dislodging two hand-painted clay magnets Holly and Keira had made for her one Christmas. So her entire *life* should be shaped around her blog now? 'Don't worry, there's plenty more I can write about,' she said.

'". . . Our fashion director's trapped in W10" doesn't have the same ring to it,' she quipped, as if Roxanne hadn't spoken.

Actually, Roxanne thought, *I live in Islington – N1.*

'What I mean is,' she continued, 'Elsa took lots more photos of me in various hideous waterproof things, so there's plenty there to keep us going.'

'Oh, that's good. I'd hate it to run out of steam, you see.' Marsha paused. 'So, er, why *are* you back? Did it do your head in, being up there?'

'Not at all,' Roxanne said quickly. 'I, er, just had to come back to help out a friend . . .'

'Ah, so it's just a fleeting visit? You're not *back*-back, then, I take it?'

'I'm really not sure,' Roxanne said cautiously. 'Erm, would you have time for a chat today, if I pop into the office?'

'Yes, of course. How are you fixed for a quick lunch?'

How was she fixed? Until recently Roxanne's life had been crammed with work-related events, her diary a mass of scribbles and mysterious symbols which had signified something when she'd drawn them, although she could never quite remember what that was. But from now on that diary was blank. The very sight of it was at once panic-inducing and rather thrilling. 'Lunch would be lovely,' she replied.

And so Roxanne got ready for a meeting with her editor, feeling oddly in limbo as she did so. She was going to the office – but not to do any actual work. She was still on leave, yet carefully ironing a pink and white Paisley-patterned top to wear with a neat grey linen skirt, plus low black heels. It wasn't exactly a sabbatical outfit. It was the kind that would attract a great deal of 'get you, up from London!' attention in the Red Lion in Burley Bridge.

On her way out of the building, she stopped and knocked on Isabelle's door.

'Ooh, you look smart,' Isabelle remarked. 'Off on a date, are you? Meeting Sean?'

'Later,' she explained. 'He doesn't know I'm back, though. I know it's a bit silly as we only saw each other a couple of days ago, but I thought I'd surprise him with a visit.' She patted the hefty bag slung over her shoulder. 'He still hasn't taken the book I bought him for his birthday so I thought I'd deliver it personally.' In fact, she had already planned the scenario. She would turn up at his block, press his buzzer and call out, 'Delivery for Mr O'Carroll!' through the intercom to his flat.

'He'll be delighted,' Isabelle remarked, not entirely convincingly. 'So, is this you back for good? I still feel terrible about you rushing back home just for me.'

Roxanne shook her head dismissively. 'Please don't. It's actually the best thing, I think. I wanted to be with you after what had happened, and now I'm here, I think it's best that I see Marsha and find out exactly where my job's going – if I have a future on the magazine at all . . .'

'Of course you do!'

Roxanne smiled. It was kind of Isabelle to say so, but a slightly delusional elderly woman, whose own 'career' may or may not have been entirely fictitious, knew nothing about the inner workings of a fashion magazine. 'We'll see,' she said. 'I'd better dash. She's taking me to lunch.'

326

The greeting Roxanne received as she walked into the office suggested she had been away for months.

'She's back!' Tristan announced loudly, causing a ripple of excitement at the unexpected sighting of their esteemed fashion director.

'Are you just visiting us?' Serena asked with a grin.

'Or have you come to take us all up to Yorkshire with you?' chipped in Kate. 'Please say you've got a coach parked outside . . .'

'Yes, smuggle us out of here,' Serena hissed.

'What's been going on?' Roxanne murmured.

'Come into the cupboard,' she commanded, 'and we'll tell you all about it.'

In they snuck, like giggling children: Roxanne, Serena, Kate, Zoe the beauty editor and Tristan the art director – not into an actual cupboard, but the fashion cupboard, as it was known: the small, windowless room where clothes for shoots were stored. It was quite a squeeze in there, as it was home to several heavily laden rails, plus numerous bulging carrier bags of clothes and so many shoes piled up haphazardly that they made Roxanne's collection at home seem rather organised and restrained.

'So, why are you back?' Zoe wanted to know. 'Tell you what – if I'd been given a sabbatical like that, I don't think you'd ever see me again . . .'

Roxanne dispensed a brief summary of her elderly neighbour's burglary trauma, adding that she'd asked Marsha to spare her some time today.

Serena folded her slim brown arms and gave her an ominous look. 'Well, you might as well know, Rox – the place is a bloody disaster.'

'What d'you mean? What's happening?'

'Shall I just say rats, sinking ship?' She paused for

effect. 'In the past two weeks, eleven advertisers have pulled out.'

'But why?' Roxanne asked. 'They haven't even seen the new-look magazine yet. As far as they're concerned, we're just doing what we've always done, and they've always been perfectly happy with that . . .'

'Word's got around,' Kate added. 'You know what it's like. It's all, "Oh, they're turning it into a trashy rag now that Roxanne's left . . ."'

'But I haven't left!' she exclaimed. 'I'm just on a break—'

'Yes, but that's what everyone thinks,' Serena cut in. 'That's the big news.'

Roxanne was astounded that anything she did in her professional life would ever be considered newsworthy. 'Do they? Why would they think that?'

'Because it was all so sudden,' Zoe ventured, 'and they put two and two together. You know, Marsha arrives, brings in a no-mark like Tina over – erm, in a senior position – and suddenly, you're gone.' She shook her head. 'If you were going to spend a quarter of a million advertising in a glossy magazine, wouldn't you want to know there was someone brilliant in charge of the fashion?'

Roxanne nodded. 'I suppose so.'

'So it's kind of shaken everyone up,' Serena added.

'The word going round is you've been sacked,' Tristan added, pulling an alarmed face.

'God, really?'

'A lot of people are very upset,' added Kate gravely.

'. . . Because you *are* the magazine,' Serena added dramatically, at which Roxanne grimaced.

'Oh, come on – that's not true. I'm just a part of it and it could rattle along perfectly well without me.'

There followed a barrage of protestations from her

colleagues about how brilliant she was – *indispensable* – which Roxanne was keen to call to a halt, so she quickly changed the subject: 'Have any of you read my blog?'

'We all have!' Zoe exclaimed.

'Did it scare you, the level of glamour I was projecting there?'

'Oh, it's hysterical,' Tristan said with a grin. 'Those massive hairy hiker socks! And those waterproof trousers, my God . . .'

'Good on you for sending yourself up,' Kate remarked.

'So, how *was* it up in the frozen north?' Tristan wanted to know.

Roxanne smiled. 'It was . . . well, I suppose it wasn't quite what I expected, which sounds weird because I lived there for the first eighteen years of my life. I mean, I know the place. At least, I *thought* I knew it—'

'Ah, there you are, Roxanne!' Marsha had appeared in the doorway and was staring at them in the manner of a malevolent gym teacher who had just caught them passing around a cigarette. 'What *is* this? The gang hut?' Everyone laughed stiffly. 'Roxanne, shall we go now?' Marsha prompted her. 'I mentioned to Rufus we were meeting today, and would you know it?' She rolled her eyes to the cracked polystyrene tiled ceiling. 'He's only muscling in on our cosy lunch.'

Roxanne had never been for lunch with Rufus, the publishing director who controlled several high-profile magazines in her company's portfolio. She had barely spoken to him, in fact, because, unlike publishing directors in other companies she'd worked for, he rarely lowered himself to making an appearance on the editorial floor. On the rare occasions when he was spotted, he always looked rather uncomfortable at being surrounded by all those mysterious creative types with their messy desks and piles of clothes strewn everywhere. However now, as the three of them strode through Soho, making their way towards Piccadilly Circus, Rufus seemed terribly keen to get to know Roxanne. This was utterly baffling to her. Why was this red-haired, faintly sweaty man in a Paul Smith suit even bothering to join them at all?

'Marsha tells me you're from Yorkshire,' he said, as they found themselves all clumped together awkwardly on a terribly narrow pavement which would lead them to Marsha's restaurant of choice.

'Yes, that's right,' Roxanne said pleasantly.

'Not got much of an accent, have you?' he suggested.

'No, well, I left a very long time ago. A scarily long time, in fact. Pre-internet. Pre-mobile phones!' Agh, what was she saying that for? She guessed that Rufus was in his late thirties. Now was not the time to allude to her lengthy career, bringing with it the suggestion that she should be quietly shuffled off to the retirement home for clapped-out fashion types.

He beamed at her. His own accent was rather bland home counties. She had never acquired the knack of being able to distinguish one region from another; to her, it was all lumped together as 'the south'.

'I do like northerners. Straight-talking, hard-working and honest,' he went on, which made her smile. He could make her sound like a miner if he wanted to. 'So, how long have you worked for us?'

'Ten years,' she replied.

'Gosh. And with fashion, does it all roll around again and again, so, basically, we're just recycling the same old stuff every few years?'

She noticed Marsha giving him a quick, exasperated look. 'Well, not exactly,' Roxanne explained. 'Yes, styles do come round again but there's always a different edge, a new take on a look. For instance, if you look at seventies fashion, the original stuff was all cheap and nasty polyesters with an awful lot of brown and orange floral prints, whereas today, we wouldn't dream of . . .' she tailed off as his eyes glazed over. She had lost him already, this head honcho who wanted to have lunch with her, and they weren't even in the restaurant yet. What was she babbling on about *polyester* for?

They reached the restaurant and filed in, with Marsha leading the way and saying very loudly, and ostentatiously, that her secretary had made the booking that morning. It was the kind of place where no one – not even Roxanne, with all her connections – could possibly get a table unless they booked five months ahead. But Marsha could, *on the day*, and not just any old table but the much-coveted booth.

They took their seats and Rufus immediately ordered an eye-wateringly expensive bottle of Chablis. Drinking at lunchtime, Roxanne mused. How very old-school. Or perhaps he'd heard about her energetic display at Sean's party and hoped to be treated to some tipsy dancing? They all ordered their food rather hurriedly – their order taken by a girl so languid and beautiful, Roxanne had to stop herself from suggesting she contact a model agency.

'So, with all the changes going on,' Rufus said, clearly eager to get down to business, 'I thought it was important to get a feel for what's happening with the key team members.'

'Well, I have been keeping you informed,' Marsha said tightly.

He fixed her with a stare. He had narrow, light blue

331

eyes and a sturdy jaw; a particularly masculine face, Roxanne thought. 'Yes, but I'm not quite understanding why you've packed Roxanne off for the entire summer,' he remarked.

Marsha cleared her throat and repositioned the white porcelain salt cellar. 'No one's been *packed off*, Rufus. Roxanne, erm, wasn't sure about the new direction we're taking and mooted the possibility of resigning so we decided it might be a good idea for her to just take an extended break while Tina settles in . . .'

Now Rufus turned to Roxanne. 'And then what? What sort of role are you expecting to return to after this so-called break?'

'That's why I asked to see Marsha today,' Roxanne explained, 'just so we can be clear about it because at the moment, I don't know.'

'We talked about Roxanne supporting Tina,' Marsha said quickly, 'keeping a tight rein on departmental costs and setting up competitions.'

'Yes, but I didn't exactly agree on that,' Roxanne asserted, surprised by the conviction in her own voice.

Rufus nodded and laced his long fingers together. 'That doesn't surprise me. From where I'm sitting, no one is terribly clear about anything at all.'

Marsha flushed. Rufus seemed to be studying her face, and Roxanne glanced between them. There was something going on with them, she decided; some kind of tension there. Marsha's appointment as editor had seemed an odd choice, seeing as she came from a diet magazine and had no experience of the glossy fashion market – and Rufus would have been responsible for that. She wondered now if he suspected he had made a mistake. But why offer her the job in the first place?

332

'Roxanne and I agreed it was the ideal time for her to take a sabbatical,' Marsha muttered.

'But it hasn't been ideal, has it?' Rufus remarked, rather too loudly. 'There's a rather worrying rumour flying around that you sacked her . . .'

'Yes,' Marsha cut in, 'but I've been telling everyone that's not true—'

'And in less than two weeks,' Rufus thundered, 'we have lost so much advertising revenue – not to mention goodwill – that we might as well throw in the towel right now and admit we're buggered as a financially viable operation.'

The two women stared at him. Roxanne shuffled awkwardly in her seat. If he wanted to give Marsha a dressing down, she would rather not witness it: this was not how she'd planned for her meeting with Marsha to go. All she'd wanted was to get to the bottom of whether there was still a role for her at the magazine.

'It's been calamitous, I'd say,' he added, eyes narrowed to slits. 'We are utterly *screwed*. Wouldn't you agree, Marsha?'

'I wouldn't say it's calamitous exactly,' Marsha replied, her cheeks flushing deep pink.

'Well, I'd say it was. I don't know how else to describe it, frankly.' Rufus turned to Roxanne. 'You've heard about what's been happening, I assume?'

'Erm, a little bit,' she replied.

Their food arrived – all little mounds of things, with artistic dribblings of sauce and a liberal dusting of micro-herbs. Rufus speared a charred cauliflower 'steak' that, Roxanne had happened to note, cost almost ten pounds.

'So you'll know we're in deep shit,' he added.

'I understand things aren't looking good at the moment,'

she ventured, not sure how to play this, 'but I suppose it is very early days.'

'Yep.' He nodded. 'Early days and already it's clear that bringing in Tina Court was *completely* the wrong move.' His head whipped round to face Marsha.

Her mouth seemed to wilt. 'We're trying to get things on track,' she murmured.

'Yes, but how?'

Although the situation was hardly conducive, Roxanne made an attempt to tuck into her smoked trout. In fact, she wondered what the purpose of this awkward gathering actually was. Did Rufus simply want to humiliate Marsha in front of her? She couldn't understand what he hoped to gain by this.

'I think Tina just needs time to settle in,' Marsha replied.

'Well, what *I* think,' Rufus boomed, 'is this is the ideal opportunity – while the three of us are together – to figure out a plan of action, and it seems clear to me that we need Roxanne back on board as soon as possible.'

'Roxanne was never *off*-board,' Marsha asserted.

He turned to Roxanne as if Marsha hadn't spoken. 'Could you come back immediately, forget about this ridiculous sabbatical thing Marsha cooked up?'

'Erm, I'm not sure,' she replied. 'Actually, I wanted to talk about my role on the magazine. You see, if it's going to be all about budget and competitions, then I'm not sure there's a job for me at all.'

'Of course there is,' Marsha exclaimed, turning briefly to Rufus. 'I agree that we need Roxanne back right away . . .'

'And I'd go one step further,' Rufus said. 'I'd suggest that Tina's appointment has been an utter disaster. I assume she's still on probation, isn't she?'

'Er, yes, of course,' Marsha said quickly.

'Okay. Well, I think it's best for all that we admit it hasn't work out, and she leaves with immediate effect.' He fixed his gaze upon Marsha across the table. 'It would make sense for Roxanne to step into her shoes right away – as fashion-director-in chief, or whatever title you made me conjure up out of thin air for that dreadful woman.'

'But . . .' Marsha stared at him. 'Are you sure . . .'

'It seems clear that Roxanne is the face of the magazine,' he charged on, spearing a cube of balsamic-splattered sweet potato, 'and for us to regain the trust and goodwill of our advertisers, we must show that we are fully committed to her. And *that's* why we're promoting her to a new and more prominent role.'

Marsha nodded mutely. Her lunch was uneaten. Of course, she didn't really consume anything at mealtimes; just that steady supply of pastries at her desk. However, today she hadn't even touched her *cutlery*.

'What sort of role are you thinking about?' Roxanne asked, eager to remind him that she was, in fact, still there.

Rufus looked at her in surprise. He had already chugged a large glass of wine, and now the waitress had glided over to top him up. 'Well, we can't have someone on that senior level just producing shoots. Any old stylist can do that. We can promote one of your team to take care of the beautiful pictures . . .'

'I thought all that was being got rid of anyway,' she remarked, 'and it was all figure-fixing underwear from now on?'

'I think we might have been a little hasty with that,' Marsha said quickly.

'So what we need now,' Rufus continued, nostrils flaring,

'is to have someone out there, representing us, meeting with all the major advertisers and convincing them that we are the number one fashion brand about to move into an exciting new era.'

Roxanne blinked at him, trying to take all of this in. So far, she had barely touched her glass of wine. Now she took a generous gulp. 'So, I wouldn't plan and direct shoots anymore, then?'

'No, you are *far* too important for that. You'll be our brand ambassador, our figurehead . . .'

'A figurehead?' she exclaimed. 'Like on a ship?'

He guffawed, and a little fleck of something shot out of his mouth. 'Ha. Yes. A life of lunching and schmoozing and being lovely and charming to everyone. I hear you're very popular in the industry, Roxanne?'

'Or, er, I wouldn't say—'

'No need to be bashful. It's obvious that you're made for this role . . .'

'Er, thank you,' she muttered, trying to read Marsha's expression. The woman looked as if she'd just been kicked. 'I'd rather just go back to my normal job, though, if that's okay.'

Rufus frowned and shook his head. 'Sorry, but no – we need to make a big statement here, to win back everyone's confidence. Marsha can promote that girl, that *Serona* . . .'

'Serena,' Roxanne corrected him.

'Yes, her – and then you can take the much more senior role. Obviously, we'll be talking a substantial pay rise,' he added, jabbing at a runner bean, 'won't we, Marsha?'

'Oh, of course,' she replied, lips pursed. 'So, um, I assume this is fine with you, Roxanne?'

Rufus waved for the bill, as if such a piffling matter of *whether she actually wanted to do this* was of no concern.

'I'm not sure actually,' she murmured.

'Sorry? What?' Rufus tugged a company credit card out of his wallet.

'I'm very flattered that you think of me in that way,' she explained, 'but if it's okay, I'd like to take some time to think it over and get back to Marsha first thing tomorrow.' Roxanne knew that this would seem insane to them: she'd basically just been offered a promotion on a plate, but neither Marsha nor Rufus seemed to care about what she wanted to do.

He frowned, clearly put out. 'I don't see what else we can offer you. Is it the salary?'

'No, it's not that . . .'

'Because I know we haven't talked an actual figure, but if we said . . .' He shrugged, as if it was nothing. 'We can certainly match Tina's, can't we, Marsha?'

'Yes, of course . . .'

'Well, that's substantially more than you're on now, Roxanne,' he said grandly. 'We're probably talking something in the region of a fifty per cent rise. Obviously, I realise a role like this would be a big change for you. But trust me – we'll make it worth your while.'

She nodded, and Rufus paid the bill. Marsha pointedly avoided eye contact with Roxanne as they left the restaurant.

So, Roxanne reflected, she would no longer have a creative role. She would be a 'figurehead', coaxing all those recently departed advertisers back to the magazine, thus raking in a vast amount of money for the company and, so it would seem, for herself.

A fifty per cent payrise. She could hardly get her head around that. Crazy money, really, for a job she could do standing on her head. So why was she experiencing a huge wave of fashion guilt?

Chapter Thirty-One

They parted company outside the restaurant. Marsha and Rufus headed back to the office, and Roxanne wandered into a smart boutique, more because it was there than because she was particularly interested in looking. In fact, she didn't quite know what to do with herself now. She stared at a rail of tops in various shades of sludge, then stepped back outside again, finding herself drifting towards the office simply out of habit.

She could go back in and hang out with Serena and Kate – but then, they would want a full account of what had happened at lunch, and she had yet to make sense of it herself. Plus, as she didn't have any actual work to do, she would just be floating about aimlessly. She slowed her pace to more of an Isabelle-style amble, with no particular destination in mind. The photography book was weighing heavily in her shoulder bag. A shot of normality was what she needed now, she realised – like hearing Sean's voice. She stopped and fished out her mobile and called him.

'Hey, honey, everything okay?' He sounded distracted. But then, it was 3.20 in the afternoon, and he'd be working.

'Yes – just wanted to say hi, really. It was good to see you the other day. Sorry if I seemed a bit flat when you left Della's place. I'd just hoped you'd stay longer . . .'

'Oh, darling, me too. It was such a pain, honestly – bloody Louie. But I'll be up again soon, promise.'

She smiled. 'Hope so. So, um, what are you up to?'

'You're very inquisitive about my comings and goings today, aren't you, darling? You already asked what I was doing tonight . . .'

'Haha, yes,' she babbled. 'Just wondering, you know. You should be flattered that I'm so interested . . .'

'I *am* flattered,' he said, and she could tell he was smiling. 'Um, nothing terribly thrilling to report, though. I'm just catching up on reams of admin at home. Tax, accounts . . .'

'I thought that's what you paid an accountant for?' she remarked.

'Yeah, but they still need all the info from me, unfortunately. Plus, there's a ton of invoicing . . .'

'I thought Britt did all your invoicing?'

Sean chuckled. 'Hey, what is this? The time management bureau? I still have to get involved, you know . . .'

Roxanne smiled, shifting her weighty bag onto the other shoulder. It was so heavy, it felt as if it had created a groove there. 'So, um, you're just staying in tonight, are you?'

'Yep, looks like it. Recovering from the tedium of all this paperwork . . .'

'Poor you,' she murmured. 'You might have to anaesthetise yourself with booze.'

'I was planning on it.' He paused. 'All okay then, babe?'

Ah – a hint that he wanted to get back to work now.

'Yes, darling. I'll let you get on. Bye, honey.'

'Bye for now.'

In fact, she was happy to finish their conversation before Sean noticed that the background noises around her sounded terribly urban, and not remotely what you'd expect during a dog walk in the hills. She turned onto Charing Cross Road, which was home to several second-hand and antiquarian bookshops. It wasn't a part of town she was in a habit of exploring; she was usually too busy darting from one appointment to the next. She certainly wouldn't usually have stopped to gaze into the window of one such shop, which specialised in nautical books and charts of the ocean.

In the window sat a terribly fragile-looking wooden model of a ship with mottled calico sails and a carved figurehead. So that was what Rufus had mapped out for her, was it?

She wandered onwards, past yet more bookshops – one filled with art books, another focusing on trashy pulp novels of the 50s and 60s, with terrified-looking women on their covers and titles such as *Swamp Women* and *The Monster in the Lake*. Who knew there were so many specialised bookshops? When Della had first mooted the idea of the cookbook shop, Roxanne had thought she was out of her mind.

Now her attention was caught by a small selection of vintage cookbooks in another shop window. Although it was nothing to rival Della's emporium, Roxanne was intrigued enough to step inside. The cookbooks occupied just one small shelf, and most seemed to be about baking. *Party Cakes Made Easy, The Baking Powder Bible, Nanny Violet's Sweet Recipes*. Spotting *The Treasury of Fermented Breads* – the book Michael had been after when she'd met him, she smiled and leafed through it, the warm, slightly biscuity smell of old pages transporting her back to her sister's bookshop, and triggering another pang of regret about not turning up for Michael's lunch yesterday. Still, he would understand and by now, he would have forgotten all about it.

Della had texted to say she had got home safely, and that all was well up there. Roxanne pictured the bookshop, milling with customers all admiring the new extension, everything ticking along fine without her.

Well, of course it was. She had merely dropped in, helped out a bit and dropped back out again. Back here in London was where she belonged – yet already, she was wondering when she might return to Burley Bridge.

She paid for *The Treasury of Fermented Breads,* deciding she would send it to Michael, as a sort of sorry/thank you gift. Then she left the shop, pausing to pull out her phone and call Amanda.

'You're back?' her friend exclaimed. 'What's happened?'

'Oh, a drama with Isabelle downstairs – her flat was broken into and trashed . . .'

'Poor Isabelle. How awful . . .'

'She'll be okay,' Roxanne said, 'once the place has been redecorated. Can you believe they spray-painted everywhere?'

'Oh, no!'

'So, there's been that . . .' Roxanne paused, now picturing her friend trying to teach her class of twenty-eight seven-year-olds. 'Sorry – I've just realised you're still at work. How thoughtless of me—'

'No, it's fine – the bell's just gone and I'm about to go home. So, I take it you're going back to work, then?'

'I'm not sure. I've just had a meeting with Marsha and Rufus, the publisher. They want to promote me, would you believe?'

'Wow! You mean to be editor?'

'No – as a senior-floating-about sort of person. I'd schmooze the advertisers, be a *brand ambassador* . . .' She sniggered.

Amanda laughed. 'An ambassador? Like the one who always had Ferrero Rochers at his parties?'

'That's it! You are truly spoiling us . . .' They chuckled over the ridiculousness of it.

By the time Roxanne finished the call, her bag was weighing even more heavily now with the addition of the fermented bread book.

Rather than lugging it around any longer, she decided to head straight over to Sean's place at King's Cross. After all, he was at home, drowning in paperwork. After all that tedious invoicing he would be *overjoyed* to see her.

She strode towards the tube now, stopping to buy a decent bottle of white wine for her and Sean to enjoy on his roof terrace on what had turned out to be a warm and pleasant summer afternoon. How decadent, she thought with a smile. She had already had a glass at lunch – Rufus had polished off most of the bottle – and the thought of getting tipsy in what was definitely still the daytime seemed rather naughty and fun.

Quickening her pace, and wishing she was wearing her ballet flats rather than these silly heels, she passed a row of cheap, dismal-looking shops, in which staff were probably working in miserable conditions on zero-hours contracts. How could Roxanne feel so reluctant to take on a job which amounted to wall-to-wall expense-account lunches? How could she possibly feel hard done by when, just a few feet away, a young woman was curled up in a grubby sleeping bag, with a sleeping Alsatian and a couple of ripped carrier bags lying at her feet?

As she clung to the rail on the tube carriage, she wondered what she would do about Rufus's offer. No alternative had been suggested. What if she didn't *want* the figurehead role? She would talk it over with Sean – and Amanda, too, when they could get together. It was all rather overwhelming. In fact, the person she really wanted to sit down and talk to was Della, who was two hundred miles away with a shop to run.

Roxanne emerged from the tube and strode briskly towards Sean's apartment block. By now, she had decided against pretending to be a delivery person. She would simply surprise him instead, and perhaps they would go out to eat later. Like Roxanne, Sean never seemed to have much food in his fridge but luckily there were plenty of lovely little places nearby. When he first moved in, choosing the flat for its proximity to his studio, King's Cross was pretty shabby. However, now the warehouses were all prestigious apartments, and the tatty Victorian former-railway buildings had been turned into buzzing bars, restaurants and artists' studios. London had changed so much since Roxanne had moved here twenty-nine years ago. It seemed as if there were barely any tatty little corners left.

She had reached his block. It was a huge, solid building – a former garment factory converted into desirable canal-side apartments. Rather than buzz the intercom at the main front door, she pushed it and found that, as was usually the case, it was open. She trotted upstairs – Sean lived on the top floor – looking forward to chilling out with him now after her hasty departure from Burley Bridge and the dramas of Isabelle's burglary. They just needed to hang out together, she decided; to reconnect and relax, without him having to rush off somewhere. That's what she got for falling for a man who was perpetually 'crazy-busy'.

Roxanne rapped on his door and waited. For a few moments, there was no sound at all. She knocked again.

'Hello?' came his voice from the other side of the door. She grinned, deciding to remain silent. She heard muttering, then Sean saying, 'Just a minute.' There was some pottering around, then the twiddle of the handle as the door opened.

'Hi, darling!' She beamed and took in the sight before her. Sean was standing there, wearing a dressing gown and he didn't look happy. In fact, his face had frozen and she knew, instantly, that she was the last person he wanted to see.

'Rox! What the hell?'

She stared at him. 'What's wrong? What's going on?'

He stepped back, still neglecting to invite her in. 'Nothing. Jesus. I just didn't expect you, that's all.'

She blinked at him as he tightened his dressing gown belt. 'I thought you liked surprises,' she added, her heart pounding now. 'You surprised me, when you came to the bookshop party. So, can't I come in?' Her voice was tight and high and sounded as if it was coming from someone else.

Sean's face had coloured. As he opened his mouth to speak, Roxanne saw movement in the hallway behind him. It was Britt.

'Oh!' Britt gasped, looking startled.

As the two women locked gazes, a series of quick-fire thoughts darted through Roxanne's mind: *She's his agent. She's often here. They're just friends.*

Another dart: *But she is wearing only her bra and pants.*

Roxanne dragged her gaze back to Sean, who was exhaling dramatically and sweeping a hand over the back of his head.

344

'You're supposed to be in Yorkshire. What made you come here today?'

'I came to bring you your present.' She was blinking rapidly as she took the bag from her shoulder and pulled out his book. 'So . . . how long has this been happening?'

His face crumpled, and he glanced round as if Britt might still be standing there and could speak on his behalf, but she had run into his bedroom.

'It's nothing really,' he muttered after what felt like an eternity, at which Britt reappeared, wearing a blue shift dress now.

'That's nice,' Britt growled, picking up her jacket from a chair in the hallway, pulling it on and striding past them. 'I'll leave you to explain everything, Sean,' she added, pulling a brittle little smile before clattering off down the stairs.

Sean stared down at his bare feet. Terribly attractive feet, Roxanne had thought just two days ago. 'Rox, look – it's not what you think,' he muttered.

'How do you know what I'm thinking?'

'I just . . . well, we didn't plan it, you know. It just sort of happened, with you going away.'

She peered at him, unable to form words for a moment. And slowly, it started to make sense: why he had been so keen for her to go to Yorkshire, so un-bothered by the prospect of there being two hundred miles between them for several months.

'Poor Sean, all abandoned by his girlfriend,' she remarked coolly.

'I didn't mean that. I just meant—'

'Don't lie to me,' she snapped. 'This has been going on for way longer than the time I've been at Della's.'

He cleared his throat and reddened even further. It had

just been a hunch, but clearly, she was correct. 'It's not a serious thing,' he insisted. 'It's just – you know. Sort of sporadic . . .'

'And what about us, then? I mean, are we *sporadic* too?'

'Of course we're not! I love you, Rox . . .'

'Oh, do shut up.' She looked down at the book she was gripping. She was seized by an urge to whack it over his head but she knew it could quite possibly kill him, and that being able to joke about murdering her photographer boyfriend with a photography book really wasn't worth going to jail for.

'You've brought my book,' he said weakly, noticing it for the first time. 'Thanks, darling. That's really thoughtful of you.'

She looked back into his eyes. Her heart was banging so hard it was a wonder it hadn't dented her ribs. 'Hope you enjoy it,' she said, flinging it with all her might so it landed with a loud crack against his hall wall, as she turned and hurried away.

Chapter Thirty-Two

Despite the fact that she was wearing heels, she decided to walk home. She needed some proper brisk exercise to help her to make sense of things. Walking was good for a person, she mused, especially on a bright, blue-skied day like today. Especially when your bag was lighter – because she was carrying just a small volume on fermented breads and not a whacking great photography book. Especially when you could finally admit to yourself that the man you had been seeing for the past nine months probably wasn't making you as happy as you tried to convince yourself he was.

This was a man who freaked out if she left so much as a spare pair of knickers at his flat. Who okayed Marsha and Tina being on his party guest list when he knew darn well that Tina was being brought in to the magazine over Roxanne's head. He had harangued her for drinking too much and sneered at her love of Abba.

And, to top it all, he had been sleeping with his agent for God knows how long.

Perhaps she should have been more angry or upset.

However, as she detoured to follow the towpath, she felt only a sense of calm and possibly even relief.

Maybe she had known all along that there was someone. She had certainly known, deep down, that things would never move on – and that really, he wasn't the right man for her. Sure, he was a step up from Ned Tallow, in that he had a proper job and didn't steal cacti from garden centres. But was that her sole criterion for a boyfriend these days? She would be better off alone.

Across the canal, in a cobbled courtyard, a photo shoot was taking place. There were two models – older women, easily in their sixties and both incredibly elegant in smart cotton dresses and flat shoes. Roxanne approved of this trend of using models of all ages. Isabelle could easily be a model, she decided; she certainly had the bone structure, elegance and poise. Roxanne stood and watched the shoot, relieved that everyone was too engrossed in their work to notice her, because she realised after a moment that the photographer was Yasmin Morrel, whom she had worked with several times. She would prefer to avoid any awkward shouting and waving across the canal.

Roxanne could tell, even from across the water, that the shots would be lovely. The women moved beautifully and the gentle sunlight played in their silvery hair. This was what she loved about her job – making gorgeous pictures. She could never take on Rufus's 'ambassadorial' role, she realised that now. She would call Marsha to tell her so, and then she would resign – and to hell with it. Roxanne knew she could freelance as a fashion stylist; she knew virtually everyone in the industry, and had all her decades of contacts and experience behind her. It would tide her over if nothing else. But then, she couldn't shake off the image of Della in the shop she had created from just a collection of old books. Could Roxanne also create something she could call her very own? An idea began to form in her mind: of a beautiful boutique filled with new and vintage clothing, but other things too – like the delicate tea sets she had rescued from Rosemary Cottage when no one else had wanted them, and stored in her oven ever since.

Beautiful old things – to wear or just to enjoy. Was that such a crazy idea? By the time she turned into her street, Roxanne had designed the whole place in her head. Would such a boutique work in Burley Bridge? she wondered. A few years ago she would have said no, but then, the place had changed, thanks to Della. The village seemed filled with possibilities now.

As she crossed the street towards her block, something caught her eye on the pavement ahead. It was a record. She thought she had gathered them all up, but now she spotted several more, still lying in the street. People must have been messing about with them, she realised: throwing them around. She gathered them all up. One was a blues compilation, another a live Billie Holiday album. The third depicted a stunning young woman on the sleeve, wearing a sparkly dress, a string of tiny pearls and matching earrings. She was singing into an old-fashioned microphone and this album, too, was a live recording.

Isabelle Jerome: Live at the Palladium.
Isabelle Jerome?

Chapter Thirty-Three

One week later

Although a wonderful neighbour in many ways, Isabelle could be incredibly frustrating. She had ducked out of answering Roxanne's barrage of questions, muttering that it was 'just an old record' and that she hadn't known where it was. Roxanne knew she was fibbing, and only now – with nothing else to distract them – could she finally persuade her to tell the truth.

They were travelling north together by train to Heathfield, where Della would meet them and take them back to Burley Bridge. The two women were on holiday together; at least, after resigning, Roxanne had decided to return to Yorkshire for a bit, and it occurred to her that Isabelle would never get around to having her flat redecorated unless she took charge and booked someone to do it. With Isabelle's slightly reluctant permission, she had booked a painter and decorator and persuaded Isabelle that she could enjoy a few days up north while he got on with the job. When she returned to London, her flat would be freshly painted with all the terrible evidence of the burglary gone.

In the meantime, Roxanne could finally apologise face to face to Michael for standing him up the other day. The thought of seeing him again made her smile. Of course there was the slight chance that he might be a little cross with her; he hadn't returned her calls, after all. She would have to wait and see.

But now, she fetched teas from the buffet car and, when she settled back into her seat, she decided it was time to find out all about Isabelle Jerome.

In fact, it was the surname of the love of her life, Isabelle told Roxanne as the train sped north. That was the name she performed under, and also why Roxanne had never found any evidence of Isabelle's career as a jazz singer when she had done a little searching online.

Monty Jerome, a jazz saxophonist, had played on the album Roxanne had found. That was why Isabelle never listened to it. He had died of a sudden heart attack on stage fifteen years ago and she couldn't bear to hear him play.

'I left my husband for Monty,' she explained as they sipped their tea. 'He was devastated, but he did get over it and married someone else fairly quickly. Unfortunately, Simon never forgave me.'

'Your son Simon?' Roxanne asked.

She nodded. 'Well, he was only ten when it happened, and of course, it was terrible for him. I'd been having an affair, you see. Monty and I often found ourselves performing on the same bill, and we just fell madly in love. We tried to resist each other but it was terrible. It broke our hearts.' She blinked at Roxanne, her eyes misting at the memory. 'When I left my husband, I took Simon with me, but he was never happy and went to live with his daddy a few months later.'

Roxanne touched her hand across the table. 'How awful for you.'

'It was my own fault. I deserved it, really . . .'

'Yes, but you loved this man, didn't you?'

'Monty? Oh, yes. We loved each other very deeply for the rest of his life.'

Roxanne nodded, taking this in. Was it worth losing your child to be with the man you loved? she wondered. She had no idea. But she realised now that whatever she'd had with Sean – or anyone at all – was nothing compared to Isabelle's adoration of this man.

'Oh, I have something for you,' Isabelle said, delving into the large canvas bag beside her. She pulled out her own record and handed it to Roxanne.

'I can't take this!' she exclaimed. 'Surely you want to keep it yourself, even if you don't play it?'

Tears shone in Isabelle's dark eyes as she shook her head. 'Music is meant to be played, Roxanne, and anyway, you really must have it. You rescued it, after all.'

They were met at Heathfield station by Della, and had dinner at the Red Lion where Isabelle took charge of the jukebox and enthused over the pub's rustic charms. Then the three of them strolled slowly back to the flat above the bookshop. Exhausted after the journey, Isabelle excused herself just after ten, and retired to bed in the spare room. Roxanne was spending the night on the sofa, which was fine with her. Della had tried to insist she took her bed, while she slept in the living room, but Roxanne wouldn't hear of it. Della's sofa was big and squashy and perfectly comfortable.

And now, with Isabelle's soft snores drifting out of the spare room, Roxanne set off, relieved that Michael hadn't sounded remotely annoyed with her when she had called just before the train had pulled into Heathfield station. He'd seemed delighted, in fact. It was his fault, he'd insisted, for dropping his mobile on the kitchen floor, and of course he would love her to pop round later. No – it didn't matter how late it was.

She buzzed the door.

Michael's face broke into a huge, wide smile as he opened it and beckoned her in. 'Back so soon!' he said teasingly.

'I just couldn't stay away,' she said with a grin as they headed upstairs to his flat. 'Oh – and I brought you a present.' She handed him the book, and he gushed his thanks and turned the pages reverentially.

'This is wonderful, Roxanne! Thank you. It's a real classic, you know – and very rare.'

'Well, I hope you enjoy it.'

In his living room now, he poured them glasses of wine, then they sat beside each other on the sofa, and Roxanne told him everything that had happened since she'd seen him last – about her job, and Sean, and what on earth she might do next.

'I'm thinking of possibly opening a shop of my own,' she ventured. 'I've seen how happy it's made Della and I think . . . I really think I could make it work. Is that crazy?'

He laughed. 'Perhaps I'm the wrong person to ask. But, you know, there is a vacant shop at the moment, just down the road – the one next to the greengrocer's . . .'

'Really? I might take a look while I'm here. You know, in some ways my editor's right. Glossy magazines are lovely things but they had their heyday a while ago. I think it's time for something new.'

353

'I really believe in just following your instinct,' Michael murmured, 'and doing what feels right.'

'Yes, me too.' She sipped her wine and looked around the room. It was cosy, just the right side of cluttered, with shelves of books and clusters of photos of Elsa and Jude crowding the mantelpiece. 'I notice you have a record player there,' she remarked.

'Oh, yes – Elsa just bought it. Isn't it funny how young people are mad on vinyl again?'

'Yes, it is.' She pulled the album from her bag. 'D'you mind if I put this on?'

'No, not at all. Here, I'll do it for you . . .' He took the record and placed it carefully on the turntable. There was a crackle as the needle hit its groove, a gentle piano introduction, and then the most beautiful, soulful and smoky voice filled the room.

Roxanne looked at Michael as he settled back beside her, her heart seeming to flip as his eyes met hers.

'How long are you staying this time?' he asked.

'I'm really not sure,' she replied. 'Isabelle's travelling back the day after tomorrow, but I'm planning to be here a while longer.'

He nodded, and his hand brushed against hers. She smiled, and that's when she found herself looking at him properly, knowing he was about to kiss her and wanting him to, very much.

His lips met hers, and her head seemed to spin as they kissed and kissed, with the beautiful music playing. They kept kissing through track after track, all sense of time lost until, finally, she pulled back and became aware that the record had finished.

Michael smiled. 'That was lovely,' he murmured.

Whether he meant the kiss or the album, she wasn't

sure. 'Yes, and the music was wonderful too,' she said with a smile.

Michael chuckled and took hold of her hand, kissing her so softly on the lips, she thought she might dissolve. In that moment, Roxanne felt more certain than ever before that, right now, this was exactly where she belonged.

'Who was it anyway?' he asked, winding his arms around her and holding her close.

'She's a friend of mine,' Roxanne replied. 'Her name is Isabelle Jerome.'

Loved *The Little Bakery on Rosemary Lane*?

Then join Della, Roxanne and friends, and curl up with the rest of the *Rosemary Lane* series . . .

Out Now!   **Coming soon!**

Looking for more? Get your hands on Ellen's other wonderful books, writing as Fiona Gibson.

What if your first love came back on the scene . . . thirty years later?

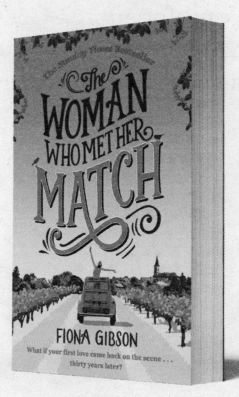

A wonderfully funny novel, perfect for fans of
Jill Mansell, Joanna Bolouri and Milly Johnson.

Have you ever wanted to escape from it all?

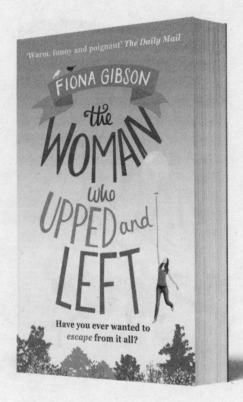

A warm, funny read for fans of Carole Matthews and Catherine Alliott, Fiona writes about life as it really is.